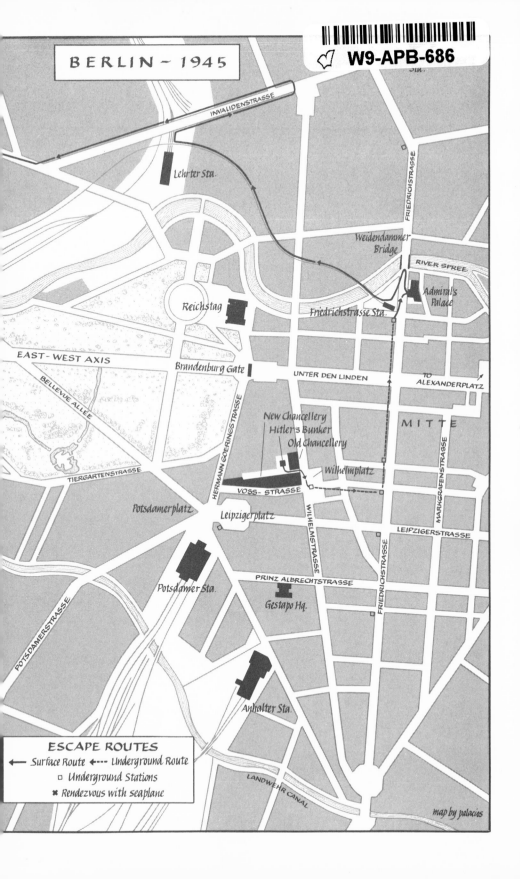

BERLIN ~ 1945

W9-APB-686

INVALIDENSTRASSE

Lehrter Sta.

FRIEDRICHSTRASSE

Weidendammer
Bridge

RIVER SPREE

Reichstag

Friedrichstrasse Sta.

Admiral's
Palace

EAST-WEST AXIS

BELLEVUE ALLEE

Brandenburg Gate

UNTER DEN LINDEN

TO
ALEXANDERPLATZ

MITTE

MARKGRAFENSTRASSE

New Chancellery
Hitler's Bunker
Old Chancellery

TIERGARTENSTRASSE

Wilhelmplatz

VOSS- STRASSE

HERMANN GOERINGSTRASSE

WILHELMSTRASSE

Potsdamerplatz

Leipzigerplatz

LEIPZIGERSTRASSE

POTSDAMERSTRASSE

Potsdamer Sta.

PRINZ ALBRECHTSTRASSE

Gestapo Hq.

FRIEDRICHSTRASSE

Anhalter Sta.

ESCAPE ROUTES

← Surface Route ◄--- Underground Route
□ Underground Stations
✻ Rendezvous with seaplane

LANDWEHR CANAL

map by palacios

Books by Walter Winward

Seven Minutes Past Midnight
Hammerstrike

Seven Minutes Past Midnight

Walter Winward

SIMON AND SCHUSTER
NEW YORK

Copyright © 1980 by Walter Winward
All rights reserved
including the right of reproduction
in whole or in part in any form
Published by Simon and Schuster
A Division of Gulf & Western Corporation
Simon & Schuster Building
Rockefeller Center
1230 Avenue of the Americas
New York, New York 10020
SIMON AND SCHUSTER and colophon
are trademarks of Simon & Schuster

Designed by Irving Perkins
Manufactured in the United States of America
1 2 3 4 5 6 7 8 9 10

Library of Congress Cataloging in Publication Data

Winward, Walter.
    Seven minutes past midnight.

    1. World War, 1939–1945—Fiction. I. Title.
PZ4.W7945Se 1980 [PR6073.I58] 823'.9'14 79–26613
ISBN 0–671–24932–0

This book is dedicated to the memory of my wife's father, the late Colonel Otis Edward Maitland, Military Intelligence.

"But for our premature surrender [in World War I], Germany would have gained an honorable peace and there would have been no postwar chaos. This time we must not give up five minutes before midnight."

Adolf Hitler to his generals, January 1945

PROLOGUE

November 1944

The Special Operations officer, whose real name was Greenleigh but who for the purposes of this trip was traveling under false identity and nationality documents, watched the plainclothes German courier cross safely back into his homeland. Then the Englishman turned away. For better or worse, the operation was off and running.

There was not too much two-way traffic between Germany and Switzerland at that point in the war, and what there was was watched carefully by troops of the *Sicherheitsdienst*, or SD, the SS Security Police, on the German side. Most Germans who passed through the frontier post had legitimate business in the neutral country—at least, business that had been franked as official by a high authority, although it was common knowledge that the majority of it involved the transfer of currency to numbered accounts. In the depraved world of National Socialism, this was not regarded as unusual. If the war went badly, funds would be required to carry on the struggle at some future time; they would also be needed to provide members of the SS with living expenses elsewhere. And there was no doubt that Sturmbannfuehrer Klaus Bauer was an officer of that elite organization, even though one set of papers pronounced him to be a Swedish citizen. That too was legitimate, simply to avoid awkward questions on the Swiss side of the border. His real papers were franked by SS-General Kaltenbrunner's department, the RSHA, or Reich Main Security Office.

Nevertheless, the SD Untersturmfuehrer who readmitted Bauer to the Reich took his time, scrutinizing each page of the entry document carefully before finally allowing the Sturmbannfuehrer to pass through. Time of entry was noted as 12:22 P.M.

Being so close to the Swiss frontier, this part of Germany had been left severely alone by Allied bombers, and Bauer found it hard to believe that less than a hundred miles away some of the fiercest fighting of the war was taking place.

Halfway down the hill, making for the public telephone booth at the foot, he glanced over his shoulder. The SD Untersturmfuehrer was about forty or fifty meters behind, accompanied by a senior NCO. Both men were carrying MP 40 submachine guns.

Bauer forced himself to relax. It was coincidence, that was all. His papers were quite in order. If the Untersturmfuehrer had suspected that anything was amiss, he would have held him at the border post. They were going for lunch or a beer; it was that time of day. Still, it was better to be safe than sorry.

He stopped, making it obvious that he would wait for them to catch up. But the Untersturmfuehrer waved his hand negatively. Nothing sinister in that either. They simply had private matters to discuss, and he was far senior to either of them in rank. His presence would make them feel uncomfortable.

At the foot of the hill he entered the telephone booth. Later it would be established that he spent six minutes on the phone, talking in an agitated fashion to the person at the other end. And so engrossed did he become in the conversation that he did not notice the Untersturmfuehrer and the NCO waiting for him until he hung up and stepped outside.

"You want something of me?" he demanded.

The younger officer seemed almost embarrassed.

"I'm sorry, Herr Sturmbannfuehrer, but I must ask you to accompany me to SD Headquarters. I have reason to believe that you are engaged in treasonable activities."

Bauer tried to bluff it out. "You will just about live to regret this impertinence. I am on important business for the Reich."

"Nevertheless, I must ask you to come with me."

Bauer nodded slowly, as though accepting the situation. He saw the other two visibly relax, and at that moment took to his heels.

Unfortunately, there was nowhere to run to, no side streets to disappear down, and the SD NCO had already been given his instructions coming down the hill. He fired a short burst from the MP 40 and at that range could hardly miss. When they reached Bauer he was quite dead.

A truck was called for and Bauer's corpse taken to SD Headquarters, where it was stripped and searched. His clothing contained nothing except his Swedish papers and his SS pass, which was strange in itself. No money, no photographs or letters, no cigarettes or matches. It took a sharp-eyed doctor to spot the ink marks on the inside of his left wrist and a magnifying glass to decipher the symbols. They simply said, LONDON—and gave some figures that were obviously a radio frequency.

In due course the papers pertaining to the case found their way to Berlin and into the In tray of Hauptsturmfuehrer Sepp Langendorf. Although an officer in the SD, Langendorf had desk space in the Prinz Albrechtstrasse HQ of the Gestapo, with which organization the SD was closely linked.

The report from the frontier guard stated that initial inquiries had revealed no trace of a permit being issued by the RSHA for Sturmbannfuehrer Bauer to visit Switzerland. Furthermore, there was no record that Sturmbannfuehrer Bauer actually existed. The name and papers were obviously fakes, but the dead man's true identity had not been established.

Hauptsturmfuehrer Langendorf resolved not to refer the case to a higher authority. He had a radio frequency and access to a listening post. All he had to do was wait.

By keeping the matter to himself he was breaking all the rules. Had he acted otherwise, the course of the war, and certainly the peace, would have altered dramatically.

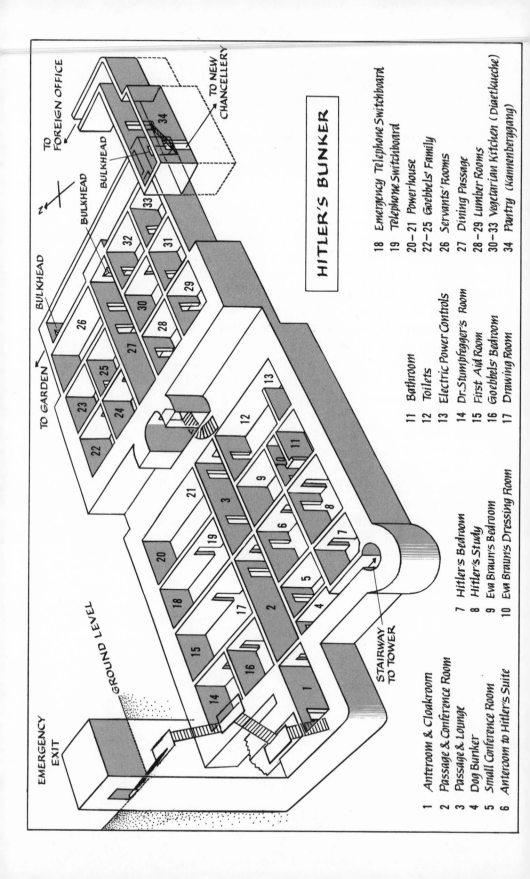

HITLER'S BUNKER

EMERGENCY EXIT

GROUND LEVEL

TO GARDEN

TO FOREIGN OFFICE

TO NEW CHANCELLERY

BULKHEAD

STAIRWAY TO TOWER

1   Anteroom & Cloakroom
2   Passage & Conference Room
3   Passage & Lounge
4   Dog Bunker
5   Small Conference Room
6   Anteroom to Hitler's Suite

7   Hitler's Bedroom
8   Hitler's Study
9   Eva Braun's Bedroom
10 Eva Braun's Dressing Room

11 Bathroom
12 Toilets
13 Electric Power Controls
14 Dr.Stumpfegger's Room
15 First Aid Room
16 Goebbels' Bedroom
17 Drawing Room

18 Emergency Telephone Switchboard
19 Telephone Switchboard
20 – 21 Powerhouse
22 – 25 Goebbels' Family
26 Servants' Rooms
27 Dining Passage
28 – 29 Lumber Rooms
30 – 33 Vegetarian Kitchen (Diaetkueche)
34 Pantry (Kannenberggang)

ONE

Not entirely because of the freezing temperature and the bitter wind blowing the length of Wilhelmstrasse, most Berliners chose to walk with their heads down these days. It was better not to look, for the city was in ruins, a tribute to the accuracy of the terror bombers. Moldering walls with gaping windows reared up like tombstones amid acres of debris for as far as the eye could see. It seemed that the Reich Chancellery, stretching the whole length of Voss-strasse, from Wilhelmplatz to Hermann Goeringstrasse, was the only building left intact. Not many saw this as a miracle.

Those scheduled to attend the afternoon conference were already entering the Chancellery, the military through one door, Party members through another. Once inside the high entrance hall they were faced with a bleak prospect, one made even drearier by the miserable illumination shed by the few remaining lights. The carpets, paintings and tapestries that had once graced the hallway had long since been removed for protection from Allied air raids. Most of the windows were covered with cardboard.

At the head of the corridor leading to the anteroom in the conference area, SS troopers of the *Fuehrerbegleit-kommando*, Hitler's hand-picked personal guard, armed with machine pistols, demanded that all visitors, regardless of rank, hand over their side arms and open their briefcases. It was now January 27, 1945, but Count Klaus von Stauffenberg's attempt to assassinate Hitler six months earlier was still fresh in the minds of many. The extreme security measures applied to everyone. Even the last to arrive, Generaloberst Heinz Guderian, Army Chief of Staff and commander of the Eastern Front, was not exempt.

15

By 4 o'clock the anteroom was filled with military and political leaders of the highest rank. A few minutes later the doors to the Fuehrer's office were thrown open and Reichsmarschall Goering led the way inside.

Though the office was spacious, it was sparingly decorated. At one end French windows were draped with gray curtains, and drab carpets covered most of the floor. In the middle of one wall stood Hitler's massive desk; behind it, his black-upholstered chair faced the Chancellery garden. The most senior conferees seated themselves in heavy leather chairs while their aides or lesser members either stood or found straight chairs.

At 4:20 P.M. Adolf Hitler shuffled in. Those who had not seen him for some time were shocked by his appearance. Shoulders stooped, his left arm hanging limply, he was hard to accept as the leader who had given them dozens of military and political victories. Only the pale blue eyes occasionally flashed with the old hypnotic power.

Those without personal knowledge assumed that his useless left arm and general appearance were the result of the July bomb plot. Others knew that it was his right arm which had been injured at Rastenburg and that the condition of his left was a recent phenomenon.

He sat down gingerly and glanced slowly around the room. His gaze took in Goering, whose redness of face seemed to indicate a heavy session with the schnapps bottle in the anteroom. Near Goering sat Feldmarschall Wilhelm Keitel, chief of the OKW, the High Command of the Armed Forces, derisively nicknamed Lakeitel—from *Lakei*, lackey—by his fellow officers. Behind Keitel was his Chief of Operations, Generaloberst Alfred Jodl.

The Deputy Leader of the Party, Martin Bormann, sat alone, silent as always, but Guderian was chatting amiably to his own adjutant, Major Freytag von Loringhoven, and Hitler's, Sturmbannfuehrer Otto Günsche.

Seemingly absorbed in a thickish document and heartily loathed by most of those present, Himmler's liaison officer at the Chancellery, SS-Brigadefuehrer Hermann Fegelein, was feeling the effects of a massive lunch. The younger officers called him Flegelein—after *Flegel*, lout—but only behind his back. Fegelein was married to Gretl Braun, sister of Hitler's mistress, Eva, and was a man quick to take offense.

Outside in the anteroom, the commander of the SS guard for the day checked against his list that all those who were due to arrive were in fact now closeted in the Fuehrer's office. Anyone else wishing to gain entry would have to have a compelling reason or be prepared to wait until the conference was over.

If it could be called a conference at all, he thought. Twenty-odd people, only half a dozen of them of the front rank, hardly constituted a major policy-making meeting.

There was a time when the corridors of the Chancellery had regularly echoed the footsteps of the most powerful men in Germany, perhaps the world. Men like Reichsfuehrer Himmler, recently appointed commander of Army Group Vistula; Ernst Kaltenbrunner, chief of the SD; Artur Axmann, head of the Hitler Youth; Admiral Canaris, former head of the Abwehr, and Admiral Doenitz; SS-Brigadefuehrer Walter Schellenberg, Himmler's chief of espionage; and Albert Speer, Minister of Armament and War Production. Men like Dr. Goebbels, Minister of Propaganda, and Foreign Minister von Ribbentrop. Even Rudolf Hess.

But no more. Hess, of course, had gone mad and defected to the British, and Canaris was in a concentration camp, or dead, for his part in the July plot. But of the remainder, most either had offices in Berlin or were regular visitors to the capital, yet they rarely visited the Chancellery. No doubt the Fuehrer had his reasons for keeping them away. Up to a year ago, Hitler would have trusted most of them with his life—but that was before Von Stauffenberg's treason. Now he watched everyone for signs of betrayal, and who was to say who would be next to play Brutus?

Beyond the closed doors Hitler tapped the desk with a ruler and brought the conference to order. "Begin," he commanded.

Guderian got to his feet. His report was a dismal affair from beginning to end.

Two weeks earlier, on January 12, three million Russians, more than ten times the strength of the armies that had landed in Normandy on D-Day, had attacked a force of three-quarters of a million Germans along a 400-mile front stretching from the

Baltic right down the middle of Poland. Supported by artillery and led by seemingly endless columns of T-34 tanks, they punched a massive hole through the unprepared and poorly equipped Germans.

In the extreme north, Marshal Chernyakhovsky's Third White Russian Front (the Soviet equivalent of an Army Group) pushed for Königsberg in East Prussia. On his left, the Second White Russian Front, led by the mercurial Marshal Rokossovsky, smashed its way into Danzig. On Rokossovsky's left the most talented of them all and the man the Germans feared most, Marshal Zhukov, in command of the First White Russian Front, spearheaded the assault on Posen, which stood in the way of his ultimate goal, Berlin. Finally, on the extreme southern flank, Marshal Ivan Konev's First Ukrainian Front was moving quickest of all. In its path stood the POW camp at Sagan, Stalag Luft III, which held 10,000 Allied airmen.

Within two weeks of the initial Soviet push, Generaloberst Reinhardt's Army Group North, the main target of Chernyakhovsky and Rokossovsky, was overrun, and the Fourth Army under General Hossbach was in full flight. But the main assault in the center, that led by Zhukov, was the one causing the greatest concern to the OKW, especially Guderian. Army Group Vistula had been hastily formed to plug the hole Zhukov had made, and from the beginning Guderian had objected to the order that gave Himmler, whose highest rank prior to the advent of the Nazis was that of sergeant major, the command. Hitler had overruled him and was now living to regret his decision. The Reichsfuehrer-SS had ill-advisedly drawn up his battle lines running east–west, from the Vistula to the River Oder, and Zhukov merely bypassed him. On the morning of January 27 the First White Russian Front was less than one hundred miles from Berlin, with only the Oder as the last major obstacle.

For more than an hour Guderian tried to impress upon the conference the seriousness of the situation in the east, but Hitler seemed more interested in the Stalag Luft III POWs.

"The camp must be evacuated. The Russians must not liberate them. I can't have ten thousand Allied fliers roaming around loose." An adjutant left to relay this order to the camp commandant.

Hitler was also concerned about reports of Russian atrocities against civilians. These were increasing daily. What had started as a trickle was now a flood.

"I have it on no less an authority than Kaltenbrunner," he intoned, "that Stalin has given his troops absolute license to rape and murder. In fact, the political commissars attached to each unit are there partly to ensure that that particular direction is carried out."

"With due respect, Fuehrer, this is neither the time nor the place to discuss such matters." Guderian made a despairing attempt to refocus Hitler's attention on the conduct of the war.

"With due respect to *you*, Herr Generaloberst, I think it is. It is precisely because the Russians are the kind of subhuman race to take full advantage of a license to pillage that I declared war on them in the first place."

Guderian gave up. Hitler was off and running on one of his favorite topics, and Guderian knew that it was useless to try to interrupt him. He also knew that this afternoon's session would be like so many that had gone before, where trivia were given importance and matters of immediate concern relegated to the scrap heap. Hitler was like a man dying of cancer reaching for an aspirin: it would do him no good, but at least it was familiar.

The conference ended at 6:50 P.M. with nothing of value discussed, let alone decided. Guderian's report was virtually ignored, as all he had to offer was bad news. The situation in the west was no better, but nevertheless forty minutes was spent discussing whether Generaloberst Kurt Student should retain command of Army Group H in the Netherlands and whether Oberstgruppenfuehrer Paul Hausser was still up to his job.

After Hitler left, the remaining conferees retired to the anteroom to drink coffee and schnapps and eat the sandwiches prepared by orderlies. Few had any real doubts that the writing was now well and truly on the wall.

Guderian and Freytag von Loringhoven were the first to move out into the cold Berlin night, heading for Zossen, twenty miles due south of the capital. Brigadefuehrer Fegelein followed them soon afterward. His first job was to report the tenor of the meeting to his chief, Himmler. And while neither Goebbels nor Von Ribbentrop nor Kaltenbrunner officially had observers at the conference, each had his unofficial representative in the room and was in full cognizance of what had occurred by 8 o'clock.

It took Grand Admiral Doenitz and some of the others a little longer. Nevertheless, by 9:30 on the evening of January 27, most of the Reich's senior Nazis, both military and political, had verbatim reports of the Chancellery meeting, and an hour later the man to whom Sturmbannfuehrer Bauer had spoken on the telephone, code-named Valkyrie by British Intelligence, had decided to act.

At 11:27 P.M., the senior NCO at the listening post set up by Hauptsturmfuehrer Langendorf was half asleep. Like his fellow watch keepers, who manned the monitoring station in shifts, he was quite convinced that Langendorf was mad. They had been at it for ten weeks now, night and day, without so much as a bleep on the frequency.

But at 11:28 the NCO was wide awake. Someone was sending Morse, and that someone was very close, to judge by the strength of the signals. He was not a trained operator, however; the lack of rhythm and speed in the dots and dashes proved that. Neither did the text make any sense: a series of five-letter groups that were doubtless in code. There was no acknowledgment from the other end.

By 11:45 Langendorf had the message form in front of him, and while drinking filthy ersatz coffee went over it again and again. Not yet twenty-four years of age, the Hauptsturmfuehrer was rumored to have taken an unhealthy interest in youthful SS troopers, but he was nevertheless feared by most of his subordinates and known to be a devoted follower of Hitler and a relentless pursuer of the Reich's enemies.

Two things struck him immediately about the message. The first was the obvious one: that without the help of a trained cryptographer he was going to get nowhere. Code breakers were in short supply in Berlin at this stage of the war, but he thought he knew someone who might assist him.

The second point was less obvious. Although the NCO had no knowledge of the fake Klaus Bauer or the reason for his watch keeping, he had said that the signals were very strong. On the logical assumption that London was on the receiving end, that meant access to a powerful transmitter, no doubt mobile and therefore impossible to trace by direction-finding equipment. But it did lead to a terrifying conclusion: only someone of considerable rank would be able to commandeer such a transmitter, which meant that this treason—there could be no other word for it—was being committed at the highest level.

The signal was received in England at Bletchley Park, Buckinghamshire. The land on which this mansion stood had once been a Roman encampment and later granted to Bishop Geoffrey by William the Conqueror after the Battle of Hastings. The house itself was a mere sixty years old, and hidden in the farmland surrounding it were webs of radio antennas. It was here that the SOE, the Special Operations Executive, sometimes known as the Baker Street Irregulars, kept open lines of communication between the Allies and Axis/Axis-occupied countries.

Once on a message pad, the signal, still in code, was handed by an orderly to the Duty Officer. This man, a one-armed captain in his early twenties, recognized by the triple-S that it was an "eyes only" communication and by the prefix whose eyes they were.

He placed the signal in a sealed envelope and summoned a dispatch rider. Forty minutes later, in a house in London's Mayfair, the envelope was in the hands of Brigadier Greenleigh, known to most of his communicators only by the code name Nemesis.

It took Greenleigh less than three minutes to decipher the message, which read:

To: NEMESIS   CVX/014/SSS/29000/Z/27.1.45
From: VALKYRIE
            AM READY TO IMPLEMENT OPERATION
            HORSETRADE AS OUTLINED.

In spite of its brevity, Greenleigh spent three-quarters of an hour studying it and considering its implications. Finally he picked up the telephone and requested an immediate interview with the Prime Minister. Although it was by now well into the small hours, Mr. Churchill would have to be told about this latest development without delay.

The Prime Minister listened carefully. He was a good friend of the SOE officer, but this was the first he had heard of Operation Horsetrade since Valkyrie had originally communicated with British Intelligence six months earlier. As far as he was concerned it had not gone any further, but now he was being told that Greenleigh had actually made a clandestine visit to Switzerland and met with a German courier in November. It could well be that the Yalta Conference, only a few days off, was occupying most of his waking thoughts, but he was very short with his visitor.

"I should have been kept informed," he rasped in his peculiar lisping voice. "I should have been told that matters had progressed this far. This sort of thing is a Cabinet decision at the very least. If it got to Mr. Attlee's ears that the SOE are trying to do a deal with a ranking Nazi, we should all be in trouble. He would never believe that I knew practically nothing about it. Neither, for that matter, would President Roosevelt or Marshal Stalin. Good God, the Marshal is already suspicious of Anglo-American intentions."

"With the greatest respect, Prime Minister," said Greenleigh, "there was very little more to tell you before an hour ago. The Swiss meeting was merely a feeler, to see what our reactions would be. If the Ardennes push had gone better for the Germans, we should have heard no more about it. This signal is the first to state unreservedly that Valkyrie wants to do business. Besides, I had to check his authenticity. You wouldn't have thanked me if the whole thing had turned out to be a hoax."

"Undoubtedly not," admitted Churchill. "There's no chance of that, I suppose?"

"None at all, sir. Via his courier, Valkyrie has already given us a mass of information which we were able to verify from independent sources. Now he wants to buy his freedom with more—much more."

22

"I'm sure he does. But I'm afraid we're not in the market."

Greenleigh gritted his teeth and recalled a rather unkind comment Lloyd George was reputed to have made about Churchill. "Winston has half a dozen solutions to every problem and one of them is right. The trouble is he doesn't know which it is." The war would doubtless be over in a few months and with it, possibly, the old man's task. But the business of intelligence went on forever. Yesterday's enemies were tomorrow's friends, and vice versa.

"If I may make an observation, sir . . ."

"Please do."

"It may well be that Marshal Stalin is suspicious of Anglo-American intentions, but I think we should be equally suspicious of his. According to the latest reports his forward troops are within striking distance of Berlin. I don't see him giving up any territory he gains, no matter what he says. When this war is over we don't want the Russians sitting in our back garden. More important still, we need to know where Stalin considers that back garden should be. It could be Calais and it could be that he's willing to fight for it, for all we know. All right, I admit that's an exaggeration, but hard intelligence on the Marshal's future plans is something Valkyrie can give us. And please remember, Prime Minister, that he also says he can provide us with a comprehensive list of highly placed German agents in the U.S.S.R., those who can be turned and who would be willing to work for us when Germany is defeated. Such a list would be of inestimable value."

"As no doubt are the location of Germany's hidden gold reserves, the escape plans of other ranking Nazis, and countless other matters," grunted Churchill. "Yes, yes, Greenleigh—you told me all this months ago, although I still don't fully understand why a German should know more about Stalin's postwar plans for Europe than our own intelligence services."

"Because this is not just *any* German, sir. This is a man who has spent his whole life compiling dossiers of one kind or another. He probably has a man or two in the Kremlin itself. If he fails or has overstated his case, he knows we'll execute him."

"An end I would thoroughly approve of," said Churchill. "I don't like rats of any description, no matter what class of ship they're deserting. I especially don't like this particular rat. I know his record. It is far from laudable."

Greenleigh sighed inaudibly. The old man wasn't thinking straight. To hell with escape plans of other Nazis, gold reserves and the rest of it, it was vital to learn what Uncle Joe had in mind for Europe.

Churchill pulled at his dewlaps. "I understand your reasoning, Greenleigh; don't think me a fool. To your way of thinking I should even make a pact with Adolf Hitler if it could be of some benefit to this country. But I'm afraid I don't see it like that. The Nazis have caused us endless loss of life and destruction of property, and I intend to see they pay for it, every last one of them, with their lives. Besides, you're making the assumption that Zhukov will be in Berlin before Montgomery. I'm afraid I don't agree. I know President Roosevelt doesn't see the strategic importance of Berlin the way we do, but he has assured me that we shall be there before the Russians. I agree that our armies should push as far east as possible fast and in strength. That is what we are doing. Our 'back garden,' as you choose to put it, will be a long way from Calais, I assure you."

Brigadier Greenleigh was far from convinced, but Mr. Churchill was the final arbiter in such matters and could not be argued with. Nevertheless, when encoding a reply for Berlin he was careful not to shut the door irreversibly.

To: VALKYRIE   CVX/014/SSS/29000/Z/27.1.45
From: NEMESIS
                HORSETRADE NOT YET FEASIBLE. POLITICAL
                CONSIDERATIONS PRECLUDE IMMEDIATE DECISION.

TWO

To: NEMESIS   CVX/007/SSS/22000/Z/28.1.45
From: VALKYRIE
    DO NOT UNDERSTAND PHRASE POLITICAL
    CONSIDERATIONS. IS IT YES OR NO.

To: VALKYRIE   CVX/014/SSS/27000/Z/28.1.45
From: NEMESIS
    REPEAT IMMEDIATE DECISION IMPOSSIBLE.

To: NEMESIS   CVX/020/SSS/30000/Z/28.1.45
From: VALKYRIE
    MUST I APPROACH THE AMERICANS.

To: VALKYRIE   CVX/011/SSS/26000/Z/29.1.45
From: NEMESIS
    AT YOUR OWN PERIL. ABSOLUTE DEADLINE WAS
    AGREED AS MID APRIL.

To: NEMESIS   CVX/010/SSS/18000/Z/21.1.45
From: VALKYRIE
    UNDERSTOOD BUT AM CONCERNED ABOUT SECURITY.

To: VALKYRIE   CVX/001/SSS/31000/Z/29.1.45
From: NEMESIS
    BE ASSURED UTMOST SECRECY GUARANTEED.

To: NEMESIS   CVX/009/SSS/17000/Z/29.1.45
From: VALKYRIE
    WHEN MAY I EXPECT A POSITIVE ANSWER.

To: VALKYRIE   CVX/26000/SSS/23000/Z/29.I.45
From: NEMESIS
        IT MAY TAKE WEEKS. BUT PLEASE REMEMBER THERE
        IS ONLY ONE LIFE RAFT AND THIS IS IT.
        ACKNOWLEDGE.

To: NEMESIS   CVX/008/SSS/24000/Z/30.I.45
From: VALKYRIE
        UNDERSTOOD.

THREE

At a little before 5 A.M. on the morning of January 30, Mr. Churchill and his staff arrived in Malta aboard a Skymaster—a U.S. C-54 transport. The purpose of the Prime Minister's visit was a four-day conference with American military and political leaders prior to the Big Three meeting in Yalta.

In the meantime, General Eisenhower had drawn up his final battle lines for the invasion of Germany, stretching along the German border from Holland to Switzerland. Pride of place in this last assault was to be given to Field Marshal Montgomery's 21st Army Group in the north. On Monty's right flank was Lt. General Omar Bradley's 12th Army Group, comprising the U.S. First and Third Armies. In the extreme south Lt. General Jacob L. Devers was given command of the 6th Army Group.

Eisenhower's strategy called for Montgomery to lead the main attack through the Ruhr, while Bradley made a secondary assault farther south via Frankfurt am Main. Field Marshal Alan Brooke, Chief of the Imperial General Staff, had already expressed concern at the plan, fearing that the secondary offensive could become as important as the first, thus weakening Montgomery. It had not escaped his notice that Bradley's Third Army had as its commander Lt. General George S. Patton, and it was unlikely Patton would accept being part of a subsidiary force.

By midmorning on January 31 the Zhukov spearhead had reached Landsberg, a mere stone's throw from the River Oder. Before noon, advance units were on the outskirts of Küstrin, east of the river but nevertheless only fifty miles from the Reich Chancellery. A hundred miles farther north, the technical director of the Peenemünde rocket station, Dr. Wernher von Braun, was holding a secret meeting with his chief assistants. It took them no time at all to decide that when the hour came, they would head west and surrender to the Anglo-Americans.

At 9:35 A.M. on February 2, the cruiser U.S.S. *Quincy* sailed into Valletta Harbour, Malta, with President Roosevelt on board. The following day, via a circuitous route, the President and Prime Minister flew to the Crimea for the Yalta meeting with Stalin.

On February 4 an unnamed officer on Keitel's staff wrote to his wife that the Chancellery was an incredible sight. There were deep craters everywhere, fallen trees, masses of debris. The entrance hall on Wilhelmstrasse was now completely destroyed. Water was in very short supply, and he advised his wife, if at all possible, to lay in stocks of food, especially green vegetables. The Russians were getting closer and he was worried about the future.

With good reason. As Stalin was to tell his guests a day or so later, the Russians had been treated worse, far worse, than even the Jews. One example he gave was that of Stalag 11A at Neubrandenburg; of the original 21,000 Russian captives, only 4,000 remained. The rest had starved to death.

The unnamed German officer was a little premature in worrying about the future—his own, anyway. The letter to his wife was intercepted by the SD. He was accused of defeatism and summarily shot in the Chancellery courtyard.

On the morning of February 9, Zhukov established a bridgehead on the Oder between Küstrin and Frankfurt an der Oder. The first of the Russian troops crossed over to the west bank of the river the same day.

Between February 8 and 10, Montgomery's northern thrust, Operations Veritable and Grenade, got bogged down on the Nijmegen–Kleve highway. German combat engineers had sabotaged the Roer dams, causing the area to be flooded and a monumental traffic jam to develop.

The final formal dinner of the Big Three conference, with Churchill as host, took place on the evening of the tenth at the Prime Minister's Vorontzov Palace headquarters in Yalta. A communiqué was issued the following day, and the leaders departed. The Anglo-Americans appeared to have wrung concessions from Stalin, and Roosevelt was particularly enthusiastic. Churchill was not so sure. Briefly, on the flight home, his thoughts turned to Operation Horsetrade.

It took two weeks for Veritable and Grenade to get under way, but on February 23 troops of Lt. General Simpson's Ninth Army crossed the Roer River and Lt. General Brian Horrocks' XXX Corps took the twin towns of Kleve and Goch. Two days later the 30th Infantry Division controlled the Hambach Forest, and through the hole made by the foot soldiers poured the 2nd and 5th Armored Divisions, racing for the Rhine. The Anglo-American forces were still west of the river, however, and over three hundred miles from Berlin. Zhukov's Russians were across the Oder and only fifty miles from the capital.

Although the description "Iron Curtain" would later be used by, and eventually attributed to, Churchill, it was actually Goebbels who originated it. In an article in *Das Reich* dated February 25, 1945, he wrote: "If the German people surrender, the Soviets will occupy . . . the larger part of Germany. In front of this enormous territory, an iron curtain will go down. . . ."

Within the next ten days it appeared as if both Germans and Anglo-Americans were paying heed to the clubfooted doctor. Having outrun his supply lines, Zhukov was held up at the Oder. In front of him, all available German forces had been assembled into two armies under the command of General Busse and Baron Hasso von Manteuffel. In the west, the Allies were pushing even harder, and on March 7 troops of Brigadier General William Hoge's Combat Command B crossed the Ludendorff Bridge over the Rhine at Remagen, 55 miles south of Düsseldorf.

Between January 27, the date of the first intercepted transmission, and March 20, the day Himmler was replaced as commander of Army Group Vistula by Generaloberst Gotthard Heinrici, Hauptsturmfuehrer Langendorf had collected enough message flimsies to paper a room. But he was still no nearer to identifying the traitor than he had been at the beginning.

He had tried using DF equipment to establish the location of the German station, but as he had suspected, it was mobile, and the signals never on the air long enough to make it possible to track it down.

Neither had his cryptographer proved much use. Langendorf had told him nothing, just that breaking the code was of vital importance, but eventually the cipher officer had to admit defeat. Both sender and receiver, Langendorf was told, seemed to be using a one-time pad, a method that was virtually uncrackable—unless, of course, Langendorf wanted to put in a request for more manpower.

This Langendorf refused to do. It would mean going to the top, and at the top could well be the man he was looking for.

He would have to use the old methods, the well-tried ones: those of keeping his eyes open and watching for a pattern in someone's behavior that was out of character. It would be a long, arduous process, particularly as he was compelled to work alone and had other duties as well; but he had solved trickier problems in the past.

Somewhere a man was putting on one face and hiding another. One day he would make a mistake.

At 2200 hours on March 23, the 1st Commando Brigade, wearing their traditional green berets and scorning helmets, crossed the Rhine in amphibious carriers at Wesel, spearheading Montgomery's Operation Plunder. As insurance, an airdrop, Operation Varsity, was also planned, and shortly before dawn on March 24, men of the British 6th Airborne Division took off from their base in East Anglia. A little later, the first of the transports carrying the U.S. 17th Airborne Division were also on their way. By early afternoon on the twenty-fourth, units of Plunder and Varsity had linked up.

Hitler's daily conference, scheduled for early evening March 23, did not get under way until 2:30 A.M. on the twenty-fourth. It was a small affair and the topics under discussion verged on the lunatic: whether to widen the road through the Tiergarten to enable it to be used as an emergency landing strip; whether General Walther Wenck, injured in a car smash in February, was now fit enough to replace Guderian; and how soon sixteen or seventeen Tiger tanks could be repaired. Sixteen or seventeen!

On March 28, at roughly the same time as Guderian was being relieved of all his duties by Hitler, General Eisenhower, the Supreme Allied Commander, made a momentous decision and changed his basic strategy. Instead of pushing for Berlin as fast as possible, he would surround the Ruhr area and launch his main attack to the southwest, toward Leipzig and Munich. This turn of events undoubtedly pleased senior American commanders such as Bradley, Patton and Simpson, as it gave the initiative to U.S. forces. The drive to the southwest would have to be led by Bradley and would necessitate the return to him of Simpson's Ninth Army, currently part of Montgomery's 21st Army Group. Now it was Monty who was to be reduced to a subsidiary role. Instead of spearheading the attack on Berlin across northern Germany, he was to swing northwest and seize Lübeck. It was rather like asking Wellington not to defend Waterloo because Napoleon wouldn't like it.

Although the decision to allow the Russians to occupy Berlin was defended by Eisenhower on the basis that the capital had no real strategic importance, it could be argued that there was another reason behind it. As Patton had remarked to Major General Hobart Gay early in March, one day Ike would be running for President, and an assault on Berlin would undoubtedly cost many American lives. That sort of track record behind a candidate was hardly the easy way to the White House, and neither was allowing the senior British commander in the field to take all the glory.

But whatever Eisenhower's true motives, the fact remained that, as Brigadier Greenleigh had predicted in January, when the war was over the Russians would be sitting in the back garden. Where the fence would be was anybody's guess.

On the afternoon of March 30, after receiving a cable from Eisenhower in which the Supreme Commander defended his decision once again and stated firmly that it could not be changed, Churchill sent for the SOE officer. He got straight down to business.

"You've heard what the Americans are up to?"

"I have, sir."

"It seems that you were right and I was wrong."

Greenleigh was much too experienced to allow a trace of a smile to creep in. What had happened was yesterday's news; he was concerned only with tomorrow.

"It could have worked out the other way round. You were not to know that Eisenhower would not push for Berlin."

"I am the Prime Minister," said Churchill haughtily. "It is up to me to divine the intentions of allies and enemy alike. I did not do so."

Greenleigh remained silent. Churchill relit one of his huge cigars and exhaled clouds of smoke.

"Valkyrie," he said. "I assume you've been keeping in touch."

"Regularly, sir. Though his signals are somewhat longer than mine."

"And they say?"

"That his situation is now extremely precarious and that he needs a decision; that if we want to do business we'd better do it quickly. Bear in mind that he doesn't want to come out yet; he merely wants a firm commitment that we'll bring him out when the time comes."

"And you have been replying?"

"More or less that he'll have to wait."

Churchill studied his fingertips. "Tell me again what he has to offer and what he wants."

Seizing the opportunity with both hands, Greenleigh explained in brief, terse sentences.

Valkyrie wanted immunity and anonymity. He also wanted money. In return he would betray the whereabouts of other Nazis and the hidden gold hoards. But the major prize was a complete breakdown of Russian intentions in Europe.

When he had finished, the Prime Minister shook his head wearily. "He's no fool, that's obvious. He knows my mind. President Roosevelt is not a European and is also a sick man. But my God, if it ever came out . . ."

"There's no reason why it should, sir. All told, fewer than half a dozen people are aware of the operation."

"What about those who go in and fetch him out and fulfill the other conditions?"

"There are ways, Prime Minister."

32

Churchill nodded. "I expect there are. Would you use SOE operatives?"

"Perhaps one, as a courier. But the state Germany must be in at present almost certainly means using troops. Only a handful, perhaps, but it would probably be wiser for them to be led by someone with extensive combat experience. Getting in might not be so bad, but getting out with Valkyrie in tow will be a bloody sight more difficult. It would have to be done fast, too—a commando-style operation; otherwise any information Valkyrie has will be outdated."

"Have you anyone in mind?"

"Major Lassiter, sir."

"Lassiter, Lassiter?" The Prime Minister recognized the name but could not put a face to it. "You've used him before, haven't you?"

"Frequently."

"Then you'd better warn him to stand by. You'd also better signal Valkyrie. I'll leave you to choose the words."

Mr. Churchill put down his cigar.

"I need time, Greenleigh, time to think this through and time to see if all the persuasive oratory I am apparently famed for cannot change the minds of the President and the Supreme Commander. I must ask you to buy me that time. If we are to do this, we must do it without the knowledge of our allies. But it cannot be done lightly. I am being forced to choose between allowing a Nazi thug to escape the rope he justly deserves and a potentially Communist Europe. Do what you can."

To: VALKYRIE   CVX/019/SSS/21000/Z/30.3.45
From: NEMESIS
        EXPECT FIRM POLITICAL DECISION SHORTLY. CAN
        VIRTUALLY GUARANTEE IT WILL BE FAVORABLE.

FOUR

At the time of asking, Major Jack Lassiter was a hundred miles inside Germany, sitting in the passenger seat of a pilfered Wehrmacht jeep and racing for Lippstadt, on the River Lippe, a town thirty-odd miles east of Dortmund. Behind the wheel Corporal Mike Gallagher chewed a match end and concentrated on keeping the vehicle on the road and out of bomb and shell craters, while sprawled across the rear seat Sergeant Harry Fuller nursed an MP 38 submachine gun and sang quietly to himself about the long and the short and the tall. Although it was still a couple of hours to dusk, flashes of gunfire in the southwest could easily be seen, and the steady rumble of explosions heard, as Feldmarschall Model's Army Group B tried to break out of the Ruhr before it was encircled and trapped.

"How far now?" asked Fuller.

Lassiter knew the answer to that without having to refer to his map or the jeep's odometer. "Five miles, give or take a few hundred yards. Ten or fifteen minutes, provided Gallagher doesn't get held up by too many red lights."

"Let's hope we don't bump into the Yanks."

"Amen to that."

Although all three men had crossed the Rhine at Wesel with their own unit, the 1st Commando Brigade, on March 23, they now wore German infantry combat uniforms and rank insignia. To avoid unnecessary feats of memory, they all kept, as they always did, the same ranks they held in the British army. Thus Lassiter was a major, Fuller an Unteroffizier, and Gallagher an Obergefreiter. It wasn't a flippant comment from Fuller, the desire to avoid the Americans. Although strictly speaking they were quite a few miles behind the Jerry side of the front, the line was fluid, and the Yanks would doubtless have long-range recce patrols somewhere around. Both Lassiter and Gallagher spoke fluent German without accents, and Fuller had more than enough to get by on. That fact, together with their uniforms and the vehicle, more or less neutralized the threat from the Germans. But bowling along in an open-topped jeep was an invitation to any GI with a bazooka and a grudge to settle the score. Which would not only put them in the graves none of them was quite ready for; it would make the last week a complete waste of time.

After being among the first of the Operation Plunder troops to reach the east bank of the Rhine, the three were left cooling their heels for five days while it was ascertained whether the mission they had been partly briefed on in England was still viable or necessary. Eventually it was decided it was, and shortly after midnight on March 29 they were given their final instructions by the Brigade Intelligence Officer.

They were to proceed to Lippstadt by way of Münster and Gütersloh. Regrettably, transport of the sort they needed was not available; they would have to pick up their own en route. At an address in Lippstadt they were to contact Helen Rand, known locally as Gerda Stein. Mrs. Rand had been infiltrated into the town, ostensibly as a refugee, in January, and had subsequently sent back invaluable information on German troop movements both to and from the Ruhr. She now had class A intelligence on the precise location of Model's rear ammunition warehouse. It was felt desirable by the brass that this dump be destroyed, but it could not be done from the air, as the Germans had resorted to the old trick of painting red crosses on the flat roofs of half a hundred warehouses. The brass wanted no mistakes.

There were also a couple of other matters Major Lassiter might like to take into consideration. Rumor had it that Model was soon to attempt a breakout in the direction of Paderborn. Lippstadt stood between the heart of the Ruhr and that town. Secondly, Mrs. Rand had reported that she was under surveillance. She was not sure how long she would be able to stay at her present address. A day or two at the most.

Twenty minutes later, the three of them slipped away, doffing the camouflage smocks that covered their Wehrmacht uniforms as they went. Heading in the general direction of Münster, they aimed to put as much distance as they could between themselves and the Brigade before daylight. Commandos were not choirboys, and no wearer of the green beret would think twice before slitting what he assumed to be a German throat.

The foremost of Lassiter's immediate problems was transport. Several times in the small hours they came across a column of German vehicles, parked at the side of the road. But on each occasion they gave men and machines a wide berth; there were too many Jerry troops standing around to permit them to consider larceny on a grand scale. What Lassiter was looking for was a straggler, someone who'd been left behind by the main column because of engine or other trouble.

It was getting toward dawn before he found what he wanted: a solitary jeep with its hood open. The driver had his head deep inside the guts of the vehicle, while his partner squatted on the running board, smoking. For both of them, the war was a million miles away.

Lassiter gave it five minutes. The last thing he wanted was to put these two out of action and find another couple emerging from the trees at the side of the road. But eventually he decided that the pair were alone.

Motioning to Fuller to stay where he was and give them covering fire if needed, Lassiter gestured to Gallagher to take the one on the running board.

Sixty seconds later, it was all over. Moving quickly but with a stealth born of long experience, Lassiter could hear his man humming softly as he approached. Because the German's head was partly concealed by the jeep's hood, Lassiter could not go for the jugular. He settled for an upward thrust to the heart from the rear. His aim was off, and at first the knife struck bone. But he twisted his wrist viciously and the blade found its target. He was rewarded with a slight cough, like that of a man clearing his throat of annoying phlegm, and the German died.

Lassiter turned swiftly to see if Gallagher wanted help, but the corporal was already wiping his favorite weapon, a length of piano wire on rope toggles, on the other dead German's tunic. The action was as much a gesture of contempt as the need to cleanse the wire of blood. Gallagher spoke fluent German as the result of a marriage between an Irish father and a German mother. But in 1936, when the boy was barely into his teens, his mother had made a trip to Germany to visit relatives and had never come back. Investigation later proved that she had got caught up in a Brownshirt demonstration in her hometown of Munich, receiving a severe beating simply for being in the way. She died soon afterward of her injuries, and her husband slowly drank himself to death over the next eighteen months.

Thus at fifteen Gallagher was orphaned, and, now, at twenty-two, he had served under Lassiter, a decade his senior, for the last three years. An inch under six feet tall, he was as strong as a bull. He was also an expert in demolition. He had his own reasons for fighting the war the way he did, and Lassiter never questioned them.

A man who knew more about engines than he did about the workings of his own body, Sergeant Fuller fixed the fuel-feed problem in minutes. Soon after daylight, they were skirting Münster to the south and making for Gütersloh, forty miles to the east, where they ran into delays.

Stuck in the middle of the main highway between the Ruhr and Hannover, Gütersloh turned out to be crawling with troops, mostly regular army but with a sprinkling of SS. Without proper movement orders, Lassiter was not in the least anxious to hang around, but he had little choice in the matter. Sometime the previous evening, apparently, a flight of P-51 Mustangs had shot up and bombed the town, and the roads east to Paderborn and south to Lippstadt were temporarily blocked by damaged vehicles. There was nothing to do but sit tight. Fortunately, nobody was much interested in them; they were just three more lost souls among many.

Interrupted by further sorties of P-51s and Mosquitoes, the German pioneer squads required all that day and most of the next to clear up the debris and open the roads. Thus it was not until midafternoon on the thirtieth that Lassiter was given the okay to drive south to Lippstadt. The German military police-man couldn't have cared less about papers. As a traffic controller he was more concerned that he would still be there when all the others had gone.

As far as was possible, Mike Gallagher, who had spent the

night hours "acquiring" jerry cans of gasoline, kept his foot down for the twenty-odd-mile drive, and now, as Lassiter's wrist-watch ticked up to 5 P.M., they were approaching the outskirts of Lippstadt.

The RAF and the U.S. Eighth Air Force had paid several visits here too, but possibly because the town was on the small-ish side or possibly because of the warehouse roofs daubed with red crosses, the only real damage appeared to be around the railway station. And that was old stuff. It was doubtful if Lipp-stadt had seen a bomb in weeks.

Gallagher brought the jeep to a halt. As always in these mat-ters, it was better to be out in the open, where you could be seen and your business assumed legitimate. No one paid them any attention. Small groups of civilians went about their busi-ness, and near the station a handful of small children were play-ing King of the Castle on a mound of rubble. It could have been a small town anywhere save for the constant rumble of gunfire from the west and the Tiger tanks that were prowling the streets. Fuller counted six of them. Of German infantry en masse, however, there was little sign. If Model expected to break out from the Ruhr in this direction, he would receive scant help from the rear.

Lassiter unfolded his hand-drawn street map. This had been assembled from a prewar guide and local intelligence and was not really of much practical use. But it was better than nothing.

He had more or less worked out the quickest route to Min-denstrasse when Gallagher muttered, "Watch it."

Lassiter glanced up. Coming toward the stationary jeep were two SS troopers. When they got closer he observed that the elder of the pair wore the collar tabs of an Unterscharfuehrer, or sergeant, while the younger had the single chevron of a Sturmmann, or lance corporal. But he was dismayed to see that both were displaying SD cuff diamonds. If Amt III, the official designation for the *Sicherheitsdienst*, was here in force, Helen Rand could well be in big trouble. And not only Helen Rand.

The Sturmmann walked slowly round the vehicle like any peacetime London bobby, but the Unterscharfuehrer planted himself in front of the jeep and raised his arm in the Nazi salute.

"Heil Hitler."

Lassiter returned the salute. "Heil Hitler. What can I do for you?" He kept his voice deliberately cold. Apart from the fact that he outranked this pair considerably, there was no love lost between the Wehrmacht and the SS. The Unterscharfuehrer would think it most odd if Lassiter were too friendly.

"It's more a question of what we can do for you, Herr Major. You appear to be lost."

"Far from lost. I have business with Oberst Raschke, who I believe is quartered in Mindenstrasse."

"Raschke, Raschke?" The senior NCO shook his head. "No, I don't believe I know the name."

"There's no reason why you should. My information is that he arrived here only this morning."

"Then he should have reported to SD Headquarters. It is now standard procedure that all army officers above the rank of major report to Standartenfuehrer Geisler on arrival in Lippstadt."

"On whose authority?"

"On the authority of the Standartenfuehrer himself."

Lassiter levered himself out of the jeep. This had gone far enough. It would be papers next, travel documents, movement orders, of which they had none.

He faced the Unterscharfuehrer. Lassiter was a couple of inches over six feet, half a head taller than the German, and considerably broader. His dark hair beneath the field cap was covered with dust, and the face, in the NCO's opinion, was one that had seen many a battle. So it had, but not in the way the SD man assumed.

Involuntarily the German took a pace backward.

"I won't ask you your name," said Lassiter, his eyes never leaving the other man's, "because if I learn it I shall be compelled to report to Standartenfuehrer Geisler that he has an obstructionist in his ranks."

His examination at an end, the Sturmmann rejoined his companion. Lassiter included them both in a blistering dressing down.

He pointed a finger west.

"Can you hear that?" he demanded. "That's the sound of Feldmarschall Model fighting the Americans. Oberst Raschke is on the Feldmarschall's staff and I have an urgent message for him. If he does not receive it, there is a possibility that the whole of Army Group B will be trapped in the Ruhr, and if I am delayed any longer the responsibility for that catastrophe will be yours—as I shall make quite clear to any court of inquiry. I need not tell you what will happen then. Not only will the pair of you be shot, but your families will be incarcerated in a concentration camp until they're too old to care. If you want that to happen, continue as you have been doing. If you do not, kindly direct me to Mindenstrasse and get back to the sty from which you undoubtedly came."

The Unterscharfuehrer was nobody's fool. Like many non-commissioned officers in the security arm of the SS, he had risen from the ranks by keeping his nose clean and obeying orders. He knew authority when he saw it and wanted no trouble. It did not occur to him, as it would not have occurred to any other man in his position, that the officer now berating him was anything other than he purported to be.

"I apologize, Herr Major," he stammered. "It was not my intention to be obstructive. But you must understand that we have been warned to look out for deserters. Now that the Americans are so close, there are many who do not wish to fight to the end."

Lassiter decided to rub it in and give him both barrels. Get him jittery and he might reveal something he shouldn't.

"*Deserters!*" he raged. "Are you implying that we are deserters? I'll have your head, you son of a malignant sow! If we were going over to the enemy would we be sitting in the middle of Lippstadt?"

"No, Herr Major."

"No, Herr Major. And you . . . ?" Lassiter turned on the Sturmmann. This one was little more than a boy and wanted to hear nothing of firing squads and concentration camps.

"No, Herr Major." A pair of heels clicked deferentially.

Lassiter took a couple of deep breaths. He'd made his point; there was no percentage in overplaying it.

"Good," he said in a normal voice. "Then perhaps one of you will direct me to Mindenstrasse."

They almost fought each other for the privilege. It was a fifteen-minute drive away, down by the river, and apparently the HQ of Geisler and the SD were on the same street. Lassiter had never met Helen Rand, but he had to admire her guts. There were no medals in that line of work.

He swung aboard the jeep. But before giving Gallagher the go-ahead, he risked another question. The presence of the SD in such a small town disturbed him, and it would be useful to know their strength. He would have liked to ask the location of the ammunition warehouse also, but that was tempting fate too far.

"Tell me," he said, "what's the SD doing in a place like this anyway? With a Standartenfuehrer in command, there must be a regiment of you. I wouldn't have thought you had that many deserters to cope with and might be better employed in the front line."

The Unterscharfuehrer was now anxious to curry favor with this bad-tempered major, especially at the mention of the front line.

"Until a few days ago, sir, there were just five of us, commanded by an Untersturmfuehrer. Then there was some talk about radio messages being picked up, and the Standartenfuehrer arrived. It cannot be too serious, however, as he brought only his driver."

Too bloody right it was serious, thought Lassiter. From a small detachment commanded by a second lieutenant to the sudden appearance of a full colonel. Things were not looking too healthy for Mrs. Rand.

"Spies," he scoffed. "Radio signals. If I had a Reichsmark for every spy I'd heard of but never seen captured, I'd be as rich as Reichsmarschall Goering. Heil Hitler."

Leaving both Germans with their arms in the air, Gallagher moved the jeep off on cue. "Jesus Christ, Skipper, that was better than the pictures."

"Bloody right," agreed Fuller. "Another couple of minutes and they'd have given you the keys to the city. I don't care much for security colonels turning up, though. What d'you think it means?"

"I dunno," said Lassiter, "but I just hope to Christ we're not too late."

Depending upon the way you looked at it, Lassiter was to think some time afterward, they were too late by about twenty minutes. Unlucky, perhaps. On the other hand, had they arrived twenty minutes earlier, they too might have been swept up in the net. In any event, as they passed number 23 Mindenstrasse at 5:45, there was a black staff car parked in front of it, a pennant fluttering from its hood. Even as they watched, a woman in her middle forties was bundled roughly into the street by a couple of SS troopers and thrust into the back seat. Overseeing events from the sidewalk were two jackbooted officers: a bespectacled Standartenfuehrer and a much younger Untersturmfuehrer.

Gallagher needed no advice to keep going, though he kept his head and held the speed of the jeep down to a steady 30 m.p.h. Mindenstrasse was a long street with what appeared to be few side turnings. He didn't want to panic anyone into firing at them with a submachine gum. With houses on both sides to take the ricochets, they'd be picked off like fish in a barrel.

"Try not to make it too obvious, but tell me what's going on, Harry," said Lassiter over his shoulder.

Fuller half-turned in his seat. "The two officers are getting into the staff car. It's coming this way. The troopers are walking, same direction."

"That figures. Geisler's HQ is in this street too, remember. Watch where the car stops. I don't see any flags."

"It's still coming . . . still coming. . . . Now it's stopped and they're getting out. I've got it . . . small gray building. Looks like a private house."

"Fine. Keep driving, Mike," said Lassiter. "I've got to think this thing out. How's the fuel situation, incidentally?"

"No problem. Where do you want me to go?"

"Make it the station."

While the two NCOs sat in the jeep and smoked in silence,

42

Lassiter paced up and down and pondered his next move—if there was one.

The area around the station was more or less deserted. The kids had finished their King of the Castle game and gone home, and the crew of a Tiger tank a couple of hundred yards away seemed more interested in their card game than in anything else. At 6 o'clock a foot patrol—Wehrmacht, not SS—put in an appearance but made themselves scarce on seeing a fully fledged major with something on his mind. You could never tell in this war: one minute you were on garrison duty, the next you were fighting the Russians. It was best to keep out of the way.

By 6:15 Lassiter was ready to admit defeat. He hated doing it, but Brigadier Greenleigh's orders had been specific. Find and destroy the ammo dump if you can; otherwise, target of opportunity.

Lassiter was not normally a man who paid much attention to rigid orders; he improvised as he went along. But without Mrs. Rand, there was no warehouse, and he could see no way of getting her out of the clutches of the SD.

He walked slowly over to the jeep.

"I think we'll have to abort. We can assume that the lady in the staff car was Mrs. Rand, and I'm sorry for her. But there's nothing we can do to help. She knew the risks and took them, and without her we're lost. There must be fifty or sixty warehouses in town, and you can bet your life the one we want hasn't got a convenient sign painted on the door. We could wander around for days without locating it, and by tomorrow that Unterscharfuehrer might have got over his nerves and be asking questions about the nonexistent Oberst Raschke."

"We should blow the shit out of something," said Gallagher. For two days he had been carrying around his explosives, detonators and time fuses, now safely stashed under his seat in the jeep, and he was reluctant to go home without using them. "Even if it's only that SS HQ."

"And Mrs. Rand?"

"We'd be doing her a favor."

"Maybe—but we don't know what else they've got in there. They could have a small ammo dump of their own. Set that off and you might destroy the whole street, innocent people and all."

"They're bloody Germans," muttered Gallagher.

Lassiter did not reprimand him. In any other unit a remark like that to a senior officer would have earned a subordinate a sharp rebuke. But it didn't work that way for those who served under Lassiter. Anyone was allowed to say precisely what he thought. Lassiter was a leader not because of the crown he customarily wore on his shoulder but because of ability. He had joined the Royal Marines in the ranks at the start of the war, had transferred to the commandos and had been commissioned in 1940. He had a DSO and an MC to his name, as well as half a dozen Mentions in Dispatches. He was an official hero, though he would have blanched at this description. Anyone who has fought in a war knows that DSOs and MCs are handed out there for acts which would merit hefty prison sentences in peacetime. He had killed many times, ruthlessly and indiscriminately, and sometimes the blameless had suffered. But he was still against the murder of innocents if it could be avoided.

Sergeant Fuller tapped Gallagher on the arm, an unmistakable sign to cool it. He understood Lassiter's thinking. The only real way out of the dilemma was to liberate Mrs. Rand, and there was no way that the three of them could storm Geisler's HQ. They might dispose of some of the troopers, but Mrs. Rand would be dead before they could reach her. And so would they.

It was one thing to defy the odds. It was another to commit suicide.

Lassiter climbed aboard the jeep. "I noticed a side road on the way down from Gütersloh. It's no more than a track on the map, but it looks as if it leads in the general direction of Münster. We'll take that and try to avoid any further traffic snarl-ups. Take it easy, Mike. I'll find you something to reduce to rubble."

44

FIVE

They had been traveling for half an hour in silence, none of them happy that they had abandoned their primary target and the unfortunate Mrs. Rand.

The tree-lined road was empty of other traffic; little wonder, as it was in a poor state of repair. Its surface was pitted and broken, the result of age and neglect as opposed to bombs and shells. But its general direction was north and should bring them out west of Gütersloh, between that town and Münster.

"What the hell's that?"

Lassister's mind was elsewhere, and Fuller, who could sleep on a bed of nails, was catching up on some rest in the back. But Gallagher's sharp eyes were scouring the countryside as well as watching the road.

"What's what?" Lassiter was quickly alert.

"Over there." Gallagher dropped down a gear and pointed to a gap in the trees. Beyond it lay a track which led up to what appeared to be a small farmhouse, and stationary in the court-yard, totally unconcealed, was a vehicle with an unmistakable star on the side. American.

"Looks like a Yank half-track."

"That's what it looks like to me too. What the hell's it doing there?"

"I haven't a bloody clue." Lassiter made a rapid decision. "Let's go and find out."

"Are you kidding, Skip?" Fuller was rubbing his eyes. "The way we're dressed they'll shoot us first and find out who we are later."

"Not if we use our heads. Besides, I'd rather face a handful than a division. This could be one of the long-range recce patrols we were worried about earlier. If it is, I'd like to know where the rest of them are."

"Reconnaissance. Not a chance." Fuller shook his head emphatically. "One vehicle and no guard. It's probably been there for years."

"There hasn't *been* an American here for years, Harry. Put the motor in the trees, Mike. We'll walk the rest of the way."

The farmhouse was three hundred yards off the road, but there was no need to approach it directly. It was a simple matter to come in via the trees and outbuildings without being seen.

Lassiter couldn't make it out. If it was a recce patrol, it seemed the height of madness to park the half-track without any camouflage cover whatsoever. Or without posting a guard. Then again, the Yanks were a law unto themselves. He'd once seen, shortly after D-Day, a tank commander, a captain, leap from the cockpit of his Sherman in a street where the bullets were flying and dive into a shop, emerging a couple of seconds later with a bottle of brandy in each hand.

Rounding a barn just thirty feet from the main house, Lassiter suddenly held up his hand and ducked back. There was a guard, although the last thing he was doing was keeping watch. Dressed in combat fatigues with his steel helmet pushed well back from his face, he was peering through the window, seemingly absorbed by some activity inside the house.

"Take him, Harry," ordered Lassiter. "Don't hurt him, but make sure he doesn't get noisy. He might be the real McCoy, but if we can dress up in fake uniforms so can anyone else."

Fuller nodded, handing his submachine gun to Gallagher.

They watched him cross the courtyard. A Londoner born and bred, Sergeant Fuller had served as a regular soldier for the last ten of his thirty-one years, with Lassiter for four of them. After the debacle at Dunkirk, he transferred to the commandos, reasoning that only that elite force would be seeing any action for a while. Somewhere in Bayswater was a marriage, which had failed, and two children, who hadn't. Above average height with fair hair and blue eyes, he looked more German than most Germans. Lassiter used him a lot when there was a stretch of open ground to be covered. Somehow—and Lassiter had never quite worked out how the phenomenon operated—he became part of the landscape, finding shadows where there were none and moving with incredible speed. One second he was by your side, the next he was where you'd told him to go. And even on reflection no one could ever remember seeing him cross from A to B.

As happened now. Hardly, it seemed, were the instructions out of Lassiter's throat when the young GI was being bent backward, reaching with desperate fingers for the brawny forearm that was crushing his windpipe, stifling any possible cry for help.

Fuller jerked the GI to one side as Lassiter and Gallagher reached the window. "Take a look," he said in German.

The curtains were half drawn, but one glance was sufficient for them to see what had been holding the GI's interest. The room beyond was a kitchen, and thrown across the table, her legs wide apart, her skirt up by her hips, was a young German girl. She could not have been more than fifteen. Her head lolled to one side, but her eyes were wide open, her state of cataleptic shock obvious. Straddling her was a muscular sergeant, his trousers around his ankles. His hands were beneath her buttocks, and he was pulling her onto him, then letting her go, rapidly, savagely. Lounging on straight chairs and swigging from a bottle, which they passed to and fro, were a couple of PFCs.

The sergeant was in the act of climaxing when Lassiter burst in through the kitchen door, but he whipped away from the girl as some part of his brain received the danger signal. His erection fell like an old tree when he saw he was facing three German soldiers, each brandishing a submachine gun with the safety off. He moved a couple of shuffling paces in the direction of his carbine before realizing the futility of the gesture. Finally, he opted for standing perfectly still.

The two PFCs were transfixed, either too shocked or too stupefied with drink to do more than gape.

Fuller heaved the so-called lookout into the middle of the room. He fell in a heap and stayed there, awaiting the inevitable bullet. The sergeant found his voice then and began yelling about sonsabitches who couldn't keep their fuckin' eyes open. Gallagher silenced him with a hefty blow to the stomach, using the gun butt.

Lassiter spoke in English while keeping his accent heavily

German. Somewhere at the back of his mind an idea was being born.

"So, the brave Americans are taking their revenge on children, are they?"

"Fuck off, Kraut." Rubbing his guts, the sergeant decided he had nothing to lose by being belligerent. He was going to die anyway. "She's just getting what you've been handing out to the French and the Poles and the Czechs for the last six years. You didn't hear her screaming, did ya? She was getting to like it."

Lassiter issued some rapid instructions to Fuller in German. "Get her into another room and feed her brandy or something. Ask her if she's got any parents or relatives around."

The girl had not moved from the table. Gently, Fuller pulled down her dress and picked her up in his arms. There was a bruise on her temple, her lower lip was bleeding and her breathing was dangerously shallow. But the worst damage would be in her head.

He closed the door behind him.

"Pull your pants up and sit over there," Lassiter ordered the sergeant. "You have nothing to boast about anyway."

The American did as he was told.

"Are you going to kill us?" asked one of the PFCs.

"Perhaps not—not if you tell me what I want to know. For example, where is the rest of your unit?"

"You keep your fucking mouth shut, Abrahams," snarled the sergeant. "One word out of you and I'll see you in front of a firing squad."

"Fuck you, Mancini. You're no longer in charge of this detail."

Abrahams and the other PFC, ably aided and abetted by the youngster on the floor, couldn't get the words out fast enough. They were part of the 2nd Armored Division on a reconnaissance patrol. They had been ordered to stay only a couple of miles ahead of the division, but Mancini, who was "a medal-hunting bastard," had pushed on. Abrahams reckoned the rest of the division was between six and ten miles behind them.

Lassiter was going to ask them what sort of speed the division was making when Fuller returned, alone. He shook his head and said, in German, "The girl's dead. I don't know whether it was shock or that crack on the skull one of these bastards gave her. There's no one else around."

"That makes it simpler."

"What are you going to do with them?" asked Gallagher.

"I'm going to take them in," said Lassiter, "back to Lippstadt. Let's see if Geisler can find a use for them."

It was almost dark by the time they reached Mindenstrasse, but not dark enough to cloak the hive of activity in front of the building that housed the SD. The black staff car was parked at the curb, and into its massive trunk boxes of documents were being loaded.

Traveling back seven to the jeep had proved a tight squeeze, but none of the four Americans jammed across the back seat, covered by Lassiter and Fuller from the front, had made any move to escape.

Gallagher cruised to a halt a hundred yards from the gray building. "Looks as if they're pulling out." Although neither he nor Fuller knew what was in Lassiter's mind, it seemed obvious that the major wanted them to continue in German, and this was the language Gallagher used.

"Typical SS. They'll leave the Wehrmacht to do the fighting while they scarper."

"They won't leave the ammo dump, surely to Christ," muttered Fuller.

"They don't give a shit about the ammo," Lassiter said. "You know what these people are like. They're not Waffen SS, they're the other sort, political. The ammunition's got nothing to do with them. If Model can fight his way through to it, it's his. If he can't—well, that's no business of theirs. Drive up to the front door. Let's see what Geisler has to say when we present him with four prisoners."

A brace of SS troopers, boxes in their arms, stared in amazement as Lassiter marched the four Americans at gunpoint up the short flight of steps and into the house. Geisler was nowhere to be seen, but the Untersturmfuehrer was in the passage, directing operations.

Lassiter did a rapid head count. Two troopers on the sidewalk and two plus the Untersturmfuehrer in the passage. There was no sign of the Unterscharfuehrer and the Sturmmann they had met earlier in the day, so presumably they were still out on patrol. A total of six enlisted men and one second lieutenant, therefore, accounted for everybody, including Geisler's driver. The only person missing was the Standartenfuehrer himself, and there could be little doubt as to what he was up to. Lassiter demanded to see him.

The Untersturmfuehrer hesitated. "I regret that that will not be possible, Herr Major. He is . . . er . . . otherwise engaged. We have been ordered to empty the building of our more valuable files. There are rumors that the Americans are only a few miles away."

"They're more than rumors." Lassiter indicated the prisoners, who were now looking considerably shaken in the presence of so many SS uniforms. "These four belong to a reconnaissance patrol I captured earlier. With proper interrogation they will doubtless yield valuable intelligence. I must hand them over to the senior SD officer before going on."

"You can hand them over to me. I'll see they're properly dealt with."

I'll bet, thought Lassiter. He shook his head. "I must see Standartenfuehrer Geisler."

"That is not possible, Herr Major. He is questioning an enemy agent we picked up earlier."

"Where? Which room?"

"Herr Major . . ."

"It's your head if you don't tell me. If your superior officer is still conducting an interrogation when American tanks roll into Lippstadt, you'll be dangling from a lamppost long before you become a POW."

The Untersturmfuehrer saw some sense in this. He pointed along the corridor, to a closed door at the far end.

Motioning to Gallagher and Fuller to remain where they were, Lassiter strode down the passage. Aware that he was being watched all the way, he rapped politely on the door and pushed it open.

Standartenfuehrer Geisler was in his shirt sleeves, smoking a cigarette. Helen Rand was tied to an upright chair, naked to the

50

waist. There were cigarette burns and weals on her torso, and her face was a mass of blood and bruises. She was alive, but in bad shape.

Geisler turned at the sudden intrusion. "What the goddamn hell—"

"Herr Standartenfuehrer," began Lassiter, closing the door behind him. As he did so he noticed that it was covered with some kind of thick insulating material. It was a typical SD and Gestapo precaution. Whatever went on on the inside would not be heard on the out.

After that he did not mince matters. Before Geisler could say anything more, Lassiter hit him between the eyes with the muzzle of his MP 38. The SD colonel staggered and fell, out cold.

Lassiter pulled what remained of Helen Rand's blouse up around her shoulders and set about cutting her bonds.

"How bad is it?"

It was very bad. She was barely conscious, but she knew an English voice when she heard one. "All right," she answered faintly.

There was another question Lassiter had to ask.

"Do the SD have their own ammunition supply in the building?"

In no more than a whisper, she told him they did not.

Lassiter half-opened the door and called along the passage. "The Standartenfuehrer wishes everyone in here immediately. Hurry."

Gallagher and Fuller were sufficiently experienced to know that they had to be last in, and in under thirty seconds one junior SD officer and four very bewildered troopers were disarmed and facing the wall.

Events had moved far too fast for the Americans. They hadn't a clue as to what was going on until Lassiter spoke to Gallagher in English.

"Tie 'em up, Mike. Use their belts and make sure it's a good job. Geisler too. He's the gent with the bump on his head."

Sergeant Mancini's mouth dropped a foot. "You're *British*?"

"That's right."

"Then what the hell's all this about?"

"I needed you to get me in."

"So now you'll let us go, right?"

"Wrong. You killed that girl back at the farm."

"She was a fucking German, for Chrissake."

"She was also a child." Lassiter helped Mrs. Rand to her feet. He could sense her summoning up her last reserves of strength. "Can you stand?"

"I think so. Have you come for the warehouse?"

"That's the general idea, but now we can take you out as well. Shake it up, Mike, we haven't got all day."

"Just about finished. What about the Yanks?"

Lassiter didn't hesitate. The Americans were guilty of a filthy crime against a kid. At least, three of them were and the fourth by association. Besides, he needed their uniforms. When the job was over his group couldn't head in the general direction of the 2nd Armored Division dressed as Germans.

"They stay. Tell your men to strip down to their underwear," he ordered Mancini.

"You can't leave us here, you bastard."

Lassiter was in no mood to argue. Any minute now the patrolling Unterscharfuehrer and the Sturmmann could put in an appearance.

"We can do this the easy way or the hard way," he said. "Either you strip off or I shoot you. This is a soundproof room, so no one would hear a thing. Please yourself."

The other three looked at Mancini for a lead, but the sergeant had seen enough trained killers to know that Lassiter would carry out the threat quicker than spitting.

"Do it," he said quietly.

Fuller gathered up the uniforms while Gallagher bound the Americans, back to back in pairs. As a final refinement he looped spare lengths of piano wire around each pair's throats tightly. One false or sudden movement and someone would end up headless.

All in all they had been in the building under ten minutes when Lassiter pulled Gallagher to one side. He explained in whispers that he wanted a diversion fixed up and what form it should take.

"Can do?"

"No problem. Take me a couple of minutes, maybe five."

"Get on with it, then."

Gallagher went out.

"What about gags, Skip?" asked Fuller.

"Not necessary. No one will hear them from in here. In any case, I'll be sitting outside the door for the next half hour. If anybody becomes ambitious they also become dead. Take Mrs. Rand and the uniforms out to the jeep, Harry. I'll see you there shortly."

Alone with the Germans and the Americans, Lassiter walked across to Geisler. He was still unconscious. Lassiter kicked him in the ribs, hard, to make sure he wasn't faking.

"You'll swing for this, whoever the hell you are," said Mancini, but there was no conviction in his voice.

"Maybe," said Lassiter from the door, "but I wouldn't bank on it."

Gallagher was on his knees in the corridor, sorting through the complex materials of his specialty.

"Harry says you're staying here, Skip."

"That was just for their benefit. We'll be moving off as soon as you're ready."

"Another minute."

It was totally dark outside now, and Lassiter had difficulty making out Fuller and Mrs. Rand in the jeep, which the sergeant had driven forty or fifty yards away from the SD HQ. Certainly, from a distance no one would be able to tell that one of the occupants was a woman, not now that Fuller had put a Wehrmacht greatcoat over her shoulders.

"How far off is the warehouse?" asked Lassiter, scrambling aboard.

"A five-minute drive." Fuller had fed her some brandy from a bottle filched from the farmhouse, and she sounded better. Not much, but better.

"Guards?"

"Just two, at the front. The red crosses are enough. They don't want to make it obvious from the air that the place is surrounded by troops."

"Good. Can you stand the pain for a few hours more?"

"Do I have a choice?"

Gallagher came out at a run. "I've set it for ten minutes, to be on the safe side."

Lassiter checked his wristwatch. "Should be plenty."

Mrs. Rand, understanding, looked at him. "The Americans too?"

"They're the same breed. Let's go, Mike. Mrs. Rand will tell you where."

They parked in the shadows opposite the warehouse. Lassiter could vaguely make out the guards' silhouettes as they paced up and down. If he was any judge of character, they too would be listening to the pounding in the southwest as the Ruhr was blasted to dust.

Nine minutes after leaving Mindenstrasse he climbed out of the jeep. Gallagher and Fuller followed him. Mrs. Rand stayed where she was.

"You there!"

The guards stiffened to attention at the authority in Lassiter's voice. He addressed the nearer of them.

"Is everything all right?"

"Yes, Herr Major, everything's quiet."

"You must be deaf, then."

The first guard chuckled nervously, but the second was made of sterner stuff and protested mildly as Lassiter walked around him and tried the lock on the massive steel shutters.

"You will forgive me, Herr Major, but no one is allowed in this area without a pass."

"That doesn't apply to me, you fool."

"It applies to everyone, sir. Those are my orders."

"Then your company commander is an idiot. Doesn't he realize that at this point in the war some orders are out of date before the ink's dry?" Lassiter was mentally totting up the seconds. If Gallagher had set his fuses correctly, there were about ten seconds to go before the big bang.

"We've had reports of saboteurs in the vicinity, and my detachment is here to make sure—"

That was as far as he got. Right on cue, the gray house in Mindenstrasse went up with an earsplitting roar. Sheets of flame leaped skyward. The warehouse was a good half mile from the eye of the explosion, but even so it seemed like the end of the world. In the jeep, in spite of herself, Mrs. Rand shuddered at the thought of the men, American and German alike,

54

being blasted to pieces. Her late husband had once said that this war bred no heroes, and that was the truth of it.

Lassiter feigned bewildered astonishment.

"What the Christ in hell was that?"

Both guards were looking fearfully toward the heavens.

"Could have been a bomb, sir."

"Bomb, my ass! Has there been an alert, can you hear aircraft? That was a ground explosion. Come on."

He moved rapidly away from the warehouse, followed by Gallagher and Fuller. But the two Germans stood their ground.

"What the hell's the matter with you two? They're going to need every man they can get up there."

The second guard—an Obergefreiter, they could now see— was taking no chances. His orders were explicit, and with Germanic obedience he was not going to move until they were countermanded by his company commander.

"I'm sorry, Herr Major, but if that was a ground explosion and there are saboteurs around, this warehouse is an obvious target. We must stay where we are."

Ah, well, thought Lassiter, and brought the submachine gun up to a firing position. Serves you right for being on the wrong side.

The Obergefreiter saw what was about to happen long before his companion, but he was too late to do anything about it. Lassiter's first burst cut him in half. The other trooper was trapped in a no-man's-land of indecision. Part of him wanted to fight back and part of him wanted to throw up his hands. The former was winning when Lassiter put an end to his dilemma. Then, without taking his finger from the trigger, he shattered the lock.

"Get going, Mike, and don't take all day about it. Somebody else might come to the conclusion that there are saboteurs on the loose and decide to reinforce the guard down here. We'll be with the jeep."

Gallagher raised the shutters and disappeared into the bowels of the ammo dump.

From other parts of town came the sound of automatic and rifle fire, as nervous Germans, confused by the explosion, took potshots at shadows.

"Won't be long," said Lassiter. Mrs. Rand was shivering. She had to be in great pain, but so far she had uttered no word of complaint.

"I'm all right."

"We'll soon have you out of it."

A couple of minutes passed. Lassiter and Fuller kept their eyes on street corners. The last thing they needed was for a nosy tank to poke its head in, although neither of them urged Mike Gallagher, even silently, to shake it up. Gallagher was the best and fastest demolition expert there was. He would do what he had to, and then he would leave.

"The diversion was unnecessary, wasn't it?" asked Mrs. Rand suddenly.

Lassiter had to think for a moment before he knew what she was talking about. "Not entirely."

"But the guards were to die anyway."

Lassiter did not answer.

Six minutes elapsed before Gallagher came out of the warehouse sprinting.

"I'll drive," he said to Fuller, who was behind the wheel in preparation for a quick getaway. "I want to be in Holland before that bloody lot goes up."

As it happened, they had covered fifteen kilometers on the jeep's odometer before a blinding flash illuminated the landscape. Moments later, the earth beneath them trembled massively. They stopped the vehicle and looked back. It seemed as if the whole of Lippstadt were on fire. Feldmarschall Model might or might not break out of the Ruhr, but if he did there would be no bullets for his guns, shells for his artillery or fuel for his tanks.

At a little before 6 A.M. on Easter morning, April 1, Company E of the 67th Armored Regiment, 2nd Armored Division, entered the outskirts of Lippstadt. It encountered little resistance, but the company commander was surprised to find evidence of two recent explosions. The prisoners he took were none the wiser either, and in his report he put it down to the work of partisans.

Later in the day a scouting patrol came across the abandoned half-track and the dead girl at the farmhouse. Checking the original occupants of the half-track was easy, but no trace was ever found of Sergeant Mancini and his crew. They were designated missing, believed killed.

But by this time Lassiter, Fuller and Gallagher, together with Mrs. Rand, were on their way back to England.

SIX

For the first two weeks in April Mr. Churchill wrestled with his conscience and did everything within his considerable powers to persuade Eisenhower to occupy as much of Germany as possible. The Supreme Commander refused, and to make matters worse had now decided merely to drive east and attain a general line on the Elbe. Farther than that he would not go.

Stalin, of course, was delighted with this turn of events, and in a most secret cable to Eisenhower agreed that Berlin had lost its former strategic importance. Accordingly (he wired), he planned to use secondary forces for the assault on the capital while concentrating his main attack in the area of Erfurt, Leipzig and Dresden.

That much was for public consumption. Privately, the Soviet leader was planning to hit Berlin with everything he had. An old Georgian proverb said "Acquire first, argue later." Stalin intended doing just that.

The Allies had always agreed that unconditional surrender by the Germans was all they would accept and that no private deals would be made with the Nazi hierarchy. It bothered Mr. Churchill that he could even contemplate otherwise.

On April 12 at 3:35 P.M. Central Time, President Roosevelt died of a massive cerebral hemorrhage, and in spite of the sadness he felt at the passing of an old friend, Churchill thought momentarily that he could convince the new incumbent, Truman, of Eisenhower's strategic folly. In this he was wrong.

Even so, the final straw was not laid until the fifteenth, when Lt. General William Simpson's Ninth Army was ordered to withdraw across the Elbe and hold there. Simpson was dismayed and disappointed. He could, he told correspondents later, have been in Berlin within twenty-four hours.

58

For Churchill that settled the matter. For some reason he could not divine, the Americans seemed quite prepared to let Stalin do what he wished in Europe. He immediately called Greenleigh and told him to "get on with it."

To: VALKYRIE   CVX/003/SSS/14000/Z/15.4.45
From: NEMESIS

      OPERATION HORSETRADE ACTIVATED WITH IMMEDIATE
      EFFECT IN ACCORDANCE WITH PREVIOUSLY AGREED
      MODUS OPERANDI.

SEVEN

Unknown to either London or Berlin, ears other than those of Hauptsturmfuehrer Langendorf had been monitoring the signals between Valkyrie and Nemesis, though for the moment the eavesdroppers had nothing more than a meaningless sheaf of coded messages. If the bastards were using a one-time pad or something similar, Major General Jake Bellinger reckoned he stood about as much chance of cracking the cipher as Paul Robeson did of getting elected to public office in Mississippi. About all his team had succeeded in establishing so far was that somebody had a hot line going between the two capitals. Which disturbed Bellinger. The British were doing or trying something he didn't know about, and that could only be bad news.

Now aged forty-four, Jake Bellinger had found himself whisked out of a combat command and given two stars when Major General William S. Donovan's Office of Strategic Services, the OSS, was officially given that title in June 1942. For the past three years, with only a couple of trips out of the country to relieve the monotony, his headquarters had been the American Legation in Berne, Switzerland, and Swiss food and wine had put on poundage around his midriff that hadn't been there when he commanded his own regiment. He'd had more hair then, too, but he guessed a lot of men who'd started this war with a full head were now as bald as billiard balls.

He chewed on a hangnail and considered the problem.

Fact: that someone in Berlin was transmitting to London at irregular intervals. Fact: that someone in London was transmitting back. Fact: that he had precious little else to go on. Not enough, certainly, to go to Mr. Dulles and ask him to make a few waves via Washington.

Officially Special Assistant to the Minister at the Berne Legation, Allen Dulles was in fact chief of the OSS in Switzerland and, as such, Jake Bellinger's superior. He was not a man to be interested in unsubstantiated guesswork, not ever, but especially not now that his gout was kicking up. "Don't talk to me about instinct, Jake. Come back when you've got something solid, when you've cracked the code." That would be Allen Dulles' reaction, and it was fair enough. Intelligence organizations could exist only by dealing in hard knowledge, not rumor or sixth-sense brainwaves or the fact that the sun was in Sagittarius. Except in this case, Jake Bellinger had a feeling . . .

Bellinger pressed the buzzer of the intercom on his desk. "Chuck, will you come in here a minute?"

The door opened before Bellinger had time to get his cigar going properly, and Major Charles Fodor came in without knocking.

Fodor was one of the few people on OSS strength in the Legation whom Jake Bellinger actually approved of. Six feet tall and just under thirty, Fodor was a Californian by birth. That he had spent most of his childhood and adolescence in a sunny climate was revealed by a strong face that never entirely lost its tan, regardless of where he was serving. Give him a couple of days in the sun and his fair hair turned almost white.

Until recently he had served in a combat capacity with the U.S. 17th Airborne Division, but back in January somebody had pulled his name from the hat, seen that he was university educated and fluent in German, Italian, French and Russian, and given him the option of either being seconded to the Berne Legation or being shipped back to the States to teach rookies how to jump out of aircraft. He had opted for Berne after being assured that the shortage of linguists was only temporary and that doubtless he would be returned to his unit within a couple of weeks. Which was as close to a downright lie as staff officers ever came. Unless a miracle happened, he was an office boy for the duration, and his frustration was aggravated now that the 17th Airborne had dropped on the Rhine as part of Operation Varsity on March 23. While the rest of the division would be in at the kill, he was cooling his heels.

"Yes, sir?"

"Sit down, Chuck." Fodor pulled up a chair. "Having any luck with the London thing?"

"None, sir. As I tried to tell you when I got here, what I know about cryptanalysis—"

"Spare me the agony, Chuck. You're not here to do the donkey work. You're here to make sure the PFCs and the Ivy Leaguers stick to their guns."

"A job for a second lieutenant."

"When we can find one who speaks four languages, you're on your way. Until then, you might as well quit griping. It's not going to get you anywhere. If they'd left me out in the field, I'd have a division, maybe a whole army, to myself by now. We do what we're told to. Ike and Patton get the headlines; you and I are the unsung warriors. Look on the bright side: there's not much decent tail available in the Ruhr right now. Between you, you and Scipioni should be having the time of your lives. Anyway, let's drop the whole subject. Just fill me in on how far you've gotten."

"As I said, nowhere. As far as I can see, they've tried everything. It's got to be a one-time pad. We don't even know which language they're in. It could be Navajo. The boys are clean out of ideas, and I haven't got any to feed them. It's occurred to quite a lot of them, though, that why don't we just ask the British? Christ, they're supposed to be our allies. Give them the frequency and the dates of transmission and ask them what's going on."

Bellinger tried blowing a smoke ring and failed.

"Can't be done. It may have escaped your notice, Chuck, but we're not too popular with our British friends anymore. When Ike changed his strategy and gave up the idea of Berlin, the name of the game became noncooperation. The British would either tell us to go to hell and mind our own business or say the signals are from one of their SOE guys."

"Which is probably the case anyway."

"But isn't."

Fodor looked at his commanding officer with interest.

"Don't get me wrong," Bellinger continued. "I don't know any more than you do. But after three years sitting in this chair, you develop a nose for something that doesn't smell right. It's like doing a recce. The road ahead may be quiet and you've been given hard intelligence that there isn't a Kraut for miles, but you know as sure as the world is round that there's trouble lurking up front."

Fodor nodded. He'd had that feeling many a time. It had saved his life more than once.

"This is more than just routine, Chuck," said Bellinger. "I know it is. I don't know what and I don't know why, but there's something here we should be in on."

"Then I guess it's time to get back." Fodor shrugged. "Though I don't see it doing any good. Unless we get lucky, we don't stand a chance of cracking it."

In the cipher department everyone was hard at work when Fodor returned, though not all of them, of course, were working on the London–Berlin intercepts. One or two of them weren't working on intercepts at all, although Joe Scipioni, with whom Fodor shared an apartment, was doing his best to give the impression that the phone conversation he was engaged in would end World War II. Fodor knew better. Scipioni was using his huskiest come-hither voice, which could mean only that he was setting up his evening's entertainment.

"Forget it." Fodor put his hand on the cradle, breaking the connection. "Whatever you've promised her she's not going to get."

"Promised who?" Scipioni's dark brown eyes filled with injured innocence. "That was a possible contact."

"I don't doubt it. Neither do I doubt which part of her you'd be coming into contact with. But not tonight, Josephina. We have work to do."

"Shit," said Scipioni. "I knew I should have listened to my ma and fought on the other side."

"War's hell, as the man said."

But for the fact that a couple of adventurous grandparents had emigrated to the New World around the turn of the century, Lieutenant Giuseppe Scipioni—Joe to his friends—could well have been fighting on the other side. As it was, he had enlisted as a soldier as soon as the United States entered the war, been granted a field commission in 1943 and transferred to the 17th Airborne after figuring out that it was better to be flown there than walk there. He spoke fluent German and Italian, and at the time of Fodor's seconding to Berne had been included in the package at his friend's insistence. This was not so much to keep Scipioni out of the firing line; Fodor had a much more devious reason than that. Having served in the army for the duration, he knew that the brass make promises one minute and break them the next. Once they had a certain Major Fodor on the Legation strength, they were unlikely to let him go until, and unless, they could find a replacement. Fodor's scheme was to get Lieutenant Scipioni noticed, get him promoted, then get the hell out of it himself, back where the action was.

Unfortunately, it hadn't worked out that way.

Scipioni had taken to Switzerland rather more than to his work. Now aged twenty-four, with his dark good looks he was much in demand, and it was a rare evening that he didn't have a female companion for bedding. As far as he was concerned—always bearing in mind that he was as useful here as anywhere else—he couldn't give a damn if he never heard a shot fired in anger again, though as a paratroop officer he had been one of the best.

"Okay," he said reluctantly, "what the hell's so urgent to prevent me getting laid?"

"This London–Berlin business, that's what the hell's so urgent. If we don't come up with an answer soon, Bellinger's going to have a fit."

"Then there's no problem," said Scipioni. Fodor looked at him. "We can't get in touch with London, right? They'd tell us to go jump, right?"

"Right."

"Then it's simple. We pick up the phone, ask for long distance and call the Reichstag. . . ."

Fodor heaved a book at him.

If it was important to Berne to know what was going on in Berlin, many of that capital's inhabitants wanted to know what was happening on the outside. Hard news was at a premium for the average citizen. All he could do was sit tight and keep faith, as Goebbels' daily broadcasts urged him to do, and wait for the relief of the city and ultimate victory, as the Propaganda Minister also promised. It would be a long road, but God was on their side and the Fuehrer was still at the helm.

Not that Hitler knew much of what was happening in the real world. At the end of March he had abandoned his office in the Chancellery, which was now almost in ruins, and had sought shelter in the huge underground Bunker fifty feet beneath the Chancellery garden.

Constructed during the war, the Bunker was on two levels. It could be reached from within the Chancellery itself, by stairs leading down through the pantry, nicknamed *Kannenberggang* after Artur Kannenberg, Hitler's butler. A second entrance, closed by an airtight, watertight bulkhead, led to another stairway with access to the garden of the Foreign Office. A third bulkhead led directly into the general dining passage of the upper level.

There were twelve rooms in this section, six on either side of the dining passage. None of them was larger than a biggish closet, and they were mostly used to store lumber and as servants' quarters, though one served as the *Diaetkueche*, or vegetarian kitchen, where Hitler's meals were prepared.

At the far end of the dining passage a stairway led downward to the second level. This was slightly larger than the first and was known officially as the Fuehrerbunker, Hitler's own private hideaway.

The Fuehrerbunker consisted of eighteen rooms, most of them small and uncomfortable, separated by a central passage, which was divided in two by a partition. The area on the near side of the partition was used as a general sitting room, and off it were offices, lavatories, the guardroom, an emergency telephone switchboard and the powerhouse. Beyond the partition lay Hitler's exclusive domain, where none might enter save by invitation. There the central passage became a conference room where the Fuehrer presided over his daily staff meetings. A door on the left led to a suite of half a dozen rooms, living quarters for Hitler and Eva Braun. Hitler's mistress had a bed/sitting room, a bathroom and a dressing room, the Fuehrer a bedroom and a study. The sixth was an anteroom.

65

Also on the left of the passage was a tiny map room, sometimes used for small conferences. Next to this was a narrow box, known to those who used it as the Dog Bunker; this acted as a rest room for Hitler's personal bodyguard. Beyond the Dog Bunker, a ladder gave access to an unfinished observation tower.

On the right of the passage were the quarters of Hitler's doctors, Morell and Stumpfegger, and Stumpfegger's first-aid room. Finally, at the far end of the passage, four flights of concrete steps led up from a cloakroom to the Chancellery garden. This was the emergency exit all the Bunker's occupants hoped they would never have cause to use.

Apart from the Fuehrerbunker, there were other hideaways beneath the complex of government offices. The one below the Party Chancellery was occupied by Martin Bormann and his staff, together with a sprinkling of officers and SS guards. A third housed Brigadefuehrer Mohnke, commandant of the Chancellery, while Goebbels and his entourage sheltered under the Propaganda Ministry.

In the guardroom on the lower level of the Fuehrerbunker, the off-duty SS troopers and NCOs were listening to Scharfuehrer Kurt Scheller torment Sturmmann Fritz Eismann about what was likely to happen to Eismann's family when the Russians got to them. The young Sturmmann's parents and girlfriend lived in a tiny village a few miles southwest of Frankfurt an der Oder, and he had not heard from any of them for several weeks.

". . . They rape everything in sight," Scheller was saying, "never mind what age she is. Anything between thirteen and seventy. And once they've screwed the ass off them, they slit their throats. I wouldn't give much for the chances of that girl of yours, or your mother. I wouldn't give a pfennig for your goat if you've got one. Believe me, those Ivans don't care where they shove it."

Scheller roared with laughter at his own wit and was rewarded with a grin or two from some of the others. He scratched his cropped head and searched his mind for further ammunition.

Like most Waffen SS men who had seen a lot of active service, Scheller looked considerably older than his twenty-five years. To a casual observer he might seem nothing more than a braggart and a bully, but this was far from the case. He had served with the SS Panzer division Totenkopf in Latvia, Lithuania and Russia, where he had won two Iron Crosses, First and Second Class, and two *Panzervernichtungsabzeichen*, the gallantry badge awarded for the single-handed destruction of a tank without antitank weapons. He was six feet one inch of muscle and fanaticism, one of those more than willing to die for Hitler if the time came.

"Mind you," he went on, coming up with a new barb, "not all the women out east are against a little rape here and there—and looking at Eismann you can understand why. You hear a lot about the refugee columns flocking west, but what you don't hear about are those going east, to get in on the fun. . . ."

"Sit down and give your brains a rest, Scheller. You're starting to repeat yourself."

The speaker was Ernst Zimmer. He too was a Scharfuehrer, but it was unusual for senior NCOs to cross swords in front of the lower ranks.

Scheller, at any rate, could not believe his ears.

"Are you talking to me?"

"That's right. I'm telling you to shut up because I'm sick of hearing your voice. If it were your home in front of the Ivans you wouldn't think it so much of a joke."

The remainder of the guardroom looked on with interest. In size and physique there was little to choose between Zimmer and Scheller, though the former was a year older and had a bullet scar running across his right temple. But more, much more, to the point, Zimmer had once been an officer and wore the coveted Knight's Cross at his throat. He had seen action on both eastern and western fronts and had served under such legendary commanders as Sepp Dietrich and Wilhelm Mohnke. The Knight's Cross had been earned in the Rostov offensive in 1941 and the bullet wound in the Russian counteroffensive which pushed the Germans out of the city and across the Mius River.

Scheller held his ground, but there was much less aggression in his voice when he said, "If it were my home in front of the

Reds, you can bet your life I wouldn't be sitting on my ass here. I'd be over the goddamn hills and far away, whether they shot me or not."

Zimmer decided not to press the argument. There would be fighting enough before the month was out.

He pushed back the table and got to his feet. "Come on, Fritz, let's take a walk."

Scheller watched them go, the bastards. Given any luck, they just might get caught in a *Tommi* air raid.

They left the Bunker by the *Kannenberggang* exit and walked up Wilhelmstrasse in the direction of Unter den Linden and the Brandenburg Gate. Everywhere they looked it seemed as if there were a building on fire or smoldering or about to crumble, and the smell of death and decay was ubiquitous.

They picked their way carefully through the rubble.

"Do you think Scheller's right—about the Russians?" asked Eismann. The Sturmmann was not quite twenty-one. He had seen action, sure enough, but as far as Zimmer was concerned he was still little more than a child.

Zimmer shrugged. "They're not all ballet dancers, Christ knows, but maybe they're not as bad as Goebbels makes them out to be." He was lying, of course; the Ivan was tough, battle-weary and out for revenge. "There's nothing you can do about it anyway, so take my advice and forget it."

"How the hell can I? You said it yourself—how would anyone else feel if his family were between the Russians and Berlin?"

"That was just to shut Scheller's mouth. He can keep only a single idea in his head at one time, that bastard."

"Maybe he was right, though."

"Right how?"

"About just getting up and going, making for Frankfurt whether they shoot me or not."

Zimmer took hold of his friend's arm and gripped it fiercely. "Don't talk like a bloody fool. That's exactly what Scheller would like you to try. You wouldn't get outside the city limits before the SD had you dancing a jig. Take a look."

Eismann saw where Zimmer was pointing. Hanging from a lamppost in a side street, quite dead and in full view of everyone, were two army officers. Pinned to each of their chests was a hand-written sign which stated, "This man was a defeatist."

68

Eismann shuddered. Such sights were not uncommon in Berlin these days, but it was really a sign of the times, or his own preoccupied state of mind, that he had not noticed the corpses until Zimmer drew his attention to them.

"The SS don't hang their own," he said, attempting to reassure himself.

"Don't you believe it. We're Waffen SS on secondment to garrison and guard duties; the lynch parties are led by political and security officers. Apart from the fact that we all wear the SS runes, we've got more in common with the RAF than we have with them. If you think Scheller's a hard bastard, Christ help you if you ever fall afoul of the SD, especially someone like Langendorf. He just might let you live long enough to regret it."

They had had several brushes with the SD Hauptsturmfuehrer during the last few weeks. As well as his other duties, Langendorf sometimes led one of the Special Patrol Groups, those responsible for the execution of defeatists and traitors—which meant anyone whose documents were out of order. It was Langendorf's habit, when such a patrol was called for, to grab any off-duty SS man he could find. Scheller was always a volunteer, but Eismann and Zimmer had been roped in once or twice. So far their luck had held: everyone's papers had checked out. But there had to be a first time they would be called upon to tie the noose.

They walked on. People made way for them. It might be true, in the field, that the Waffen SS was merely an elite fighting force, no more given to atrocities or criminal behavior, except in certain well-documented cases, than the average German soldier. But that was in the field. In Berlin, as far as civilians were concerned, every SS man wore the same sleeve eagle and was therefore to be feared.

"He'll stick a knife in you one day—you know that, don't you?" said Eismann suddenly.

"Scheller?"

"Yes."

"Not if I stick him first. Besides, that's an old quarrel. I've learned to live with it."

Not so old, thought Eismann, shaking his head as a pair of ragged urchins approached, their hands outstretched. Not forgotten, either.

He, Zimmer and Scheller were all serving together in the Totenkopf when Zimmer received his field commission early in 1944. The entire division was short of junior officers, and it was a toss-up between Zimmer and Scheller as to who got promoted to Untersturmfuehrer. It was a case of two Iron Crosses and a brace of tank medals against a Knight's Cross, and the smart money was on Scheller. But the regimental commander wanted brains as well as brawn and raw courage, and Zimmer got the nod.

Convinced that he had been outmaneuvered unfairly and now in the ignominious position of having to call his onetime equal "sir," Scheller took advantage of every opportunity to embarrass the new section commander. He made impossible suggestions for frontal assaults on securely held positions and openly sneered when Zimmer turned them down as suicidal.

But Scheller's turn came.

In August 1944, when the Totenkopf was part of the IV Panzer Corps during the time it tossed the Russians out of Warsaw and across the Vistula, Zimmer's section was ordered to attack a Russian machine-gun emplacement. Having been promoted partly for intelligence, Zimmer used it. The Ivans were well dug in. He would simply lose his own life and those of his men, and the Ivans would still be there. He therefore broke off radio contact and ignored the order.

Scheller, of course, reported him, and Zimmer was lucky to escape with his life. Had it not been for an exemplary previous record as well as the Knight's Cross, he would have been shot on the spot. As it was, he argued his case with considerable skill and received no greater punishment than a busting to the ranks.

Even the demotion did not last long. Men of Zimmer's ability were in short supply, and within six months he was again a Scharfuehrer, much to the chagrin of Scheller.

The pair came to a halt at the junction of Wilhelmstrasse and Unter den Linden, just east of the Brandenburg Gate. This was a Berlin neither of them recognized: blazing buildings filling the air with a thick dust, wrecked cars and trucks, men swinging from gibbets.

"Let's get the hell back," said Zimmer. "This is more depressing than the damned Bunker."

EIGHT

The exterior of Greenleigh's Mayfair house was like any other in that most fashionable of London's districts. There were no soldiers guarding the entrance, no flags fluttering from the windows. To all intents and purposes it was the town residence of a fairly wealthy bachelor who had something to do with one of the Ministries.

Few visitors learned that the house opposite was also owned by Special Operations and that all Greenleigh's callers were checked out from a second-floor window. Entry was usually by appointment only. If someone turned up unexpectedly or at the wrong time, he was scrutinized with the thoroughness of a surgeon looking for a tumor before the men on the second floor buzzed Greenleigh's secretary to give her the okay. Anything suspicious and one of the lookouts went down into the street and asked the caller his business. The other man kept an eye on affairs via the telescopic sights of a sniper's rifle.

Once through the front door, opened automatically from within, the visitor was met by Greenleigh's secretary, Miss Anstruther, whose aristocratic features seemed to indicate blood of the purest blue going back several centuries. In her late thirties, Miss Anstruther was primly good-looking in a *Country Life* sort of way. Operatives who called at the house held varying opinions regarding the state of her virginity. Some said she was saving it for the right duke, others that she performed services of a strictly nonsecretarial nature for Greenleigh himself. Whatever the truth of the matter, she offered no clues. She greeted everyone with a tight smile and a brisk "Good morning" or "Good afternoon" before ushering the visitor up to Greenleigh's Operations Room on the first floor, as she had done with Major Lassiter several minutes earlier.

"Our American cousins are still puzzled about those GI uniforms you turned up wearing," Greenleigh was saying, sucking the stem of an unlit pipe. "Apparently their Divisional G2 didn't believe your explanation about finding them in a warehouse in Lippstadt."

"Didn't he, sir?" Lassiter's report on the Lippstadt raid had naturally not included the business at the farmhouse and the Americans' subsequent fate on Mindenstrasse.

"He did not. He is concerned that his boys, as he chooses to call them—the original wearers of the uniforms, that is—were captured by the Germans and disposed of."

"Which was probably the case."

"Probably, probably. I've signaled him, of course, that I accept your version entirely. But then, I'm a much more credulous character than U.S. Army Intelligence."

Lassiter smiled into his brandy.

The Operations Room had once been a drawing room, and Greenleigh thought it inappropriate to remove the original furnishings just because there was a war on. In consequence, Lassiter was sitting on a Louis Quinze chair and drinking his brandy from a Regency goblet, as were the SOE officer's other visitors. This pair wore plainclothes but held military ranks: Colonel Martin and Lieutenant Colonel Devereaux. Lassiter knew them both by reputation.

Martin was short, pink-faced and plump, and looked like a banker who approves overdrafts without fuss. But that was just surface camouflage. Inside, he was as hard as nails. He had spent three years in Occupied France, organizing sabotage groups and preventing internecine quarrels between the various underground movements. Devereaux, given a slightly darker suit, could have passed as an undertaker or a bad-tempered factory owner in a Dickens novel, but he too had spent much of the war in an undercover role in Europe. Once, as a guest of the Paris Gestapo for a week, he had willed himself into a long-lasting state of semiconsciousness as a barrier against pain. The Gestapo had eventually freed him as guiltless, but the thumbs of both hands, broken in a vise, would never be the same again.

Lassiter too was in civilian clothes, and a casual observer could have been forgiven for thinking that what he was witnessing was a quiet evening drink shared by four acquaintances. The only concession in the Operations Room to what Greenleigh sometimes referred to as "this nonsense in Europe" was a huge wall map behind his desk. This showed the steadily shrinking Reich being crushed between the hammer of the Russian forces and the anvil of the Anglo-Americans.

"Mrs. Rand is coming along splendidly, by the way," said the Brigadier. "I spoke to her earlier. She's out of it for the duration now, of course, but she did ask that you pop your head in to see her if you had time. I had to explain that that might not be possible for a little while."

"Sir?"

"You seem to have acquired an interesting knack of getting into and out of Germany unscathed, so I hope you won't mind paying a return visit."

Lassiter listened in silence for the next five minutes, but in actuality Greenleigh told him very little—just that he wanted Lassiter to head a team which would go into Germany and pick up a top Nazi defector. Not even that, really. The team would simply act as an escort, on the way in, for an SOE courier, and on the way out for the courier and the defector, whose code name was Valkyrie. In Berlin itself, the courier would handle all other matters. Lassiter would merely be there to ensure that nothing went wrong, though he would have absolute operational control.

"Berlin, sir?" Lassiter threw a quick glance at the map. In a few more days, a week or two at the outside, the German capital would be surrounded by the Russians. Getting in would be one thing; getting out a different matter entirely.

Greenleigh understood. "I know what you mean. Still, we'll cross that bridge when we come to it. All I want to know for the present is whether, all things being equal, you think you can do it."

Lassiter was momentarily puzzled. This wasn't like Greenleigh. Outside his normal combat role with the 1st Commando Brigade, Lassiter had performed special assignments for SOE a dozen times in the last four years. It was usually a question of being given the job and getting on with it. Blow up that bridge, destroy that warehouse, ambush that convoy.

"What Brigadier Greenleigh is trying to say," put in the cadaverous Devereaux, "is that this operation is somewhat different from others you've been on."

Lassiter thought he understood. "You're asking me if I have any scruples about bringing out a top Nazi."

Devereaux nodded. "Precisely."

"Am I to be told who it is?"

Greenleigh shook his head. He'd considered this carefully, but eventually opted against it. Lassiter would find out sooner or later, and there was nothing to be done about that. But if he had the misfortune to be picked up by the Gestapo or one of the other security agencies going in, it was better he know as little as possible.

"No. We do not consider that advisable."

Lassiter understood that too, but he was nevertheless suddenly irritated at being treated like a first-year philosophy student asked to discuss the implications of Socrates drinking hemlock.

As far as he was concerned, it had been a long war. Throughout the whole of it he'd done unsavory things which he'd managed to square with his own conscience. He possessed his own morality, no doubt made more flexible by the last six years, and it had nothing to do with these people. He'd trained himself to be hard and uncaring because the alternative might mean a bullet in the back of the skull. It was high time Greenleigh learned the rules: they were allowed to give him tasks to do, men to kill; why he went was his own affair.

"If you don't mind my saying so, sir," he said coolly, "I'm an operational officer. I go where I'm told to. When I no longer wish to be an operational officer, I'll let you know."

Devereaux's face reddened. He seemed about to make some remark when Greenleigh waved him to silence with an impatient gesture. "Good," he said, pushing the brandy decanter in Lassiter's direction, "good."

Lassiter helped himself to a refill. "How many men will I be taking?"

"That's rather up to you, but I'd suggest no more than four or five," answered Greenleigh. "You'll travel faster that way."

"My own choice?"

"Absolutely. I don't think I've made myself quite clear, Major Lassiter. Within certain limitations, this whole operation is yours from beginning to end. We'll give help where it's needed, of course, and there are other considerations which must be fulfilled from our point of view. But the rest is up to you."

"I'll want Sergeant Fuller and Corporal Gallagher, for openers."

Greenleigh smiled reassuringly. "I rather gathered as much. They'll be standing by. And to simplify your other choices, I've drawn up a list of people you've worked with before. I'm afraid it's rather a short list. Some are on other assignments and some are dead."

He handed Lassiter a typewritten sheet of paper. It was a short list: only eight names in all.

His eyes were drawn to four at the foot of the sheet. They were bracketed together in pairs, and against each entry was a green asterisk. Major Joe Kennedy and Sergeant Bill Holmes; Captain Alex Dunbar and Corporal Dougal Maclean. The brackets meant they always worked as pairs; where one went, so did the other. He had no idea what the asterisks signified.

"I thought Captain Dunbar and Corporal Maclean were in Yugoslavia."

Greenleigh raised his eyebrows. "You're remarkably well informed. They were, until six weeks ago. Regrettably, they were both wounded and shipped home."

"Badly?"

"They've recovered now, if that's what you mean. The green ink, incidentally, indicates that those four are in the country and available. The others I'm not sure about."

Lassiter considered the matter. Availability aside, it was a toss-up between Kennedy and Holmes on the one hand, Dunbar and Maclean on the other. He could ask for all of them, but that would make the team top-heavy. Greenleigh was quite right in suggesting no more than four or five. This sort of operation demanded a small, fast-moving unit.

"Kennedy and Holmes, Dunbar and Maclean. Either pair. I'll leave it to you. Whoever's available and wants to come."

"Good. I'll get my secretary onto it later."

"You're quite happy taking just four as well as yourself?"

Colonel Martin spoke for the first time since the introductions.

"It's either four or a brigade," answered Lassiter. "If I've chosen the right four we won't need the brigade. If I haven't, a few more won't make any difference."

Martin nodded. "I need to know exact numbers because the next step is to decide how you go in, whether as civilians or in German uniforms. Unless you have any strong feelings one way or the other, let me tell you our thoughts on the subject.

"There are arguments for and against both, but on balance the scales come down in favor of being in uniform. For a start, you'll be able to carry weapons quite openly. Second, where we manage to infiltrate you will depend upon where the front is at the time, but it's bound to be a long way from Berlin. You'll have a lot of ground to cover both going in and coming out, and that will mean using a vehicle. Petrol is in extremely short supply, and a civilian with his own transport would be regarded with suspicion. Apart from that, we're getting reports that the authorities are closing many roads to all save military vehicles. So a jeep or a one-tonner it will have to be, which of course entails wearing uniform. We could furnish you with Gestapo papers, of course, and let you travel in mufti, but that would still make you fair game for anyone else with a uniform and a gun. The papers would doubtless get you through, but you'd still be stopped and questioned. The less you're stopped and questioned, the more chance you'll stand. Even expertly forged papers might not stand up to constant scrutiny."

"Major Lassiter has been across before, Peter," said Greenleigh, fumbling to get his pipe lit.

"Of course he has. I'm sorry; I'm really just thinking aloud." Colonel Martin inclined his head apologetically at Lassiter.

"The snag about wearing German uniforms, of course," he went on, "is that the Russians are closing on Berlin at a hell of a rate. There are a lot of factors to be taken into consideration, but you'll almost certainly run across the Red Army at some point. Needless to say, you can't tell them what you're up to and that you're British. You'll have to play that part by ear. Avoid trouble if you can. If you can't, well . . ." Martin made a chopping motion with the blade of his hand. "With any luck at all you'll be in and out before the Russians encircle Berlin, but if

76

you're not we have one or two other ideas which we'll go into at a later date."

"What about the Germans themselves?" asked Lassiter. "I had a brush with the SD in Lippstadt, and I've heard reports that they're hanging deserters on sight. They've got a pretty loose interpretation of what constitutes desertion, too. Get caught in the wrong place with the wrong papers and they string you up first and worry about it later. If we're pulled up heading for Berlin, somebody might get the idea we're quitting the war zone."

Lieutenant Colonel Devereaux fielded that one.

"I doubt if anyone with desertion in mind would head east, towards the Russians, but I think we've covered it in any case. It seems to us that the best way to avoid the unwelcome attentions of the SS is to make your team fellow members, the theory being that you hide something dirty in a dung heap. You'll be rigged out as officers and men of the SS Panzer division Das Reich, which is second only to the Leibstandarte Adolf Hitler Division in prestige. As far as we know, the Das Reich is currently involved in the fight for Vienna, but you'll be provided with documents giving you business in Berlin."

"Any special reason for choosing that particular division?" asked Lassiter.

"One or two. It happens that the division's previous commander, Gruppenfuehrer Werner Ostendorff, is no longer at the head of things. We're not quite sure whether he's been killed or has fallen from grace, but since March 9, Standartenfuehrer Rudolf Lehmann has been divisional commander. They don't usually hand over divisions to the SS equivalent of a colonel without promoting him, so it seems logical to assume that the appointment is a temporary one. In any event, it's a confusing situation, which can only work to our advantage."

Lassiter squinted at the wall map. "Vienna's a hell of a long way from Berlin," he pointed out.

"True enough," said Greenleigh from behind a cloud of blue smoke, "but we won't put you over there, you can rest assured of that. As you might expect, the western front is very fluid at present, the situation changing hourly." He thumbed over his shoulder. "That map was accurate as of 0900 this morning, but I doubt if it is now. Vienna's merely background information. Wherever you go in, it will be as close to Berlin as it is humanly possible to place you. Which leads us directly to *when* that will be."

Greenleigh replaced his pipe in its rack and peered over half-moon spectacles at Lassiter. The young major could not know it, but he was shortly to embark on what could be the most fruitful mission of the war.

"I'd like you to get going as soon as possible, naturally, but I'm afraid that everything rather depends upon Valkyrie himself. He's just as anxious to get out as we are to have him, but for reasons I can't go into it's not safe for him to make a move yet. We'll just have to wait and see. I'm sorry to be so vague, but you'll be given a proper briefing nearer the time.

"Meanwhile, take a few days' leave. Make the most of it, because before the end of the week I'll want you to go down to one of our houses in Devon. All of you, that is. You'll have the place to yourselves, of course, because I don't want anyone else seeing five British soldiers running around in SS uniforms—apart from the guards, that is, who are used to such sights."

Greenleigh pushed back his chair.

"While in Devon, you'll spend all your waking hours being briefed by our own people on every aspect of the SS division Das Reich, as well as one or two other matters. You'll go over the campaigns you've fought in, order of battle, commanders down to battalion level. You'll speak nothing but German and handle nothing but German weapons. You'll be tutored by a team of experts who know more about the SS in general and Das Reich in particular than those organizations know about themselves. They'll kit you out, give you new ranks, new identities. Use every day as though it were your last."

Greenleigh stood up and came around to the front of the desk. Lassiter stood also.

"I can't impress upon you enough the importance of this operation," the SOE officer said, "but I can tell you that sanction for it comes from the very highest level. The *very* highest. When you get to Devon you can tell the others everything I've told you, but you must emphasize that this is a purely British venture. No one else is in on it. Not the Americans, Russians,

French, Poles—no one. For the purpose of this exercise, they're your enemies."

Greenleigh walked Lassiter to the drawing-room door. There were no handshakes or goodbyes. The SOE did not function that way.

"Stay in touch with Miss Anstruther by telephone. She'll keep you up to date."

Although it was mid-April, it was still cold enough for the three SOE officers, when Lassiter had gone, to indulge in another brandy apiece. Glasses filled, Greenleigh said: "Well, gentlemen . . .?"

"A good man," said Martin. "I don't think you could have made a better choice."

"Needs to learn a little respect, though," muttered Devereaux. "Even in the commandos they're taught to say 'sir' once in a while."

Greenleigh snorted impatiently. "Good Christ, Arthur, I thought you had all that First World War shit knocked out of you in France. What do you think we're running here, a private club for public-school boys with good table manners? Let me tell you something about Lassiter that's not in his dossier. As he's a natural linguist, it's not immediately apparent that he was brought up in the slums of Manchester. Before the war he married a London girl and made his home here. They had a couple of daughters, aged three and two respectively in 1940. The wife and the two children were killed in the Blitz while Lassiter was away, and it's to his eternal credit that he did not go to pieces or treat every German with a psychopathological hatred. He did, however, become a machine. He may not touch his forelock enough for you, Devereaux, and you might not want him at a postwar houseparty. But let me tell you something: he's the most efficient killer I've ever come across."

Killing was far from Lassiter's mind as he turned out of Curzon Street and into Shepherd's Market.

Although it was still early evening, the prostitutes were anxious to get off to a flying start. Rumor had it that the war wouldn't last much longer, and with its end would vanish the

Yanks. A girl had to make sure of her nest egg before the geese flew home. Being on the make in postwar Britain wasn't going to do much for the retirement fund.

Being tall and broad-shouldered, Lassiter was a natural target for the whores, who called invitingly to him from the depths of shop doorways. But after a cursory glance in the direction of whoever had offered what last, he walked on. Eventually he went into a pub.

The heavy drinking wouldn't start for a few hours yet, but even so there were enough customers waiting to be served to keep the two barmaids fully occupied. With a pound note clutched firmly in his fist to attract attention, Lassiter took a look around. This was one of the haunts of the more expensive whores. The proprietor didn't mind risking his license provided the girls were discreet and paid him a weekly sum for the privilege of using the place.

Lassiter counted four girls waiting for trade. Two he dismissed immediately as being the wrong type. The third was a possibility, but it was the fourth who held his attention. Though sitting down, she seemed to be quite short. An inch or so over five feet would be his guess. Her hair was blond, bottle variety but tastefully done. She wore a short skirt and an open-necked beige blouse. On her head, in the current fashion, she'd perched a tilted beret, French-peasant style.

He nodded amiably in her direction and raised his hand in a drinking gesture. She smiled and mouthed, "Gin."

Once served, he carried the drinks across to her table and sat down. She swallowed half of hers in a single gulp. "Cheers."

Close up, she was much younger than he'd first thought, but that was neither here nor there.

"You busy for the next hour or so?" he asked.

"Not if you're not."

"Good. We'll go when you've finished your drink."

"Anxious, aren't you?"

"Not so many questions. I'm not paying you for questions. What's your name?"

"Fiona."

I'll bet, thought Lassiter.

They were on the street in less than five minutes. The girl

said her own place was a ten-minute cab ride away, or they could use a local hotel she had an arrangement with. He would have to pay the fee for the room, but it wouldn't amount to much more than the cab fare.

Lassiter said he didn't care, he'd leave it to her.

"The hotel, then."

They walked on.

Lassiter was conscious of the fact that since his wife's death his sexual experiences had been exclusively with whores. He was also partly aware that this had something to do with being unwilling to enter into a relationship with an ordinary woman, something which could well become permanent. He was totally unaware, however, that every whore he went with was on the small side and fair-haired. The two he had automatically rejected in the pub as being the wrong types were tall and dark-haired. His wife had been tall and dark-haired.

NINE

To: VALKYRIE   CVX/005/SSS/17000/Z/16.4.45
From: NEMESIS
          UNIT FORMED. LANDFALL BERLIN FLEXIBLE AND
          DEPENDENT UPON HOSTILE ACTIVITY BUT SUGGEST
          CONJUNCTION TEN/TWELVE DAYS FROM NOW.
          ACKNOWLEDGE.

To: NEMESIS   CVX/011/SSS/23000/Z/17.4.45
From: VALKYRIE
          UNDERSTOOD. CONJUNCTION NOT ONLY DEPENDENT
          HOSTILES YOUR END HOWEVER. CONDITIONS HERE TO
          BE CONSIDERED. YOUR UNIT TO BE SELF-SUFFICIENT
          UNTIL ALREADY AGREED MOD. OP. POSSIBLE.
          ACKNOWLEDGE.

To: VALKYRIE   CVX/019/SSS/20000/Z/17.4.45
From: NEMESIS
          AGREED. STAND BY.

TEN

In the cipher department of the American Legation in Berne on April 17, the lights were still burning although it was after 10 P.M. The code room was staffed on a twenty-four-hour basis, but it was unusual to find an analyst still slaving away at that hour. Marvin Newbegin was an exception.

Like many cryptanalysts, Newbegin lived in a curious half-world of ciphers, codes and anagrams, acrostics and hieroglyphics. He was familiar with most branches of cryptography and had both originated and broken codes based upon systems as far apart as reversed Shakespearean sonnets in the Cyrillic alphabet and the times of the tides at Charleston, South Carolina. He was fully aware that what one man could put together, another could take apart.

Mostly.

The single exception was the one-time pad, whereby the encoder used the key sentence or passage once only. With the one-time pad there was no chance of establishing a pattern, no way of seeing, for example, how often the letter E, the most commonly used in the English alphabet, turned up. With a one-time pad, a man needed luck; but then, all cryptanalysts relied upon a certain amount of that. They were systematic people, of course, but some of the most spectacular results were achieved by men dredging up from their unconscious scraps of information stored there since childhood.

Flexibility was the key to cryptanalysis. Become rigid in your approach and you stood no chance, which was the reason Marvin Newbegin's desk blotter and scratch pad were invariably covered with doodlings. Naturally there were machines available to take over some of the heavy work, but they were in their infancy. In any case, like many traditionalists, Marvin believed that a machine was only as good as its operator. It could shorten the process of code breaking, but only if you fed in the correct information. And if you had the correct information, you didn't need the machine.

Though still younger than forty, Marvin Newbegin was a traditionalist. Unless it had been around for several thousand years, he was not interested, and it was no accident that his specialties were ancient languages and mathematics. For his doctorate, he had written a thesis entitled "The Mathematical Content and Geometric Euphony of Aramaic." He was a godsend to the cipher section and a pain in the ass to his wife, to whom he had not written in several months and whose latest letter, dated March 8 and still unanswered, lay open on his desk as a constant reminder that he must do something about it today. If he didn't, the doodles he had made in its margins would soon render it unintelligible. But the first line was enough to put anyone off: "I have just returned from a visit to Cousin George . . ." Christ, it was hard to get enthusiastic about that. Cousin George (wife's cousin) was an idiot and a bore, and what was worse, was very soon to be a millionaire idiot and bore, having seen his small two-man business grow to massive proportions since 1941.

Newbegin sighed and returned his attention to the Berlin–London intercepts. The latest were on top of the pile, one dated April 16, the other two April 17. And they were as incomprehensible as ever.

While debating whether he should give it another few hours in case, as sometimes happened, the conscious mind became so tired that unconscious thoughts, and occasionally answers, filtered through, he picked up a pencil and begin writing on his wife's letter, as he had done so often during the day. Though he was totally unaware of what he was doing, after a couple of minutes the opening sentence looked like this:

I have just returned from a v i s i t to Cousin George . . .
A BCDE FGHI JKLMNOPQ RSTU V WXYZ . . .

In the blank space above "Dearest Marvin . . ." he scrawled UIFATR, which, if this were a code, would spell MARVIN, allowing for A = I, B = H, and so on. For want of something better to

84

do and because he had that sort of mind, he tried the same code on the kind of key words that might appear in a message between England and Germany. BERLIN became HEFTTR. Which did not make any immediate sense, as both L and I would be represented by the letter T. But he pressed on. London translated as TNRVNR, and SECRET became REAFEO.

He was still only half conscious of what he was doing, but when he focused and glanced down at his scribblings he thought he saw something familiar about the letters REAFEO. It was impossible, of course—the result of overtiredness or imagination. Either that or he had grown punch-drunk with the hundreds of different combinations he had tried. But cryptanalysts are nothing if not thorough, and he resolved to check it out.

In a dun-colored folder were transcriptions of every intercept, and he began by working backward. Which was a mistake, for on one of the very last he came to appeared the letters REAFEAS. It wasn't REAFEO, but it was close. *If* this were a code, it could be the noun SECRECY from the adjective SECRET.

He tried it, using the same system as before. It was lunacy, but it worked. SECRECY transcribed as REAFEAS.

For a moment he closed his eyes. It just wasn't possible that a code based upon the opening lines of a letter from his wife was the one being used by London and Berlin. He'd made a mistake, or it was a million-to-one shot.

Very slowly he counted up to fifty before writing down the entire coded message exactly as it had been intercepted. He ignored what appeared to be a call sign. He also ignored what were probably the sender's code name and that of the recipient.

The text was in groups of five letters, but that was pretty standard. It prevented cryptanalysts from picking up obvious words such as "and" and "the."

When written down on a clean sheet of paper, it looked like this:

HEIRR/MFEVM/OUNRO/REAFE/ASUMI/FIROE/EVIII.

Decoded, it read:

BEASS/UREDU/TMOST/SECRE/CYGUA/RANTE/EDZZZ.

Be assured utmost secrecy guaranteed. The three "Zs" at the end were just to fill that group.

Still a very long way from understanding the concept, he was nevertheless unwilling to look a gift horse in the mouth. Full of excitement, he pounced on the second message and tried the same technique. He was alarmed when nothing happened. What began as gibberish stayed gibberish.

Thinking quickly, he realized that the second intercept had its origin in Berlin. It was therefore highly probable that it was in German and indecipherable by the use of an English sentence as the key. But the next ex-London message . . .

He tried it. Nothing. A jumble of meaningless words that refused to reveal their secret.

His heart hit the floor. He was almost there, yet he was still a million miles away. In that one simple sentence lay the clue which would break the cipher wide open, but he couldn't see it.

I have just returned from a visit to Cousin George . . .

No; he was wrong there, for a start. Wherever the answer lay, it had nothing to do with his wife's letter. Or Cousin George. The key was the first twenty-six letters. *I have just returned from a visit* . . . That was all he needed.

Fresh out of ideas, he helped himself to a cup of coffee from the pot in the main office and looked at the deciphered message again. Well, it was only partly deciphered. He hadn't bothered with the call sign because it wouldn't mean anything and he had overlooked the sender and the recipient completely in his anxiety to get to the guts of the text.

But that was soon resolved. Or should have been—but wasn't.

Applying the same principles to the coded names of the sender and the recipient got him nowhere. Which could mean only that Berlin and London were using a different code for the addressee and sender than they were for the body of the text. But why? It was unusual, to say the least, to use two different ciphers in the same message. The call sign told him nothing. In this case it was cvx/001/sss/31000/z. It might have been written in Martian for all it meant to him.

He lit a cigarette and blew smoke at the ceiling. Judged by the state of the near-empty packet, it was his thirty-seventh or thirty-eighth of the day. He had promised his wife months ago that he would give up smoking or at least cut down, but he couldn't afford the virtue of abstinence right now.

86

He stared unseeingly at the untidy heap of message forms. Somewhere in there was the answer, a common denominator, but he was damned if he could see it. Being a methodical worker, however, he sorted the forms into two piles, in order of interception. The left-hand pile contained those from London, the right-hand those from Berlin. Some were quite short, a couple of words; some lengthy. A quick riffle through and a trial dip were enough to tell him that the code based upon the sentence in his wife's letter had not been used again, and that the only recurring factor was the call sign. It always began cvx, always ended with z. The sole difference in each message was the figures, separated by triple s.

Those on the first sheet, the one he had solved, were 001/sss/-31000. Another ex-London was 014/sss/27000. Yet another 011/sss/26000. If there was a pattern, it was far from an obvious one. There was nothing unusual in numbering messages, of course, to ensure that none went astray. Thus if Berlin received 001 followed by 003, the addressee would be aware that 002 was somehow missing. But the numbers were evidently not a checking device. They jumped all over the place, seemingly at the whim of the sender. Except that no one who had evolved a code such as this was guilty of whimsy.

He thought about the sentence again. *I have just returned from a visit* . . . It was very odd to base a code on something as banal as that. One-time pads were normally composed of a random jumble of letters underneath which could be written the alphabet. Sender and recipient had copies of the same pad. On Day One, Page One was used; Day Two, Page Two. All designed to prevent a cryptanalyst from building up a continuous picture. *I have just returned from a visit* was something you'd write in a letter, as indeed his wife had written. The only problem with that was that there were not a hell of a lot of letters floating between Berlin and London at this point in the war.

It could be a line from a book, but . . .

He almost fell out of his chair as this thought occurred. A book. Why not? That method had been used before, and it was almost impossible to crack without going through every line in every book that had ever been written. But why shouldn't the long arm of coincidence have played a role here? It was a perfectly ordinary sentence . . . *I have just returned from a visit* . . .

He examined the figures in the call sign again. The lowest used was 001 and the highest to date 31000. Discounting the zeros, that left 1 to 31, roughly the number of chapters in the average book. Why shouldn't the figures, which were not consecutive and seemed to serve no useful function, tell the recipient which chapter to use as the basis for decoding? That would make sense. The figures on the deciphered message were instructing Berlin to use the first chapter in an already agreed-upon book as the key. That would account for 001. The 31 was a command to use that chapter in the reply or . . . or, better still, that that chapter was to be used for decoding the names of the sender and the addressee.

The more he thought about it, the more it made sense. The deviser of the code had opted not to use the same basis for both text and names for fear that with the repetition of the names, an analyst might get lucky and ascertain certain letters. It was also a dual guide to authenticity.

If, for example, the analyst broke the text code, as he had broken it, by luck alone, and if he decided to send a fake message on the same radio wavelength, the recipient would know it to be a phony because the address code would not check out.

Marvin Newbegin lit his thirty-eighth or thirty-ninth cigarette of the day and brushed away the cobwebs from his tired mind.

He was convinced he had it, or something approximating it. What he was looking for was a book that began Chapter One with the words *I have just returned from a visit* . . . It was a seemingly impossible task at first glance; English literature was not his subject. He was going to need help, lots of it, and he was sure Jake Bellinger wouldn't mind being disturbed for something as important as this.

He picked up the phone.

Two hours later they were still at it, only just beginning to realize the magnitude of the task. One corner of the code room had been cleared of everything but empty desks and tables. On top of these were piled a mountain of books, filched for the purpose from the Legation library. A dictionary of quotations, originally thought to be the key, had long since been reduced to holding Styrofoam coffee cups. The air was thick with cigarette and cigar smoke.

On having his after-dinner brandy session interrupted by Marvin Newbegin, Jake Bellinger had roped in everyone who wasn't actually nailed down, and from cipher clerks upward the room was a parade of long faces and fraying tempers. Not least of those who would cheerfully have murdered Newbegin were Chuck Fodor and Joe Scipioni.

Fodor in particular had been making up for lost time. If he couldn't see active service in one way, he was going to see it in another.

The latest on the list of consolation prizes was a redheaded divorcee (Translation Section) from Milwaukee, a woman in her mid-twenties with a positively staggering figure. She had refused several invitations to an intimate dinner at the apartment, but had finally accepted the one issued that same afternoon.

The meal was nothing exceptional, but after the second bottle of wine she started to loosen up. Two brandies later she was not only giving the high sign that she was willing to stay the night, she was also complaining she felt hot and would it be all right if she slipped into Fodor's robe.

Then Bellinger had phoned. Fodor had contemplated abandoning subtlety and settling for a quickie, but he shortly rejected the idea. She was worth more attention than that. She promised to stay on, amuse herself with the brandy and his jazz collection until he returned, but he wasn't sure he believed her.

For Scipioni it was even worse. In his own section of the apartment he had been within seconds of scoring when the call came. Fodor was merciless, hammering on the door until it was opened. What majors couldn't have, neither could lieutenants, and Scipioni's expression was currently that of a tethered ram.

About the only thing to have emerged from the session so far was that while the OSS in particular and the Legation staff in general might be rich in men with field experience and those with degrees in mathematics, engineering and languages, no one had majored in English literature. Of course, Marvin

Newbegin could be wrong. The cipher key did not have to be based upon a book. Even if it was, it did not have to be a famous book or a classic or even one written originally in the English language.

"This is ridiculous," snarled Bellinger, chomping on an unlit cigar and glaring red-eyed around the room. "I've as good as told Mr. Dulles that we'll have this thing cracked by tomorrow morning, and I'd better not have to tell him I was wrong. You guys are supposed to be educated, for Chrissakes. I'm a soldier, I don't have to be, but you guys have got around five hundred years in college between you. What the hell were you doing with yourselves all that time, jerking off?"

"There have been a lot of books printed since the fifteenth century," someone piped up.

"I know that," said Bellinger. "I can see that just by looking at this fucking table. But we're not looking for a lot of books; we're looking for one."

"It doesn't even have to be a book," said Fodor. "It could be a diary, a notebook, something like that. It's not the sort of sentence you'd open a novel with."

"Not a twentieth-century novel, anyway," someone else chipped in.

Bellinger turned on him. "Go on. What do you mean by that?"

"Well," said the speaker, "I don't know a lot about the subject, but it strikes me that that's the sort of gimmick nineteenth-century writers used to open up with. First-person narrative direct to the reader. Dickens, say."

"I've been through Dickens," Scipioni said. "Opening lines of first chapters, anyway. Apart from the fact that it is now my considered opinion David Copperfield was a faggot, it's not Dickens."

"I'm not saying it is. I'm just saying that that's the kind of method nineteenth-century writers adopted. Maybe it'd be an idea to list from A to Z all the old-timers we can think of and take it up with a librarian in the morning."

"I promised Mr. Dulles he'd have his answer by morning," Bellinger reminded the group.

"I don't think that's possible, sir," said Fodor. He'd had enough and could sense that even the major general would go along with a reasonable suggestion. Part of him wanted to get back to his unfinished business before she went off the boil, and part of him, the professional part, realized that they could sit up until the sun rose and get no further.

It had been a reasonable, if impetuous, idea to drag them all in on the off chance that someone would recognize the lines, but as that hadn't happened, consulting a librarian seemed a sensible alternative.

"There must have been thousands of books published last century," he told Bellinger, "even if we're right on that. We're going to need professional help. We could spend a hundred man-hours looking for something a librarian could tell us in a second. If you like, I'll make it my personal business to do just that in the morning."

Bellinger sighed the long sigh of a man who knows when he's licked.

"All right," he said, "pack it in."

The Milwaukee redhead was as good as her word and was still waiting when Fodor and Scipioni returned to the apartment. Better still, she was now in Fodor's silk robe. Fodor was a broad-shouldered individual with a deep muscular chest, but she jutted through the thin material in ways he never had.

"Hello and good night," said Scipioni, and disappeared in the direction of his own bedroom at the run. The door banged behind him.

Fodor sank onto the studio couch beside the redhead and accepted the proffered brandy snifter.

"You smell of tobacco," she complained.

"Meaning you want me to go and brush my teeth."

"Meaning nothing of the kind, Chuck Fodor. I've been saving you up and tonight's the night. If you'd kept me waiting any longer, I'd have been forced to commit an unnatural act or two. What I mean is, let's not do it face to face, not the first time. Let's put some of the fires out; then you can think about cleaning your teeth."

She slipped out of the robe and bent over one arm of the studio couch, spreading her legs in erotic invitation and rearing her buttocks.

"Don't be all night about it," she whispered.

Whether he knew it or not, Fodor was tired and had a lot on his mind. In consequence, although she did most of the work, weaving figure 8s around his erect phallus, it was not one of his better performances. He came beautifully in a long shuddering stream before he really wished to and before she was ready, but in some perverse way this seemed to please her rather than disappoint her. Had he been the stud to end all studs, she would have chalked up just another good lay. As it was, she had done something for him, satisfied him unselfishly, and it made her happy.

They went into the bedroom, where he allowed her to undress him. She made a noisy meal of it in more ways than one, but only part of his mind was on the magic she was making. He was conscious that he was muttering that goddamn sentence—*I have just returned from a visit*—but it took him several seconds to realize that she too was speaking, something about the solitary neighbor she would be troubled with.

He sat up. "What was that you said?"

"I was finishing your sentence for you."

"What sentence?"

" 'I have just returned from a visit to my landlord . . .' You quoted that, or most of it."

"Quoted what?"

" 'I have just returned from a visit to my landlord, the solitary neighbor I shall be troubled with.' "

He gripped her arm until she winced with pain. "You mean you know the lines—they're from a book or something?"

"Of course they're from a book. What's the matter with you? You're hurting me."

He let go of her and struggled to get his mind into gear. "Now give it to me gently," he said. "Those lines are from a book, are they?"

"Certainly. *Wuthering Heights.* Emily Brontë."

"And where do they come in the book?"

"They're the opening lines. Why—you don't think I can quote the whole damn book, do you?"

"But how the hell do you know them? How can you remember them?"

"I grew up with the book. Christ, it's probably one of the

92

most romantic stories ever written by a woman for women. Don't you know anything?"

By a woman for women. Jesus H. Christ, thought Fodor, how stupid could they get? There had been nine or ten people in the code room, all men. They had torn apart almost the whole of the Legation library, but he'd lay odds that no one present had thought of a woman writer. They'd looked at Dickens, Tolstoy, Melville, Zola—but no women.

He levered himself from the bed.

"Where are you going?"

He began putting on his pants. "You're beautiful and I love you, but I'm afraid that this is not a night that's going to figure in your memoirs."

ELEVEN

Everything fell into place.

Fodor's phone call to Bellinger got the major general out of bed on the double, though he vowed to have the junior officer's balls for door chimes if this turned out to be a wild-goose chase.

On learning that Scipioni was also at hand—though moaning like a bastard—Bellinger decided not to bother with the rest of the cipher staff with the exception of Marvin Newbegin. It was Newbegin who had kicked the whole thing off with his suggestion of a book, and he deserved to be in at the kill.

Getting hold of a copy of *Wuthering Heights*, in English or German, proved far from easy. There wasn't one in the Legation library, a fact they verified by reference to the index but confirmed by awakening the officer whose duties included those of librarian. This man—a junior career diplomat with rheumy eyes—suggested they try a bookseller friend of his who lived in Berne's Viktoriastrasse. The bookseller stocked works of every description, though his main source of income was pornography, with a heavy emphasis on sadomasochism.

The diplomat took pains to make his own position quite clear. "Don't think I have any interest in such things myself, but if you want him to open his shop at this hour in the morning you'll need a lever. The Swiss are pretty moral about these matters, and I don't think his wife and daughters would care to learn how Poppa brings home the rent."

It was 4:30 on the morning of April 18 when Fodor and Scipioni pulled up outside the bookseller's apartment in an unmarked Legation car. Middle-aged and fleshy, the man was angry at being disturbed at such an hour and uncooperative until Fodor leaned on him with a little blackmail. Not only would the criminal police be informed of the pornographic sideline, but Fodor would make sure that both wife and daughters received copies of the magazines in question.

Being Swiss, the man backed off. As a country, Switzerland exists—then as now—rather as a pimp does. It takes no risks, merely a cut of whatever is going.

The bookseller became all smiles, albeit they were a little forced. Of course he would do anything to assist the liberators of Europe; and yes, he was sure he had copies of Brontë's works in both English and German. As for the other matter, he hoped that Fodor and Scipioni, being Americans, would appreciate that a man had to make a profit wherever he could in these troubled times.

They were back at the Legation and in Newbegin's cubicle in the code room by 5:15, a volume each of *Wuthering Heights* in English and German in Fodor's briefcase.

While Bellinger sucked at an unlit cigar and ran relays between the cubicle and the coffeepot, Fodor, Scipioni and Newbegin split the coded message transcriptions into three heaps. Fodor and Scipioni took those emanating from Berlin, as their German was fluent, far and away superior to Newbegin's. After the cryptanalyst explained what was required, they retired to separate desks and proceeded.

There was a moment's panic when the opening lines of Chapter 31 failed to crack the code names of sender and addresses, but Newbegin quickly tried the last lines of the same chapter: ". . . and migrated together into the stirring atmosphere of the town . . ."

And there it was. Sender: Nemesis. Recipient: Valkyrie.

Experience and familiarity increased their speed, and by 7:20 they had all they needed to know. Or most of it, rather. It was obvious that a deal was being made under the cover name of Operation Horsetrade, though the details were still a mystery. Neither did they know who Nemesis and Valkyrie were. But one thing was patently obvious: whatever Operation Horsetrade involved was due to take place very shortly.

Jake Bellinger collected the decoded flimsies and sorted them into date order, the first intercept at the top. Allen Dulles wasn't going to like this one little bit.

"Thanks," he said to Newbegin. "I'm not sure what sort of

citations are handed out for this sort of work, but I'll see you get some kind of recognition."

The cryptanalyst nodded his acknowledgment. He felt unbearably tired and elated at the same time. It was such a simple code—but they all were, once you had the answer.

"It wasn't only me, sir," he said generously. "If Major Fodor hadn't established the title of the book, we could have been here till Thanksgiving."

Bellinger turned his gaze on Fodor, slumped in a chair and looking as if he'd died a week ago. Next to him, Scipioni was already asleep.

"Maybe you're right," said Bellinger, "but from the condition of that pair they've already had their rewards."

Meetings with the OSS chief usually took place in Dulles' apartment, overlooking the River Aare. It was only a few minutes' drive from the Legation, and there was no nonsense about using unmarked cars. Bellinger arrived in style, in a Cadillac flying the Stars and Stripes. Since a Swiss newspaper had published a story late in 1942 that Allen Dulles was head of an American secret service in Berne, anyone who was not entirely blind knew of the house and its occupant.

Bellinger was shown into Dulles' study a few minutes after 8 A.M. He thought of telephoning first, but he knew Dulles would have taken that as an insult. As far as could be ascertained the man never slept, though possibly the pain from his gout had something to do with that.

He was sitting on a low couch, his left leg stuck out in front of him, resting on a pile of pillows. The omnipresent pipe was in his mouth, the room full of smoke. For a man still in his early fifties he didn't look too healthy. He was perspiring heavily, and behind the rimless spectacles his pupils were mere pinpricks. Bellinger wondered what sort of drugs he was on.

"Sit down, Jake," he said. "What have you got for me?"

Bellinger pulled up a chair and passed over the sheaf of decoded flimsies. On top he had handwritten a short report, summarizing the contents, stating his conclusions and giving credit to Newbegin and Fodor for their part in getting the job done. This Dulles read last.

"*Wuthering Heights*, eh?" he said finally, chuckling. "The British are developing a sense of humor."

"If you can call it that," muttered Bellinger. "No wonder it took us all night to crack it; only the Limeys would choose a woman. If it had had been us, we'd have made it Hemingway or someone with balls."

"And they'd have had the answer within an hour," said Dulles drily. "Okay, what do you make of it all? I see what you've written down, but I'd like to hear what you've got to say in greater depth."

"I don't think there's much I can add," said Bellinger. "The messages explain themselves. The British are attempting to conclude a deal with a top-ranking Nazi. What the deal involves or who the Nazi is we have no way of knowing. Yet. But unless they've told us about it—and nothing's come across my desk— they're breaking the basic agreement we have with them."

"Which is?"

"That intelligence material is shared and that neither side negotiates with the Krauts on any terms other than unconditional surrender. It seems from where I'm sitting that they're trying to pull a fast one."

"And we object to that."

It was more of a statement than a question, but Bellinger answered it anyway. "We do. Unless Harry Truman's changed F.D.R.'s policy."

"He hasn't. It's still unconditional surrender, which is what I tell every Nazi emissary who comes knocking at my door."

Bellinger nodded. It was no secret in the service that some of Himmler's hirelings had been trying to negotiate a private settlement via Dulles. He was relieved to hear from his chief that no such arrangement was contemplated.

A thought struck him. "It couldn't be, could it," he asked, "that having failed to make any headway with us, Himmler is trying the British?"

"I don't know."

Dulles filled his pipe and got it going. From behind a cloud of tobacco smoke he flicked through the sheaf of documents until he found three he was looking for. He removed them from the bulldog clip and passed them across to Bellinger.

"Do you see any significance in those?"

The messages were datelined 28 January, 30 March and 15 April. The first said that Horsetrade was not yet feasible owing to political considerations, the second that a favorable political decision could be virtually guaranteed, and the third that Horsetrade was in operation with immediate effect in accordance with previously agreed modus operandi.

"Not a hell of a lot," said Bellinger, "seeing that we don't know what this previously agreed m.o. is. That must have been arranged before we were on to them."

"Or by courier. Almost by definition the m.o. is bound to be complicated. It would involve a long transmission, something nobody in this business is fond of. I think it more likely that some sort of meeting was arranged between one of Valkyrie's stooges and London. That is one significant factor, yes, but there are others. Look at the dates of those intercepts.

"In January London was virtually saying the operation wasn't on. By March 30, they're signaling that a favorable political decision is virtually guaranteed. And on April 15, it's all systems go. . . .

"The dates are important, Jake, especially the March one. The signals was sent just two days after Ike decided not to take Berlin."

Dulles puffed away at his pipe.

"A moment ago you were talking about the basic agreement we have with the British—sharing intelligence and not negotiating under any banner other than unconditional surrender. They're breaking it, evidently, but they must feel mighty pissed off that Ike broke his word to them."

"It was never a hard-and-fast promise to go for Berlin," protested Bellinger. As a soldier, even though attached to the OSS, he felt it his duty to defend the Supreme Commander.

"All right, I know the wording was something about prosecuting the war to the utmost and destroying Germany's means of sustaining an army in the field. But you can't name me a single senior commander, British or American, who didn't assume that taking Berlin was an important part of that brief, pushing as far east as possible."

"It's open to interpretation."

"The hell it is, Jake. You know and I know why Ike changed his strategy, but the fact remains that the British think he's making a mistake. For that matter, so do I. If Stalin gets his T-34s onto the North German flatlands, he may decide not to stop until he reaches the North Sea."

Bellinger was horrified. "He'd have to go through half the entire Anglo-Allied forces first. Good Christ, you're not suggesting that's what's on his mind?"

"I'm saying I don't know. I'm also saying that as we're giving him most of the territory east of the Elbe, he might decide he can bluff or force his way into some of the real estate west of the river too. I'm suggesting that the British have every right to feel sore. If I were they, so would I. If your allies won't help you, you've got to help yourself.

"Now, I don't know who the hell this Valkyrie is or what he's got to offer, but I'm not going to blame the British for making the sort of deal I'd make myself under the circumstances."

Bellinger was silent for a moment or two. "You mean we're just going to file these documents and forget we ever saw them?"

"The hell I mean that," retorted Dulles. "Pour yourself a drink, Jake, and let's thrash this thing out. Mine's a Scotch and soda."

Bellinger glanced at the study clock. It was 8:30 A.M., a bit early for anyone to be hitting the hard stuff. Fuck it, he thought, and mixed two stiff ones.

Dulles sipped his appreciatively and rearranged his leg on the pillows.

"Now let's see what we've got," he said. "One: the British have agreed with a ranking Nazi to make a deal. We don't know what they're getting or what they're giving in return, so speculation in that area is futile. Two: the deal is about to come off, but we don't know how or where. We can hazard a guess at that, however. Two of the later messages mention a conjunction, and the one from Valkyrie talks about the unit's being self-sufficient. Which seems to indicate that Valkyrie is to be met by some person or persons and information or whatever exchanged. Three: I doubt very much if Special Operations is doing this on its own authority. Remember the phrase 'political considerations.' That has to mean Churchill himself, which makes Valkyrie one very big fish.

"Which leads me to four: we've got to get in on the act."

"We?"

"Me, you, the OSS."

Bellinger was staggered. "You mean you're going to let this thing ride; you're not going to tell the British to lay off or we'll blow the whistle?"

Dulles shook his head sadly. "Jake, Jake—how long have you been with us? Two years, two and a half? When are you going to learn you're no longer a soldier? You're in intelligence now, and in intelligence there are no rights and wrongs, only results."

"That's not what Washington says."

"Agreed. I've had clear directives from the White House to do nothing that would offend Stalin. If the entire German General Staff were to walk in here tomorrow and offer to surrender their land forces in exchange for a few tickets to South America, I'd have to tell them to get lost." Dulles pointed his pipe at the two-star general. "But Jake—if I can pick up a top Nazi and justify it by saying that all I was doing was keeping a friendly eye on the British—well, who knows what I'd learn? This war's not over yet and won't be until the last Kraut lays down the last gun. After that, it'll be a question of keeping Uncle Joe off our backs until we're ready for him. Who knows what a top Kraut could tell us?"

"They'll pillory you," said Bellinger. "When the brass find out, they'll put you in a mincer and grind you to hamburger."

Dulles disagreed. "They would, yes, if I made the deal myself, but that's not the case, is it? Not if we time it in such a way that it becomes clear I had no means of stopping Horsetrade, that all I could do was climb on the bandwagon and protect U.S. interests."

"But it's bound to come out eventually," predicted Bellinger. He had served under Dulles for close to three years, but it had never been demonstrated to him more clearly than in the last five minutes that as far as intelligence work went, he was a child. A soldier saw things in black and white; not so men like Dulles. What was black yesterday was white today.

"Come out where, Jake?" asked Dulles, draining his glass. "If anyone learns about it, it will be the President and perhaps one or two of his advisers. They'll examine it carefully, see if it's likely to become front-page news and cost them votes, then act accordingly. If they can see an advantage and it's free, they'll take it, believe me."

He shook his glass under the military man's nose, more to take his mind off what seemed to be a double shuffle than out of any great need for a refill. But Bellinger misread the signs and topped up the glass.

"Jesus," he said, sipping his own drink, "it's a hell of a world."

"You've known that for six years. It's part of our job to make it a better one, and to do that, in this case, we must start with the British. Now, who do we know in SOE who would come up with a fancy name like Nemesis for a cover?"

"Greenleigh," answered Bellinger without hesitation. "I've been thinking about it since that first message was decoded. At this level the case officer could only be one of four people. Greenleigh, Bryant-Jones, Brophy or Ellis. But my two dollars is on Greenleigh."

"I'm inclined to agree with you."

Dulles put a match to his pipe and puffed away for a few moments. "All right," he said eventually, "this is what we do."

Bellinger listened in silence for the next five minutes while Dulles outlined what he had in mind. Finally, the major general said, "And if it's not Greenleigh?"

"It is. I'd stake my other leg on it. But if you draw a blank there, try the same tactics on the others. You should be able to get their whereabouts from Lincoln in the London Embassy. He generally spends more time watching our so-called allies than he does at his desk."

"When do you want me to go?"

"Today. As soon as possible. Pass that yellow folder over to me, will you?"

Bellinger did so. Dulles opened it and turned over a couple of pages. Bellinger could only half-see the contents, but they were, in part, maps. It would be Dulles' update on the latest troop movements on the western front.

"I guess you'd better hop across the border to France and fly from there," said the OSS chief. "The latest I have is that the French First Army under Marshal Tassigny is east of Strasbourg and just north of Kehl. Patch's Seventh Army is east of Tassigny. The whole situation's a bit fluid, however, and we don't want you running into what's left of the Luftwaffe. I'll send a messenger across to the Legation with the location of the nearest military airfield as soon as I can. In the meantime, I suggest you pack a few things and tell the boys you're going on a trip."

Bellinger rose to take his leave. He had copies of the messages, which was just as well. Dulles evidently had no intention of returning those on his lap.

He paused by the door. "We may be right in identifying Greenleigh as Nemesis," he said, "but what about Valkyrie? Any ideas who that might be?"

Dulles smiled wearily and shook his head. "Not one. But if it turns out to be Hitler, I'll listen."

TWELVE

The staff meeting at an end, Churchill beckoned Greenleigh into a quiet corner. Men far senior in rank to the brigadier moved discreetly away. When the Prime Minister wanted a private conversation with someone, he brooked no eavesdroppers or interruptions.

Churchill hunted through his pockets and produced a cable. It was from Anthony Eden. The Foreign Secretary and the British Ambassador to the United States, Lord Halifax, were in Washington for discussions on an Anglo-American communication to Stalin concerning Poland. In complete violation of the agreement made at Yalta, the Soviet leader appeared to have no intention of telling his puppet government in Warsaw to enter into talks with exiled nationalist Poles in England, in particular Mikolajczyk. As far as the Prime Minister was concerned, it was yet another example of Stalin's saying one thing and doing the complete opposite. Poland might not yet be a de facto satellite of the Soviet Union, but it wasn't far from it.

Part of the cable read:

> MY IMPRESSION FROM THE INTERVIEW (WITH
> TRUMAN) IS THAT THE NEW PRESIDENT IS HONEST
> AND FRIENDLY. HE IS CONSCIOUS OF BUT NOT
> OVERWHELMED BY HIS NEW RESPONSIBILITIES. HIS
> REFERENCES TO YOU COULD NOT HAVE BEEN WARMER.
> I BELIEVE WE SHALL HAVE IN HIM A LOYAL
> COLLABORATOR. . . .

Greenleigh handed back the cable, puzzled. This sort of thing was not within his sphere of competence.

"Yes, sir?"

The Prime Minister grunted. "My impression, I regret, is not that of the Foreign Secretary," he lisped. "Naturally I believe President Truman to be a friend of ours, but he owes a greater loyalty to his own people. In spite of what Eden says, his attitude to Marshal Stalin is much the same as that of President Roosevelt. You might be interested to know that I have spoken to President Truman again since receiving the Foreign Secretary's cable. I urged him to instruct Eisenhower to push our armies as far east as possible and hold. I also urged him to take Berlin, but he replied that he completely supports the Supreme Commander's strategy."

Mr. Churchill shook his head in despair.

"I understand President Truman's dilemma, of course," he went on. "He is hoping for Soviet participation in the war against Japan at a time when it will be most useful to the Americans. The Russians have it within their power to delay entry into the Far East war until U.S. troops have done most of the dirty work. He is therefore loath to upset Stalin. But I think he misreads the Marshal. Stalin appreciates strength. Neither does he want Japan sitting at his back door."

Churchill glanced around the conference room. There were several senior officers waiting to attract his attention, and he realized he had already spent too much time with the SOE brigadier.

"What I'm trying to say, Greenleigh," he concluded, "is that Horsetrade is now more important then ever. I can accept the wrath of our American friends, accusations of double-dealing, if I can prove to them once and for all that Stalin has territorial ambitions in East and Central Europe that make Hitler's policy of *Lebensraum* seem like that of an acquisitive child seeking more space on a crowded beach for an extension of his sand castle."

Nodding farewell, Churchill moved away. He was immediately buttonholed by a rear admiral, who waved a batch of papers at him.

Collecting his briefcase from the anteroom, Greenleigh privately thanked God that he was not a politician. His job was merely to carry out orders, not dictate policy. He had his own worries, true, but they were minuscule compared with those of the Prime Minister, who had to answer not only to his colleagues and allies but to history.

It was such a lovely morning for mid-April that he decided to walk to the Ritz, where he had a date for preluncheon drinks.

Sara Ferguson was already there when he arrived. She was, he thought as he crossed to meet her, an extraordinarily beautiful woman.

"Good morning, Brigadier," she smiled up at him.

"Good morning, Mrs. Ferguson."

He flagged down a passing waiter. "Two extremely dry sherries, if you please."

Five minutes went by in small talk until the drinks arrived.

"Your very good health," said Greenleigh, raising his glass.

The woman left hers on the table. "It's not like you to be evasive, Brigadier," she said softly. "Neither, flattering though I'd find it, do I think you invited me here solely for the pleasure of my company."

"You could always see through me," chuckled Greenleigh. "And you're right, of course." He was suddenly serious. "I'm afraid I have a most unpleasant chore for you, my dear."

Half an hour later he put her in a taxi, apologizing for the fact that he was too busy to buy her lunch.

Miss Anstruther was not there when he got back to the house. There was a note on her desk to say she would be out until 2 P.M. The same note also said that there were three urgent messages awaiting him.

Upstairs he helped himself to a generous goblet of brandy before sitting down. It was too early for serious drinking, especially without any food in his stomach, but somehow he felt in need of it.

The first message was from Major Lassiter. He had called to say that he had had more than enough of London and leave and would it be all right if he set off for Devon that afternoon? If it was and if he could have a car made available, he would take Sergeant Fuller and Corporal Gallagher with him.

Greenleigh smiled to himself. Typical Lassiter, anxious to get on with it. There was one man for whom the war was far from over, possibly never would be.

The second message was much more serious. Major Kennedy and Sergeant Holmes had been killed in a motor accident the previous evening. A third man, a civilian, had also received fatal injuries. The driver of the lorry was not to blame, according to police reports already received. His vehicle had simply got out of control. Miss Anstruther, on her own initiative, had put out an immediate call for Captain Dunbar and Corporal Maclean to report to this office. She hoped she had done the right thing. She had not told Major Lassiter about the deaths. He and Major Kennedy had been reasonably close friends, and she felt that the information should come from Brigadier Greenleigh himself.

Greenleigh drained his glass. Of all the bloody things to happen. Kennedy had been in almost as many tight situations as Lassiter and had come out unscathed.

He banished these thoughts from his mind, as he had trained himself to do over the years. He had seen many good and brave men go to their deaths, and to lament each and every one of them would drive a man insane.

The third message, though seemingly the most innocuous of the bunch, brought him upright in his chair. It was from a Mr. Lincoln at the American Embassy. Mr. Lincoln wanted to know if Brigadier Greenleigh could see Major General Bellinger soonest—2:30 that same afternoon if it was possible, as Major General Bellinger had to be back in Berne by evening.

It at least necessitated another brandy, and Greenleigh topped up his glass. Bellinger's arrival could only be bad news.

At precisely 2:29, Miss Anstruther came through on the intercom to announce Major General Bellinger's arrival. Forty-five seconds later he was in the room, the two stars on his shoulder sparkling obtrusively.

The pair shook hands. Because of the similar nature of their respective organizations, they had met on many occasions before, mainly in Switzerland during the tough, dark years of 1943 and early 1944. Frequently the SOE and the OSS had identical objectives in mind, and it was necessary to liaise closely to avoid duplication of effort. Greenleigh was aware that the British were looked upon as poor relations in the intelligence and counterintelligence business, referred to irreverently as "that bunch of hotshot amateurs across the pond." Americans never seemed to understand that a show of amateurism was an essential part of the British character. Hadn't somebody once said that they treated their games like a war and their wars like a game?

"You're putting on weight, Jake."

"It's all that damned Swiss fodder. I swear to Christ that if I have to sit through another five-course meal before this war's over, I'll burst."

"It must be hard." The irony was lost on Bellinger. "Brandy?" offered Greenleigh.

"Fine. You not having one?"

Greenleigh shook his head. He had managed only a sandwich lunch and he wanted no alcohol fogging his brain when Bellinger got to the point.

They exchanged small talk for a few minutes. Who was doing what to whom and where; how long the war would last; and why didn't all Germans do what Feldmarschall Model had done and shoot themselves now that the game was up?

Eventually Bellinger made his move.

"We're on to this *Wuthering Heights* business," he announced casually.

Greenleigh's stomach turned a somersault, but he managed to feign bewilderment. "What *Wuthering Heights* business?"

"Come on, Harry, quit stalling. We've got chapter and verse. All we need now is the commas and the periods."

Greenleigh winced at the contraction Harry from Henry, but realized he had to be thankful for small mercies. For much of 1943 Bellinger had called him Hank.

"I really don't know what you're talking about."

It was worth a try, he thought, though it was unlikely to get him anywhere. The OSS had obviously intercepted the radio messages between Bletchley Park and Berlin. They'd cracked the code, too, though they must still be in the dark to a large extent. If they were not, there would be no pussyfooting around about commas and periods. Neither would Bellinger have come alone. The American was a good man, but he wasn't top of the totem pole. If they had all the answers, Dulles himself would have been on the hot line.

"Bullshit," snorted Bellinger. "We've had our cryptanalysts working twenty-four hours a day on those signals and we know all about Horsetrade and Valkyrie. We know something's going on, but—I'll be frank with you—we don't know what or with whom. That is information we've got to have, that I've got to take back with me."

"Otherwise?"

"Otherwise Dulles blows the whistle. Whether he blows it to the President or Ike or the Joint Chiefs of Staff doesn't matter. When word gets out that you're negotiating with Nazi brass, you can kiss the operation goodbye. You won't be shaking hands with your pension, either."

"You've got no proof we're negotiating with anyone, certainly not with a ranking Nazi. You've picked up a couple of coded wireless signals and you're jumping to conclusions. For all you know Valkyrie is one of our own men in Germany."

"We thought you'd say that, but it won't wash. Christ, you must think I come from Cleveland. You've set up or you're about to set up a high-powered deal and it's not with Hitler's barber. Proof we haven't got, but they don't put someone of your rank on bread-and-butter jobs."

"You're jumping to conclusions again. I admit Valkyrie exists, but that doesn't make me Nemesis."

Bellinger grinned wickedly. "I didn't say anything about Nemesis."

Greenleigh could have bitten his tongue off, but he tried to make the best of it. "I'd be bound to know the code name of the senior officer. It doesn't mean it's me."

"I'll try the others if you like. I'll try Bryant-Jones, Brophy and Ellis. It's got to be one of you, and sooner or later I'll pin that one down. You can all lie till chickens fuck ducks, but I'll get there somehow. If I don't—well, you'll hear the shrieks from the White House in Piccadilly. Something's happening or about to happen and we want in."

"We?"

"The OSS."

Some of the scum began to clear from the surface.

Allen Dulles was not concerned on moral grounds that SOE had an open line to a topflight Nazi. He was only worried that he might not be let in on the act. Whether he would sabotage the entire operation if he were not allowed American presence was open to conjecture, but on balance Greenleigh thought it likely. His mind would work like this: anything the British knew that the OSS did not could only work to the detriment of the United States; he had therefore nothing to lose by putting the skids under Horsetrade.

But Greenleigh had at least one ace. Sabotaging Horsetrade would be the very last resort, in much the same way a blackmailer sent the incriminating photographs to the unsuspecting wife only when the husband refused to pay up. Like the blackmailer, Dulles would prefer to be part of the operation rather than anything else, which gave the SOE officer a lever. The OSS might accept a compromise, a small gain rather than an uncountable loss. Against that was the certain knowledge that the Prime Minister would be in all sorts of trouble if there were a leakage. He could maintain until his dying breath that his subordinates had acted without proper authority, but President Truman would be unlikely to believe him. Politics didn't work that way. The President would feel justified in taking equal unilateral action anywhere he wished, which was exactly what Mr. Churchill did not want. It was difficult enough levering small concessions out of the Americans without making matters worse.

There was, however, an interesting side element. Truman would have no truck with such a deal as was being contemplated with Valkyrie. He might accept the intelligence gratefully once it was all over and provided it could be kept a secret, but it would be more than his political life was worth to give it the go-ahead. He was a new President, he might even turn out to be a good one, but he had been in office less than a week and was still feeling his way. If there were points of doubt, he would be conservative in his approach.

Dulles would know this. It therefore meant that he was willing, assuming he could wangle OSS participation, to keep his President in ignorance. In many ways that put the SOE and the OSS on the same side.

But it would need a lot more consideration. Ideally Churchill should be informed of this latest development and become the final arbiter, but Greenleigh recalled how difficult it had been to obtain the PM's consent in the first place. He would abandon Horsetrade in its entirety if he suspected that word of it might reach the White House.

"How long have you got?" he asked Bellinger.

"Before I'm due to fly back? A couple of hours, maybe three."

"That'll do."

Greenleigh depressed a switch on the intercom. Miss Anstruther responded immediately.

"Yes, sir?"

"Have my car and driver round front in five minutes, will you?" said Greenleigh. "Tell him I'll be wanting the guided tour, two-star American general style. He'll understand."

"We going out?" asked Bellinger.

"Just a short ride. I want to show you something."

Bellinger knew something of London from private visits made during the thirties, but since the outbreak of war his duties had kept him elsewhere. He had seen a little of the devastation caused by the Luftwaffe and Hitler's V-rockets during the drive down from the airfield in Hertfordshire, and prior to his secondment to the OSS he had held a combat command in the Pacific. He was therefore no stranger to bombed-out buildings. Even so, the farther the car traveled east, the more he was shocked by the sights he witnessed. This wasn't some town in the middle of France or the Low Countries; these weren't aerial photos; this was London.

Without any prompting from Greenleigh, the driver worked his way through the side streets up to Oxford Circus, where he turned right into Oxford Street. From there, by way of Holborn and Cheapside, he made for that square mile of the capital known as the City. So far, not so bad. St. Paul's was still standing, and the West End had never been a direct target for the Luftwaffe. Nevertheless, night bombing was a long way from being an exact science, and many of the stores, those still standing, still bore scars earned in the Blitz. Beyond Whitechapel, however, the pattern changed.

When Goering switched his tactics from attacking fighter and bomber bases and radar installations to an all-out assault on the capital, his prime objective had been the East London docks. September 7, 1940, saw the first heavy raid in this zone, carried out by 625 bombers and 650 single- and twin-engined fighters. Not all the payload scored bull's-eyes, even if that was the intention, and beginning at the western extremity of the Commercial Road, in many cases whole streets had been razed, entire communities wiped out. Not a house, nor a shop, nor a pub remained unscathed, and it wasn't hard to imagine that beneath the debris lay skeletons which would not be found for another decade, if ever.

"It's difficult to compile an exact figure," said Greenleigh in a monotone, "but a rough estimate has put civilian deaths in the United Kingdom alone at around one hundred and fifty thousand from bombs and rockets. I don't want to rub it in, Jake, but it wouldn't take long to come up with a comparable figure for, say, New York. Nil, I believe the answer is."

He thought of adding that Great Britain and her Commonwealth, by themselves, had been at war for two years before the United States came in. He decided not to. There was no point in putting the major general's back up, not if he hoped to salvage Horsetrade and prevent the OSS from having more than nominal participation.

Bellinger dragged his eyes away from the wreckage. It certainly didn't make an honest man feel good to see what the British had been going through while the America Firsters were banging their drums in Washington. In any case, it was a fact of life and couldn't be altered.

"I presume all this is leading somewhere," he said. "I presume you're not giving me the five-dollar tour to prove some philosophic point I wouldn't understand anyway."

Greenleigh smiled to himself. "Quite correct, I'm not. I just wanted you to see for yourself what was happening to these people in 1940 and 1941 because as a result of that they deserve something in return. Note that, Jake; *they* deserve something. Not the French or the Poles or the Dutch or even the Americans."

"I'm still not with you."

Greenleigh sighed. "What I'm trying to say is that Horsetrade is a British operation. Valkyrie approached us, not you. What he has to sell may turn out to be of no value whatsoever, but if it is worth something it's the British who are going to benefit by it."

"No way, Harry." Bellinger shook his balding head vigorously. "You're not going to con me with cheap theater. What happened in 1940 has no bearing on what's happening today or next year. Besides, I've got my orders—and you'd better not make the mistake that Dulles is kidding. I've got to go back with something to show him. If I don't, he'll blow your operation sky high. So you'd better think about it hard."

Greenleigh had already done that during the drive across London. He was a realist. If he were in Dulles' position and had a lever, he would do exactly the same. But there wasn't a chance in hell that the OSS was going to take over the operation. He would give them enough to satisfy them, but no more. Go beyond that point and it wouldn't be worth snatching Valkyrie, as he would simply be spirited away to the States. Bellinger was bright enough to understand that. So was Dulles.

The bargaining began.

"I'll allow you to bring in two men and no more," proposed Greenleigh, "none of them to be your usual cloak-and-dagger boys. Special Operations has worked out the details, but that's as far as our involvement goes. Apart from the courier, all our men will be regular military personnel. And don't try putting uniforms on two of your goons. We're not stupid. We'll spot them as soon as they step off the plane. Two and two only, both German speakers."

"How many on your team?"

"Five plus the courier."

"Then we should have five."

"No." Greenleigh was adamant. "Eight including the courier will already make the unit overmanned from the original conception, and any more will just complicate matters."

Bellinger argued for several minutes but eventually agreed to a total U.S. complement of two.

Privately he was delighted. He had expected to be allowed— if allowed anything—one observer. The extra man was a bonus.

"Joint operational command?" he suggested.

Greenleigh laughed scornfully. "Not at all. My senior officer is to be the sole commander, and if something unfortunate happens to him, authority will devolve on my junior officer. Which brings me to another point. Lassiter is only a major, so I don't want your senior man wearing stars. He's to be a major also. I'd prefer a captain, but I'll allow you a major.

Bellinger mentally scratched the name Lassiter on his cuff.

"Okay," he said, "that settles the personnel. Now all you've got to tell me is where they're going, when they're going, who they're going to meet, and why."

But Greenleigh had played this game before.

"The precise nature of Horsetrade and the identity of Valkyrie I am *not* going to reveal," he said, "and you can lose your injured-dog look. I'm not holding out on you. None of my party, not even the courier, will have that information either. If the operation's a success, everyone will find out sooner or later. If it isn't, it won't matter."

"You're asking us to go in blind?" wailed Bellinger.

"Of course I am, and if you'll use your head, Jake, you'll understand why. These things have a habit of leaking, as I've just found out to my cost. If you knew the identity of Valkyrie and what's involved, how long do you think it would remain a secret? I know the way you people work—everything in triplicate. Sooner or later some file clerk or other would catch sight of the name, and that would be that. I've conceded all I'm going to concede, far more than I wished, and if you don't like it you can shove it right up your fat Swiss-fed ass."

Bellinger glanced out the window and thought about it. Unobserved by either of them, Greenleigh's driver had made a U-turn at some point and they were now back at Oxford Circus.

Greenleigh's proposals were less than Dulles wanted but more than he, Jake Bellinger, could have hoped for an hour ago. And when a man thought about it, it wasn't such a bad arrangement. Select the right officers for the job and Mr. Dulles would have all he wanted.

As the driver turned into Regent Street, Bellinger made up his mind.

"You've got a deal," he said. "Let's finalize the details over another brandy."

It was almost midnight by the time Jake Bellinger arrived back in Berne. Not having slept for most of the previous night and having been unable to grab more than a catnap on the flight down, thanks to a pilot who thought he was Eddie Rickenbacker, he was exhausted. But his day was far from over.

Dulles was waiting for him at the apartment, pipe in one hand, whisky and soda in the other, left leg extended. Light-headed, Bellinger wondered how he took a crap.

"Help yourself to a drink, Jake."

Bellinger declined. In his present state, a drink would more than likely put him to sleep.

"No, thanks. We'll get right down to it, if that's okay with you."

"Fine."

Bellinger gave him the details of Greenleigh's offer. If he expected his chief to complain that they hardly knew more now than they had known twenty-four hours ago, he was wrong. Dulles seemed more than happy with the arrangement.

"Nice going, Jake," he said finally. "You did well. I've had dealings with Greenleigh before, and he's a tough bastard. If he'd told you to go to hell, I wouldn't have been surprised. I'm not honestly sure I like the idea of a British major being in command of the operation, but I guess there's nothing we can do about it. Do we know anything about this man Lassiter?"

"Doesn't mean anything to me."

"Nor me. Still, we'll check him out. All we have to decide now, then, is who goes for us."

"Major Fodor," said Bellinger without hesitation. "You know how he's always bitching to get back on the firing line—well, here's his chance. He speaks fluent German, he's the right rank, and officially he's still part of the 17th Airborne."

Dulles took his pipe from his mouth. "Perfect. An officer with OSS experience who's not OSS at all. Couldn't be better. What about the other one?"

"I suggest we leave that to Fodor."

"Fine. Let's have him in."

"Now?" Dear Jesus, thought Bellinger.

"Of course now. If he's got to report to this place—where is it?—in Devon the day after tomorrow, he'll need all the time he can get."

THIRTEEN

The house belonging to Special Operations stood in the middle of Dartmoor, within easy hiking distance of the River Dart. The nearest major towns were Plymouth and Devonport, fifteen or so miles to the southwest, and Exeter, about twenty miles northeast. On a clear day it was possible to see the village of Princetown, site of the top-security prison, from which, from time to time, a long-term convict escaped. Usually he did not get very far. The moor was a hostile place at the best of times, home of sudden swirling mists and bottomless bogs. Many a man making a bid for freedom was more than happy to see again the comparative comfort of his cell.

In 1938 the original owner had died, leaving the property and its surrounding acres to heirs who had no intention of living so far from civilization. Three times in the latter months of that year and twice in the spring of 1939 it had come up for auction, on each occasion failing to reach anywhere near its reserve price and once attracting no bidders at all. Finally, in May, the real estate agent engaged to make the sale approached the War Department. With a flash of genius never to be repeated in his uneventful life, he sold the property for the very reasons no one else would buy it: it was big, it was ugly, it was isolated. It was also ideal for the planning of clandestine operations, and contracts were exchanged.

In midsummer, workmen moved in and built around the property an eight-foot-high wall which cost almost as much as the house itself. Soon afterward, notices advising hikers of the dangers of unexploded mines appeared in the area. There were no mines, of course, but the warning signs served to keep away itinerant shepherds and small boys looking for adventure.

A single massive gate set in the wall allowed access to the grounds, and once inside, the occupants were invisible from what passed as roads in these parts. The guard consisted of handpicked Royal Marines who had learned to turn a blind eye to the mysterious happenings they sometimes observed. They were billeted away from the main house, and as far as they were concerned they were overseeing a training establishment for foreign nationals. Which sometimes was not so far from the truth. For example, the operation against Reinhard Heydrich, chief of the SD prior to his assassination by Czechs Jan Kubis and Josef Gabeik in 1942, was planned in one of the upper rooms and rehearsed on the north side of the estate, behind the firing range. Thus the presence of "guests" who frequently spoke any language but English as a rule did not disturb the leathernecks. Neither did the variety of uniforms their charges wore.

Lassiter, Fuller and Gallagher, the latter driving the car provided for them by Brigadier Greenleigh, arrived at the house in the small hours of April 19. It had been a lousy, boring journey down from London, and all three wanted nothing more than to hit the sack. But the Royal Marines color sergeant who scrutinized their papers insisted that the CO wished to see them before they turned in. He had stayed in his office specially. Lassiter told him to lead on in a tone he would not normally have adopted with a senior noncommissioned officer, particularly a Royal Marine. But he was feeling bloody-minded as well as tired.

His ill humor was occasioned only partly by the stupid, unfair manner in which Major Kennedy and Sergeant Holmes, after surviving so much, had died. A soldier learned to live with such things, though he hoped to Christ that no malevolent deity had his eye on Captain Dunbar and Corporal Maclean, due to arrive sometime during the afternoon of the nineteenth.

What had angered him most was the last-minute addition of the Americans. Eleventh-hour changes were never uncommon in any operation undertaken for the SOE, but on this occasion he had felt bound to say that he was far from keen.

"We're becoming top-heavy," he had told Greenleigh. "Not only that, but it means we'll have to work with people we don't know."

Greenleigh sympathized. He was well aware that men like Lassiter got into and out of sticky situations unscathed because they didn't have to watch their backs, because each member of the team knew what the others would do and could act accordingly.

"I know, and I'm sorry. But I'm afraid it was forced upon me. I've made it quite clear, however, that you'll be in full operational command and should anything happen to you, Captain Dunbar will take over. But more than that was impossible. You'll just have to spend some time getting them acquainted with your methods."

Privately, Lassiter resolved to do just that.

The CO turned out to be a one-armed lieutenant colonel in his mid-forties. His left breast was a mass of decorations and campaign ribbons, though he wore no regimental insignia. He introduced himself as Owen and asked them to make themselves comfortable. He apologized for having to see them at this late hour, but it was essential, as it might be his last opportunity to fill them in on one or two details and house rules.

"You see, I'm no more than nominally in charge of this establishment," he said, smiling pleasantly. "A sort of shopkeeper, you might call me. I take care of the day-to-day running of the place and make sure the bootnecks don't get bored and set fire to the armory, but apart from that I'm more or less redundant. Your real masters here you'll meet in the morning. There are three of them, and I'll allow them to introduce themselves. You'll find that they will not be in uniform, but please don't treat them as idiotic civilians who know no better.

"We're pretty informal here. You won't be required to salute, and nor will you, Major Lassiter, return a salute if you receive one. I doubt if that situation will arise, however; I understand you'll be running around in German uniforms most of the time, and I've yet to see the day when a Royal Marine salutes a German. You'll be damned lucky not to get a bayonet in the backside.

"We have messes for officers and NCOs, of course, but I'm afraid you won't be using them. It'll all be explained to you in full tomorrow, but I guess you'll be eating separately from the rest of us."

"What about tonight, sir?" asked Lassiter. "We've been on the road for eight hours and we're pretty hungry."

"Tonight's an exception," said Owen. "A hot meal's been prepared. The color sergeant will show you where when you leave."

The lieutenant colonel glanced down at a pad on which he'd scribbled a few notes.

"Just two other things. Although you don't officially start until tomorrow at reveille, Brigadier Greenleigh asked me to tell you that from tonight you will speak nothing but German. That includes private conversations as well. And secondly, each morning you're to spend an hour on the firing range with one of our instructors. You will, of course, shoot nothing but German weapons."

Lassiter nodded his appreciation at this. Almost certainly they would have a lot of classroom work to do, and it would be easy to forget that they were essentially soldiers. A week or ten days or however long it was before Greenleigh gave them the green light was a long time for a man to be away from a weapon.

Lieutenant Colonel Owen stood up. The others followed suit.

"Apart from your instructors, who are quartered separately from you in the east wing of the house, you will be quite alone up there. Even I'm not allowed inside, I'm afraid, once one of Brigadier Greenleigh's little schemes is under way. I mention this because, as it's a very large house, for the moment I've allotted you single rooms each on the second floor."

"Thank God for that," muttered Fuller. "You'd have to hear it to believe it, the way Gallagher snores."

"In German, if you please," said Owen, dropping into that language himself.

Reddening, Fuller repeated the sentence in German.

Owen nodded approvingly, although Fuller had stumbled over the verb "to snore." He studied each of them, one by one, before glancing down, or so it seemed, at his missing arm.

"Needless to say," he said, "I know nothing of the reason for your being here or where you'll go afterward. Nor do I wish to know. But I do wish you good luck."

Lassiter led the way out of the room. The Royal Marines

color sergeant was waiting for them a discreet distance from the door. "This way, sir," he said.

"*Danke, Herr Feldwebel,*" said Fuller.

Immediately after breakfast, which they prepared themselves in the huge kitchen on the ground floor, their instructors appeared. As expected, they were in civilian clothes, and there was no doubt in Lassiter's mind that they were not army personnel.

They introduced themselves as Messrs. Browning, Gray and Keats—another of Greenleigh's little games, and phony names to be sure. In his late forties the eldest of the trio, Browning also appeared to be the senior in status. At any rate, he did the talking. All conversations were conducted in German.

"Good morning, *meine Herren*, and welcome. My colleagues and I are not quite sure how long we'll have you, though we understand it could be a week. It could, however, be no more than a few days, so we must use each one to the full.

"During your time here we shall endeavor to teach you all we can about the Waffen SS in general and the Das Reich Division in particular. Anything that is not fully understood, please ask. Needless to say, we do not know why we are imparting this information. I mention this for security reasons only, in case you think we are privy to the operation you will soon undertake and ask us questions. We are not.

"In a moment you will be kitted out in Waffen SS field uniform, after which you will make your way to the firing range. There you will meet the weapons instructor, Sergeant O'Halloran. In spite of his name, he too speaks fluent German, and you will use that language at all times. Sergeant O'Halloran is the only man you will have any communication with during your stay here. The Royal Marines are well enough trained not to talk to you, but should any one of them forget his position and make an approach, you are to ignore him and report the matter to one of us. As far as you are concerned the Marines do not exist."

They followed the Poets, as they were soon to be called, into an adjacent room. Laid out on a trestle table were heaps of Waffen SS field uniforms of all shapes and sizes: caps, tunics, trousers, breeches, boots. Most of them were well worn, and it took no great feat of imagination to deduce that their original wearers were either dead or in captivity. Try as he might, however, Lassiter could find no trace of bloodstains or bullet holes.

Browning referred to his clipboard.

"Your new identities and service records will come later, but for the moment I think it's advisable that you adopt Waffen SS ranks identical to your own."

"That's the way we usually work," said Lassiter.

"Good. In that case, Major, you are now a fully fledged Sturmbannfuehrer."

On cue, Mr. Keats stepped forward, eyed Lassiter up and down as he estimated his size, and quickly selected an armful of garments and passed them over. "I'll leave you to fit your own cap and boots," he said, "but most officers in the Das Reich prefer the old-style cap, without the spring."

Lassiter glanced down at the tunic. On the left-hand side of the collar four stars connoted his rank; on the right-hand side was a grinning skull.

"Wrong tunic," he said laconically. "Only the Totenkopf Division wear the skull. The others wear the SS lightning flashes, the runes."

Keats took the tunic from him with an expression of puzzlement. "Now, how the devil did that get there?" he asked of no one in particular, but it had obviously been some kind of test.

Gallagher and Fuller were swiftly kitted out. As a corporal, Gallagher became an SS Rottenfuehrer, with the almost universal symbol of two chevrons to connote his rank. Sergeant Fuller became an Unterscharfuehrer, wearer of a single star on his left-hand collar patch.

"Details such as cuff bands, proficiency badges and decorations are the province of Mr. Gray," said Browning, "and will be dealt with later. But for the moment I simply want you to get accustomed to wearing your new uniforms. When you've changed, perhaps you'll make your own way across to the firing range. I'll see you back here later."

Sergeant O'Halloran turned out to be a huge individual, six feet four or five at least, with a broken nose. Whether he was actually Irish they never found out, as his German was better than that of Lassiter, who considered his perfect.

The firing range was a walled area some seventy yards by thirty, the butts being approximately fifty yards from the firing point. The targets were man-sized replicas of British and U.S. infantrymen. As any member of the 1st Commando Brigade could hit a man-sized target at fifty yards with a catapult, it soon became obvious that the object of the exercise was not to test their skill but merely to familiarize them with the weapons they would from now on be using.

Set out on a groundsheet were five different weapons: a bolt-action rifle, an automatic rifle, a submachine gun and two handguns. The three men recognized them as respectively, the Kar 98K, the FG 42, the MP 38, the P 38 and the PO 8, or Luger. O'Halloran lifted the MP 38. In his huge hands, it looked like a toy.

"Probably the best submachine gun you'll ever come across," he said, "and known quite incorrectly as the Schmeisser, even in Germany. Not that it matters, but for the record Hugo Schmeisser had nothing to do with its design or early manufacture. He had a hand in the later version, the MP 40, but nothing to do with this. Nevertheless, as everyone calls it the Schmeisser, we'll do the same."

He tossed it at Gallagher, who caught it deftly.

"Tell me what you know about it."

Gallagher was no stranger to the weapon and answered easily. "First submachine gun to have a folding butt, first to be made without any wood in its stock. Weighs around nine pounds and has a thirty-two-shot detachable magazine. Cyclic rate 500 rounds per minute with a muzzle velocity of 1,250 feet per second."

"Very good," said O'Halloran. "Drawbacks?"

"It's a single-column feed, which makes it liable to jam when you can least afford it."

"It's also bloody expensive to make," said O'Halloran, "which is why the Krauts introduced the MP 40. You won't find many MP 38s around, but anyone who's got one has been in the Waffen SS a long time. It's loaded," he added. "Let see what you can do with it."

Although standing at an angle to the target, Gallagher had

turned and was shooting almost before the words were out. He let fly in five- or six-shot bursts, punching holes through the chest of his selected target.

O'Halloran was very much impressed.

Fuller was handed the Kar 98k and told to strip it. Made by Waffenfabrik Mauser AG of Oberndorf-am-Neckar, this bolt-action weapon was the standard German rifle. Fuller had seen dozens like it, frequently pointing in his direction. He had it in pieces in under twenty seconds, chanting the litany as he went.

"Length just over three and a half feet, unloaded weight eight pounds nine ounces. Barrel length almost two feet, with four grooves and a right-hand twist. Magazine takes five 7.92-milli-meter rounds in an internal box, which wouldn't be much use to me if I was in a hurry. Give me the Lee-Enfield Number 4 Mark I any time. It's a bit longer and a bit heavier, but it can fire twice as many rounds with near enough the same muzzle veloc-ity."

"Never mind that," said O'Halloran. "Let's see what you can do with five, middle target."

Fuller threw himself to the ground, legs spread in the classic V position. It was standard procedure to go for a body shot, but Fuller was a marksman and went for the head. He achieved a one-inch group above the right eye.

"Clever bastard," muttered O'Halloran.

Lassiter was next on the list, being told to pick up the FG 42 and get on with it. Weapons were Lassiter's hobby as well as the tools of his trade, and he startled O'Halloran with his knowledge of the automatic rifle's history, from its development by Rheinmetall-Borsig AG of Düsseldorf as an assault rifle for Luftwaffe paratroops to its falling out of favor with the German High Command because of the expensive and time-consuming manufacturing process.

O'Halloran stared open-mouthed while Lassiter told him that it fired from an open breech when set to automatic in order to avoid cook-offs, premature discharges caused by the round's overheating in the chamber. It had been the first service rifle to be made with a straight-line configuration. In spite of the light bipod and integral bayonet, he, Lassiter, could see why the High Command, apart from expense and time, had given it the thumbs-down as a mass-produced weapon. The magazine fed from the side, rather like the Sten, which tended to unbalance the gun. But for all that, with a cyclic rate of 750 rounds per minute, a muzzle velocity of 2,500 feet per second and a detachable magazine containing twenty 7.92-millimeter shells, it was a nice weapon in a tight corner, provided you were close enough.

To prove his point, Lassiter advanced halfway down the range before squeezing the trigger. As he enfiladed from right to left, the others could see lumps flying off each target. Had the targets been men, not one of them would have got up.

O'Halloran shook his head. "There doesn't seem to be a hell of a lot I can teach you people about these things."

The hour went by swiftly. In turn, they each handled, stripped, assembled and fired every weapon on display, though none of them was very keen on the handguns. Georg Luger might be a genius, and the latest version of Carl Walther's P 38 better than anything the Allies had produced, but the fact remained that a handgun was a handgun and its efficacy like throwing eggs at a Sherman tank when the chips were down. Nevertheless, O'Halloran had his orders and kept them at it until it was time to go.

"Who's responsible for cleaning all these?" asked Lassiter before they left the range.

"I am," answered O'Halloran. "I'd have made you do it if I didn't think you knew what it was all about, but I reckon you could give me lessons. Still, same time tomorrow."

It was only a couple of minutes' walk from the range to the house, but Lassiter, in the lead, froze when he pushed open the door. Standing in the hallway were two SS men, the taller of the pair a Rottenfuehrer, the smaller a Hauptsturmfuehrer. In spite of the fact that the rational part of his mind told him that all was well, instinctively he reached for a weapon he did not have.

The Hauptsturmfuehrer stepped forward to where it was lighter. "We got here early," said Alex Dunbar.

Because the arrival of Dunbar and Maclean and the fitting out of the pair of them had slowed down the morning schedule, Browning gave the five men fifteen minutes to themselves while he set up the equipment for his opening address. He repeated, however, that all conversations were to be in German.

In the manner of these things, the two officers got their heads together in one corner of the room, which henceforth would serve as a communal common room for military and civilians alike, while the three NCOs formed a semicircle around the open fireplace. Someone had thoughtfully provided a giant pot of coffee, and pretty soon this was being drunk, cigarettes smoked, stories exchanged.

Lassiter had not seen Dunbar, then a lieutenant, since the middle of 1944, since the action in which the young Scot had gained the bar to his MC on Lassiter's recommendation. Like many of his countrymen, he was a dour and dogged fighter, marvelously suited, if Lassiter was any judge, to the mountain warfare he must have been involved in with Tito's guerrillas in Yugoslavia. Lassiter estimated that he was now twenty-five or so, though his twinkling brown eyes, boyish good looks and air of indefatigable enthusiasm made him appear younger. He wasn't very big—five feet ten or thereabouts—or heavy—about 160 pounds—but he made up for that with fierce resolve and determination. Equally important, he spoke fluent French, German and Italian, and had added, according to Greenleigh, Serbo-Croatian to his armory. He had started his service life with the 51st Highland Division, but transferred out when Colonel Stirling called for volunteers for his newly formed Special Air Service. He was more at home, however, with the kind of freebooting operations the SOE usually mounted.

For as long as Lassiter could remember, Dunbar and Dougal Maclean had been inseparable companions in spite of the differences in rank. That they were both Scots doubtless had something to do with it, but there, to an outsider, common factors ended. Where Dunbar was on the small side, Maclean was huge —six feet three of solid bone and muscle. His reddish blond hair and deep blue eyes seemed to indicate that a Viking or two had got over the wall of the women's compound somewhere in his ancestry, but for all his size he was a hard man to rile—except when there were Germans around. Then he was a madman, charging forward regardless of risk, blood-curdling Highland yells issuing from his throat.

He was two or three years younger than Dunbar and had joined up as soon as he came of age. Somehow he had found himself in North Africa with that bunch of pirates, the Long Range Desert Group, but he had asked for a posting to the SAS because, as he put it, he was "sick to death of bloody sand." In the SAS he had met Dunbar and they had become firm friends. Neither had seen a hell of a lot of leave in this war, but what they'd taken they had spent at one or the other's home. Dunbar was godfather, and proud of it, to Maclean's young son, now aged two.

"Greenleigh mentioned that you and Dougal caught a couple of bullets," Lassiter said.

"Yes, he warned me you'd probably ask about that, but they were really no more than flesh wounds. We got a bit careless and overconfident in the hills, that's all."

"Must have been a bit more than a scratch, or they wouldn't have shipped you home."

"We were more or less due to leave anyway. The Germans have had it in that neck of the woods and Tito can handle anything the Nationalists want to throw at him. It was the ideal time to go. Besides," grinned the Scot, "you seem to have hogged all the action that's left in this war."

"Greenleigh told you what it was all about, then?"

"He gave Dougal and me some of the background. We're going to capture Hitler or something, aren't we?"

Mr. Browning came back into the room. "When you're ready, gentlemen."

FOURTEEN

The morning session came to an end shortly after midday. Using slides, Browning and Gray had taken them through an abridged history of the SS in general and the Panzer division Das Reich in particular, taking pains to point out the essential differences between the Waffen SS and the concentration-camp guards. Members of the former were elite fighting troops; the latter, sadistic thugs and murderers. To Lassiter and the others, they were all Germans.

The team's lunch, provided by the Royal Marines and left in mess trays by the front door, was hot and filling, which was about all that could be said for it. Afterward, the five men retired to the common room.

Dunbar took a cigarette for himself and tossed the packet on the table for the others to help themselves.

"I must say," he remarked, "that there doesn't seem to be a hell of a lot of urgency about this operation. Brigadier Greenleigh showed Dougal and me a situation map in his office; the bloody Russians have almost got Berlin surrounded. If Valkyrie's so anxious to get out, I can't see why he doesn't make a run for it while the corridor's still open."

Lassiter had already worked this out for himself.

"The way I see it, he must be someone pretty close to the top, maybe in Security or a member of the High Command. He can't just walk out without someone spotting he's missing and putting the balloon up. He's got to sit tight and take his chances."

"I'd feel a damned sight happier about that if it was only his neck and not mine," said Dougal Maclean.

"I thought you were a volunteer," grinned Lassiter.

"Volunteer, hell. Mr. Dunbar's the one who volunteered; I just got dragged in." The huge Scot's eyes twinkled. "One of these days we're going to have to do something about a system that says where the master goes, so does the man. It's bloody feudal."

"Master and man my ass," snorted Dunbar. "Do you know, Jack—"

"Hold it," said Lassiter.

Dunbar saw where he was looking; they all did. Standing in the doorway, clad in British Army battle dress and pointing a Thompson submachine gun in their direction, was Gray. He just stood there, immobile. Neither did any of the others move.

Ten seconds elapsed before Gray said, "Ratatatatat. Well done, gentlemen," he added sarcastically. "You're all dead. You've been wiped out before you're even off the ground. You've been told that you're to think of yourselves as Waffen SS from now on, and you calmly allow a British soldier to walk in on you. If that happens in Germany, you won't get a second chance. A British infantryman is not going to wait while you explain that you're really on the same side."

He turned on his heel and marched out.

Mike Gallagher said it for them all. "Am I being stupid, or does that clown expect us to start killing our own people?"

Mr. Keats took over the afternoon session. Where Gray was the expert on the Das Reich's commanders and the actions it had fought in, Keats had made a study of badges, awards, decorations and regimental insignia.

"You might think it's the kind of thing that can be learned by reading a book for a couple of hours, gentlemen, but believe me, it's not. Following a German tradition that goes back several centuries, the Wehrmacht and the Waffen SS like bedecking themselves with badges and ribbons. In much the same way as you would be suspicious of a British officer wearing his MC to the right of his DSO, so someone masquerading as a German could find himself having to answer a lot of awkward questions if he pins his Iron Cross to the wrong pocket. Equally, by quickly recognizing some of the more common symbols, you can learn whom to avoid. The Security Service, for example, wear the initials SD in silver-gray thread on a black diamond low down on their left sleeve. Similarly, the piping on their caps is of a toxic green color, though if you can see that you're too damned close."

Keats did not mean it as a joke, and no one laughed.

"Another group to avoid are those who wear a chevron on their *right* sleeve. Not their left, mark you, where chevrons of rank are worn by Rottenfuehrers and Sturmmanns, corporals and lance corporals. But a chevron on the right sleeve is known as an *Ehrenwinkel*, or Old Campaigner's stripe. That is mostly worn by people who joined the Nazi Party or the SS prior to Hitler's accession to power in January 1933. Some were awarded later, but be wary of all of them. They've been Nazis a long time."

Keats told them how all NCOs from the rank of Unterscharfuehrer upward wore a length of silver braid 9 millimeters in diameter around the tunic collar. "They also wear a single pip on the left-hand side, as Fuller is wearing now. Take a good look at him, you other noncommissioned officers, and remember it. In a flap you might think a single pip represents a second lieutenant, as it does in the British Army, but if you call a sergeant "sir" it'll be the last mistake you ever make. Note also that you're all wearing the German eagle on your left sleeve. It's a quick and easy way of recognizing an SS man, as the SS are the only formation to wear the eagle in that position.

"We'll go into the question of decorations for you later in the week, but I might as well tell you now that the *Ritterkreuz*, the Knight's Cross, will probably be awarded to one or two of you. It's worn round the neck, of course, and we won't be handing them out just because they look pretty. A Knight's Cross holder is someone very special even at this late date in the war. The medal can open doors to him that are closed to many others.

"Lower down the scale in awards for bravery are the Iron Cross First and Second Class. The higher of these two decorations is worn on the left breast pocket, the lower as a ribbon through the tunic buttonhole. Any Waffen SS man who has survived the war thus far will almost certainly have one of them and probably both, especially in the Das Reich Division.

"The only other major combat awards for nonspecific deeds are the Close Combat Clasp, which is self-explanatory and worn above the left breast pocket, and the wound badge, which is worn on the pocket itself. This comprises a swastika-charged steel helmet over crossed swords within an oak wreath.

"More specific awards for gallantry are the tank-destruction badge, the *Panzervernichtungsabzeichen*, and the *Tiefflieger-vernichtungsabzeichen*, the badge for shooting down an enemy aircraft with a hand-held weapon of a caliber of less than 1.2 centimeters, which was instituted in January this year. Both of these badges are worn on the right sleeve, and their wearers are either extremely courageous men or lunatics. Whichever category they fall into, if you run into trouble with one you're likely to have a fight on your hands."

There was more in the same vein. Badges for snipers, badges for marksmanship. Awards for this, awards for that. Finally Keats held up a cuff band with the words DAS REICH upon it in block capitals.

"This is worn by all personnel of the division who are not members of the regiments Deutschland, Germania, Der Fuehrer and Langemarck, who wear their own cuff band. It's been decided that you will wear the plain Das Reich. The regiments I've just mentioned are the crack infantry and Panzer-grenadier units of the division, but that doesn't mean to say that all civilians and others you will be trying to impress will recognize the names immediately. Everyone, however, will know your uniforms and the words Das Reich. It should be enough to keep them well out of your way."

Later that evening, Lassiter, Dunbar and Maclean were alone in the common room. The three civilians had business of their own to attend to and had excused themselves right after dinner, another feast of incompetence from the Royal Marines' kitchens. Gallagher had professed himself in need of an early night, and Fuller, whose German was the weakest of the bunch, was memorizing a long list of compounds Lassiter had written out for him. No one had said anything about a ban on alcohol, and Maclean had produced a bottle of malt whisky from his kit. None of the three men bothered with water, and there was, at the moment, about a third of a bottle left—two good slugs apiece.

"I'd give a month's pay," said Dunbar, "to see the expression on one of those bootnecks' faces if he looked in through the window right now. Three Waffen SS men with their feet up supping Scotch."

"You'd probably get a grenade lobbed at you," said Maclean slyly in a dig at Lassiter's Royal Marine origins. "You know what marines are like—they don't think. They see a German uniform and they start throwing things."

"I'm happy to say," commented Lassiter. "The day they start reacting slower than that, I'm joining the Catering Corps."

"Of course, if we saw them first," mused Dunbar, "it would be up and at 'em with the Schmeissers, according to Poet Gray."

"And he's right, of course." Lassiter swirled the last of the Scotch around his glass before dispatching it. "If we meet up with anyone other than Germans, it's going to take a firefight to get us out. We'll just have to keep our eyes and ears open."

Somewhere in another part of the house, a telephone rang half a dozen times before the receiver was picked up. A moment later Browning shouted that the call was for Lassiter. "There's an extension in the hallway."

Dunbar waited until he was out of the room. "He's changed, Dougal. I swear to God it took me a minute to recognize him this morning."

"Losing your wife and bairns to the Luftwaffe isn't a recipe for keeping you in one piece. I know what it would do to me. It's a surprise to me that he's still alive."

"I didn't mean that. Christ, that was five years ago, and we've seen him a dozen times since then. I can't put my finger on it exactly, but he's a bloody sight harder than I remember him."

"I'll settle for that. No offense, but for getting into and out of tough situations, Lassiter's top of the class."

"Let's hope so."

Lassiter came back, shaking his head. "The Brigadier," he said, "to tell me that the Americans are on their way. They'll be here sometime tomorrow. Is there any more whisky?"

Maclean refilled his glass. "Well," he said, "if we run out of things to do in the evening, we can always listen to them tell us how they won the war."

Six thousand feet over France, Lieutenant Scipioni still couldn't believe that he was going back into the fucking war.

He had a mental picture of a newspaper headline which read, LAST MAN TO BE KILLED IN WORLD WAR II OFFICIALLY NAMED AS GIUSEPPE SCIPIONI.

"It's gonna take me a long time to forgive you for getting me involved in this, Chuck," he said to Fodor, sitting beside him in the belly of the plane, for the hundredth time.

"Quit bitching. It's my problem as much as yours. I asked for the best man they had, and you came somewhere after the busboy, who was busy with the garbage. In any case, you'd only have got into trouble if I'd left you in Berne. It might have escaped your notice, but girls can get pregnant, you dumb Wop."

"That sort of trouble I can handle." Scipioni tried another tack. There was always a chance Fodor would turn the plane around. "Anyway, I'm not sure I agree with the morality of this whole business—pulling some Kraut general's chestnuts from the fire."

"Morality, Scipioni? You've got the morals of a Twelfth Street hooker. All you're worried about is not having any place to put your cock for a few weeks."

"Well, there is that."

"Maybe you'll get lucky and some Kraut'll shoot it off."

Scipioni closed his eyes. "You're a great comfort, you know that?"

FIFTEEN

April 20 was Hitler's fifty-sixth birthday, and Germans were reminded of the fact by a broadcast speech from Goebbels, who told his listeners that they had the Fuehrer to thank that Germany still existed. "Wherever our enemies appear," he intoned, "they bring poverty and sorrow, chaos and devastation, unemployment and hunger. . . . On the other hand, we have a clear program of restoration which has proved its worth in our country and in all other European countries where it had a chance."

He acknowledged that the war was nearing its end, but foretold that in a few years Germany would flourish again. "Her ravaged countryside will be studded with new and more beautiful towns and villages inhabited by happy people. We shall once again be friends with all nations of goodwill. . . . Order, peace and prosperity will reign. . . ."

Even more astonishingly, this gratifying state of affairs was to come about not by a German defeat but by a victory, for if ". . . history can write that the people of this country never deserted their leader and that he never deserted his people, therein lies victory."

Accustomed over the years to the art of doublethink, Berliners took all this with a very large pinch of salt, though few voiced their private thoughts. To do so was to invite the unwelcome attentions of the SS. It was better to pay lip service to the doctrine of ultimate victory than to walk around without a head, though if Goebbels saw Berlin as representative of success, God help them all if they were ever beaten.

The capital was a blazing ruin filled with the stench of death. Spacious avenues were a mass of rubble, streets pockmarked with huge craters. Neither parks nor boulevards contained trees that were other than charred stumps. And above everything hung a pall of black smoke.

The Charlottenburg Chaussee, that broad avenue which cut the center of the city in half from east to west, was littered with the mangled wreckage of burnt-out cars and trucks. The chariot of victory atop the Brandenburg Gate was twisted beyond recognition. East of Unter den Linden, which itself was being consumed by fires past and fires present, virtually nothing remained of the domed palaces, the pillared libraries and museums. The Tiergarten, the world-famous zoo, resembled a World War I battlefield, with the animals either dead or dying. Only the huge antiaircraft control tower had somehow escaped more than superficial damage.

Moving south, Wilhelmstrasse, though still out of range of Russian artillery, had not been missed by the bombs; neither had the Chancellery, although most of the offices were no longer occupied; business was being conducted from underground cellars and bunkers.

There was no escaping the dreadful heat, no shutting out the fearful noise of air-raid sirens, though why anyone wanted to bomb the city any further was beyond most Berliners. Indeed, it had been decreed in London and Washington on April 16 that the bombing of German cities was to cease. Except for Berlin. The capital was to be pounded until it capitulated, and squadrons of Mosquitoes, among others, were over the city three or four times a day, harassed by what remained of the Luftwaffe. Me 109s, which were taking off and obtaining fuel and servicing from God knew where, continued to tackle vastly superior numbers of Russian and Anglo-American fighters.

Everywhere a man looked there were corpses. The sanitation department had found it impossible to keep up with the burial of the dead. Even if it had had enough gasoline for its trucks, it had not enough men to drive them. And even if they could be driven, it would take hours to weave through the shattered streets, hours more to take the bodies to a municipal dump.

The living formed continuous breadlines. What remained of three million inhabitants required food, and not even the appearance of the RAF or the USAF would drive them from their queues. To stay might mean sudden death from a bomb, but to leave promised certain starvation. The limited provisions would not go far.

There was no water in the mains any longer, and thirst had to be quenched at the pools that had formed in bomb craters. There was no gas or electricity—except for the privileged few—to boil the water and thus reduce the risks of typhoid and cholera. The best that could be done was a tin can over an open fire. Of fires there were plenty.

At night the Berliners slept in cellars, underground passages, improvised tents—or simply in the open. Subway stations had become communal dormitories, and those who could grab a space rarely left it. Families became primeval groups; the wife guarded the bed space with the eldest and strongest of the children while the husband went off to hunt. It was a lottery. He might return with nothing; he might be one of the lucky ones who reached the head of the queue before supplies ran out. Murder for a loaf of bread was commonplace, for in this insane world it mattered not that someone died provided your own family lived. Near Alexanderplatz a girl of eighteen was kicked to death by a gang of youths for the brown-paper parcel she was carrying. It turned out to contain nothing but old newspapers—her portable bed and blankets.

The bombs (and later the shells) were undiscriminating in their choice of target. Hospital patients were incinerated just as easily as soldiers. Those who died were the fortunate ones, for there were no bandages for the wounded, no medicines for the sick.

The barricades, trenches and tank traps around the inner city were manned by old men and youngsters of the *Volkssturm*, the Home Guard. The few with rifles had no ammunition, and a length of iron bar was the commonest weapon. Not that a million rifles would have done much good. The Russians were less than twenty-five miles away.

Nevertheless, it had been decreed that Berlin would fight to the last man—or woman or child. Day and night, SS troops roamed the streets looking for deserters and defeatists. Suspicion and proof had long been the same thing, and without adequate papers a man was doomed. Bullets were at a premium, but each patrol carried a coil of rope.

Other SS men guarded the precincts of the Chancellery and the Bunker. Those of the *Reichssicherheitsdienst*, under the overall command of Brigadefuehrer Rattenhuber, were responsible for the personal safety of the Nazi leaders. Second-line troops of the SS *Begleitkommando* under Obersturmbannfuehrer Schedle were there to make sure that no one penetrated the triangle bounded by Hermann Goeringstrasse, Wilhelmstrasse and Leipzigerstrasse without good reason. But on this day of all days, many ranking Nazis had business in the Bunker.

Throughout the afternoon Hitler received a variety of visitors and well-wishers. Among them were Himmler, Goering and Goebbels, Admiral Doenitz, Generalfeldmarschall Keitel and Generaloberst Jodl; late arrivals were Von Ribbentrop, Bormann and Albert Speer. There were some who could not make it; they were elsewhere in the city or just outside it, directing its defenses.

In the Chancellery garden he met a delegation of the Hitler Youth under their commander, Artur Axmann. He thanked them all and decorated some for their efforts on his behalf.

At the reception afterward he was particularly affable to Keitel. "I will never forget you," he said. "I will never forget that you saved me on the occasion of the July Plot and that you got me out of Rastenburg."

Keitel could not bring himself to reply directly, but managed to say that negotiations for peace should be initiated at once, before Berlin became the last battlefield.

Hitler would have none of it. Even if Berlin fell and he with it, the fighting must go on.

"Time and time again," he said, "I've tried to arrange a peace, but the Allies won't. Ever since 1943 they have demanded unconditional surrender. My personal fate is naturally of no consequence, but any man in his right mind must see that I cannot accept unconditional surrender for the German people. We must do everything to get past this crisis so that new weapons may yet bring us victory."

These were brave words from a man who had not left the precincts of the Bunker in weeks, who had seen nothing of the devastation afflicting the city nor the misery of its ordinary inhabitants, who continued to move imaginary brigades around his situations board.

Throughout the day Hauptsturmfuehrer Langendorf watched them come and go, the mighty and the less so. He witnessed the arrival of envoys from those who could not be there in person. And somewhere among the dozens who were present to pay tribute to the Fuehrer was, he felt sure, a Judas. Somewhere there was a handshake or a pretty speech that conveyed one emotion and meant the opposite; somewhere there was a letter that did not reveal the writer's true feelings.

But he was as far away as ever from discovering the identity of the traitor, for he could not go to Brigadefuehrer Rattenhuber or Obersturmbannfuehrer Schedle with his suspicions. For all he knew they were the guilty ones or, worse, part of a conspiracy.

In any case, his best weapon—his only weapon if he was honest with himself—was to keep his eyes open. Whoever the treacherous bastard was, he was not in it alone. The business on the Swiss border was proof enough of that. He had used a go-between before, and it was odds on that for any further dirty work he would use one again. All he, Sepp Langendorf, had to do was watch for a pattern to emerge, watch for actions that were out of character. The servant would then lead him to the master.

In the meantime, there was a war to be fought. Berlin was virtually under siege, and there were those prepared to capitulate rather than fight. They had to be stopped. The miracle weapons promised by the Fuehrer would be ready any day now, and it was up to Berliners, soldier and civilian alike, to keep the Ivans from the gates until they could be dealt with once and for all.

With Langendorf as he left the Bunker were Scharfuehrers Scheller and Zimmer and Sturmmann Eismann. All four men carried MP 40 submachine guns, but it was the length of rope, coiled around Scheller's shoulder like some obscene aiguillete, that caused the patrol to be given a wide berth. The All Clear signaling the end of the RAF's latest bombing raid had sounded minutes earlier, and those Berliners who had elected to take cover were now beginning to emerge. They held back, however, until Langendorf and his men passed. It was better to risk death under a collapsing building than to fall afoul of the SS.

Halfway up Wilhelmstrasse, Scheller pointed skyward. North of their position, a dogfight was in progress. Now that the RAF had departed, it was the turn of the Russian fighters to harass the German ground forces, though in this case three Ivans had been jumped by a single Me 109. It was a hopeless situation for the Messerschmitt from the start, however, and even as they watched, it received a mortal blow and spiraled down, smoke pouring from the fuselage.

"The Luftwaffe never were any fucking good," muttered Scheller callously.

They were not the only Special Patrol Group out that afternoon, and as they turned right into Unter den Linden and picked their way through the rubble toward Alexanderplatz, on all sides they saw evidence that the SS had had a busy day.

Between the Brandenburg Gate and Friedrichstrasse, Fritz Eismann counted a dozen new corpses hanging from lampposts. Several of them were youths in their late teens and all of them had handwritten cardboard signs around their necks. "Thus perish all traitors." "I did not believe in ultimate victory." "I was guilty of hoarding."

Grotesque in death, several of them seemed to be smiling. Eismann knew that this was an illusion, a trick of rictus, but part of him couldn't help feeling that they were smiling for another reason—because they were out of it. For them there would be no more bombs and shells, no more burning buildings, no more choking in the filthy dust that covered the whole city.

It was unbelievable that Germans could do this to other Germans, but if they could, what would the advancing Russians do to the civilians they captured? Each day that passed, radio and written bulletins told of the atrocities that were being committed by the Ivans. No longer content with merely raping the women, when they'd finished they mutilated their victims with knife or bayonet. He'd heard tales told by refugees of seeing lines of burly Slavs queuing for their turn at the prettiest girls and of how they were mounted time after time, on many occasions long after they were dead from shock or pain. It was being said that Stalin had given his troops carte blanche to do as they liked, and he shuddered to think of what had happened or was happening to his girl and family. If only there were some way of knowing.

"Don't think about it," muttered Zimmer, reading his mind. The pair were a few paces behind Langendorf and Scheller, and a quiet conversation was possible. "It won't get you anywhere."

Zimmer was worried about his friend's mental state. It would take very little to push Fritz Eismann right over the top, and not for the first time he thought it a mistake on the part of the SS *Führunghauptamt* to dragoon Waffen SS troops into doing security work. The argument in favor of it, of course, was that the war had reached a critical stage and that everyone during his so-called off-duty periods had to take a turn in ferreting out deserters and defeatists, hitherto the exclusive province of the SD.

So far their group had been lucky—if that was the word for it—as none of its patrols had come across anyone whose papers had not checked out. Which was just as well, for with the possible exception of people like Langendorf and Scheller, everyone viewed these hanging patrols with barely disguised horror. Even men who had seen bitter combat on a dozen fighting fronts, hardened men whose personal courage was not in dispute—even they had been known to go quietly into a corner and vomit at the conclusion of a "successful" day.

There was no way out of the trap, of course—that was the problem; there was no way an SS officer or trooper could refuse to obey an order and hope to remain alive. It was useless for the Allied Powers to say—as many a clandestine listener to the BBC had heard them intone—that each man was responsible for his own actions, that an order which was a criminal order was no order at all and should be disobeyed. Then what? A firing squad for the insubordinate and a concentration camp or worse for his wife and children.

Continuing along Unter den Linden, from time to time, at

138

Langendorf's behest, the patrol stopped and questioned and asked to see the papers of various individuals and groups, both those in uniform and those out of it. To a man, those interrogated wore an expression of fear and hoped their documents were up to date, that they had not offended against some new rule.

Langendorf himself did the questioning, and he took special pleasure in making himself obnoxious to the younger of the women they came across. Not in the least interested in women himself, he nevertheless gave the impression that his greatest desire was to use their bodies. It was degrading to see their response. Without exception, each girl's expression said that if there was something amiss with her papers, she was willing to offer herself for any sort of perversion provided she was allowed to go free.

Langendorf took full advantage of his position of power. Where Unter den Linden crosses the River Spree, he deliberately hurried the questioning of a gang of youths in order to cross the road and accost a pretty blonde in her twenties. Gesturing to the others to remain where they were, he planted himself in front of her and held out his hand. Her documents were quite in order, but before returning them he said, "My senior NCOs are particularly interested in fellatio. Do you know the word fellatio?" The girl blushed furiously but nodded. It would not be the first time. "And if necessary you would have no objection to performing that act on them?"

"Necessary, Herr Hauptsturmfuehrer? Who is to judge the necessity?"

"They will, of course. Their needs will decide the necessity."

"Then it would be foolish to object, wouldn't it?"

Langendorf let her go. It was no fun if they were acquiescent.

A little later he had better luck with a woman who was dragging two small children in her wake. To her he suggested that, for money—a trifling sum, more of an insult than a fee—she should be prepared to accommodate the whole patrol. "There are plenty of bombed buildings around. Anywhere will do."

"And my children, Herr Hauptsturmfuehrer?"

"They can wait elsewhere, naturally."

The woman paled with embarrassed anger, and Zimmer

stepped in quickly. This one was a fighter. If Langendorf pushed her she would give as good as she got, but the final arbiter would be the butt of the SD officer's submachine gun.

"If the Hauptsturmfuehrer will permit me," he began—but Scheller interrupted him.

"Shut your mouth, Zimmer. When an officer's talking you keep quiet until you're spoken to."

Zimmer didn't hesitate. He moved a couple of paces forward and slapped the children—both under five years of age—hard around the face. There was a moment of shocked silence before they began howling.

Langendorf looked at Zimmer in astonishment.

"What the hell d'you think you're playing at?"

Zimmer had to raise his voice to make himself heard above the cries. "Just trying to get the woman to be a bit more cooperative, sir."

"Cooperative! Since when did you start making decisions around here?"

"Sorry if I made a mistake, sir. . . ."

"Sorry! I'll make damn sure. . . ." Langendorf turned on the woman, who had a protective arm around each child and a look of hatred in her eyes for Zimmer. "For Christ's sake, take those whining brats out of my sight!"

The woman hurried off, talking soothingly to her offspring. Zimmer sighed with relief. She would never remember him with anything other than disgust, but he'd probably saved her from getting beaten or worse.

Dismissing the incident, Langendorf checked his watch. The patrol had been out an hour, and it would probably be another hour before the *Tommis* came back with more bombs. Still, they could be early, and he had no wish to be caught so far from the safety of the Bunker with an air raid in progress. It was time to press on. The patrol had not yet earned its keep for the day.

They continued east, stopping people at random. Langendorf thought he'd struck oil when he confronted a young man of obvious military age wearing civvies. But it transpired that he was totally deaf and had a card to prove it.

With the time approaching 5 P.M., Langendorf was beginning to think that Berlin was now devoid of deserters and defeatists, looters and hoarders. But at the junction of Alexanderplatz and Alexanderstrasse he found his first victims.

There were two of them, each carrying a bulging gunnysack, and it was sheer bad luck that they happened to step from a gutted building at precisely the same moment as Langendorf's patrol rounded the corner. There was no mistaking the SS uniforms—but neither, for the two men, was there any point in making a run for it. Less than ten yards separated the groups, and Scheller already had the safety off his MP 40 and was holding it in a manner that invited the pair to run at their peril. They chose not to. Instead they stood stock still, not dropping the sacks, not raising their hands. If it's possible for fear to cause immobility, these two were scared stiff.

Eismann felt sick to his stomach. There could be only one outcome to this encounter, and he dreaded it.

"Well, well, well," murmured Langendorf, walking slowly around the pair. They were quite young, late teens or early twenties, and while neither was wearing a uniform, it was perfectly obvious that they had served—and in that case should still be serving—in the Wehrmacht. It was one thing to discard regulation tunics and trousers; with so many deaths due to the bombing, civilian replacements were not hard to come by if a man wasn't fussy about stripping a corpse. But footwear was a different matter; in the correct size it was at a premium, and these two were still wearing their army-issue boots.

"Open the sacks, Zimmer," said Langendorf. "Let's see what our two little squirrels are hoarding for the winter."

Zimmer complied, emptying the contents into the roadway. Both sacks contained bread, a dozen or so loaves. Their condition was a long way from perfection, but bread was bread.

"What's the name of your unit?" snapped Langendorf. "Or rather, the unit you used to belong to before you decided running away was easier."

"I swear on my mother's life, Herr Hauptsturmfuehrer, that we are not deserters." The taller and more commanding of the two answered for both of them. "We were caught out in the open when the *Tommis* came over earlier and we took shelter in there." He pointed to the building they had just left. "It must once have been a bakery, because we found the bread in an oven. Quite by accident."

"And you intended to hand it over for distribution, of course."

"Of course."

"I see. For that, naturally, you will be rewarded, but in order to reward you we shall need your names. So your papers, if you don't mind."

The spokesman hesitated. "I regret, Herr Hauptsturmfuehrer, that they were destroyed in a bombing raid and we have not yet had time to obtain replacements."

"Of course you haven't," said Langendorf softly, and for a moment both men's eyes glittered with hope.

"Nevertheless, you can see I have a problem here, can't you? I have on my hands two young men of military age whom I find without documents but carrying stolen bread."

"It could hardly be called stolen, Herr Hauptsturmfuehrer."

"Did it belong to you? No. Therefore it's stolen. But that's not my greatest problem. My greatest problem is that I have two criminals but only one rope. I'm rather afraid that one of you is going to have to be shot."

Both men paled beneath the dust and grime that covered their faces, but Langendorf's sadistic so-called problem was solved for him by the smaller of the two blurting out, "I'm sorry, Hans"—and taking to his heels.

For a moment the suddenness of this action took everyone by surprise, but Scheller was too old a hand to be caught completely off guard. Before the youth had covered thirty feet, he had dropped to one knee to steady himself and fired a short burst. At that range he couldn't miss. At least half a dozen bullets took the youth in the middle of the back, but his momentum carried him forward for another few strides. Finally he pitched forward, coughing up lumps of pink lung tissue.

Scheller did not go over to check. He had seen enough dead men to know that this one wouldn't be getting up.

The noise of the shooting had attracted the attention of others, however, and from a dozen derelict buildings fearful faces peered. Mostly they were not interested in the dead man. Mostly their eyes were upon the bread.

"You whore's son!" The surviving deserter spat into the dust.

Langendorf ignored the insult. "String him up," he said. "Over there will do. No, not you," he added, as Scheller uncoiled the rope from his shoulder. "You two."

While Zimmer and Eismann frog-marched the doomed prisoner to the lamppost on the far side of the street, Scheller was instructed to search the man he'd shot for some form of identification. Langendorf stayed where he was, next to the bread.

Zimmer was carrying the rope. Beside him, Eismann trembled as he walked.

"I can't do it, Ernst," he muttered. "I don't care what they do to me, I can't hang someone."

"Shut up, you idiot," hissed Zimmer. And then to the prisoner: "Run for it, you stupid bastard."

"You'll shoot me."

"It's better than being hanged. Believe me, it's better than choking to death."

The deserter hesitated before making up his mind. Then suddenly he was ten yards off, arms tucked into his sides, knees high. Across the street Langendorf was bellowing at the top of his voice.

Zimmer could see that the man was making for a gap in the fallen masonry, and part of him wanted not to squeeze the trigger of his submachine gun until the fugitive had more of a chance. But another part of him preached survival.

Firing from the hip, he let loose a long burst, making absolutely certain he was on target. It wouldn't help the deserter any if he was only wounded. Langendorf would string him up anyway.

Later on, he wasn't quite sure whether he'd screamed at Eismann to shoot also, for his own protection. But whatever the truth of the matter, a fraction of a second after Zimmer began firing, so did Eismann.

Watching from the far side of the street, his own weapon on the ground beside him as he searched the other body for documents, Scheller estimated that the deserter had been hit by perhaps fifteen, perhaps twenty bullets. It had to be that many. Anything fewer would not have nearly torn the man in half.

Hauptsturmfuehrer Langendorf couldn't have cared less

whether it was one bullet or a thousand. He'd wanted a lynching—*pour encourager les autres*—and he'd been robbed of it.

Later that same evening, Eismann told Ernst Zimmer that he was getting out.

"You're a lunatic," said Zimmer. "You saw what happened today."

"It's precisely because of that that I'm going. I can't take any more, Ernst. It's not only because one of these days I might actually have to tie the rope; it's also because I've got to know what's happened to my family."

"You won't get five miles. If Langendorf doesn't get you, the Russians will."

"It's a chance I've got to take. There's nothing for me here. There's nothing for any of us here, if we were truthful. It's all over."

"When will you go?"

Eismann's eyes lit up. "You mean you'll come with me?"

"No, I didn't mean that. There may not be anything for me here, but there's nothing on the outside either. But if you let me know when you're going I'll try to cover for you, give you a couple of hours' start."

"I don't know," said Eismann. "Tomorrow, the next day, the day after that. I'll have to wait for an opportunity." He peered at Zimmer anxiously. "You won't give me away, will you? I mean, you don't want to know when I'm going so that you can tell Langendorf?"

"My God," said Zimmer, "have we come to that?"

Two days later Eismann had gone, though Zimmer was sure his friend had waited too long. On the afternoon of the previous day, the twenty-first, the Russians were so close that shells from their heavy artillery were landing within the city limits, and Marshal Zhukov's advance columns were approaching Oranienburg, site of the Sachsenhausen concentration camp, nineteen miles north of the capital.

SIXTEEN

It has been said that throughout the war the American and British military cooperated poorly. In some cases this was true, but while Lassiter had an open mind on the matter, it was one headache he could do without. The operation would be just that much more difficult.

Nevertheless, he got on well with Chuck Fodor from the moment the two Americans walked through the gates of the Devon house on the morning of April 21. Fodor was a hardened soldier; plenty of combat experience with a tough outfit. But Scipioni was the other side of the coin. In an army where cockiness and near-insubordination are a way of life, he'd made a career of it. Deep down he meant no real harm, but he was young and had spent too much time enjoying the fleshpots of Switzerland. His complaints about the food and the lack of proper heating in the house were delivered with something akin to self-mocking humor, but to the others, particularly the British NCOs, he was a pain in the ass.

Harry Fuller summed it up. "He's getting under our skin, Skip. To hear him talk, we've been doing nothing for six years except wait for the Yanks to pull our chestnuts from the fire. But he's an officer and we're not, so we just sit there and take it. I dunno how long that'll go on, though; I think Dougal's about ready to clobber him and to hell with the court-martial."

Lassiter could see their point, but there wasn't a lot he could do about it. He was stuck with the Americans and that was that. Moreover, while Scipioni sailed close to the mark, he never went beyond it.

Chuck Fodor kept out of it. Dulles had made it quite clear that Lassiter was the operational commander, and Fodor wanted to see what kind of commander he was going to be. In a few days all of their lives might hang on one of Lassiter's decisions, and Fodor wanted to find out whether it was worth listening to the commando major or whether it was better to run the other way.

Part of the trouble was that Scipioni was nobody's fool when it came to physical fitness or handling weapons. If he'd fallen down in either of those departments, Lassiter would have got rid of him in an hour and to hell with what Greenleigh or anyone else said. But he was good.

The second morning on the range, now dressed as an Obersturmfuehrer in the Waffen SS, he achieved a one-inch group at fifty yards with the Kar 98k Mauser almost as fast as Mike Gallagher did with the FG 42 automatic. When challenged by Sergeant O'Halloran, who couldn't believe his eyes, to do it again, he did so with contemptuous ease.

That same afternoon Lassiter took them all, with full packs and rifles but in British Army fatigue gear, on a twenty-mile hike across the moor. Spending so much time learning the battle order and the various et ceteras of the Das Reich and standing still on the range, it was easy to become flabby. And there might come a time when they'd have to run like hell for it.

Twenty miles was nothing to any commando or member of the SAS, and even Chuck Fodor had managed to keep in shape during his time in Berne. But Scipioni was a revelation.

His personal habits should have put him flat on his back after eight hundred yards. He smoked a couple of packs of cigarettes a day and was always first to the drinks table when work was over. But after fifteen or so miles he suddenly said, "The hell with this. It's getting late." And having said it, he broke into double time.

There was not much to choose between in the relative fitness of the others, but it was generally conceded that Dougal Maclean's long legs got him to wherever he was going a bit faster than anyone else. Without waiting for any kind of signal from Lassiter, the big Scot took off in pursuit of Scipioni.

He could have saved his breath. Whether going downhill or uphill, Scipioni always kept a hundred yards ahead. After the first mile he increased this to two hundred. Lassiter had deliberately chosen a route that kept them off any sort of footpath, and Scipioni had never been outside the immediate vicinity of the estate in daylight. By rights, therefore, he should have at least had to think about the direction in which he was traveling. Not a bit of it. Straight as a stone from a slingshot, he made for the house.

Maclean wasn't that far behind him, but by the time he arrived Scipioni was already out of his fatigues and heading for the showers.

There wasn't a hell of a lot you could do with a man like that. He might get on everybody's nerves, but he was an indisputable asset to any team.

All seven men were on the range. Sergeant O'Halloran had managed to pick up a Walther Gew 43 automatic rifle from somewhere, and he was anxious that they familiarize themselves with it. None of them had seen one before, as this weapon, the logical successor to the Gew 41 (W), was used mainly as a sniper's rifle on the Russian front. With Germany now being squeezed like a nut, however, it was possible they would come across one or two, and it was a hell of a good weapon when handled properly.

Lassiter was first in line and rattled off his ten shots at a reasonable speed. This done, he walked forward with O'Halloran to examine the target. For security reasons they never used a butts party, and the accuracy of the weapon or the extent of the rifleman's skill could be judged only close up.

"It's pulling to the right," said Lassiter.

"I think maybe it's you, sir," said O'Halloran. "It's a pound and a half lighter than the 41. An extra half-ounce pressure on the trigger will be enough to swing it out of alignment."

Lassiter said he'd remember it.

Mike Gallagher was next. Having overheard the conversation about pressure, he took his time and achieved a tight group for a rifle that had not been zeroed for him personally.

After Gallagher it was a toss-up between Dunbar and Scipioni regarding who went third. The American held out his hand to take the rifle from Gallagher, but Dunbar stepped in front of him. "Rank before beauty, sonny."

It was an idiotic remark to make, but for some reason Dunbar had been jumpy and irritable for the last twenty-four hours. He'd said he had a cold coming on, but Lassiter nevertheless made a mental note to have a quiet word with him later.

Scipioni wasn't put out in the least. He gave a tiny mocking bow and a big grin through very white teeth.

"Yeah, I guess the way you were shooting this morning you'd better go before the experts."

The barb went home. Possibly because of his incipient cold, Dunbar's scoring had been well below par at the earlier session.

The Scots captain blushed furiously and snatched the weapon from Gallagher's outstretched hands. He accepted a fresh magazine from O'Halloran and slapped it home. Then, almost without taking aim, he fired shot after shot into the cardboard target.

The action seemed to calm him, for when he was finished he grounded the rifle quietly and walked forward with O'Halloran.

There was an uncomfortable hiatus before Scipioni gathered up the weapon and, playing to the gallery, aimed it in the general direction of the butts.

The next thing anyone remembered was an explosion as the gun went off. Automatically Dunbar and O'Halloran hit the dirt while everyone else stared thunderstruck at Scipioni, who was looking at the Gew 43 as though he couldn't believe his eyes or ears.

But Dunbar believed his, all right. When he picked himself up and realized that both he and O'Halloran were unhurt, he came back toward the firing point like an Olympic sprinter.

Suddenly everyone was talking at once.

From Fodor: "You idiot! What the hell are you tryin' to do!"

From Scipioni: "Dunbar didn't take his ten! There was a round in the breech! How was I to know?"

From Gallagher: "Jesus Christ, we've got to teach the stupid bastards basic firearms drill!"

From Fodor: "That'll be enough of your lip, soldier!"

Less than ten seconds had elapsed between the time the rifle went off and the time Dunbar arrived at the firing point. His face was white and he was trembling with rage. He was ready to do murder—and might have done it if Dougal Maclean had not got hold of him.

"The stupid sod tried to kill me!" he shouted. "Jesus Christ, you mean we've got to go into Germany with this bunch of Girl Guides? We'll be dead in ten minutes! Maclean, if you don't let go of my arms, I'll have you cleaning latrines for the rest of your life!"

Lassiter had already let it go on far too long before pulling rank. He hated doing it, but his team was rapidly disintegrating. What four days earlier had been a fully coordinated outfit was now a shambles. It was partly Alex Dunbar's fault. Whatever the circumstances, you didn't go around calling junior officers "sonny," and you never left a rifle with a cartridge in the breech. But it was mostly Scipioni's fault. Nothing had been the same since the Americans' arrival. Scipioni might be the greatest shot in the world and as fit as Paavo Nurmi, but a team survived because of its corporate and interdependent qualities.

He stepped up to Dunbar. Maclean looked at him anxiously. His first loyalty was to his fellow Scot and friend, the man he knew best and had served with longest. He hoped Lassiter would not force him to make a choice.

"Let him go," ordered Lassiter.

Maclean did so warily, but had the good sense to place himself between Dunbar and Scipioni. The SAS officer rubbed his arms and glowered about him like a lion just out of reach of the Christians.

Lassiter took him to one side and quite quietly said, "Alex, get the hell out of here or I'll see *you* clean latrines for the rest of your days. And if you ever pull a stunt like leaving a round in the breech again, I'll make sure your next posting is catering officer at Colchester."

Dunbar opened his mouth to protest, but thought better of it. Nodding curtly, he left the range.

Lassiter waited until he was out of sight. "You," he said to Scipioni, "come with me. Chuck, keep everyone at it."

For the making out of reports on the progress of the team and other administrative matters, Browning had allotted Lassiter an office on the ground floor of the main house. Once inside, he shut the door behind him.

"Sit down," he said to Scipioni.

"It was an accident, Major," said the American, taking the initiative.

Lassiter looked him up and down. "An accident. How long have you been handling weapons, Scipioni?"

"All my life. I was brought up with them. Look, you don't have to lecture me. I know you never point a rifle unless you intend to use it."

"But you did. You were making a grandstand play, and the result could have been the death of Dunbar or O'Halloran. You were, in short—as you have been since you arrived—behaving like an asshole."

"Hey, now look here—"

Lassiter half-rose from his chair. "No, you look here. That door's closed and we're alone in this room. If I hear anything spout out of that big mouth of yours that I don't like, I'm going to give you the worst beating of your life. And don't think I can't or won't do it. Understood?"

Scipioni considered it for a few seconds. "Understood," he said finally.

Lassiter sat back. "The way I hear it from Major Fodor," he said, "you didn't volunteer for this operation."

"Damn right I didn't. You think I'm crazy or something? For me the war was over until somebody pulled my name from the hat."

"That's fair enough. But to set the record straight, I didn't want you either. Neither of you, for that matter—except in the case of Major Fodor I think it'll work out. But with you it won't. I'm getting rid of you. You're going back to wherever the hell it is you came from."

Scipioni sat bolt upright. "You can't do that."

"Can't?"

"Well, what I mean is . . ." Scipioni thought furiously. "Christ, if you kick me out somebody's going to want to know why, and that's my ass in a sling."

"Highly likely. But what the hell do you care? You want out, I'm giving you out."

"That's not what I said. I said I didn't want to come in on something as crazy as going into Berlin at this stage of the game. But now I'm in I've got to stay in. Jesus Christ, they'll court-martial me. They'll put me in the stockades and throw away the key."

"Again highly likely."

"Then you can't do it."

"You keep using that word, Scipioni. Get it through your head that for this operation I can do any damned thing I please —from commandeering fifty Lancasters to making you sing 'Happy Birthday' to Hitler. I can keep you here or send you back as the mood takes me. You've done nothing but make a bloody nuisance of yourself since you arrived, and for my money you'd be a liability in Berlin. Anyone who can't jump when I say jump is no use to me."

"Maybe," said Scipioni. "And maybe," he added craftily, "you're stuck with me whether you like it or not."

"How's that?"

"I'm only guessing, of course, but whatever the deal is between your boss and my boss, I'd lay odds your boss didn't like it. Fodor and I aren't here by invitation. We're here because somebody put some pressure on somewhere. And whoever put that pressure on once can do it again. You try to get rid of me and you're going to get a lot of flak from upstairs. You'll be picking shrapnel out of your ass for a month."

"We can get a replacement."

Scipioni shook his head. "No time. Christ, Major, I listen to the news too. The Russians have got Berlin almost surrounded. Another forty-eight hours and it'll be locked up tighter than a virgin's knees. If whatever we're supposed to be doing is going to happen at all, it's got to be pretty damn quick. You haven't got time to get a replacement who speaks German, give him a new identity, drill him on weapons and the SS. You're over a barrel, Major."

Lassiter thought about it. The little bastard was right, of course.

"All right," he said finally, "I accept the logic of your argument. I can't send you back. But there is one way I can make sure you don't cause any more trouble."

"How's that?"

"I can shoot you."

Scipioni's eyes widened with astonishment. "You've got to be kidding!"

Lassiter remembered the Americans in Lippstadt. "No, I'm not," he said quietly. "You almost killed Dunbar a few minutes ago. The same thing could happen to you. I'm holding a rifle, it's pointing in your direction, my finger slips, and you're minus a head. Don't make the mistake of thinking I wouldn't do it. That thought could be your last."

Scipioni saw he meant it and shivered in spite of himself. "So I've got to go around watching my back from now on."

"No, you don't. What you have to do is keep your mouth shut. You don't complain about the food or the heat or the booze or anything else until this thing's over. You don't treat the NCOs like servants. You think twice before you even give the time of day. And you go and find Captain Dunbar right now and make your peace. Because if you fall down on any of those things, I swear to Christ you'll be coughing up your lungs before the day's out."

Scipioni nodded slowly and got to his feet. He paused with his hand on the doorknob. "What if Dunbar doesn't go for it?"

"He will. You're never going to dance at his wedding, but he's been a professional a long time. Provided you keep your end of the bargain, he'll make it work until you're both civilians again and can beat the shit out of each other."

"If we get that far. For my money we're all going to end up being fried in Berlin."

"If you feel that way, you can still take the other option. Being court-martialed is better than being dead."

"Not in our stockades."

Late the following afternoon, the twenty-fifth, Browning received a telephone message to say that Brigadier Greenleigh was on his way and would be arriving sometime during the evening. He was bringing the courier with him.

Lassiter instructed everyone except Fodor to check his kit and get packed up. They were as ready as they'd ever be. Each man had a completely new identity and an impeccably forged set of papers. Each man knew as much about the Das Reich as it was possible to know without having served with the division. Each man felt a peculiar tingling in his palms.

"It's on, then," said Fodor when he and Lassiter were alone.

"Looks like it. Though I'm damned if I know how we're going to get in."

"I'm more worried about how the hell we're going to get out. Tomorrow, the next day, the Russians will have Berlin in a box."

"Maybe that's part of the courier's job. One thing's for sure: Greenleigh's not going to send us all that way for no reason."

"You met him, the courier?"

"No. Greenleigh likes to play things pretty close to his chest."

They helped themselves to a drink apiece. Fodor sank his in one and smacked his lips appreciatively.

"You ever speculated on who it is, this Valkyrie?"

"No."

"Not even curious?"

"Of course I am, but I learned a long time ago not to waste time on problems I can't answer."

"Like the morality question?"

"What morality question?"

"Risking our necks to save the skin of some Nazi general."

"Who said it was a general?"

"No one. But it has to be, I guess. Anyway, doesn't it bother you?"

"Greenleigh asked me the same question a couple of weeks ago. I told him I was an operational officer. I go where I'm told to go."

"Obeying orders? There are going to be a lot of Germans saying that when the War Crimes people get off the ground."

"It's true enough, anyway. The only difference between our side and theirs is that I'm on one and not the other."

"That's a hell of a cynical statement."

"So what do you want from me—philosophy? If I had my way I'd hang the lot, beginning with the politicos and working downward from the General Staff. But I haven't got my way. It may sound naive and stupid, but somebody, somewhere has decided that this particular German is going to be useful to us—just as they decided that bombing the shit out of Dresden was going to be useful. I don't have any beliefs anymore, Chuck —I go where I'm pointed."

"That's a terrible thing to say."

Lassiter thought briefly of his dead wife and children, then just as quickly dismissed them from his mind. As he'd told

Fodor a moment ago, he no longer wasted time asking questions to which there were no answers.

"So it is," he said.

They were all together in the common room when they heard Brigadier Greenleigh's car draw up. Lassiter, Fodor and Sergeant Fuller in armchairs, Gallagher, Dunbar and Maclean by the fireplace. Scipioni was sitting quietly some distance from the others. He had reached an uneasy truce with Dunbar, but so far had kept his own side of the bargain, his mouth shut.

Of Browning, Gray and Keats there was no sign. Their part in the proceedings was over. Anything that happened or was spoken about from now on was not for their ears.

No stranger to the house, Greenleigh came directly into the common room.

"Good evening, gentlemen," he said in English.

Behind him stood the courier, at whom Lassiter was staring as though he'd seen a ghost. She walked straight over to him, her hand outstretched.

"Hello again, Jack."

Sara Ferguson smiled up at him.

SEVENTEEN

No," said Lassiter.

The others turned their astonished gaze from the woman to Lassiter then back to the woman again.

She was, they estimated, about five feet eight, taller by a couple of inches in her heels. Her age they surmised as late twenties, though her facial bone structure was so finely molded, so full of determination and character, that she could have been four or five years older and it would not have shown. Although they couldn't see clearly from where they were standing, most of them guessed correctly that her eyes were green and that she had a few generations of Celt in her lineage. On her head she wore a silk scarf, which, when she pushed it back, as she did now, revealed dark hair cut to the shoulders. Her fawn raincoat was unbelted and open, but even the chunky sweater and tweed skirt beneath could do nothing to disguise the fact that she was one of those rare women who would look better undressed than dressed.

Lassiter had not seen her for three years, since her husband, Alan, then a captain and Lassiter's company commander, was killed while serving with Lord Lovat's Number 4 Commando on the Dieppe raid. Prior to that he had been a frequent visitor to the Fergusons' house in Scotland, but later he had lost touch with the widow. She had written to say she was going to Canada. At the time he had thought it just as well. In looks she was not unlike his dead wife, and as she was vulnerable after the death of her husband, a situation could have developed that neither of them was ready for.

"No," he repeated. English was to be the common language now.

Brigadier Greenleigh did not have to ask what the negative meant. "I was rather afraid you'd say that, but this is no place to discuss it. Have you got somewhere private the three of us can talk?"

"My office."

"Lead the way. You'd better come along too, Major Fodor."

In the office Greenleigh automatically made for the chair behind the desk. He gestured to the others to sit where they wished. Sara Ferguson fumbled a cigarette from her handbag and held it while Fodor flicked his lighter. She smiled her thanks.

"All right, Major Lassiter," said Greenleigh, "let's have your objections. Make them brief. We don't have an awful lot of time."

"They should be perfectly obvious, sir. When you mentioned a courier I assumed it would be a man. The whole mission is going to be difficult enough without involving a woman. It's not just Sara—Mrs. Ferguson—I object to. I'd feel the same about taking any woman."

"Why?"

"Why?" Lassiter looked at the SOE brigadier as though he had suddenly sprouted an extra head. "Because I can't guarantee her safety, that's why. And neither can I be constantly looking over my shoulder to see if she's all right."

"You won't have to. I don't think I'm violating the Official Secrets Act when I tell you that Mrs. Ferguson has spent more time in Germany during this war than even you have. She has learned to look after herself. The proof of that is the fact that she is sitting here today."

"I'm not talking about cloak-and-dagger stuff where an agent can disappear into the woodwork and remain in what I believe is called 'open' concealment for weeks. If you say so, I'm perfectly prepared to accept that Mrs. Ferguson is good at that. But we're talking about a different kind of operation, a commando-style assault where we go in, pick up the German and get out again as quick as Christ'll let us. Good God, we've spent every waking hour of the past week learning to act and talk like officers and men of the Waffen SS. We adopted that role because, as you pointed out at the beginning, it will give us greater freedom of movement in Germany. How the hell are we supposed to trek halfway across the country with a woman in tow?"

"That no longer applies, Major Lassiter. There'll be no trekking halfway across Germany with or without a woman in tow. You'll be going straight into Berlin."

"Jesus Christ," muttered Fodor, "how the hell are we supposed to do that?"

"It will be explained later," answered Greenleigh. "In the meantime I want to set Major Lassiter's mind at rest concerning Mrs. Ferguson.

"As I said a moment ago, she can look after herself. She was selected for the mission because she is the best available operative. Until a couple of days ago I had no idea you two knew each other. When I found out, I too had my doubts. I dismissed them. Mrs. Ferguson has the qualifications we need. She speaks fluent German and knows Berlin intimately. She has made a study of the personal dossiers of Germany's military and political leaders, though I hasten to point out that she has no more idea than you of Valkyrie's true identity. She will not be taken in by a fake, however. If, as seems very unlikely, this whole operation turns out to be a confidence trick mounted by a minor official to save his own skin and with nothing to give in return, Mrs. Ferguson will realize that. Equally, even though unaware of his identity as of now, she will know him to be a man of considerable importance the moment she sees him. It's too late to change the courier, Major Lassiter, even if I wished to. Time, as you will shortly realize, is extremely pressing, and Mrs. Ferguson has been thoroughly briefed regarding her part in the operation."

"And what about her cover?" demanded Lassiter. "What explanation do we give for seven SS men carting a woman around with them?"

"I'll let Mrs. Ferguson answer that. It's something she worked out for herself, a stratagem she's used successfully before."

"I'm a camp follower," said Sara, stubbing out her cigarette. "It's not unusual at this stage of the war to see small groups of soldiers with women in their company. The women provide the obvious service for the men as and when needed and in return receive protection and food. No one will think it the least odd to see a woman surrounded by SS troops."

"You're talking about Berlin tarts," said Lassiter. "You don't qualify."

"Too British?"

"Too beautiful," offered Fodor.

Sara smiled in acknowledgment of the compliment.

"Thank you, but I can change. You won't recognize me by the time I've mussed up my hair, taken off my makeup and climbed into some different clothes. In any case, as a backup plan I shall be carrying credentials giving me business in Berlin. Again as a courier/agent, of course, but this time working for the Gestapo."

"Besides," put in Greenleigh, "you—we—have no choice. As I said, time is pressing. By tomorrow you'll be in Berlin."

The SOE officer got to his feet. Fodor and Lassiter followed suit. Only Sara remained seated.

"May I have a few words in private with Major Lassiter, Brigadier?"

"Of course. Make it brief, though. Come on, Fodor—you and I will go and explain to the others why they've got a woman along. Though why anyone should object to a Continental trip with Mrs. Ferguson I have no idea."

"Nor me, sir," said Fodor with feeling.

There was a moment's awkwardness after the door closed. Sara broke it by offering her cigarettes. Shaking his head at the lunacy of it all, Lassiter took one and lit both.

"You're looking well, Jack," said Sara. "A bit more than three years older, but that's only to be expected, I suppose. I thought of you often, but I'm afraid I balked at trying to establish your whereabouts. You could have been dead, and I'd rather not have known."

"What happened to Canada? Last I heard you were about to sell up and disappear."

"I nearly did. After Alan was killed I almost went to pieces. It didn't seem to matter much while you were still around, because, I suppose, I was leaning on you. But after your leave was over I just wanted to get out. The house wasn't the same and wouldn't be again. I tried drinking, but I never was very keen on it. I used to get sick before I'd had enough to anesthetize myself. I tried charity work, but there were too many other middle-class wives and widows doing the same thing and better."

She stared out the window. Beyond the high walls that surrounded the grounds it was possible to see, in the growing dusk, parts of the moor. It was not unlike the Scottish Lowlands.

"I received quite a lot of gratuitous advice, as you might expect," she went on. "It was all well meant, and mostly it took the same form: sell the house and furniture, leave the country, start afresh elsewhere. Well, that seemed sensible enough, so I took it. The house was more or less sold—at least, I'd had a very good offer for it—when I received a visit from one of Lord Lovat's friends, no doubt on the advice of the Clan Chief himself. Without saying so directly, he made me feel that what I was really doing was running away—which was true enough, of course. A great many women had had their husbands killed in the war, but they weren't in such a privileged position as I. They didn't have houses to sell or money in the bank, and there was no one in Canada or America to help them forget it all and begin again. They had to stick it out, and if people like me—he actually used that expression—couldn't do the same it was going to be hard luck on poor old Britain. Oh, he really turned the screws. He all but said that Alan would have died for nothing if I wasn't around to wave flags on victory day. I suppose he was trying to make me feel ashamed—but it transpired that that wasn't all he was trying to do.

"You know, I expect, that SOE had a pretty active recruiting system in the universities and so on, and were forever tracking down graduates who were otherwise not engaged?" Lassiter nodded. "Well, he was one of their recruiting officers and it soon became clear that I was to be his newest acquisition. He'd done his homework thoroughly and found out that I was fluent in three languages and had traveled a lot, especially in France and Germany. To cut a long story short, I gave up the idea of Canada before he left the house that afternoon and signed on the dotted line. They gave me the whole course—radio, codes, the lot—and before I knew where I was I was parachuting into France.

"I can't go into too many details, of course, but for the past two and a half years I've spent more time in Germany and Occupied France than I have at home." She paused. "I've even killed a couple of men."

He looked at her steadily. It seemed impossible to believe that the Sara Ferguson he remembered presiding over a dinner table had been responsible for another human being's death. But when he saw her eyes he knew she was telling the truth.

"I'm telling you this," she said, "so that you'll understand I know my job and that I won't be a liability. I'm not the same person I was three years ago. Neither am I a foolish twenty-year-old looking for excitement. I'm twenty-nine and I know what I'm up against. I also know that this time tomorrow I'll be scared stiff. But it has to be done, and I'm the one they've chosen to do it. Or rather, we are. I only found out forty-eight hours ago that you were leading the team, but it gave me a good feeling. I can't think of anyone with whom I'd feel safer."

Lassiter smiled for the first time. It was the same old story: what you couldn't change you had to put up with.

"I don't know whether I should hug you for being here or horsewhip you for being a bloody fool," he said.

"It had better be the hug. You didn't even shake my hand a little while ago."

He embraced her. She was, he was surprised to find, trembling.

"Come on," he said, pulling away. "We'd better get back before someone misinterprets our absence."

At the door he paused. "Tell me," he asked, "when Greenleigh found out that you and I knew each other, did the pair of you sit down and discuss my probable reaction?"

"It's possible," she said cautiously.

"And which of you decided that it might be a good idea if you had a couple of words with me yourself in private?"

"I did, I suppose."

"Working on the theory that if you couldn't persuade me to take you along, Greenleigh wouldn't stand a chance, rank or no rank?"

160

She lowered her eyes. "Something like that."

"I'm glad you've got the grace to blush."

"Berlin is almost completely surrounded, gentlemen," Greenleigh was saying twenty minutes later.

He had affixed a large map of the city center and suburbs to the wall. On it were broad arrows showing the positions of the advancing Russian forces. One of Zhukov's columns was just east of the city; another was sweeping down from the north and looked as if it would meet up with Konev's southern spearhead within the next twenty-four/forty-eight hours.

"That is the situation as far as we know it as of 1500 hours today. It could change very rapidly, of course, but it will not change in our favor nor that of the Germans, whose interest in the Russian positions is identical to our own for the purpose of this operation. Militarily, Berlin is a dead duck. There is no way in by road, certainly not for men dressed in uniforms of the Waffen SS."

He paused before delivering his bombshell.

"I have therefore decided to fly you in."

He waited for the commotion this announcement caused to die down, finally obtaining complete silence by holding up his hands.

"I understand your feelings, gentlemen, but believe me, there is no other way. None of us expected the Russians to move so fast, and we couldn't go until we were called for. That call came this morning. You have to be in and out with Valkyrie by April 30, which is the date our planning people estimate the Russians will have raised the Red Flag in Wilhelmstrasse. Bear that in mind, all of you—just in case something happens to Major Lassiter or Captain Dunbar. If you are not out of the city by April 30, there is a good possibility you will not be coming home."

He let this sink in before picking up a pointer and tapping the map.

"There are three possible landing zones. Gatow airfield over here in the west, which is about fifteen miles from the city center; Tempelhof in the south, which, as you can see, is considerably closer; and the East–West Axis which runs through the center of the city. Until recently this was no more than a broad avenue, but in the last few days the lampposts and trees and wreckage and other possible hazards have been removed to produce a satisfactory runway. We've had reports of transports seen taking off and landing.

"All three zones are under more or less constant shellfire, of course, and my own preference is for Tempelhof. Gatow is likely to be overrun before we can get you there, and the East–West Axis, while putting you slap-bang in the middle of where you want to be, is likely to draw too much attention to your arrival. As you will appreciate, there are not too many German aircraft flying into and out of Berlin these days, and those which succeed in penetrating Soviet air cover are immediately the center of attention, as mostly they ferry in ammunition or food. Tempelhof, however, is only an hour's fast march, regardless of the conditions, from the Reich Chancellery. If you can commandeer a vehicle, all well and good. If you cannot, you can still reach your objective without too much delay. The final decision, however, must be left to the pilot."

"What if Tempelhof and Gatow have both been taken and the East–West Axis is under artillery fire?" asked Dunbar.

"Then I'm afraid you'll have to abort. This is not a normal military operation, gentlemen; there can be no alternative plan. If you cannot get in, that's the end of it."

"Parachutes?" suggested Fodor.

Greenleigh shook his head. "Not practical, I'm afraid. We considered it carefully, of course, as you've all had jump training. But you can imagine the effect on the German defenders if they see eight paratroopers descending on their city. They'll assume you're Russians and take potshots at you. You'd be dead before you hit the ground. No, if you cannot land, the operation is off."

"Suits me fine," grinned Dougal Maclean.

Greenleigh joined in the general laugh. "I think I'd feel the same in your situation."

"It'll be a German aircraft, of course," said Lassiter.

"Yes. A Junkers 52, the old Iron Annie. We captured quite a few intact, and there's one waiting for you at Eindhoven in Holland, which is about 350 air miles from Berlin, or a couple of hours at cruising speed. The Ju 52 has a normal range of 930 miles, but we've fitted extra tanks to add a couple of hundred, just to be on the safe side. Apart from other considerations, the crew has to get back."

"What about fighter activity, sir?" asked Scipioni. "Our own people, that is. If we're flying along in a Junkers 52, some hotshot might want to take a crack at us."

"As far as the RAF and the USAAF are concerned, they've been given the route and the time of takeoff and told to let severely alone any unidentified aircraft flying on your heading. You'll get no trouble from them. But for obvious reasons, we cannot forewarn the Russians. You may run into some hostile activity once you cross the Elbe. You will be flying at night, however, which will help to some extent, and the closer you get to Berlin, the easier it will be. Now that their own ground forces are so close, the Soviet Air Force has largely taken a back seat. Don't get me wrong; it's not going to be a milk run. But we've managed to get the best pilot and copilot the RAF can muster, so you'll be in good hands. It might be worth bearing in mind that they've got as hard a task as you. They've not only got to get you in and put you down; they themselves have got to take off again. Getting in might be relatively easy; getting out will be ten times as difficult."

It was an obvious cue, and Lassiter took it. He asked the question that was in all their minds.

"How does that apply to us, sir? Assuming we pull it off, how are we to get through the Russian blockade? If they're knocking on the door now, they'll be inside the house in a couple of days."

"I'm afraid I don't know," said Greenleigh. He saw their expressions of bewilderment. What the hell was he trying to give them? They could get in, but they couldn't get out. "Only Valkyrie knows the escape route, and he's kept it to himself for pretty obvious reasons. If you don't turn up he'll doubtless try to make a break for it himself, though his chances of succeeding alone and unaided are remote. Furthermore, if you don't take good care of him—even at the expense of your own lives—you will not get home. He is being clever and cautious, gentlemen, which no doubt you would be in his position."

"Christ," said Fodor, "that beats all, doesn't it? We've not only got to save the bastard's neck, we've got to trust him to lead us out."

"Precisely, Major," said Greenleigh. "But don't forget that this is no ordinary Nazi we're talking about. If he doesn't make it he's a dead man. If you don't get out, neither does he."

Greenleigh checked the mantelpiece clock. The cars to take the team back to London were due soon. It was high time he let Sara Ferguson have a word. She'd obviously convinced Lassiter she wouldn't be a liability, and to judge by the adoring look on Fodor's face he'd take her into the Chancellery itself if that was where she chose to go. But they were only two of the team.

He made a gesture and Sara stood up. She had already taken off her raincoat, but she made a play of smoothing her skirt. Seven pairs of eyes followed her every movement, and Greenleigh smiled to himself. Sara Ferguson was nobody's fool.

"My part in the proceedings is relatively simple," she began, "but I have Brigadier Greenleigh's permission to explain it to you in case anything happens to me."

There was a chorus of "God forbid."

Sara inclined her head in acknowledgment.

"As Majors Lassiter and Fodor have already been told, I shall be traveling with you as a camp follower and carrying documents of immunity which must be given to Valkyrie in person, the seal unbroken. Needless to say, they must not be allowed to fall into anyone else's hands. It's my job to pass them over and identify Valkyrie—though, like you, I don't know who he is."

She saw frowns of puzzlement on one or two faces.

"If that sounds a bit Irish," she explained, "an odd contradiction, it isn't. That none of us are being told his identity is basic security. What we don't know we can't reveal. But part of my job during the last few years has been to make a study of all Germany's top political and military figures. As I understand it, I shall recognize Valkyrie immediately and be able to evaluate his worth. If it turns out to be one of the leading forty or fifty people we all know about, I shall be satisfied I have the genuine article. If it's a third-grade civil servant, I shall know we've been duped.

"As well as carrying the documents I shall have with me a small radio transmitter—no bigger than a cigarette case, which in fact it resembles. It operates on a fixed frequency and sends out a prearranged signal, repeating it at intervals. When we reach Berlin I shall activate the transmitter. Twelve hours later —neither a minute more nor a minute less—we'll be met on the north side of the Brandenburg Gate, where the Charlottenburg Chaussee joins Unter den Linden. I don't know why twelve hours has been stipulated, so don't bother to ask me to speed up the procedure even if we're being shelled. The time lag was a condition made by the other side. It might mean that Valkyrie needs a few hours to get papers together; it might mean that he is coming, somehow, from some distance away. Have I forgotten anything?" she asked Greenleigh.

"Recognition signals."

"Oh, yes. To begin with, we'll doubtless be met by an emissary, someone who is also in on the plot. Into his opening sentence he will introduce the word Horsetrade; into ours we will introduce Mercury. Any questions?"

Maclean waved his hand in the air.

"Yes—Dougal, isn't it?"

"Yes, miss. You said a moment ago that you were explaining your part in the operation in case anything happened to you. But if it does, none of us will know if Valkyrie is a fake."

"True enough. And call me Sara, please—until we're in Germany, that is. True enough," she repeated, "but there's nothing we can do about it. You'll just have to take good care of me. Any other questions?"

"What are you doing for dinner?" asked Fodor.

Sara smiled. "The same as you, I expect—eating sandwiches in a car on the way back to London."

Greenleigh stood up as Sara sat down. "Precisely that," he said. "The cars should be here in thirty minutes. They'll take us all back to London, where you'll spend the night. Tomorrow you'll be flown by the RAF to Eindhoven, where you'll meet the crew of your Junkers. After that . . ." He shrugged. After that it was in the lap of the gods.

"Thirty minutes you say, sir?" asked Lassiter.

"About that."

"Then we've got time for a drink or two."

"At least two, Major Lassiter, and preferably three or four."

EIGHTEEN

To: VALKYRIE   CVX/015/SSS/21000/Z/25.4.45
From: NEMESIS
        UNIT MOBILE. DUE DESTINATION 26TH/27TH.
        ACKNOWLEDGE.

To: NEMESIS   CVX/009/SSS/28000/Z/26.4.45
From: VALKYRIE
        UNDERSTOOD. THIS IS MY LAST COMMUNICATION.
        FOR SECURITY REASONS THIS CALL SIGN IS NOW OFF
        THE AIR. OUT.

NINETEEN

The man known as Valkyrie had laid his plans with meticulous care. On the surface he was a diehard supporter of Hitler, one of those who had resolved to stay with the Fuehrer until the end, if necessary perish with him. With the exception of his adjutant, no one now alive knew that since the Allied landings at Normandy he had been scheming to save his own neck.

He would have to be careful, of course—now more than ever before. With the British rescue squad already on its way, it would be easy to rush things, move before it was absolutely safe to go. Which could cost him his head. Fearing last-minute mass desertions, Hitler was suspicious of everyone, even of men who had served him for more than a decade. He would be merciless toward anyone thought planning to leave the sinking ship, regardless of rank or position.

It was a terrible temptation to get out while the going was good. All being well, the British would be here in a few more hours, and logic screamed at him to make the run before the Russians finally encircled the city and made escape a hundred times more difficult. Even fifty feet belowground, as he now was, it was impossible not to be aware of the Ivans' heavy artillery pounding hell out of the city. They intended to level it, wipe Berlin off the face of the earth, and it would go ill for any ranking German falling into their hands. The obvious thing to do was get the hell out as soon as the fixed-beam signal from the British told him that they were here.

But logic and doing the obvious had never played a major part in Valkyrie's life. He was, he reminded himself, a man of instinct, and his instinct told him to sit it out. The escape route had been well planned months ago. It was as safe as anything could be in these uncertain times. Besides, if he were not available for the daily conferences which Hitler still insisted upon holding, the Fuehrer would assume the worst and have SS execution squads hunting him in no time.

It was better to wait—wait until the moment came when Hitler, as Valkyrie was certain would happen, took his own life. And if that meant the SOE operatives' having to wait also, that was just too bad.

In the meantime, there was plenty to do. There were documents to be sorted through. Some he would take with him, as his end of the bargain. But the majority would have to be destroyed.

Six hundred miles away across the North Sea, Brigadier Greenleigh landed in Hertfordshire at 1745 hours. He had intended remaining in Eindhoven until the Ju 52 took off at 2030, but a sudden urgent telephone call from London had summoned him home. No, he could not be told what it was all about across an open line, but it was essential that he return right away.

He was met at the airfield by an SOE captain in plainclothes, who introduced himself as Rutherford. Rutherford belonged to Unit Seven, which was the SOE's own internal-security organization designed to keep tabs on all operatives from the brigadier downward. As Greenleigh knew from past experience, Unit Seven was a law unto itself, part Military Intelligence, part Foreign Office, part secret police. It had little or nothing to do with the SOE's day-to-day activities; its sole raison d'être was to ensure that those engaged in clandestine enterprises did nothing to jeopardize the nation's security.

"What's the flap?" he asked Rutherford.

"If you'll forgive me, sir, that will be explained at our destination."

"Which is where?"

"You'll soon find out, sir."

Damned cheek, thought Greenleigh. It was high time these jumped-up traffic policemen from Unit Seven learned a little respect.

"This had better be damned important," he said curtly.

"It is, sir, I'm sure you'll see that."

At Rutherford's urging the driver gave the car the gun, and it was still several minutes this side of 1830 when they pulled up outside an address in West London.

Rutherford led the way inside and up a short flight of stairs. Guarding the door at the top was a uniformed sergeant carrying a tommy gun. Rutherford waved him to one side and pushed open the door. Seated on the near side of a large desk were Colonel Martin and Lieutenant Colonel Devereaux. Behind the desk, obviously in command of the situation, was a youngish man wearing the rank insignia of a major but no unit flashes. All three men got to their feet as Greenleigh came in. Rutherford closed the door and took up a position just inside it.

"What the hell's going on?" demanded Greenleigh.

Martin shook his head. "We've only got half the story ourselves. Major Ansell insisted we wait for you."

"Well, Major?"

"If you wouldn't mind sitting down, sir," said the Unit Seven officer.

Greenleigh did so. Major Ansell opened a cardboard folder.

"I'll make this as brief as I can," he began, addressing Greenleigh. "Have you ever heard of a gentleman who goes by the name of Jean-Claude Dessigny?"

Greenleigh was certain he had not. "No," he said. "Who the devil's he?"

"He's a man who purports to be a member of the Free French and who has lived in this country for the past six years. That was his cover story, anyway, but in reality he's been working in a minor capacity for the Russians. At least, he was until this afternoon. Working on information received from another source, Special Branch picked him up earlier—at his girlfriend's flat."

"So?"

"His girlfriend's name is Anstruther."

Greenleigh's jaw dropped a foot. "My Miss Anstruther?"

"Yours, sir. Please don't misunderstand me—I'm not suggesting for a second that Miss Anstruther is also working for the Russians. But when Special Branch realized who she was they got onto us right away. It could be a coincidence that a Soviet agent is having an affair with your secretary, but no one wanted to take that chance. In any case, she does appear to have been some kind of security risk."

Greenleigh listened in astonishment as Ansell related in a dull monotone details of Miss Anstruther's sexual proclivities. Far from the haughty upper-class virgin she appeared, she was one of those women who liked being abused, debased even. And Jean-Claude Dessigny was the man who had dished it out for the past few months.

But how much harm had been done? Greenleigh was asking himself while Ansell was still talking. Miss Anstruther's security clearance was a low one; she saw no classified documents, was privy to no secrets. About all she did was answer the door and make a few phone calls.

Jesus Christ, that might be more than enough.

"You've questioned her, of course?" he asked Ansell.

"We have, sir. The poor woman was terrified out of her wits, frightened that we were going to put her straight up against a wall. She swears she's never discussed her work with Dessigny, told him nothing, but that doesn't seem possible. What I mean to say is, it's hardly likely Dessigny would hang around if there was nothing in it for him. In fact, we're pretty certain she has told him something, though it's doubtful if she remembers or even considers it significant."

"Explain."

"Well, sir, Special Branch and ourselves have spent most of the afternoon . . . er . . . interrogating Dessigny. He proved tougher than he looked, insisting that it was all a mistake. But we got him talking eventually, though what he said didn't make much sense."

"Tell me."

Ansell referred to his notes. "He mentioned seven names. Lassiter, Dunbar, Maclean, Gallagher, Fuller, Fodor and something that sounded like Scipiani or Scipioni. There were one or two others, but they were incomprehensible." Ansell shrugged his shoulders. "You'll appreciate that we had to get a little rough with him. He wasn't in full possession of his faculties by the time we'd finished."

"Carry on." Greenleigh's face was a mask.

170

"He also said something else, something we didn't understand at first—still don't, for that matter. Three weeks ago his masters didn't appear to give a damn about what Miss Anstruther had to say or his relationship with her. But in the last eight or nine days they ordered him to put pressure on her, get out of her as much as he could concerning those names. Which seemed to indicate to us that they're on to something, something you might be involved in." Ansell paused. "Something big."

Greenleigh looked at Martin and Devereaux without seeing them. It was impossible for the Russians to know anything about Horsetrade or Valkyrie from Miss Anstruther, because, to the best of his knowledge, she had never heard either word. But they knew about Lassiter and the others. They might even know about Sara Ferguson. The big question was, however: had they done anything about it?

"Are these phones secure?" he asked Ansell.

"Yes, sir. You have to go through the switchboard, but each mouthpiece is scrambled."

"Then I must ask you and Captain Rutherford to leave us alone for a few minutes."

"Of course, sir. We'll be outside the door if you need us."

Greenleigh checked the time. There was plenty of it before the Ju 52 was due to take off.

"Major Lassiter must be given this information," said Colonel Martin. "He must be told that the Russians might be onto us."

"*Might be!*" spluttered Greenleigh. "It's a bloody sight worse than that. They could have infiltrated the team."

"*What?*"

"You heard what Major Ansell said. They only started to take a real interest in the last eight or nine days."

"So?"

"So it was eight or nine days ago that the Americans found out what we were up to."

"Good Christ."

"You're not suggesting, surely to God, that Fodor or Scipioni is a Communist agent?" asked Devereaux.

"I'm suggesting that I don't like coincidences."

Greenleigh picked up the telephone. "Get me the Duty Officer at Bletchley Park and make it fast. I'll hold on."

"Are you going to abort?" asked Martin.

"I'm going to do nothing of the kind. I'm going to give Lassiter all the information we have and tell him to watch his back."

"But—"

"Hold it," said Greenleigh. "Duty Officer? This is Brigadier Greenleigh. I want a direct secure line to Eindhoven in Holland, and I want it five minutes ago. . . ."

TWENTY

They had been airborne for an hour, flying almost due east at a height of 4,000 feet, well below the old Iron Annie's ceiling of 18,000. In many versions of the Ju 52 the five forward windows on either side of the fuselage were blacked out or omitted entirely from the design, but not in this case. Lassiter wanted to see where he was going.

Of all the transports used during World War II, the Ju 52, along with the DC-3, may justly claim to be the most famous. The Iron Annie had taken part in such major actions as the invasions of Poland, Scandinavia and Western Europe. In the Norwegian campaign alone it undertook 3,000 sorties, delivering troops, general supplies and fuel. Five hundred 52s took part in the assault on France and the Low Countries, the paratroopers they dropped capturing such vital installations as the fort of Eben Emeal on the Albert Canal. Before the war, as a heavy bomber, she had participated in the Spanish Civil War, flying some 5,400 sorties for Franco's Nationalist forces. But the two operations most closely associated with the three-engined 52s were the airborne invasion of Crete and Hitler's abortive attempt to get supplies through to General Paulus' VI Army surrounded by Soviet troops at Stalingrad.

The Iron Annie was powered by three 830-horsepower BMW 132T radial engines which gave it a top speed of 189 m.p.h. and a normal range of 930 miles. In this case, however, RAF engineers had fitted extra tanks to increase the range, and the aircraft had suffered a corresponding drop in its maximum speed. It had also lost some maneuverability as a result of the searchlights fixed to its belly. This was a refinement insisted upon by the pilot, Squadron Leader Willie Macgregor, a veteran of the raids on the Möhne and Eder dams. They were flying in at night, and it was hardly likely there would be a nice flare path illumi-

173

nating the runway. The two searchlights were therefore positioned to converge when the aircraft was precisely thirty feet above the ground. After that, it was up to those among the passengers who prayed.

The aircraft's armaments consisted of one 13-millimeter MG 131 machine gun and two 7.9-millimeter MG 15 machine guns. The standard crew complement was four: pilot, copilot/engineer, navigator and upper-turret machine gunner. On this flight, however, it was carrying only three crew members.

Flight Sergeant Paddy O'Brien was the upper gunner. A quiet youth whose cheeks looked as if they had yet to feel the first kiss of a razor, he nevertheless wore on the left breast of his uniform blouse an impressive array of decorations. On the tarmac at Eindhoven, Dougal Maclean had counted the Conspicuous Gallantry Medal and two Distinguished Flying Medals before O'Brien, suddenly aware that he was being studied, zipped up his flying jacket with a shy smile.

The copilot and engineer, who was also doubling as navigator on this trip, was Flight Lieutenant Peter Swan. Swan had completed three bombing tours over Germany, an almost unheard-of feat for someone who was walking around apparently still intact in mind and limb. Statistically, only 2 percent of fliers completed three tours, which meant that Swan was either very good or very lucky. Recalling that Napoleon had preferred his commanders to have luck above all other qualities, Lassiter sincerely hoped that Swan's guardian angel was still looking after him.

As Squadron Leader Willie Macgregor's had, apparently, always been around when needed.

By rights Willie Macgregor should not be alive at all. Long before his transfer to 617 Squadron and the Dams Raid of 16/17 May 1943, he had completed a tour and a half in Stirlings. With their pitiful ceiling of just under 20,000 feet, the Stirlings were regarded as sitting ducks for both German flak and night fighters, and on half a dozen separate occasions Macgregor had brought his machine safely home shot to ribbons. One famous incident, still talked about in Bomber Command, involved an aircraft whose starboard wing had broken off clean as a snapped twig immediately on touchdown. Later examination revealed that it was not the impact which had caused the fracture; the wing had evidently been flapping like a vulture's all the way home from the Ruhr. RAF engineers put down the fact that it had not come adrift earlier to freak air conditions, but Macgregor's crew, who knew nothing of stresses and strain, swore by everything they held sacred that the skipper had kept the Stirling airborne by willpower alone.

Long after the Dams Raid, for which he was awarded the DSO, Macgregor was in the lead Lancaster that attacked the *Tirpitz* on November 12, 1944, as the German battleship lay at anchor in Tromosfjord. A month later he brought home an aircraft which, by rights, should have gone down in flames east of the Elbe. When asked why, in view of the fire, he had not bailed out, he said that he had no intention of spending the remainder of the war in a German prison camp. His copilot gave a slightly different account. The navigator and bombardier were both suffering from serious flak injuries and were in no condition to abandon the aircraft. For the pilot and the rest of the crew to do so would have meant leaving the navigator and bombardier to die. This Macgregor refused to do.

The RAF brass took a long, careful look at the report and Macgregor's history and decided that he should be given the Victoria Cross. Macgregor agreed to accept it on the condition that he not be taken off flight duty.

Three days earlier, when Brigadier Greenleigh explained his problem to the Air Ministry, the Air Vice Marshal i/c Special Operations had no hesitation in nominating Squadron Leader Macgregor for the job. Greenleigh explained that it was an extremely hazardous mission and that he would prefer the crew to be volunteers. The RAF officer suggested he tell that to Macgregor himself.

Greenleigh arranged to do so, setting aside a whole afternoon for the briefing. In actuality it took less than five minutes.

"What sort of aircraft will I be flying?" asked Macgregor.

"It'll have to be a German transport, probably a Ju 52."

"I've never flown one. I'll need some time to familiarize myself with it."

Greenleigh's face fell, envisaging a delay of a week. "How long?"

"An hour or two. And if it's all right with you I'd like to select my own crew. Three of us should be enough."

The Brigadier had no objections. It would be hard to quarrel with a man who, before the war, had been brought up in an orphanage, who had little formal education, who wore the purple ribbon of the VC; a man who, although Greenleigh had no way of knowing it, would not be twenty-five years old until the following September.

The intercom crackled. To keep his passengers fully informed, Squadron Leader Macgregor had rigged up a p.a. system between the cabin and the belly of the aircraft, where Lassiter's party were crouched on the floor of the 52, their backs against the fuselage.

"In case anyone's interested," they heard Macgregor say above the roar of the engines, "we crossed the Weser a few minutes ago and the Leine's just below us, with Hannover coming up on the port side. So far, so good. We seem to be the only plane in the sky, but that could well change in the next forty minutes when we cross the Elbe at Tangemünde. If my information's up to date, that's where the U.S. Ninth Army's drawn its line. E.t.a. 2230."

Fifty-five minutes to go by Lassiter's watch—always assuming that neither Fodor nor Scipioni had something else planned.

He thought it improbable. In spite of Greenleigh's urgent telephone call, he felt unable to accept that one of the Americans was a Communist agent, and he had resolved to put the matter from his mind and keep his own counsel. Nothing was likely to happen, in any case, before they met up with Valkyrie, and until then they were still a team. After that he would take Greenleigh's advice and watch his back.

In the meantime, there were other things to do.

"Let's go over it again," he said, more to keep their minds occupied than through any real fear that his earlier briefing had been forgotten. "Chuck."

"As soon as we're on the deck," said Fodor, "assuming we land at Tempelhof, Maclean, Fuller and I leave the hatch first like greased pigs and take up defensive positions under the wing. We shoot to kill anyone who comes anywhere near us."

"And I do mean anyone," prompted Lassiter. "German transport aircraft are going to be at a premium, and there are likely to be hundreds of people at Tempelhof who'll see this one as a way out. Our very first job is to see that Macgregor and his crew get airborne without any trouble. This is for our own sake as much as theirs. None of them speaks German, and if they're caught on the ground someone's going to start asking questions about us. Alex?"

"Gallagher and I go next," said Dunbar. "If we see a truck or anything that looks as if it'll move, that's what we make for. If not, we give Major Fodor a hand."

"Right. But keep it flexible. If there's a truck close by but the plane's being surrounded by Germans, deal with the Germans first. These uniforms should scare the hell out of most people, but at this point they may be more frightened of the Russians than the SS. So no kidding around. I don't care who or what's involved. Anyone even looks at the plane, they get shot. Scipioni."

Since the incident on the range and Lassiter's subsequent threats a day or two earlier, Scipioni had toed the line, putting a curb on his brashness. He still had a quick tongue and a quip for most occasions, but his remarks were less designed to deliberately irritate.

"I look after the courier," he said, "and a real pleasure it's going to be, too. If I've got to take the deep six, I can't think of a better way to go."

Beside him on the starboard side of the fuselage, Sara Ferguson smiled to herself.

"I don't see why you had to give Scipioni the plum job," Fodor moaned at Lassiter, not entirely in jest. "Putting him in charge of a woman is like asking an alkie to guard the bar. No offense meant," he added hastily.

"None taken," said Sara lightly. "Though if he sees anything in me dressed like this, he must have a very good imagination."

In keeping with her role of camp follower in wartime Germany, Sara's topcoat was an old Wehrmacht greatcoat which hung below her knees. Underneath she had on a well-worn sweater and skirt, and next to her skin underwear purchased in Hamburg in 1938. She wore no makeup except a little bright red lipstick, and her hair looked in need of a good washing. Even so, she exuded an air of total sexuality, a fact that escaped no one, least of all Scipioni.

"Doesn't take much imagination, ma'am," he said archly. "If

you want to know the truth, you look a bit like Vivien Leigh in *Gone with the Wind*."

"Oh, Christ," groaned Fodor, "spare us the line, Scipioni. I don't think I can take it."

Scipioni raised his eyebrows and did a passable imitation of Gable. "Frankly, my dear, I don't give a damn."

"Okay," said Lassiter, jumping in before the two Americans went into their Abbott-and-Costello act, "let's hear the rest of it."

Scipioni was suddenly serious. "Sara's the reason we're here," he said. "If everything else goes down the tube but Sara gets where she's supposed to be, then that's okay. So I stick with her like a mother hen, with Major Lassiter as my backup. If any of you other guys get hit, that's not my responsibility. I get Sara, her documents and the transmitter into Berlin." He couldn't resist the crack. "After that, I go to the movies."

"Which just leaves me," said Lassiter. "I'll be last out. As soon as I see everything's going the way it should, I'll give Paddy the signal to close the hatch. From beginning to end, from first man to last man, the whole operation shouldn't take more than thirty seconds."

Satisfied that everyone knew his job, Lassiter relaxed, his head against the fuselage. They all looked the part—he'd say that for them.

He became aware that Sara was smiling at him from across the aircraft. There had been a time, as they both knew, when something could have developed between them, and he was honest enough to recognize that remnants of his own feelings still lingered. But this was not the moment to dwell upon them.

Thirty minutes went by before the p.a. crackled into life again.

"We're approaching the Elbe," Macgregor announced. "Would you mind coming up front, Major Lassiter?"

Lassiter made his way forward to the cockpit. The night was cloudless, the moon in its last quarter, and it was possible to make out the River Elbe and the surrounding German landmass below. A strange phenomenon took place east of the river, however. This side of it, in that area now occupied by the Allies, blackout restrictions had been eased if not lifted entirely. In consequence, it was possible to see pinpoints of light here and

178

there, pinpoints that were probably villages or small towns or airfields. But east of the Elbe, where the Germans were still fighting, it was completely dark except for the distant flashes of artillery and a larger patch of light that flickered mysteriously some way ahead and seemed to grow even as he watched.

"We've picked up something of a tail wind," Macgregor shouted, "so I've revised our e.t.a. All being well, we should be there in twenty minutes."

"Right," said Lassiter, "I'll get my people ready."

"Tell them not to move around too much. We may run into some trouble on the way in, and if that happens the first you'll know about it is when I start throwing the plane around. Anyone on their feet might get hurt."

"I'll tell them," said Lassiter. He paused, unable to take his eyes off the mysterious patch of light. "What the hell's that?" he asked.

Flight Lieutenant Swan grinned up at him. "That, Major, is where you're going. We're still fifty or so miles away, but what you're seeing is Berlin burning itself to a cinder."

"Why the flickering effect? There's no cloud."

"Smoke, Major. I was over the day before yesterday on a photo recce, and believe me, you can't see a hell of a lot until you're below five hundred feet. We've mostly stopped bombing it now. The majority of the recent damage is being caused by Russian artillery."

Lassiter returned to the others. "Start getting ready," he instructed them. "We're about twenty minutes out. When you've done that, sit tight. There might be some fighter activity going in."

Each checked his gear and his weapons, though unconsciously each had done it half a dozen times on the short flight. With the exception of Sara, who was unarmed, they all carried MP 38s—Schmeissers. The officers also wore 9-millimeter Lugers at their hips. Of the NCOs, only Dougal Maclean carried a concealed handgun in a shoulder holster. It was a habit he'd picked up in Yugoslavia and one he could not break.

When they were finished, Lassiter gave them a thorough going-over. The Poets Gray, Keats and Browning had been lavish with decorations, but on balance that was probably a plus factor. Corporals Maclean and Gallagher, each now dressed as a Rottenfuehrer, both wore the Iron Cross First and Second Class. In addition, Gallagher had a brace of *Panzervernichtungsabzeichen*—the badge for the single-handed destruction of a tank —sewn to his right sleeve. Sergeant Fuller, wearing the single collar-patch pip of an Unterscharfuehrer, also had the Iron Cross First and Second Class, and in addition wore the Winter 1941/42 Campaign ribbon in his tunic buttonhole.

Browning had decided in Devon that all the officers should be holders of the Knight's Cross, with Lassiter himself having the further honor of oak leaves—roughly the equivalent of the VC or the Congressional Medal of Honor. As well as that, Scipioni (Obersturmfuehrer) wore two Iron Crosses and the Winter Campaign ribbon. Dunbar (Hauptsturmfuehrer) wore the same as Scipioni with the addition of the Close Combat Clasp above the left breast pocket. Sturmbannfuehrers Fodor and Lassiter, with the exception of Lassiter's oak leaves, wore identical decorations: the Knight's Cross, two Iron Crosses, Close Combat Clasp, Winter Campaign ribbon, Wound Badge and Infantry Assault Badge. As a refinement Lassiter also sported, on his right sleeve, the *Ehrenwinkel*, the Old Campaigner's chevron.

Later, Lassiter was never quite sure whether Macgregor had left the p.a. system active in order that his passengers could get some idea of what was going on, or whether the whole thing was an accident. In either event, the Iron Annie had no sooner crossed the Elbe than Paddy O'Brien suddenly called out, "Trouble on the port beam, Skip. Nine o'clock."

Part of O'Brien's duties now they were over enemy territory was to scan the sky with binoculars for signs of hostile aircraft.

"Let's be a little more accurate than that, Paddy," said Macgregor. "Type, range, intentions."

"Sorry, Skip. It's just that I haven't yet got used to the idea that we're Germans. Looks like a Yak-9U fighter. Range around four thousand yards. Hard to tell what he's up to yet, but he's coming to take a closer look."

"I've got him," said Peter Swan from the copilot's seat. He too had night glasses. "Paddy's right. It's a Yak-9U."

"By himself?"

"Seems to be."

For this mission Macgregor had done his homework on Soviet fighters, the only "hostiles" they were likely to encounter, and what he remembered about the Yak-9U didn't fill him with elation. It had a speed of over 430 m.p.h. and was armed with a 20-millimeter cannon firing through the propeller hub and two 12.7-millimeter machine guns. It was extremely maneuverable, especially in tight turns, and below 20,000 feet was a better plane that the Messerschmitt Bf 109G, the Gustav. The Iron Annie was a fish in a barrel unless he could do something about it.

"Hang on!" he yelled, and put the 52's nose down. At the same moment both the fighter and Paddy O'Brien opened up.

Inside the belly of the 52, the passengers flinched involuntarily.

Traveling at over 400 m.p.h., the Yak-9U had covered 3,000 yards between the time Paddy O'Brien first spotted it and the time Macgregor put the Iron Annie's nose down. A more experienced fighter pilot would have anticipated the move and come around behind and below the 52, but these days, with the war virtually over and practically no German aircraft in the sky, anyone who could fly in the Soviet Air Force was begging to be sent up to bag at least one German before hostilities were officially ended.

It was Macgregor's good luck that the pilot of the Yak was a mere boy on only his third combat mission. By the time his ammunition reached the point where the 52 would have been had Macgregor not taken evasive action, the German transport had lost 500 feet in altitude and was banking to port.

The Russian saw none of this. In spite of the Yak's reputation for being able to turn tight, he was two miles farther on before he realized what had happened. Nevertheless, it was a clear night and it wouldn't take him long to pick up the scent.

TWENTY-ONE

acgregor kept the stick forward, sacrificing height for speed. Being a vastly experienced pilot himself, he sensed that the Russian was a novice. Nevertheless, you couldn't throw a transport around the sky the way you could a fighter, and sooner or later even a novice would catch up with them. His only hope was to push as hard as he could for Berlin, now looming larger every second, a distant conflagration that had to be seen to be believed. With the tail wind and the nose down, Macgregor estimated he was ten minutes away from some sort of landfall. With luck he would have the 52 on the ground before the Russian got the range. Failing that, the Yak pilot might well sheer off when faced with what remained of the German capital's ack-ack system.

"Any luck, Paddy?" he called out. It was just possible that the gunner had rammed a couple of shots home.

"Sorry, Skip. You took me by surprise too."

"What's he up to now?" With Peter Swan, unbidden, concentrating on navigating them safely into Tempelhof, Paddy O'Brien was, for the moment, the 52's eyes.

"He's about two thousand feet above us and five thousand yards off to starboard. He must have been going a hell of a lick. Damn near in Czechoslovakia."

"Christ," muttered Scipioni to no one in particular, "did somebody say they volunteered for this?"

"Keep me posted."

"He's turning now, Skip. He's got about three thousand feet on us at five o'clock. Same distance, five thousand yards. I don't think he's picked us up yet. Jesus Christ, he must be blind."

"He's probably learned his lesson," said Macgregor, "so we can expect something different this time. Count off the distance to me and let me know if he looks like he's coming in below and behind."

"Got you, Skip."

There was what must have been a five-second silence. For those in the belly it felt like five hours. They made a conscious effort to relax. There was nothing they could do; they were in Macgregor's hands.

"He's found us, Skip." O'Brien again. "But he's not trying to get below or behind. He's trying the same tactic. More or less beam attack from about four o'clock."

"He's probably heard what a lousy shot you are. Count it off for me, Paddy. Let me know as soon as you see the flashes from his guns or when he's at a thousand yards, whichever comes first. As soon as you give me the word, I'm going to put her in a steep bank to starboard. That'll bring the Yak shooting over the top of us, so see what you can do. It'll mean losing another few hundred feet, but it's either that or nothing."

"Roger. Four thousand . . . three thousand . . ."

"Jesus Christ," breathed Fodor.

"Two thousand . . . He's still coming, Skip." O'Brien's voice went up an octave and simultaneously they heard him open fire. "One thousand . . . *He's firing!*"

Stomachs leaped for the stratosphere as Macgregor threw the 52 into a sideslip. A dozen things seemed to be happening at once. Above everything was the scream of the props as they clawed for a hold, and in spite of a firm grip on foot and hand straps, the passengers felt as though they were about to be catapulted into orbit. There was a smell of cordite everywhere, and the rattle of O'Brien's machine guns made only marginally less noise than that coming from the Annie's propellers.

The entire incident was over in a few seconds, the 52 again flying on an even keel.

From his gun turret O'Brien could see the Yak way off to port, guns still firing. The Russian had come nowhere near hitting them, but by the same token, neither had he come anywhere near putting the Yak out of commission. He hoped Macgregor was keeping the throttles open. Even a novice would know better than to try a beam attack a third time.

On the flight deck the altimeter read 800 meters, about 2,500 feet. That was okay, fine, as far as Macgregor was concerned, but he was losing height every second, and the lower they got, the less he wanted to start stooging around with sideslips.

From the copilot's seat, in a totally calm voice, Flight Lieutenant Swan asked, "Do you want the new fix for Tempelhof?"

"Just keep me pointed in the right general direction for the time being. If our Russian friend comes back I could well end up heading for Italy."

In the belly Lassiter took stock. "Everybody all right?"

Everybody was, though there were one or two white faces to be seen.

"Sara?"

"Fine. I can do without a repeat performance, though. A large part of my insides is still up there somewhere."

"I think our Yak's getting company," they heard O'Brien say suddenly, a note of apprehension creeping into his voice.

"Be specific, Paddy. I gave up reading minds after D-Day."

"Port beam, nine o'clock and climbing. Single-motor job. I can't read . . . Half a minute . . . Jesus Christ, it looks like . . . It is . . . It's a Bf 109! It's a bleedin' Messerschmitt!"

"You sure?"

"Sure I'm sure. Jesus, haven't I seen enough 109s in my life?"

"Then for Christ's sake curb your natural enthusiasm and don't shoot at the bloody thing. For the time being, it's on our side."

"He's right," said Peter Swan. "A 109—a Gustav."

"Then we can forget about the Yak. The Germans aren't handing out Gustavs to anybody but the best."

"He's turning away," shouted O'Brien. "The Yak's buggering off. He's seen the 109 and he's heading for the deck."

"Forget him, Paddy, but keep your eyes peeled."

"Roger, Skip. Jesus, I never thought the day would come when I was pleased to see a 109."

"You can give me that course for Tempelhof now, Peter," said Macgregor. "The sooner we're in and out, the better I'll like it."

"Amen to that," murmured Chuck Fodor. "You can forget TWA. From now on I'll fly RAF anywhere."

There was a general nod of agreement for the manner in which Macgregor and his crew had handled the situation. For

184

the most part, crack ground troops had little or no fondness for the air forces of any nation, considering them to be pampered glamour boys who were never around when air cover was needed. But if that was what they went through every time they went up—well, they could keep it. The whole action had lasted no more than three or four minutes, but they were minutes the passengers had no wish to repeat.

"E.t.a. six minutes, Major Lassiter," they heard Macgregor say. "If you look out of the port side you'll be able to see what you're letting yourselves in for."

Hardened though all of them were after a long war, they were shocked by what they saw. Some twelve to fifteen miles away the German capital was an inferno, a wall of flame. Columns of smoke and ash towered several miles into the air. It seemed impossible that anything could be alive down there, yet all of them knew that what they were seeing was an illusion, an amalgam of small fires that looked like one huge conflagration. On the ground it would be easy enough to walk around from street to street, building to building. Fires could rage only where there was combustible material, and there was precious little of that left in Berlin.

"Anyone bring the sausages for the wienie roast?" asked Scipioni.

"I think you'd better come up front, Major Lassiter," said Macgregor. "It doesn't look any too healthy down there, and there might be one or two fast decisions to make."

Lassiter went forward. On the flight deck Macgregor told him to wedge himself between the seats of the pilot and copilot. "Just in case I have to indulge in a few more aerobatics."

The squadron leader pointed over to his right.

"Tempelhof's down there, just south of the city limits. I know you can't see it because of all this bloody smoke, but you'll have to take my word for it. Frankly, I don't like the look of it. You see those flashes?" Lassiter said he did; it was about all he could see. "Heavy artillery," advised the Scot, "and it seems to me to be bloody close to where the airfield is. If it were ack-ack, we'd be okay. Ack-ack would mean that the airfield is still under German control. But all I see is artillery, which has to be Russian. I'll give it a try, but I'd like you to stay up here and keep your eyes open. We won't be able to see much until we're below five hundred feet, if then, but if the place is crawling with Russian tanks it would obviously be fatal to put you down there. Not to mention that it wouldn't do *my* health much good."

"What about the alternative?" asked Lassiter.

"Well, that, as you know, is the East–West Axis, which we certainly can't see from here because of all that damned smoke. I know it of old, though. I must have flown over it a score of times, mainly to bomb the shit out of it. To be honest, I'd rather land on the deck of a carrier in a Force 9. Let me explain that from a pilot's point of view.

"It's about five miles long and a composite of four avenues: the Kaiserdamm, Bismarckstrasse, Charlottenburg Chaussee and Unter den Linden. It begins well west of the city center and finishes just beyond the Brandenburg Gate. It used to be able to take five lanes of traffic going in either direction, so width's no problem. Neither are trees and lampposts, now that Hitler's had them removed. We've had reports of one or two 52s flying in and out, but the last one was a couple of days ago. If the Russians have been plastering it in the past forty-eight hours, Christ knows what condition it's in. It could be full of holes. Trouble is, we won't know much about that until we're on the deck or committed to land, and I don't have to tell you what will happen if we run into a shell crater while traveling at speed." He threw a grin over his shoulder. "Just thought I'd let you know what we're up against."

"He's always been a cheery bastard," said Peter Swan. "Comes of eating haggis and wearing skirts."

Lassiter returned the grin. "So what do you plan to do?"

"Give Tempelhof a spin first. If that doesn't work out, try the East–West Axis."

"Can I go back and tell my people that? They're going to wonder what the hell's happening if we start bobbing up and down like a yo-yo."

"Use the p.a., if you don't mind. Just depress that switch there. I'd like to keep you at the sharp end in case something happens suddenly. Peter and I are Bomber Command; we don't really know one tank from another."

Lassiter flicked on the p.a. and briefly informed the others what was about to take place.

"Okay," he said to Macgregor finally, "let's go down."

On later reflection, the next fifteen minutes were ones that none of them would have repeated for a million pounds and a promise of immortality, though events happened so fast, the one crowding in on the next, that there was precious little time to worry about which moment was likely to be their last.

For most of the flight from Eindhoven, with the exception of the time spent dodging the Yak-9U, Squadron Leader Macgregor had flown a course almost due east. But as they approached the outskirts of Berlin, on Flight Lieutenant Swan's instructions, he banked to starboard and flew for several minutes south-southeast, to bring him well south of Tempelhof, the intention being to approach the airfield from that direction.

It was now possible to see that not all of Berlin was ablaze, that there were gaps in the flames where everything burnable had been consumed.

Over the Grunewald Forest the Russian flak started. The shooting was wildly inaccurate for the most part, but that didn't mean they couldn't be hit by a lucky burst. Macgregor could climb out of it, of course, but higher up they might run into a night fighter.

He brought the aircraft down to 400 meters, which was as low as he dared go using an altimeter that might not be dependable. The undercarriage on a Ju 52 was nonretractable, and he could well do without its brushing the tops of the tallest trees.

"Do you see anything?"

No one did. Tempelhof was somewhere below them, but it might as well have been at the bottom of a mile-deep pit. The artillery flashes were way off to the east and south, and most of the shells, as far as it was possible to judge, were landing on Berlin itself. But that didn't help. It could mean that the Russians were not shelling the airfield in order to save it for their own use later, or it could mean that tanks and infantry had already taken it. In either event, they wouldn't know a lot about it until they were down, which could be too late.

"I'm in your hands, Major Lassiter," shouted Macgregor. "One way or another I think I can get her down, but you might find yourself in amongst the Red Army."

Lassiter didn't hesitate. Conditions were much worse than any of them had been led to expect, and there was no point in coming this far to finish up at the business end of a Russian firing squad. "Try the East–West Axis," he yelled.

Aided by Flight Lieutenant Swan, Macgregor hauled on the stick to get some height. If they were still standing, there were a radio mast and a flak-control tower over by the Zoo, and there was no point in bending the aircraft around those either.

He decided to tackle the Axis west–east. This would mean landing with the wind more or less behind him, but that couldn't be helped. Depending upon the condition of the avenues he might need a lot of runway, and it would be safer to head toward the center of Berlin rather than in the other direction, where they could end up shaking hands with the Russian spearhead.

To get into position for the descent, he had to fly the reciprocal of the course that had taken them down to Tempelhof, traversing the eastern edge of the Grunewald en route. This time, however, there was no flak, because no one could see them. At 600 meters they were flying through dense black smoke, the like of which none of them had ever seen before. It was blind flying of the worst possible sort, and Macgregor hoped to Christ that his instincts and sense of direction were not about to let him down. He also prayed that the lower they got, the less dense the smoke would become.

"I've just thought of something," said Peter Swan. "What if they've mined the Axis or left the camouflage nets up to keep out Soviet gliders?"

"You're a cheerful bastard, aren't you?" snarled Macgregor. "It's not possible, anyway. They've still got some of their own stuff flying in and out."

He banked to starboard and straightened up at what he judged to be the western extremity of the Kaiserdamm. Because of the prevailing wind the smoke was practically nonexistent here, but ahead of them Berlin loomed like the gateway to hell.

"Talk about tigers jumping through flaming hoops," muttered Swan.

Macgregor eased forward the control column. Flak tower and radio mast notwithstanding, when he hit that smoke he wanted to be no more than fifty feet above the deck.

Two hundred meters . . . one-fifty . . .

Jesus Christ, but they were shifting.

"Up ahead, Skip!" Paddy O'Brien's voice came bubbling urgently over the intercom.

All three men on the flight deck saw immediately what he meant. About three-quarters of a mile ahead of them and a hundred feet below, flying a course identical to that of the 52, was a single-engine light monoplane silhouetted against the flames. Although they did not know it, and would in fact never know it, it was a Fieseler Storch carrying test pilot Hanna Reitsch and General Ritter von Greim, who had been summoned to Berlin by Hitler. Even as they watched, the Storch wobbled and put its nose down to lose another hundred feet. Seconds later it was lost in the peripheral smoke.*

"That bastard seems to know where he's going," yelled Macgregor. "We'll follow him in."

Which was not as straightforward as it seemed. While solving, in part, the problems of course and height, it created another hazard. The monoplane's stalling speed and therefore approach speed would obviously be a lot less than those of the 52. They could follow it in, all right, though they might be a damned sight closer than any of them would wish.

There was, however, no time to think. Moments after the Storch disappeared, the 52 was enveloped in smoke.

Macgregor switched on the landing searchlights instantly. At this height the altimeter was useless. Angled forward, using precisely the same technique that Wing Commander Gibson had evolved for the Dams Raids, they did not yet converge, but via the beams he could see concrete and judged his height to be a hundred feet or thereabouts.

No pilot himself, Lassiter was receiving only the sensation of tremendous speed, though logic told him that Macgregor would be keeping the aircraft just this side of stalling.

The scene changed from second to second. Sometimes they were in thick smoke, sometimes not. Over on his left he thought he caught sight of what remained of the Tiergarten, but it could

* Author's note: Accounts differ regarding the precise time Hanna Reitsch and Ritter von Greim landed on the twenty-sixth. Some say early evening, others several hours later. I have chosen to accept the latter version.

have been anywhere. He heard Swan shout, "You bloody near just took the top off the Victory Column!" And Macgregor yelling, "Shit or bust, we're going down!"

Much later, Lassiter realized that the distance from the Victory Column to the Brandenburg Gate was a little over a mile and that Macgregor, who obviously knew this, put the 52 on the ground on that basis.

It was far from over yet, however. The aircraft was still bowling along at 70 m.p.h., and they hadn't got a hell of a lot of runway to play with. Images crowded in like a fast-run film. White blobs that were faces staring stupefied at the 52, bodies lying in heaps, burnt-out trucks and tanks, trucks and tanks that were still burning, gutted buildings, a shell exploding somewhere up front and then another, Macgregor cursing as he fought to slow the aircraft, the arches of the Brandenburg Gate looming larger and larger—and flames everywhere in this world gone mad, this inferno that Dante would not have believed.

But Macgregor was winning. The aircraft was gradually slowing down and miraculously avoiding bomb and shell craters. The Gate was not coming up so fast now, and the white blobs were becoming identifiable faces.

There was no time, or need, for congratulations. Macgregor was already swinging the 52 around in a wide arc in order to be facing the other way before it rolled to a halt.

Out of the corner of his eye Lassiter saw the Storch immobile within the shadow of the Gate, surrounded by armed soldiers. Even as he watched, some of them broke away from their charge and started running toward this new arrival.

Back in the belly of the plane, Chuck Fodor already had the port hatch open and was preparing to jump out. Dougal Maclean and Harry Fuller were right behind him.

"*Niemand nähert sich dem Flugzeug!*" Lassiter shouted. Nobody was to come near the plane. He had no need to remind himself to speak in German. That was second nature. From now on all conversations would be in that language. "I don't give a sod if it's Hitler himself."

Dunbar and Gallagher went next. Unconsciously Lassiter was timing the whole operation, and so far he had no cause for complaint. The aircraft was still rolling and half the team were out.

190

He saw Scipioni disappear through the hatch and, right after him, Sara. She paused for a moment before jumping.

Lassiter gave her the thumbs-up sign.

As had been arranged in Eindhoven, once the 52 was on the ground Paddy O'Brien was to leave his gun turret temporarily in order to secure the hatch after Lassiter departed. This he now prepared to do, but before Lassiter could make a move there was a sound of shouting from outside, followed quickly by shots from several automatic weapons.

Lassiter swore violently. "Tell the Skipper to hold it, Paddy!"

In the roadway Harry Fuller was lying in an untidy heap, blood pouring from a thigh wound. Gallagher was on his knees beside him. Forty yards away half a dozen German soldiers were backing off warily, leaving two of their number lifeless. The muzzle of Fodor's MP 38 was smoking.

"What the fuck happened?" bellowed Lassiter.

"They didn't want the plane to take off," said Fodor. "Gave me some shit about ferrying out wounded and wouldn't take no for an answer."

None of the Wehrmacht troops appeared to be officers, and they seemed a lot less keen to make an issue of it now that they fully realized the newcomers were SS. But to make damned sure they remained unenthusiastic, Lassiter put a burst over their heads. They scattered and disappeared down what was left of a side street.

"How's Harry?" demanded Lassiter.

"Bad." Gallagher shook his head. Fuller wasn't going anywhere. "It's going to need attention."

"Right. Get him back on board."

Fuller was completely conscious, though in obvious pain. He made no attempt at false heroics. He knew he was out of it.

"Good luck, Jack," he said, using Lassiter's first name for the only time Lassiter could remember.

Gallagher and Dunbar bundled him aboard. O'Brien closed the hatch. Lassiter motioned everyone back.

More Russian heavy-artillery shells were landing on the East–West Axis now. Whether somehow the Soviets had got wind from a forward observation post that there were planes moving into and out of Berlin or whether it was a routine bombardment, no one ever found out. But as the old Iron Annie gathered speed, the area east of the Victory Column, where Bellevue Allee bisects the Charlottenburg Chaussee, came under fire.

Macgregor had perhaps six hundred yards in which to get the 52 to unstick, and there was never a chance he was going to make it. He tried—Christ, how he tried—but those on the ground could see what was going to happen long before it did.

They willed him to get up—Lassiter, Fodor and the rest—but willpower was not enough.

They saw the shells exploding ahead of him, patterning the road with new craters. The 52 was running directly into the barrage.

Something the size of a 25-pounder exploded off its starboard wing, the blast or fragments of shrapnel causing the plane to slue wildly.

Macgregor must have had almost the necessary speed when he hit the first crater, but almost was not enough. The right wheel of the undercarriage disappeared and the aircraft turned a somersault, one wing snapping off in the process.

At approaching 80 m.p.h., no one aboard stood a chance, and what little there was vanished when the fuel tanks caught fire and detonated. It was no consolation, but at least everyone knew they'd died quickly.

TWENTY-TWO

It was a wretched start to the mission, a poor omen as well as a personal loss, but Lassiter knew he had to snap them out of it. They were only a few hundred yards away from the triangle of streets that bounded the Chancellery: Hermann Goeringstrasse, Wilhelmstrasse and Leipzigerstrasse. Intelligence reports had it that these were being guarded by troops of the SS *Fuehrerbegleit-kommando*.

"Come on—we've got to get the hell out of here before someone decides to investigate who arrived in the 52 and started shooting the Wehrmacht."

Not that he thought a couple of dead soldiers were going to cause much of a furor. During lulls in the artillery barrage it was possible to hear small-arms fire coming from various parts of the city, and that was less likely to be Germans mixing it with advancing Russians than the SS stiffening resistance by killing the fainthearted.

Sara hadn't moved. She was transfixed, staring dully at the distant funeral pyre that was the 52.

"What a Christawful waste," she said.

Lassiter shook her by the shoulders—hard. It took a second or two, but gradually her eyes focused.

"What about the transmitter?" he asked.

"Already activated. I did it automatically as I left the plane."

It was 2250 according to Lassiter's watch. They had a little under twelve hours to wait.

"Any ideas?" he asked Sara. "You know more about the place than the rest of us."

She thought about it. "We can't use the Underground stations without attracting attention. In any case, they'll be full. I've got several contacts here, but the Brigadier asked me not to use them unless it's a matter of life or death."

Lassiter could understand that. When the war was over, Berlin was going to be in the middle of Russian-occupied territory. Anyone with intelligence training was too valuable to risk.

"Looks like a night in the open, then."

"I'm afraid so." She pointed over her shoulder. "The area around Alexanderplatz seems as quiet as anything can be in this madhouse. There's an underground passage there, too. If the Russians start shelling, we can always take temporary shelter inside."

Lassiter nodded. His team had full canteens of water and emergency rations. At a pinch, they could survive a week.

Less than half a mile away from the Brandenburg Gate, the SS trooper on duty at the radio receiver had picked up the signal from Sara Ferguson's transmitter three minutes earlier. Like the other two troopers who shared the watch-keeping duties with him on a rotating basis, he knew nothing of Horsetrade. Neither did he care that he had been given the mind-dulling task of simply listening in on a preset frequency. It was better than being "out there."

He had orders to report, under pain of death, the instant he heard anything, but he listened a moment or two longer to make sure that the signal was not going to change or be added to. It wasn't. In Morse code on a loop tape, he heard the word *Merkur* —Mercury—repeated over and over again.

Like many SS troopers, he was an unintelligent individual, a butcher's deliveryman before joining up and donning the uniform with the lightning flashes. He was vaguely aware that mercury was some sort of heavy liquid, but he had no idea that it was also the planet nearest the sun. Still less did he know that Mercury was the messenger of the gods.

Removing the earphones, he picked up the message form on which he had written the word and the time of receiving it, and left the radio cabin. Although he was many feet below-ground, it was impossible not to be aware of the heavy thump of Russian artillery. He shivered involuntarily. They would be here soon.

Halting before a door which bore the legend STURMBANNFUEH-

RER KORDT, he paused only to straighten his tunic and square his shoulders before knocking.

He was instructed to enter.

Walther Kordt was a middle-sized man of thirty-five who vaguely resembled a caricature of the elementary-school teacher he had once been. His short hair was cut high on the neck, Prussian style, though he was a Saxon by birth and a poltroon by nature.

"The signal, Herr Sturmbannfuehrer."

Kordt reached for it eagerly. "Give it to me and get out."

Alone, Kordt read the single word and noted the time of its reception. After a moment's thought, he reached for the telephone.

Although the choice of code word, along with the recognition signals, had been decided upon months earlier, Valkyrie was still amused by them. If the new arrivals were Mercury, that made Brigadier Greenleigh Zeus. Really, he thought, the British still had an overinflated sense of their own importance.

"Sit down, Kordt, sit down. To judge by the time on this, our guests arrived in the Ju 52 that was destroyed on takeoff."

"Sir?"

"The 52, Kordt, the 52. Doesn't anything that happens outside percolate through to you down here? Good God, Marshal Stalin could be holding a victory parade in Friedrichstrasse and the first you'd know about it would be when somebody shot you."

Kordt felt someone walk over his grave. That was a bit too close to home to be funny.

Valkyrie fingered the message form. "The question is, what do we do next?"

"Next, sir? I meet them as arranged and bring you the documents they're carrying. Provided they're in order, we leave."

"It's not quite as simple as that, I regret to say. You know the Fuehrer's state of mind as well as I do. If I—we—attempt to leave now, he will miss us—me—within the hour. I don't have to tell you how far we'd get if we have the SS hunting our heads as well as the Russians. It can't be risked. We'll have one chance at this, Kordt, and one only. If we fail we'll be dead. I've put too much thought into the plan to jeopardize it at the eleventh hour through hasty decisions."

Valkyrie leaned back in his chair and made a pyramid of his fingers.

"Imagine you're in a car, Kordt, and through some mischance you drive into a deep river so that you're submerged completely. The instinctive reaction is to push open the door and try to reach the surface, but the instinctive reaction is the fatal one. Even if you manage to get the door open, you will be swamped and drowned by the water rushing in.

"The correct procedure is to close all the windows and let the water seep in gradually. As the car begins to fill up you have to move your mouth closer and closer to the roof in order to breathe. Naturally this takes nerve, but it's the only sure way to escape. When the water pressure on the inside is equal to that on the outside, the door will open easily and you will float to the surface. That's what we must wait for, Kordt—equal pressure."

Kordt did not understand what his chief was talking about and cared less. "That's all very well, sir, but without wishing to give offense or question your judgment, if we don't go now we may not get out at all. I don't know whether you've seen the latest situation reports, but the Russians have virtually overrun Tempelhof in the last hour. The districts of Machnow, Niko-lassee, Zehlendorf, Schlachtensee and Steglitz are entirely in their hands, as are the Weissensee, Reinickendorf and Tegel districts in the north. The Nordland Panzer Grenadier Division in Defense Sector 111 has suffered terrible losses and is giving ground all the time. The 20th Motorized Division in Defense Sector V is reporting that tanks are through the Grunewald."

"I am perfectly aware of the gravity of the situation, Kordt, doubtless more so than you. Nevertheless, this is not the time for precipitate action. Of course, if you wish to make a solo attempt, I will have no objections."

"You know I wouldn't do that, sir."

"I think 'can't' is a more exact word. Apart from the fact that you do not know the precise recognition procedure, there is also the incident of the French hotelier's wife. I forget the details, but didn't you have him arrested and executed on some trumped-up charge in order to get the woman into your bed? You may not be as important as I am, Kordt, but you're certainly on somebody's list for a postwar noose. You'd do well to remember that and also to bear in mind that without me you wouldn't be getting out at all. You're coming only because I say so."

Kordt knew this to be unfair. A man such as his chief could not be seen talking clandestinely or disappearing for long periods at a time without someone's asking a lot of questions.

The same thought seemed to have occurred to Valkyrie.

"Still," he said with false joviality, "there's no need for us to quarrel, is there? We Germans live in a friendless world. We can ill afford to cross swords among ourselves. You'll have to trust me, Kordt—accept that I know what I'm doing."

Kordt remembered the incident on the Swiss border and hoped to God he was making the right decision.

"What do you want me to do, sir?"

"That's better."

Valkyrie thought about it for a few moments.

"I was going to suggest that we leave them to stew until I'm ready, but that might cause unnecessary complications. I'm sure the British have selected only their best people, but it's probably unwise to leave them to their own devices. In the first place, they might make the false assumption that something has gone amiss and call off the operation. Not that I believe they can get out of Berlin without my assistance, but one never knows what the British will do next. Secondly, they could accidentally be killed by our own people or a Russian shell. On balance, therefore, I think we should stick to the agreed plan—that is, meeting them twelve hours after the time of this signal. Say, ten forty-five tomorrow morning. Have you got somewhere you can keep them for a little while?"

Kordt shuddered at the phrase "a little while." He fervently hoped the chief was talking in terms of hours.

"I think so, sir. There are still one or two cellars no one knows about."

"Good. In that case, take them directly there. But make sure the cellars, or wherever you put them, are well inside the Defense Perimeter. I want our guests neither buried under rubble

197

nor overrun by the Russians when the time comes to utilize their services.

"Your contact in the morning, by the way, will be wearing the uniform of a Sturmbannfuehrer in the Waffen SS division Das Reich, whose cuff bands he will have on. He will also be wearing a head bandage. On the left-hand side of the bandage will be daubed the SS runes. The liquid will look like blood but is actually red paint. I apologize for the melodrama, but we can't have you walking up to the wrong man, can we? You will introduce the word Horsetrade into your opening sentence. He will respond with Mercury in his."

"They'll want to know how long they're expected to remain undercover, sir."

"And so, no doubt, do you. You'd better tell them two days, possibly three."

"Three days!"

Valkyrie banged the desk with his fist. How in the love of God had this timid creature attained the rank of Sturmbann-fuehrer? By blind obedience, no doubt, which was why, together with a strong sense of self-preservation, he had been chosen for his present task.

"For God's sake, Kordt, pull yourself together. The most pessimistic estimates don't put the Russians in our backyard until the thirtieth. In any case, it's not a matter for debate—by you or them. They will remain where you hide them until I say otherwise." He paused for a moment's reflection. "But you may tell their commanding officer—in case he too holds your sentiments—that you will return to collect them by the evening of the twenty-ninth at the latest. Have you got all that?"

"Yes, sir."

"Good. You might also ask them to let us have sight of the documents guaranteeing our immunity—in order that we may verify their authenticity, you understand."

"I doubt if they'll do that."

"So do I. That's the trouble with the world today—there's no trust anymore."

There was not much left of the superstructure of Gestapo HQ in Prinz Albrechtstrasse, but down below in the heavily protected cellars they were still working as if imminent defeat were a nasty piece of Allied propaganda. In every imaginable way these men of Amt III, the SD, and Amt IV, the Gestapo proper, typified the worst of Hitler's regime.

Not least among their number was Hauptsturmfuehrer Langendorf. Seated at a table in a borrowed cubicle a dozen meters below Prinz Albrechtstrasse, he had spread out in front of him every document pertaining to the unknown high-ranking traitor —from the original report on the death of Sturmbannfuehrer Klaus Bauer (although no such officer existed within the ranks of the SS) to the last coded message from the secret transmitter, intercepted earlier in the day. It mattered not to him that the city lay in ruins, that it could be a matter of only three or four days before the last of its defenses were squeezed like a nut between the pincers of Zhukov in the north and Konev in the south; that was the responsibility of others. If everyone carried out his duties faithfully, as he proposed to do, all would be well. The Fuehrer had promised that the battle groups of Obergruppenfuehrer Steiner and General Wenck were coming to the aid of Berlin, and that was good enough for him. In the meantime, he had work to do.

He saw now that it was asking the impossible to establish the name of the traitor simply by keeping his eyes open. The job was too big for one man. But the argument still held that he could not go to his immediate superiors for assistance, for fear that one or another of them was part of the plot. More to the point, even if they were as loyal as he, he would be pilloried, perhaps shot, for not reporting the matter sooner.

The radio messages were still undecoded, a meaningless mass of rubbish. The only hard evidence he had to work on was the papers found in the fake Bauer's pockets and the written report from the border post. To begin with, he went over these again, starting with the report.

The first couple of paragraphs were the usual junior-officer mumbo jumbo, designed to show how loyal and efficient the writer was. Langendorf virtually knew them by heart. His eyes danced down the page until he found what he was looking for.

Using the documents in his Swedish name but making quite certain we saw his SS papers, Sturmbannfuehrer Bauer crossed back

199

into the Reich at 12:22 P.M. Hauptscharfuehrer Hoess and I followed him, making no attempt at concealment. It is a regrettable fact of life that anonymous tip-offs against SS officers are not uncommon, being mostly made by disgruntled individuals anxious to cause trouble for the officer concerned.

Bauer did not appear worried that we were several meters behind him and even stopped to permit us to catch up. I waved him on, indicating that the Hauptscharfuehrer and I had private matters to discuss.

Quite openly Bauer entered a telephone booth. This fitted in with what we had been told he would do and what we should permit him to do. He held a lengthy conversation with the person at the other end. Hauptscharfuehrer Hoess timed it at six minutes. When he emerged from the box I challenged him.

He seemed completely taken aback and said, "You will regret this impertinence. I am on important business for the Reich."

I told him I had reason to believe he was guilty of treasonable activities and that he was to accompany me. He seemed to agree at first, but after a moment took to his heels. We shouted for him to stop, but he did not. Hauptscharfuehrer Hoess had no alternative but to open fire. (Enclosed separately please find the postmortem report, which appears to show that death was due to a combination of bullet wounds and cyanide from a capsule kept in the mouth. You will note that the medical officer is unable to state whether the capsule was bitten deliberately or whether its fracture was due to the impact of Hoess's shots.)

The SS papers in the name of Sturmbannfuehrer Klaus Bauer, as well as the Swedish documents, appear to have been issued by RSHA Stuttgart, but initial inquiries there have drawn a blank. Stuttgart has no trace of a Sturmbannfuehrer Bauer, and neither have documents for a clandestine trip to Switzerland been authorized by that office recently. I therefore judge them to be extremely clever forgeries.

Bauer carried no money or personal papers, no photographs or letters. The only other item of importance was the radio frequency inked on his left wrist. [The frequency was then given.]

It is regretted that we have been unable to ascertain the name or whereabouts of the anonymous informer, but it will doubtless be appreciated that this is not unusual under the circumstances. It is my opinion that it was a fellow conspirator; one who had, for some reason, cause to distrust Bauer or who simply wanted him eliminated.

That was the meat of the matter. There were another couple of paragraphs tacitly hinting that no matter what the front-line troops thought, commanding a border post was not an easy duty. Langendorf ignored them. Everyone had border duties these days, as the guard commander had undoubtedly found out, if he was not already dead.

Slowly he read the report again, underlining the sentences he considered important.

This fitted in with what we had been told he would do and what we should permit him to do. . . .

I therefore judge them to be extremely clever forgeries. . . .

unable to ascertain the name or whereabouts of the anonymous informer. . .

It is my opinion that it was a fellow conspirator. . .

Langendorf considered the first sentence to be far and away the most important. How had the anonymous informer known that Bauer would make a phone call and how had he persuaded the border post to let him make it? Well, that was pretty obvious, on reflection. The informer knew about it because he had already made that arrangement with Bauer. Bauer was to call his contact and let him know what had taken place in Switzerland as well as passing on the radio frequency. The informer had doubtless hinted to the border post that the authorities suspected who Bauer's contact might be and had put a tap on his telephone. It was therefore vital that Bauer be allowed to make the call before being challenged.

But it hadn't worked like that at all, of course. Bauer's usefulness had been at an end the minute he returned with some sort of deal. He could therefore be eliminated, but not before he had passed on details of the arrangement plus the frequency, which the contact was not to know that Bauer had written down.

That the fake Sturmbannfuehrer would make a run for it when challenged was a risk, but a justifiable one; he would believe that the real plot had been uncovered.

It was all rather clever. The contact had got what he wanted, and Bauer was dead.

The third and fourth sentences could almost be counted as one, and the border-guard commander had come closer than he realized in his opinion that the informer was a fellow conspirator.

I therefore judge them to be extremely clever forgeries. . . .

Langendorf examined them again, the SS papers in the name of Sturmbannfuehrer Bauer and the Swedish documents. They *were* clever, brilliantly so, right down to the last detail. They would fool anyone. If he hadn't known better and if Stuttgart had not confirmed that Bauer did not exist, he would say they were undoubtedly genuine. . . .

He sat up with a start.

But of course they were genuine! That was the point he'd been missing all along! He had assumed—wrongly, it now seemed—that the traitor was a senior Wehrmacht officer or a civilian or a scientist, someone who would have no access to anything other than forged documents. But if the bastard was a member of the Party or the SS, incredible though that might seem at first sight, then it all fell into place.

Such a man would have no need for forgeries. By pulling rank and inventing a false mission, he could have all the genuine documents he wanted, authorized and franked by the RSHA.

That would also explain why there was no record of papers being issued to the phony Bauer in Stuttgart. They would have been issued right here in Berlin—issued, for that matter, from the very building in which he was now sitting. Only if a man had genuinely joined the SS would his service sheet be kept in the city of enrollment. False documents—not *forged*, he reminded himself—were issued from the capital. And records were kept.

He mentally kicked himself for not thinking of it earlier, for being led astray by the red herring of Stuttgart, which was doubtless what the traitor had counted on.

His first reaction was to pay an immediate visit to the massive underground records section and demand to know who had authorized the false papers in the name of Bauer. But he quickly realized that that would achieve nothing. From what he had seen personally and heard on the grapevine, dossiers were being destroyed or transferred to secret hideaways at an astonishing rate, a policy he had thoroughly approved of until a few minutes ago. If the city was overrun (though any defeat would, of course, be a temporary one), it would go badly for members of the SS. It was no secret that the Allies were spreading alarming lies about the organization's activities, and no one was likely to pay much attention to a Hauptsturmfuehrer looking for a solitary file. Of course, if he made the request by telephone and promoted himself several ranks . . .

He lifted the phone and asked the switchboard to connect him to Records.

"This is Brigadefuehrer Wiedemann," he announced imperiously when the receiver at the other end was finally picked up. "Let me speak to the senior officer present."

A youthful voice came on the line, full of cautious respect for a caller who held such an illustrious SS rank.

"Hauptsturmfuehrer Koch speaking, Herr Brigadefuehrer."

Good, thought Langendorf; he'd made the correct decision. One Hauptsturmfuehrer to another would have got him nowhere.

"You are the senior officer?" he demanded.

"Yes, sir."

"Excellent. I have something I wish you to do for me as expeditiously as possible."

It was not very difficult to keep his tone of voice clipped and curt when asking for the file on Bauer. That was the manner in which Langendorf spoke to most junior officers, actual or imaginary. "Bauer was not his real name, so you may find the file cross-referenced. I require any correlative documents also."

He sensed hesitation in Koch's manner and suspected that the man was about to tell him that such a request would be difficult if not impossible under present circumstances. He therefore added quickly, "I cannot impress upon you enough, Koch, how important this file is. Odd though it may seem, it could change the course of the war, and I hold you personally responsible for finding it. I can give you twenty-four hours, no longer, to deliver it safely to my aide, Hauptsturmfuehrer Langendorf. I suggest you call him immediately to talk over any problems you're likely to encounter."

Langendorf gave his own extension number and hung up. Sure enough, in less than thirty seconds Koch was on the line. Now that he was talking to someone of his own rank, the Records Officer was more inclined to give vent to his feelings.

"What the hell's all this about your chief wanting a solitary dossier?" he demanded. "Doesn't he know it's chaotic down here?"

Langendorf made soothing noises—but not for long.

"All I can tell you is that if he says something's important, it's important. And if he says he wants it in twenty-four hours, he doesn't mean twenty-five or someone will be facing a firing squad."

"It's not possible. It would mean taking half a dozen men off other duties."

"Well, you know your own business best," murmured Langendorf, "but I can advise you that Wiedemann has just returned from a conference with the Fuehrer. Whether that has anything to do with his request to you, of course, I couldn't say."

"Jesus," muttered Koch, awestruck by the implications of failure.

"Perhaps I could get you a little more time," said Langendorf. He didn't want the man to panic and report to someone higher up the ladder that an unknown Brigadefuehrer was asking for miracles.

"Could you?"

"Another twelve hours—say, thirty-six in all."

"Try to make that forty-eight, will you? It's going to take most of that to find the relevant card index, let alone the goddamn file."

"I'll try," said Langendorf, "but forty-eight will be the absolute limit. And you'd better keep me posted on your progress. If we let him down it will be my head as well as yours."

"I'll do that. And thanks."

Langendorf hung up, well pleased with himself. It was now a few minutes after 2 A.M. on the morning of the twenty-seventh. By this time on the twenty-ninth he would have the name of the man who was selling out to the British.

At 2:25 A.M., Brigadier Greenleigh knew that he was not going to hear from Eindhoven about the safe return of the Ju 52. Even with extra tanks, the Iron Annie could afford only five hours in the air, and those five had run out at 1:30. If the plane had come down somewhere in Allied territory on the return flight, he would have been notified by now.

News was already coming in that the Russians had taken Tempelhof, and he had no way of knowing whether the 52 had met its fate after safely depositing its passengers or before. He had to assume they'd made it. He had to assume they were in and execute the remainder of the plan accordingly—that part of it which not even Lassiter knew about.

TWENTY-THREE

Fodor made his way south along Hermann Goeringstrasse toward the Brandenburg Gate, a silk scarf wrapped around the lower half of his face to protect his lungs from the ubiquitous dust which rose like mist from the pulverized brick and stone. It was 10:40 on the morning of the twenty-seventh, and the city was taking a terrible beating from the big Russian guns, though for the moment it was the west and southwest sections that were feeling the brunt of the barrage. Even so, there was always the odd stray shell to worry about, as well as the Russian dive-bombers, which had a habit of coming out of nowhere and plastering anything that looked like a target. From time to time, when it was possible to see above the flames and smoke, Fodor observed that the Russian planes were being harassed constantly by Me 109s. He wondered where the hell the German aircraft were getting their fuel from.

East of the now-gutted Reichstag he suddenly waved his arm furiously and dropped to his knees. Fifty yards to the rear, Lassiter and the others did likewise. But the armed patrol that suddenly appeared out of the smoke on the other side of the street, going in the opposite direction, paid them scant attention. They were mostly *Volkssturm*, Home Guard, and Hitler Youth; old men and boys under the command of several SS NCOs.

"Jesus Christ," muttered Dougal Maclean, and those who heard him knew that he was not only commenting on the ages of the patrol.

The city in daylight was mind-numbing, far worse than it had appeared the previous night. Then, in spite of the flames, it had given the superficial impression that only inanimate objects were being destroyed. Now they could see the truth.

Every last one of them, including Sara Ferguson, had witnessed cities under siege before, but never anything like this. It wasn't only the fires, the crumbling masonry that fell with the suddenness of an avalanche, the choking dust; it wasn't even the overall terrifying impression of noise: noise from the screaming shells, from the dive-bombers, from the dogfights going on somewhere above their heads, from steel girders buckling and splitting under the incredible heat. That was part of war, and it was surprising how quickly you got used to it, learned to ignore it almost. It was a minor assault on the senses when compared with the sight of the corpses, which were everywhere, civilians and service personnel alike, many of them mutilated beyond all recognition, many in an advanced state of decomposition; bodies of women and children, adolescents and old people, sprawled obscenely where they had fallen, an impossible task for the sanitation squads, which had in any case virtually ceased to exist.

But even the dead were a part of war that professionals were accustomed to and could rationalize, as they could rationalize the cadavers hanging from the lampposts.

It was the living that could send a man insane unless he had learned, as most soldiers had to, to switch off a portion of his brain. The slaughtered were gone, finished, out of it; they might look ugly, unlike anything that had once walked around and laughed, but at least they no longer felt anything; those who were still alive, if living it could be called, walked hand in hand with the most appalling suffering imaginable.

In the few brief moments they were crouched by the side of the road, they saw sights that would remain with them for the rest of their days, however brief, for some of them, those days might be.

For the average citizen there was, of course, no water any longer—for the extinguishing of fires, for washing, for drinking. The main supply sources had been rendered useless by bombs weeks ago, the conduits fractured by shells. To quench his thirst a man had to collect what he could from the filthy liquid that had gathered at the bottom of bomb and shell craters, as several of them were now doing some fifty or sixty yards away, among them a boy of twelve or thirteen. It seemed there was only one receptacle, which the boy had, an old iron kettle. It was not to be his for long.

One of the men snatched for it, but the boy held on grimly to his prize. The man aimed a kick at him. It missed, but in avoiding it the boy let go of the kettle. It was seized immediately by a second man, who held a swift conversation with the first. They seemed to agree that they should share the kettle and what it would hold, to the exclusion of the original owner.

The boy was having none of this and went for the pair, fists flailing. He stood no chance. One of them knocked him to the ground and, when he got up, knocked him down a second time. Then both men proceeded to kick him senseless. In a world where survival depended upon brute force and cunning, he was a loser.

There was no food, either. Whether the rations were exhausted or whether the authorities found it impossible to distribute what remained under present conditions, there was no way of knowing. But oblivious to shells or bombs from Russian aircraft, women in tattered rags wandered among still-burning buildings and poked in the rubble with long sticks. What they were looking for it was hard to say. Perhaps they knew that the erstwhile occupier of what had once been a house or shop had hoarded cans of cooked meat or fruit. Perhaps the mounds of debris had once been a store. But whatever the truth of the matter they kept at it, some with babies in their arms, some hardly more than babies themselves; some with knee-high children whose cries for sustenance or out of fear and bewilderment could be heard quite clearly, even in this asylum of noise.

Neither were there any medicines or bandages. Those with open wounds or suffering from burns had to manage as best they could, as did those who had lost the faculty of sight and could find no one to lead them or provide for them.

Many no longer cared whether they lived or died. In every street and within every ruin there were those who wandered aimlessly wherever their feet took them, not caring that the next bomb or shell or collapsing building could have their name written on it. Many, though still clinically alive, simply lay where they had fallen, whether hit by shrapnel or flying masonry or merely succumbing to typhus and cholera contracted

208

by drinking the stinking water or lingering too long near an open sewer. Perhaps, for some, hunger had removed what remained of their will to carry on. But whatever it was, when a man lay down, he was as good as dead unless he had family or friends to take care of him, to force him to survive for another few hours, another few minutes.

Any sort of moral code had long since disappeared. Women and girls of any age were prepared to sell their bodies to all comers for any kind of perversion in return for a crust of bread or shelter or protection. Those who were not prepared to give in willingly and who still retained something of their looks were dragged away forcibly by gangs of marauding youths and occasionally soldiers. In many instances the screaming victims were not even taken out of sight; they were raped where they were trapped, sometimes within yards of passersby who looked the other way and hurried on. Many women did not survive the assault. If they were very young or weak or frightened and if the gang was a large one, sometimes they died where they lay, from shock or brutality—because the perpetrators of the violence had nothing to lose.

"Jesus Christ," repeated Maclean.

The same thought crossed several minds simultaneously: that they were here in this city to help save the neck of a man who was, at least in part, responsible for much of the destruction. They were going to save him from a hangman's noose because it had been decreed by those who knew about these matters that he had a value to the Anglo-Americans. But among those who wondered at the lunacy of it all was one who had already determined that Valkyrie was not going to get away with it, that he was not going to live to enjoy the fruits of his private agreement with British and U.S. Intelligence.

Fodor got to his feet and waved them forward with an American cavalry gesture. "Get moving," commanded Lassiter.

He was tired; they all were. There had been no chance of shelter or much sleep the previous night; no way, it had quickly transpired, of taking refuge in a building with the secure knowledge that it would be there the following morning, that it would not be hit and bury them under tons of concrete. Neither had they reached Alexanderplatz. Meeting an SS patrol en route, they were warned that Russian snipers had infiltrated the district and that there was little possibility of dislodging them before daybreak.

The Obersturmfuehrer commanding the patrol had taken in the Das Reich cuff bands and inquired curiously whether the division was now in Berlin. Lassiter pulled rank and brushed aside the question, but it was apparent that his team was going to attract attention if it was found wandering aimlessly through the streets, especially with Sara in tow. They had passed other groups of Wehrmacht and SS which included women, but Sara still stood out. In spite of the mussed hair and the old greatcoat, she looked healthier and more vital than the Berliners.

In the end, Lassiter had done the only thing possible by setting up his own defense post in a side street, the theory being that in a barrelful of apples anything that looks like an apple goes unnoticed. Even so, and even with them manning it in turns, rest was out of the question for more than a few moments at a time. The appalling noise apart, with the chance of a stray shell's wiping them off the face of the earth, it was not a night for sweet dreams.

Fodor reached the junction of Hermann Goeringstrasse and Unter den Linden, and stopped. This was dangerous territory. On the south side of this section of the East–West Axis, the extension of Hermann Goeringstrasse formed one leg of the triangle that bounded the Chancellery. The area was guarded by crack SS troops, most of them determined, in spite of everything, that neither the Russians nor anyone else were going to get anywhere near their beloved Fuehrer.

Ahead of Fodor lay the Brandenburg Gate, almost unrecognizable from the photographs he had seen. Atop it, the chariot of victory was twisted grotesquely, three of its four horses looking anything but equine. Milling around beneath what remained of the superstructure were a dozen or more SS men, examining a crippled antiaircraft gun. Nearby, a Tiger tank, caught in the open by dive-bombers, was blazing. One of its crew members had been killed when half out of the cockpit, and there he remained, still burning.

Fodor took a deep breath. He felt absurdly conspicuous wearing the phony head bandage, but logic told him that it was as good a recognition signal as anything. Green carnations were definitely out.

He glanced skyward to make sure there were no Soviet aircraft about to pounce, counted to three, and made a run for the Gate.

Lassiter and the others remained on the north side of Unter den Linden. If anything went wrong, they would leave Fodor to his fate and get the hell out of it. But nothing seemed to be going wrong.

There was a moment of panic when one of the SS men left the antiaircraft gun and strolled over to the American, but it became apparent that all he was after was a few cigarettes. They saw Fodor reach into his pocket, hesitate, than hand over an entire pack.

"All we need now is for Chuck to have reached into the wrong pocket and given him a pack of Luckies," Scipioni murmured.

There was no chance of that. Thanks to Browning and his fellow Poets, even the darns in their socks were made with German thread.

Three minutes passed, and Lassiter was beginning to get worried. Fodor couldn't stand out there all day as though waiting for a tram. The contact was late.

Another minute—and Sara was first to see him, a middle-sized man in SS uniform hurrying along Unter den Linden from the east, one eye on the sky. It was hard to be certain because of all the dust and smoke, but she judged his rank to be that of Sturmbannfuehrer.

In any case, it was definitely their man. He marched straight up to Fodor and flung him a Nazi salute. Fodor responded in kind. A few seconds' conversation, no doubt to verify identities, and then the pair of them were heading back through the smoke.

Sturmbannfuehrer Walther Kordt eyed each one of them warily. Years of service with the SS had taught him that little was as it seemed. Before committing himself irrevocably, he wanted to be sure that neither the Gestapo nor the SD had somehow learned of the plot and switched their men for the British.

Finally he was satisfied. They looked like Germans, the one he had already spoken to sounded like a German, but Kordt knew that anyone who had served for long periods with the Das Reich, as these people must have to gain their medals and campaign ribbons, could not possibly appear so fit. They were the genuine article, all right, including the girl.

"Why a woman?" he asked, glancing from Fodor to Lassiter, the two senior officers present.

"The courier," answered Lassiter. "The woman has the necessary documents."

"You risk bringing a woman just to carry a few papers?"

Lassiter had no intention of telling him the truth, that Sara's intimate knowledge of the Nazi hierarchy would preclude any sleight of hand. "If they're just a few papers, you and your boss could have made your way across without them, couldn't you? You could have got out under your own steam and trusted us to be nice to you at the other end."

"Point taken, Herr Sturmbannfuehrer." Kordt held out his hand. "Well, as they're so valuable, perhaps you'd better entrust them to my possession."

"And perhaps you'll get the entire High Command to surrender to the first Russian private they see." Lassiter shook his head. "The papers stay with us. They'll be handed over to the person they're intended for and no one else."

"I am one of those people. Sturmbannfuehrer Walther Kordt."

"I sort of gathered you were. But the documents get given to the whale, not the minnows."

"As you wish."

They all ducked involuntarily as a wayward shell whistled overhead.

"Come," said Kordt, "we must leave this area. The Russians won't be happy with their present target much longer."

Lassiter stood his ground and motioned to the others to remain where they were also. "Where are you taking us?"

"To a place of safety."

"What place of safety?"

"It won't mean anything if I tell you."

"I'd rather know anyway."

"You have no reason to distrust me, Herr Sturmbannfuehrer."

"That's what you told the Czechs and Poles," said Scipioni.

"Shut up," said Lassiter. "I neither trust nor distrust you," he advised Kordt. "You don't mean anything to me either way. It's your boss we've come for, not you, so what the hell's all this about a place of safety? It sounds a bit too permanent for my liking."

"Very well," said Kordt, "it's in the cellar of a derelict building on Markgrafenstrasse, which is a kilometer or a little more in that direction." He pointed east, up Unter den Linden, away from the Chancellery area. "No one knows of it. You'll be quite safe there. It contains food and water and general provisions. . . ."

"That's not what I meant and you know it," snapped Lassiter. "The way you're talking, you've victualed the place for a month."

Kordt hesitated. "Two days," he said. "The evening of the twenty-ninth at the latest."

In spite of himself, Lassiter took a pace forward and gripped Kordt by the lapels. "Two *what?*"

"It can't be helped," stammered Kordt. "Believe me, I don't like it any more than you do, but circumstances have forced my . . . circumstances have forced us to delay."

"Patrol coming," Gallagher called out.

Lassiter glanced up. It was another of the *Volkssturm*/Hitler Youth patrols.

"We must leave here," gasped Kordt. He tried to break Lassiter's hold and failed. "Believe me, the least of our worries is Russian artillery. The SD have eyes everywhere looking for defeatists and traitors."

"We'll leave when I say we leave," said Lassiter. "Now what the hell's all this about two days?"

"You must understand there was no alternative—"

A salvo of heavy shells screamed overhead, landing just beyond the Reichstag and scattering the *Volkssturm* patrol. Lassiter had been under enough artillery barrages to realize that these were bracketing shots and that the next would fall shorter. So had Alex Dunbar.

"We'd better do as the man says and get the hell out of here," the Scot advised. "We can argue about it later."

Lassiter nodded slowly. Dunbar was right. Already the troopers around the antiaircraft gun were making for cover.

He let go of Kordt's lapels. The SS officer straightened his tunic and did his best to appear dignified. It was far from easy; he had a lot of things to be scared of.

"We must move quickly," he said.

The bombardment was on in earnest by the time they crossed Friedrichstrasse, running bent double, Kordt in the lead, panting like a man with a heart ailment, Lassiter and Dunbar next, followed by Scipioni and Sara Ferguson, side by side. Maclean, Gallagher and Fodor brought up the rear, though not more than thirty paces separated all eight of them.

The Russian batteries had got the range now and seemed intent upon leveling the area bounded by Unter den Linden in the north and Leipzigerstrasse in the south, Wilhelmstrasse in the west and, regrettably, Markgrafenstrasse to the east.

Each of them knew that they would have to get to wherever they were going pretty damn quick or they wouldn't be getting there at all.

Without warning Kordt darted across Unter den Linden, almost stumbling into a steep crater for his pains but somehow avoiding it with an agility that was the product of raw fear. The others followed. Ahead of them on the right lay Markgrafenstrasse, though where one street ended and another began it was hard to tell these days.

Kordt turned into it, ran twenty yards and stopped, hands on knees, coughing.

Lassiter jeked him upright. "How much farther?"

Kordt waved a limp hand. "Down there," he spluttered; "just this side of Leipzigerstrasse."

It was impossible to see "down there": the whole of the lower end of the street was a thick fog. And Kordt expected them to go through it.

Sara Ferguson came up, her face covered with dust and sweat. "We'll never make it," she shouted. "I know this area; it's a good half mile to Leipzigerstrasse."

Lassiter looked around desperately for somewhere to shelter.

It didn't exist. Neither, a moment later, did a wall which received a direct hit and crumbled by degrees, like a newsreel run in slow motion.

He had already made up his mind that there was nothing for it but to plow on when he felt a tug at his sleeve. It was Gallagher.

"Down there, Skip!"

Lassiter saw where he was pointing. Sixty or so yards away on the other side of the street, barely visible through the dust, a figure was waving to them, beckoning.

"You can't," protested Kordt, reading Lassiter's mind. "You don't know who it is!"

"And we can't stay here either without some of us getting killed. Is that what you want? It doesn't matter who it is, it's a better bet than this."

They ran toward the beckoning figure. When they got close they saw it was a man wearing the collar insignia of SS Obersturmbannfuehrer, one rank above Lassiter and Fodor—a lieutenant colonel in British and American terms. He was standing before what looked like the entrance to a concrete dugout, holding open a heavy door. Beyond the door was a naked light above a flight of steps that led downward.

"Get in!" he shouted, ushering them through.

Lassiter brought up the rear. When he was safely inside, he assisted the Obersturmbannfuehrer to shut the door and lock it by means of several massive iron bars.

TWENTY-FOUR

The sudden comparative silence was overwhelming, but the SS officer gave them no time to wonder where they were.

"Please continue down," he instructed. "We are not at all safe at this level."

Kordt led the way with Fodor right behind him, prodding him forward. The staircase was narrow and wooden but far from makeshift; it looked as if it had been built to stand the test of time. From top to bottom, allowing for the right-angled turn halfway, Fodor counted forty-six steps. Every inch of the route was lit by naked light bulbs, obtaining their power, presumably, from a private generator.

At the foot of the stairs they found themselves in a small anteroom, twelve feet by twelve. The floor here was concrete, but someone had made an effort and covered much of it with strips of carpet. Against one wall were a table and an upright chair, and just to the right of these items a door, firmly closed and insulated with some sort of soundproofing material. At a guess, they were fifteen or twenty yards below ground level.

The Obersturmbannfuehrer stood with hands on hips and looked them over. He was young for his rank, perhaps thirty years old. He took in the various medals and the Das Reich cuff bands and seemed impressed, though he himself wore the Knight's Cross at his throat. Finally his gaze alighted upon Sara and he nodded approvingly.

"Allow me to introduce myself," he said formally. "Obersturmbannfuehrer Joachim Harmel of the 11th SS Panzer Grenadier Division Nordland, to which I must return as soon as the Ivans have finished their target practice."

Lassiter introduced his own officers by their German pseudonyms, feeling a profound sense of unreality as he did so. He explained that Kordt was not part of their group, that they had simply joined forces when the barrage began. In accordance with custom, German or British, he did not introduce the NCOs, who, taking their cue, had moved several deferential paces to the rear and were standing roughly to attention.

"I thought the Das Reich was in Vienna," said Harmel.

"It was, and still is to the best of my knowledge," answered Lassiter. "We came in last night on a 52, but more than that I'm afraid I cannot say. Security, you understand."

"Of course. I heard about the 52." He looked at Sara again. "And the young lady?"

Although the question was indirectly aimed at Lassiter, Sara fielded it, using the backup plan. Being a camp follower would no longer hold water. It had been an acceptable cover when their stay in Berlin was likely to be measured in hours, but not anymore. They might, by some mishap, bump into this Obersturmbannfuehrer again, and the SS did not keep their women that long.

"Frau Hanna Beck," she said stiffly, "with orders to report to Prinz Albrechtstrasse. These gentlemen kindly gave me a ride in their aircraft."

The German propensity for secrecy and covert terror organizations worked in her favor, as it had worked before. No one, not even senior Waffen SS officers, meddled in Gestapo business.

Harmel visibly backed off. If the female was more deadly than the male, the Gestapo female was poison. The interest in his eyes disappeared.

"Frau Beck," he said politely, bowing from the waist.

"What exactly is this place?" asked Fodor.

"Yes, I was coming to that," answered Harmel. "You are in what used to be the storage vaults—this and the next-door room —of an art dealer, though needless to say he has not practiced his profession for years. Nevertheless, his collection was a valuable one—doubtless now the property of Reichsmarschall Goering—and he took great care of it. This part of the building was—and to a large extent still is—watertight and airtight. The walls and roof are reinforced concrete; it would take a direct hit by a bomb or shell to more than scratch the surface.

"It was turned into a fortified bunker in April 1944, mostly for the use of Party officials and the like. In the last few months, however, it has become something different." He inclined his head toward Sara. "I trust Frau Beck has seen enough of the world not to be shocked."

"Frau Beck," said Sara, with an audacity which left Scipioni, standing next to her, with his head reeling, "has doubtless seen more of the world than the Obersturmbannfuehrer. And not much of it from the security of a cellar, either."

It was doubtless the right thing to say from a supposed member of the Gestapo. Harmel's lips tightened, but he held his temper. "We have all fought the war in our own ways, Frau Beck. . . . And now if you'll follow me, gentlemen; the NCOs too, of course. There are no barriers here, as you'll soon discover."

Harmel knocked loudly on the communicating door. It was opened instantly by a youthful Untersturmfuehrer in a state of semiundress. At least, his collar was wide open and his shirt coming out of his breeches. In his left hand he held a bottle of French brandy; with his right he flung Harmel a mock Nazi salute.

That the material used to make the vault airtight and watertight had also rendered it soundproof, there was no longer any doubt. Even before they saw more of the Untersturmfuehrer than his glowing face, they heard the pandemonium coming from beyond: music, laughter, the clinking of glasses, raised voices, cheering.

Harmel pushed the junior officer roughly to one side and led them through the doorway. There they were confronted with a scene which took their breath away, which made them, momentarily, doubt their sanity. If Berlin aboveground could be equated with the last days of Rome, this was certainly the week before.

This second room was much larger than the first, perhaps eighty feet by seventy, and dimly illuminated to simulate a nightclub atmosphere. Its occupants were some thirty men and women, who were sitting at tables, lounging on sofas and even sprawled out on the carpeted floor. Few appeared sober, which was hardly surprising in view of the number of bottles of wine and spirits on display.

The majority of the men were in uniform; SS almost without exception, though here and there Luftwaffe blue and Army gray could be seen, as well as one or two individuals in civilian clothes.

Outnumbered two to one, the women were mainly naked save for flimsy wraps. Those who were as drunk as their partners were allowing themselves to be fondled in the most intimate way. Others protested, if only mildly, when a hand went outside what they considered to be public propriety.

There was evidently a ventilation system somewhere out of sight, but even so the air was thick with smoke. Not the kind that was pervading the streets above, however. This was the smoke of expensive cigars and a seemingly endless supply of cigarettes, a rare sight in Berlin at this stage of the war.

In one corner of the room, unbelievably, stood a grand piano, a Hauptscharfuehrer at the keyboard thumping out prewar medleys. Around him, in varying stages of drunkenness, half a dozen SS troopers were singing at the top of their lungs.

But it was the other end of the cellar that was attracting most of the attention.

Someone had rigged up a kind of raised stage, and on it was the floor show. This consisted of two young girls, both completely naked and neither over the age of sixteen, making love in various forms to each other and also to a naked young man on a pile of rugs. That this was not simulation but the real thing was apparent from the man's state of erection and the expression in his eyes. And if any further proof were required, it was provided quickly by the male, unable to stand the foreplay any longer, grabbing the nearer girl and making her straddle him, which she did with total abandon, easing herself down over his enlarged phallus. The second girl took up a position behind the first, fondling her breasts and kissing her neck and throat.

It was impossible for any of them, including Sara, not to be affected sexually, not to feel a sudden surge of lust at a sight that was normally buried deep in fantasy. But almost as quickly, horror supplanted desire. Upstairs the world was going mad, people in their hundreds being blown to pieces. The nuts had taken over the asylum, and it was a far from comforting thought.

Obersturmbannfuehrer Harmel led them to what passed for a quiet corner. He shook his head at those men who looked at Sara with more than casual interest.

Two tables had been pushed together and were currently occupied by a couple of SS officers and a Luftwaffe Major, debating in loud voices about whether it was possible for General Wenck to cut off the Russian supply columns. Harmel leaned forward and whispered in the nearer SS man's ear. The tables were vacated immediately. The Obersturmbannfuehrer evidently carried a lot of weight.

Feeling far from at ease, Lassiter's team and Sturmbannfuehrer Kordt sat down. There was nothing to be done but to wait until the Russian bombardment, still audible even above the present racket as a series of distant thumps, ended.

There were half-empty bottles and glasses already on the table, and Harmel indicated that they should help themselves. It would not have been logical to refuse, and Lassiter gave permission for the others to drink with a gesture. He himself accepted a glass of wine from Dunbar but hardly touched it, being more concerned that Harmel would take his duties as "host" seriously and either start to ask awkward questions or leave him no time to tackle Kordt about the two-day delay.

He need not have worried. Possibly because of Sara's presence or possibly for private reasons of his own, the SS colonel did not join them. Neither did he offer any explanation for their surroundings. Either he assumed they had all seen such scenes before or he was totally unconcerned with what they thought. In any event, he did not sit down.

"I'll leave you to your own devices, Herr Sturmbannfuehrer," he said to Lassiter. "As soon as the barrage is over I shall be leaving, as no doubt you will. In case we don't meet again, good luck."

Lassiter thanked him for his hospitality and wished him luck also.

Harmel shook his head. "Ah, it's going to take more than luck, I fear."

"Jesus Christ," said Scipioni, when Harmel was out of earshot; "I see it but I still don't believe it."

"He comes from Brooklyn," gagged Fodor. "They don't screw

220

in public *or* private back there." Then he remembered Sara's presence and muttered that she should forgive his dirty mouth.

Sara reacted in a way none of them expected. Perhaps it was because she was a woman in all-male company, but she gave Fodor both barrels for apologizing.

"Look," she said angrily, "I told you back in England that you're to treat me as just another member of the team, no favors or cleaning up your language because you're frightened you might offend my sensitive ears. If someone hears you treating me the way you'd treat a lady back home, they may just smell a rat.

"That Obersturmbannfuehrer has accepted me as Gestapo, and you can bet your life he'll tell others to steer clear of me for that reason. You may not know too much about Gestapo women, but I do. They're not the sort you say Sorry to just because you've said a dirty word."

She glanced around to make sure she was not being overheard by anyone other than those at the table.

"Before we get out of this place, one of these drunken louts may come across and start making improper suggestions. If I want him got rid of I'll make it perfectly clear, believe me. But it could well be that my judgment dictates otherwise. So if I choose to go out into the middle of the stage and let him fuck me in public, that's my business and I'll know what I'm doing."

There was a moment's shocked silence before Fodor said, "Ouch!" and looked away.

Sara felt sorry for the man, but what she had said and the manner in which she had said it were necessary. As a woman receptive to vibrations, she knew that Chuck Fodor was already more than casually interested in her. The others found her attractive, of course—there was no point in being unduly modest about it; but with Fodor it went deeper and had to be stopped. Not only was this far and away the wrong time and place: it could be fatal if the American, out of a misguided sense of chivalry, treated her other than as a cipher with a job to do.

Jack Lassiter had the right idea. Whatever he really felt was almost impossible to fathom, but she was fairly sure that his innermost feelings toward her were not those of a big brother. Nevertheless, until the time came, if it ever did, when he was free to speak his mind, he would keep those feelings hidden from her, possibly even from himself.

Lassiter understood some of the logic behind her putting Fodor through the hoop. Indeed, it was because he had taken note of Fodor's interest that he had given Scipioni the job of looking after her. But he would have added a couple of other reasons for the outburst that Sara had overlooked.

In the last dozen hours she had been shot at by enemy fighters, subjected to an artillery barrage and managed precious little sleep. Apart from that, they were a hell of a long way from being home and dry yet. She might be an experienced agent with a history of getting out of tight spots, but it was all bound to have its effect.

He laid a restraining hand on her arm. She understood and nodded curtly.

"I want to have a quiet word with Kordt here," he said generally, keeping his tone conversational. "I might have to throttle the little bastard, and I don't want anyone wandering across while I'm doing it. So if you'll maneuver your chairs into some sort of line, that'll be a help." He grinned, trying to lighten a still-tense situation. "You've got plenty to look at, so I don't think you'll be bored. Sara, you'd better sit in on this."

Kordt was already swigging brandy from a bottle. A few minutes ago he had thought that nothing could be worse than being caught in the open, far from his secure bunker, with Russian shells hurtling down. Now not only were the British arguing among themselves and uttering threats against him, he was trapped in some lunatic cellar surrounded by the SS. One foot out of place and he'd be strung up by the neck.

It was not just to keep Sara temporarily away from the sex show and Fodor that Lassiter wanted her with him while he grilled Kordt. If Greenleigh was right and one of the Americans was an enemy agent, sooner or later, in case anything happened to him, he would have to share that fact/suspicion with someone. Of all of them, he trusted Sara the most. He wanted her to hear, at first hand, everything he heard.

He removed the bottle from Kordt's trembling fingers.

"Now, you bastard, what's all this about waiting two days? Maybe all you people have been listening to too much Wagner, but it's going to be touch and go whether there'll be any city to hide in in forty-eight hours."

Kordt's eyes were slightly glazed, but he spoke with a little more confidence now that the brandy was beginning to bite home.

"It is completely unavoidable, I assure you. If it were not, do you think I—we—would want to stay? There are matters to be considered about which you can know nothing."

"Then why the hurry to get us here?"

Kordt smiled vacantly. "My dear Sturmbannfuehrer, you've seen for yourself what conditions are like outside. If you had not arrived yesterday you might not have arrived at all."

Lassiter felt like carrying out his threat to throttle the little swine, but that of course was out of the question. Kordt was the only link to Valkyrie.

"Perhaps I'd better talk to your boss in person."

Kordt was not that far gone. "I'm afraid that will not be possible, Herr Sturmbannfuehrer. Apart from the fact that he does not as yet wish to speak to you, if I give you direct access you will no longer need me as go-between."

"Neither, of course, will he," said Sara nastily, "once you've completed your task."

"Yes." Kordt looked concerned. "Yes, I hadn't thought of that."

The bombardment lasted upwards of an hour, but finally stopped with the suddenness of a switched-off lamp soon after midday. Kordt advised caution.

"The Russians sometimes cease firing for a while to persuade us that the barrage is over. Then they start again, when everyone is on the streets."

Lassiter accepted the wisdom of this and gave it another fifteen minutes.

The atmosphere in the cellar was curiously subdued now. Once the trio on stage had finished their performance, some time ago, the room had lost its sexual ambience. Whether they had walked in on the tail end of an all-night session which had exhausted everyone or whether the terror of the bombardment had released atavistic fears and lusts, Lassiter never found out. But in either event, for the last fifteen minutes the stage had been clear, the girls left unfondled. Even the pianist and the singers had become quiet. In the main, the occupants were now just drinking, anesthetizing tomorrow.

As they left, Obersturmbannfuehrer Harmel waved to them from across the room. He was very drunk and it seemed unlikely that the 11th Panzer Grenadier Division would be seeing him that day.

In the street it was the mixture as before; a few more fires, a few more craters, dazed people emerging from their funk holes, new corpses.

At the end of the column that made its way down Markgrafen-strasse, Mike Gallagher remembered some lines from a boyhood book. *Treasure Island*, he thought it was, and Long John Silver speaking; something about "Them as die'll be the lucky ones."

For the death of his mother all those years ago, he still hated the Germans with every fiber of his being. But a large part of him found it impossible not to feel compassion for the homeless and terrified women and children. They hadn't killed his mother; it was men like Kordt and his unknown boss who had done that.

The German led them across a stretch of open ground and stopped before what had once been the ground-floor door of a four-story building. The upper stories were gutted. For that matter, it seemed as if it would take a dozen strong men several hours to remove the steel girders and beams which blocked the entrance, but it transpired that these were fakes. From a distance they looked solid enough, but in actuality were made of some light alloy, painted over, and attached to the door itself. A touch on a hidden spring and the whole lot opened outward.

"Hurry," urged Kordt.

Down a short flight of stairs and into a room the size of the average sitting room. There were half a dozen two-tier bunks around the walls, a shelf full of canned provisions and even a large drum of drinking water. It might be stale, but it was not contaminated.

In an adjacent cubicle there were a chemical toilet and a primitive ventilation system. Lighting, though, was by candles.

"Lock the door from the inside when I go and don't open it to anyone," said Kordt. "You'll be quite safe here, although overcrowding may prove a problem. However, one cannot have everything. I shall be back by early evening of the twenty-ninth at the latest."

None of them liked this inactivity, but there was nothing to be done about it.

After Kordt had gone they selected their bed spaces and settled down to wait.

TWENTY-FIVE

Unknown to most Berliners, over the next forty-eight hours events were to take place that would solve their problems once and for all. Some would make worldwide headlines for months to come, others no more than a line or two in some distant obituaries column; still others, though with far-reaching effects, would never be known save to a select few.

At a few minutes after 4 o'clock on the afternoon of April 28, Benito Mussolini and his mistress, Clara Petacci, captured while trying to flee to Switzerland, were executed in the village of Dongo in northern Italy by partisans. The chief hatchet man, Walter Audisio, discarded several weapons before finding one that worked, and it was a burst of half a dozen shots from a Mas 7.65-millimeter machine pistol that finally dispatched the former Duce and his girlfriend.

Early next morning, a Sunday, the bodies of Mussolini, Petacci and other executed Fascists were taken to a half-built gas station in Milan, where they were kicked and mutilated before being strung up by their feet from an overhead beam.

News of Mussolini's death was received shortly after 9 P.M. on the twenty-eighth by a clerk of the Deutsches Nachrichten-büro, the official German news agency, which had a small office for monitoring enemy broadcasts in the upper level of the Bunker. He scribbled it out on a message form and was about to have it delivered to Hitler's valet, Heinz Linge, when it was followed by an even more shattering statement. In brief it read:

IT WAS AUTHORITATIVELY STATED IN OFFICIAL CIRCLES HERE
YESTERDAY THAT ACCORDING TO INFORMATION SENT TO EDEN
AND MOLOTOV A MESSAGE FROM HIMMLER GUARANTEEING
GERMAN UNCONDITIONAL SURRENDER BUT NOT TO RUSSIA HAS

Hitler received the news in silence and later conferred behind
locked doors with Goebbels and Bormann. When the conference was over, Hitler ordered Brigadefuehrer Fegelein, Himmler's liaison officer in the Bunker and the brother-in-law of Eva
Braun, to be brought before him.

Fegelein had been arrested by the Gestapo in his Charlottenburg house the previous day. As he was wearing civilian clothes
and carrying quantities of jewelry and money, including Swiss
francs, the Gestapo concluded not unreasonably that he was
planning to make a run for it.

He was brought back to the Bunker in disgrace and saved
from immediate execution only by the intercession of Eva
Braun, who pleaded for his life on the ground that Fegelein's
wife, her sister, was having a baby. Hitler listened to Eva, much
to the disgust of the others present, and contented himself with
stripping Fegelein of his rank and Knight's Cross.

But now the news report of Himmler's treachery convinced
Hitler that Fegelein was somehow involved in offering unconditional surrender to the Anglo-Americans. In the space of fifty
minutes he was court-martialed, found guilty of treason and
condemned to death.

This time Eva Braun kept her own counsel. She had learned
that some of the jewelry which Fegelein had on his person was
her own and that his proposed traveling companion was someone else's wife.

Minutes after sentence was passed, the former Brigadefuehrer was taken out to the Chancellery garden and shot. The officer in command of the firing squad was Hauptsturmfuehrer
Langendorf.

Since his conversation with Hauptsturmfuehrer Koch in the
small hours of the twenty-seventh, almost two days ago, Langendorf had been acting like a man on the edge of a breakdown;
jumpy, quick to anger, living on his nerves and amphetamines,
he was unable to concentrate on the simplest problems for more

than a few minutes at a time. He was within millimeters of having the traitor's name in the palm of his hand, damn it to hell, and the strain of waiting was killing him.

Koch had four hours of his original forty-eight left, and there was no doubt that he would not be delivering the goods on schedule. Langendorf had spoken to him earlier in the evening, pretending that the fictitious Wiedemann was screaming for the Klaus Bauer dossier.

"I'm doing all I can," Koch had pleaded, "but I'll need more time."

Langendorf had to bite his tongue to keep the angry frustration from his voice, remembering that now he was speaking as a Hauptsturmfuehrer and not a senior officer.

"How much more?"

"It's impossible to say. It could be found in another ten minutes, it could take another day."

"Another day! Christ, man, we'll be knee-deep in goddamn Russians in another day."

"It can't be helped. Things are chaotic down here. I'll speak to the Brigadefuehrer himself if you like."

"No, don't do that," said Langendorf hastily. "It's better that I handle him. But can I tell him that a further twenty-four hours is the upper limit?"

"You can tell him we're doing all we can."

Himmler's betrayal finally convinced Hitler that Berlin and the Third Reich were doomed, that there could be no eleventh-hour miracle by Battle Group Steiner or General Wenck. But shortly after midnight on April 28/29, with one of those sudden changes of mood which used to leave opponents and allies alike reeling, he declared that Wenck stood a chance of breaking through if every available aircraft were used to cover his approach.

With this in mind he ordered Ritter von Greim to fly to Rechlin airport and muster the planes from there. Von Greim had been wounded on the flight in, and Hanna Reitsch had brought the Fieseler Storch down. Hitler suggested that she act as pilot going out, with Von Greim as passenger.

Von Greim said it would be impossible to reach Rechlin and that he preferred to die in the Bunker.

"As soldiers of the Reich, we have a duty to exhaust every possibility," Hitler reminded him. "It is the only chance of success remaining. We have to try it."

Hanna Reitsch was not convinced. "But what can be accomplished even if we get through?"

Hitler ignored the question and kept his eyes fixed on Von Greim. Even at this late hour he still retained something of the old hypnotic power—enough, anyway, to change Von Greim's mind.

"We are the only hope of those who remain here, Hanna," said the General. "Whatever the chances of success, we owe it to them to try. Perhaps we can't help, but we must try."

As Von Greim arose from his sickbed and began to dress, Hanna Reitsch burst into tears and begged to be allowed to stay. But Hitler had said his piece and that was an end to it.

Frau Goebbels, now with her husband and six children permanent residents of the Bunker, gave Hanna two letters to her son by a former marriage. Eva Braun also gave her one written to Frau Fegelein.

The Fieseler Storch had cracked an axle during landing, but an armored car brought Hanna Reitsch and Von Greim to an Arado 96 trainer, which was hidden near the Brandenburg Gate. Hanna taxied the aircraft down the East–West Axis and took off. At a hundred feet she was picked up by Russian searchlights and came under tremendous antiaircraft fire. But somehow her luck held, and she flew off into the night.

With Hanna Reitsch and Von Greim gone, Hitler's mood reverted to pessimism. He was again convinced that the Third Reich was doomed, and in a fit of absurd sentimentality resolved to reward his faithful mistress with the marriage she had always wanted.

A minor official, appropriately named Wagner, was found in a nearby *Volkssturm* unit and the marriage ceremony performed. With Goebbels and Bormann present as witnesses, both Hitler and Eva Braun swore that they were of pure Aryan descent and were free of any impediments to marriage.

Later Hitler invited Bormann, Goebbels, Frau Goebbels and his secretaries, Frau Christian and Frau Junge, to his quarters for champagne. Others joined the party from time to time, but after an hour the Fuehrer retired to another room and began dictating his political testament and his will to Frau Junge.

In the testament he blamed everyone but himself for the war and the misery it had caused. International statesmen who either were Jewish in origin or worked for Jewish interests were at fault; so were the English, who had forced him to invade Poland because a political clique in that country wanted war for commercial reasons.

Frau Junge dated the document 0400 hours 29 April 1945.

In his personal will he left his possessions to the Party or, if the Party no longer existed, to the State. To his relatives he left everything that was of value as personal mementos or could be used to maintain their middle-class standard of living. He concluded: "My wife and I choose to die in order to escape the shame of overthrow or capitulation. It is our wish that our bodies be burned in the place where I have performed the greater part of my daily work during the twelve years of service to my people."

By midafternoon on the twenty-ninth, Russian ground forces were within a mile of the Chancellery, though every inch of terrain gained was done so against fierce SS opposition. Overhead, RAF Spitfires and Soviet Air Force Yaks eyed each other suspiciously, while those in the Bunker were preparing for the end.

Hitler's favorite dog, the Alsatian Blondi, was poisoned, and the two other dogs shot. Hitler himself supplied cyanide capsules to Frau Junge and Frau Christian and apologized for the inadequacy of his parting gift. He praised their courage and their loyalty; it was a pity, he added, that his generals lacked those very same qualities.

One of the Goebbels children came in and announced that the artillery bombardment had stopped and wasn't that good? Frau Junge patted his head and nodded, unable to tell the boy that if the Russians had stopped shelling, their ground troops must be very close indeed.

At the lower end of Markgrafenstrasse, Lassiter's party too had heard the artillery barrage cease, and none of them had to be told the significance of this new and sudden silence. They had no way of knowing how close the Russians were, that forward units were within five hundred yards of their hideout, though advancing en masse at no greater rate, for the time being, than thirty or forty yards an hour. Not that there was much they could have done had they known. Kordt had promised to be back for them by the evening of the twenty-ninth at the latest, and it was now only 5 o'clock. They would have to sit it out.

In the event, Lassiter had opted not to tell Sara of the possibility that there was an enemy agent among them. There would be nothing she or anyone else could do about it if the agent decided to kill Valkyrie on sight, though Lassiter doubted that that was to be the modus operandi. More likely, the agent would try to steer them, one way or another, toward a Soviet patrol. Whoever Valkyrie was, the Russians would much prefer him alive.

It was typical of Hauptsturmfuehrer Koch that he stuck to his task until the last. He was a young man, a year younger than Langendorf, and in spite of his rank and the SS runes on his collar, he had never fired a shot in anger.

In the early days, when the three premier SS divisions of Leibstandarte Adolf Hitler, Das Reich and Totenkopf were formed, he would not have qualified for entry. Men had to be over six feet tall and in perfect health. There were stories of would-be recruits being rejected for having a single filling in an otherwise perfect set of teeth. Koch would have been disqualified on both counts; he was a millimeter under five feet ten inches and had a mouthful of fillings.

But gradually the rules of entry had changed. With the SS taking some fearful beatings in the various eastern campaigns, officers who had hitherto occupied desk jobs were transferred to fighting units. The resultant gaps were filled by men like Koch. It had still taken pull and some bribery, but for a man who, prior to joining up, had worked as a clerk in an ordnance factory, anything to don the uniform of an elite corps and be given a rank equivalent to that of captain was worth the effort.

He would always be a clerk, of course, through and through, but somebody had to do the job, and there was no doubt of its importance. Prior to the last few weeks he had prided himself on always keeping his files in meticulous order; the Gestapo or the SD could usually have whatever they were looking for within minutes. But recently it had been bedlam. Apart from his being compelled, for security reasons, to take up temporary residence in the cellars of Gestapo HQ, a constant flow of directives were being issued from above. Burn this; see that Gruppenfuehrer so-and-so receives that; microfilm the card index system. It was little wonder it had taken him so long to find the documents Langendorf wanted.

Many of Koch's superiors had already left the building to fight whatever last-ditch battles were to be fought in and around the Chancellery Bunker complexes. Prinz Albrecht-strasse was directly in line with the Russian push from the south, but Koch wasn't worried. He'd been told that it would be the early hours of the thirtieth before the Russians actually overran Gestapo HQ, which gave him plenty of time.

Most of the files to be transferred to safer surroundings had already gone. Those to be burned as incriminating were in cardboard boxes, ready for the incinerators. It was part of Koch's task to glance quickly through them before consigning them to the flames, to ensure that nothing was burned which would be required sometime in the near future. Like many SS officers, Koch did not believe that Russian entry into Berlin signified the end of the war; it was the end of a battle, no more. When the new Germany rose from the ashes of the old, records would be needed as a cornerstone.

It was by doing his job with the utmost efficiency, therefore, that Koch had come across the Bauer documents a few minutes ago.

He had found them quite by accident, while examining the file of Sturmbannfuehrer Walther Kordt. He and Kordt came from the same town in Lower Saxony, and it was Kordt who had

232

actually sponsored Koch's entry into the SS. It was repaying a favor, therefore, to see that Kordt's service record never fell into the hands of the enemy.

But human nature being what it is, Koch flicked through the file from cover to cover, to see if there was anything written about his sponsor that he did not already know. And attached to the last pages by a paper clip was the information Langendorf wanted so desperately. No wonder they had searched in vain for it! Just because Kordt had authorized the phony documents in the name of Bauer, some fool had attached the whole file to Kordt's own.

Nevertheless, Koch was still puzzled. While fake documents were nothing new, the usual procedure was to have the request countersigned by a ranking officer in Amt III, which had not happened here. Then he saw the scrawling signature of Kordt's boss. Well, that solved the problem. No one was going to question *his* authority.

Ringing Langendorf's extension on the internal telephone system produced no response, and Koch was aware that most if not all the lines were down between Prinz Albrechtstrasse and the Chancellery, which was the other place Langendorf would be found. The Bauer papers would have to be delivered by hand.

He glanced around the room. He still had six troopers and an Unterscharfuehrer working for him, and any one of them, if he was any judge, would be only too happy to get to the relative safety of the Chancellery. But it would have to be the Unterscharfuehrer. He didn't like losing his one senior NCO, but he was a safer bet to get through than the youngsters.

He placed the papers in a brown envelope, hoping that Langendorf's superior, Brigadefuehrer Wiedemann, would understand the delay and appreciate the diligence of the Records Section.

After scribbling Langendorf's name on the envelope, he handed the package to Unterscharfuehrer Lorenz.

"You're to deliver these papers at once to Hauptsturmfuehrer Langendorf. You'll probably find him somewhere in the vicinity of the main Bunker."

Lorenz did not look at all happy about making the run on his own. The area around the Chancellery, now known as the Citadel, was heavily guarded and barricaded, thick with troops ready to shoot first and establish the identity of the corpse later. Besides, although the artillery had ceased firing, there were still dozens of Soviet T-34 tanks on the prowl, blasting all kinds of hell out of anything that moved in order to give the following infantry an easier passage. But he judged that it was foolish to look a gift horse in the mouth; he was being given a chance to quit this death trap, and he should take it.

Up to a point, he judged correctly. Willfully or otherwise, Koch's superiors had misinformed him about the speed of the Russian advance. Within the hour, while he and his SS troopers were still working furiously, a forward unit of Konev's First Ukrainian Front occupied what remained of the upper level of Gestapo HQ. Forty minutes later they were in the cellars, and soon the corridors echoed and reechoed with the noise of fragmentation grenades and submachine-gun fire.

Koch and the others stood no chance. They put up as spirited a fight as their limited experience of infantry close-quarters tactics would allow, but to no avail. A bazooka fired at point-blank range took the door off their room and stunned the occupants. Moments later, a couple of bearded infantrymen appeared. They grinned happily before killing everyone in sight.

Not that Unterscharfuehrer Lorenz had it all his own way. More often than he later cared to remember, he was pinned down in the crossfire between his own people and the handful of Russian snipers who were in the van of the assault. Hauptsturmfuehrer Koch was already dead by the time Lorenz seized his chance and charged at the command post in Potsdamerplatz, screaming that he was a friend.

Willing hands helped him to his feet. His machine pistol was taken from him and in its place he was given a rifle.

"Here, you'll do better with this until they're a hell of a lot closer." The speaker was a bedraggled Obersturmbannfuehrer.

Lorenz realized he was being asked to man the barricades. He waved the envelope in the Obersturmbannfuehrer's face.

"But I have an urgent message to deliver."

"So have we all, sonny, so have we all. But you don't win wars with love letters. I need you here."

"But Herr Ober—"

"Don't argue with me. Put the damn thing in your pocket and hang on to it. We'll be pushed back sooner or later; then you can deliver your letter."

And so it was that a few more hours would have to pass before Langendorf received the envelope with his name on it, though in the meantime he had another matter to occupy his mind.

During his week on the run, Sturmmann Fritz Eismann, in the pilfered clothes of a dead German civilian, had tried every way he knew to get out of the beleaguered city. It was hopeless; the Russians had it sewn up and were killing military and civilian alike.

His food and water had not lasted long, and eventually, unshaven and half-starved, he was found by a Special Patrol Group. He had no papers to justify his civilian status, of course, and the customary treatment for deserters (as Eismann well knew) was a stretched neck. In desperation he tried a bluff, telling his captors that he was on a secret mission for Hauptsturmfuehrer Langendorf of the SD. He knew that Langendorf would show him no mercy, but it was always possible that his friend Zimmer could somehow intercede in his behalf or that the SD officer was already dead. In either event he had nothing to lose. The patrol would kill him unless they received verification of his story.

There were still some telephone links open between the inner defense sectors and the Bunker, particularly north of the East–West Axis, where Zhukov's forces were closing at a slower rate than those of Konev in the south. It was therefore a little after 9 P.M. on the twenty-ninth that Langendorf received the call telling him that Eismann was under arrest as a deserter but had pleaded that he was on a secret mission for the SD. What should be done with him?

Langendorf was in a murderous mood. He had just learned that the Russians had overrun Prinz Albrechtstrasse, and he had no way of knowing whether Koch had got out in time, with or without the Bauer dossier.

The SD officer's temporary base of operations was one of the lumber rooms on the upper level of the Bunker. Although strictly speaking Langendorf belonged neither to Brigadefueh-rer Rattenhuber's *Reichssicherheitsdienst*, the military guard allocated to the personal protection of top Nazi leaders, nor to Franz Schedle's *Fuehrerbegleitkommando*, whose main function was to guard official buildings and the like, the Chancellery and the Bunker included, there was a great deal of overlapping of duties and authority in the latter days of the Third Reich. Langendorf had served, at one time or another, under both Rattenhuber and Schedle. He had walked the corridors of power and wielded much of it for so long that he had had no trouble at all in commandeering one of the lumber rooms for his own use as well as that of his men. It was here that he received the call from the patrol.

What should be done with Eismann?

He decided, just for the fun of it, to ask the advice of Scheller and Zimmer. There were others in the room, all hard-core SS men whose day of reckoning was about to come, but Scheller, Zimmer, Eismann and himself had all been on Special Patrols together. Besides, it would be interesting to see their different reactions.

Scheller's was immediate. "Tell them to hang him," he said.

Zimmer hesitated. "He's been through a lot, Herr Hauptsturm-fuehrer."

"So have we all. He is a coward and a traitor who has broken his oath of allegiance to the Fuehrer. Are you suggesting I let him live?"

"It's not my decision."

"Quite correct. Hang him," said Langendorf into the telephone. "His story is a pack of lies. He is a deserter. Hang him, and hang him very high."

Zimmer turned away, sick to his stomach. Langendorf had passed the death sentence and there was nothing to be done about it—except for one thing. When the time came, the SD officer would also be condemned, and the executioner would be Ernst Zimmer.

General of Artillery Helmuth Weidling, overall military commander of the overage *Volkssturm* and the underage Hitler

Youth, was the chief speaker at the Fuehrer conference that began at 10 P.M. on the twenty-ninth. Known as "Bony Karl" to associates and subordinates alike, he insisted that there were only two options open to the Fuehrer: flight or capitulation. He spoke of bitter, hopeless battles in the streets; his "paper" divisions were little more than battalions. Morale was poor and ammunition virtually exhausted. He concluded that the battle for Berlin would be all over by the following evening.

In the midst of all this, Sturmbannfuehrer Walther Kordt slipped away from the Bunker via the Foreign Office garden exit. He was quite frankly scared out of his wits. Soviet tanks had been reported approaching Potsdamerplatz and also in line abreast just south of Leipzigerstrasse. Their objective was obviously the three main north–south arteries of the city: Wilhelmstrasse, Friedrichstrasse and Markgrafenstrasse.

A political appointee as opposed to a soldier, he nevertheless knew that the phrase "line abreast" did not mean a cavalry charge. The squadrons of T-34s would not be advancing along a perfect horizontal. Some would be ahead, some behind. None would wish to get too far in front of his fellows for fear of counterattack and encirclement, and every meter of ground would be defended fiercely. This was the *Heimat*, the Homeland. It would not be given to the Ivans without a lot of blood being spilled.

Wearing a *Stahlhelm* as protection against shrapnel and falling debris, he stopped at the northern side of Wilhelmplatz, the junction of Wilhelmstrasse and Leipzigerstrasse. It seemed safe enough. There was a hell of a racket going on, of course, as if the world were coming to an end, but he had not expected a Sunday-afternoon stroll through the prewar Tiergarten. The fires made the surrounding streets as bright as day, but straight along Leipzigerstrasse was the most direct route to Markgrafenstrasse and the British commandos.

He counted to ten, ran forward a few paces, then ducked back at the sound and flash of a massive explosion somewhere over to his right. It was a delayed-action land mine, but he was not to know that. Neither was he to know that at its distance, it could not have done him any harm. Ducking back was a mistake, and it was to be his last.

Had he kept running, as a trained combat soldier would have done once the decision was made, the Soviet sniper seventy yards away on the other side of Leipzigerstrasse would not have had time to recognize the unmistakable shape of the *Stahlhelm* and draw a bead on the shadows in which Kordt was hidden. As it was, when Kordt made his next move some thirty seconds later, the Russian had a shot a raw recruit could have made.

The first round from the 7.62-millimeter SKS carbine smashed into Kordt's chest and probably killed him instantly. But for good measure the sniper put three more rounds into the prostrate figure, one through the head, from which the *Stahlhelm* had now fallen.

Kordt's hesitation had cost him his life, but he had been living on borrowed time anyway.

Much more to the point, the link between Valkyrie and Lassiter no longer existed.

TWENTY-SIX

It was just after midnight on the thirtieth when Dunbar stated the obvious: that Kordt wasn't coming. Only Sara Ferguson seemed prepared to challenge his prediction, offer an alternative explanation.

"He could have been held up. We're well below ground level, but we can hear what it's like up there—and it's a hell of a sight worse than it was two days ago. Berlin's not London. You can't expect the buses to run on time."

"You can't do that in London either," said Gallagher, "war or no war."

His remark broke the tension, and one or two tired grins were seen for the first time in sixty hours. They didn't last long. It had escaped none of them that if Kordt failed to put in an appearance, they were in trouble with a capital T.

"Let's not hit the panic button yet," suggested Lassiter. "Another hour's not going to make that much difference."

But by 1 A.M. he too had accepted the inevitable. Kordt was either dead or delayed indefinitely for reasons they could only guess at.

"All right," he said, "we can't hang around here any longer. We don't know exactly where the Russians are, but you can bet your life their ground troops and tanks are heading in this direction. We're only a stone's throw from the Chancellery, and that'll be their number one target. It's also ours. If Kordt's dead or captured, we've got to find out who he was working for, whose staff he was on; who, in other words, Valkyrie is. Don't get me wrong. I'm not doing this just for the sake of the mission. Valkyrie's the only one who has some sort of route out of this nuthouse. If we don't find him, we don't make it."

He allowed the implications of his words to sink in. Scipioni thought one of them was going mad, and he wanted to make sure it wasn't he.

"Let me get this straight. Are you trying to tell me that we march right up to the Chancellery, even if we can get inside the cordon, and start asking a few guys who Kordt worked for?"

"I'm saying more than that. The Chancellery itself is in ruins; we saw that much the morning we met Kordt. We're going underground, into the main Bunker itself."

"Jesus Christ, let me off—"

"Figure it out for yourself," Lassiter interrupted him. "We know from intelligence reports that there's not just one bunker but a dozen or more, scattered under the Foreign Office and the Propaganda Ministry as well as beneath the Chancellery. But the man we want is top brass, which means that wherever Hitler is, he won't be far away. He's not going to be at the barricades waving a machine pistol. Wherever Hitler is, that's where we'll find Valkyrie."

Chuck Fodor was shaking his head. "We won't stand a chance. The entrances will be guarded by half the SS."

"Not on your life," retorted Lassiter. "The SS are having their work cut out defending the area itself. They can't afford more than a handful of men for guard duties. Besides, you're forgetting something." He tapped the rank insignia on his collar. "We're SS ourselves as far as anyone else is concerned. They're not going to stop their own, but if necessary we'll bluff or blast our way through."

"Anyway," said Dunbar, "what alternatives do we have? We stay here and sooner or later we get blown to hell. At least outside we stand a chance."

"What about Sara?" asked Scipioni.

"I've got my Gestapo papers, and nobody's going to be questioning those. This is not Berlin 1940, remember; this is Berlin 1945 with the writing on the wall and the Vandals at the gates. The famed German efficiency is not going to be functioning the way it used to."

"We're forgetting something else." Maclean said so little for the most part that it was easy to overlook the fact that he missed nothing and spoke only when he had something to contribute. "Not all of us can go."

Lassiter told him to spell it out.

Maclean chose his words carefully. "We're assuming that Kordt is either dead or captured; but what happens if he's been delayed for some perfectly legitimate reason and doesn't get here for another couple of hours, possibly not until morning? Not all of us can stay on such a supposition, I agree, but one of us should. If he arrives back to find us gone, he'll panic—you saw what he was like under that artillery barrage. He might think we've cut and run."

"Shit," said Lassiter—but Maclean was right, of course. Someone would have to stay behind. For that matter, there would have to be two of them.

Fodor took the words from his mouth. "One won't be enough. Apart from the usual reasons of each man being able to watch the other's back, if by some chance Kordt turns up, it'll take at least two to get him out in one piece. I don't know whether any of you other guys noticed it, but it didn't look to me as though he'd carried a rifle in years."

There was a long silence. Each of them knew that the two to be left behind stood little chance of survival. Unless Kordt turned up—and none of them now believed he would, but it was a hundred-to-one bet that had to be covered—their funk hole would eventually be overrun by the Russians. They could not plead that they were Allied troops on a special mission, because that mission was aimed against the Russians. Neither could they surrender; they were dressed in Waffen SS uniforms, and the Soviets would remember only too well the carnage the SS had wreaked in the east. They would fight and then they would die.

"Anyone got any straws?" asked Scipioni casually.

They looked at Lassiter. He was their commander and his the final say on any major decision.

"Give me a minute," he said.

By rights he should exercise the power of command and make a choice, disregarding the melodrama of a lottery. But these people were his friends and comrades. Gallagher he had known for years; Maclean and Dunbar he had served with on countless occasions. The two Americans he knew less well, but they were brave men and he couldn't condemn them to death just because they were newcomers. As for Sara, she was special in many ways.

Friends and comrades, had he said? Yes—all but one. And it was because of the one who might turn out to be an enemy agent that he, Lassiter, could not be among those who remained. Under normal circumstances he might have considered it and taken his chances in the funk hole, but now that was out of the question; he had to be among those who went. So, for that matter, did Sara. That she was a woman—and an extraordinarily courageous woman at that—had nothing to do with it. She was carrying the documents of immunity for Valkyrie and was the only one who would recognize him as being the genuine article.

There was another consideration also. Whether he liked it or not and whatever Greenleigh's suspicions, this was an Anglo-American operation. However the choice was made, only one American stayed behind.

"We'll do it by lot," he said finally, "a draw from a hat. Neither Sara nor I will participate, but if it happens that Major Fodor and Lieutenant Scipioni are nominated, we draw again. Only one American remains."

No one objected to the fairness of this, but it was left to Scipioni to have the last word.

"You don't have to worry about us. We're used to fighting rearguard actions for the British. And that's a joke, for Chrissake."

Lassiter ejected five cartridges from his MP 38 and scratched a mark with his sheath knife on two of the casings. This done, he put all five cartridges in his *Feldmütze*, his field cap.

"Anyone want to go first?"

Dunbar stepped forward and rummaged in the cap. His casing was unmarked. Fodor went next; he too drew a blank.

"You get better odds shooting craps in Vegas," said Scipioni, and promptly drew one of the marked casings. "See what I mean?"

Maclean pulled a zero, and Gallagher waived the right to examine the last casing. Lassiter showed it to him anyway.

They had wasted enough time on the absent Kordt, and there was no more to spare. In any case, two men were being condemned to almost certain death, and there wasn't a hell of a lot anyone could say about that. Except one thing: if Scipioni was working for the Russians, wouldn't he have kicked up a hell of a fuss at being left behind? And if he was not, did that mean Fodor was?

Dunbar and Maclean were already at the top of the short flight of stairs, shoulders against the door, which seemed partly blocked by debris. Sara and Fodor were crowding their heels.

Last to go up, Lassiter said, "I can't give you any real advice. If Kordt turns up, make for the Chancellery area. That's where we'll be."

"And if he doesn't," said Gallagher, "I'm going to start practicing saying 'Stalin is a genius' in Russian."

They had the door open now.

"Shake it up, for Chrissake," shouted Fodor. "It's like Coney fucking Island out here."

Lassiter half held out his hand, then changed his mind. He nodded curtly and was gone. The heavy door swung shut.

Scipioni turned to Gallagher. "You don't happen to have a deck of cards, do you?"

There was nothing that could even remotely be termed a front line any longer, and it took them a dozen hours to cover the three-quarters of a mile which separated Markgrafenstrasse from Wilhelmstrasse and the east side of the Chancellery. Apart from the ever-present danger of Soviet tanks, marauding at will south of Leipzigerstrasse, Russian forward troops were advancing—if that expression can be used for a few houses at a time—in broken columns. Here and there, companies of Konev's First Ukrainian Front would be up to a hundred yards ahead of the companies on either side, creating a "bulge" effect, a head to be lopped off by the defending Germans whenever a counterattack could be mounted. Neither German nor Russian was much concerned about whom he shot at; anything that was not instantly identifiable as friendly was fired upon, and the Russians in particular seemed to have declared open season on everything north of Leipzigerstrasse. Konev's spearhead companies probably suffered as many casualties from his own light artillery as from anything the Germans threw at them.

Progress for Lassiter and the others was agonizingly slow. Although to begin with it was still night, the flames of Berlin made it as bright as day. Every mound of rubble was suspect, every glaring skeleton of a building a potential hide for a sniper. Sometimes they would cover a dozen yards in as many seconds; others they were pinned down for up to an hour.

Every moving figure was treated as an enemy because, to them, that was exactly what he was. On six or seven separate occasions one or another of them fired at and hit a man whose nationality they would never establish.

As always, the noise was appalling, the stench of death and decay ubiquitous. From all sides, even though it seemed impossible that anything could be heard above the tumult of artillery and small-arms fire, came the screams of the dying or those who were about to die.

After the first couple of hours the pattern of advance became automatic. Find cover, be it no more than a heap of bricks, scout visually the next stretch of ground, then go like hell until it was crossed. The order never changed either. First Lassiter, in case they were running into a Soviet machine-gun nest, then Sara, before any potential sniper suspected that there was more than one of them; Dunbar and Maclean next, going together, and Fodor, after a suitable interval, bringing up the rear.

Throughout it all Lassiter never ceased to be amazed at Sara's resilience. The noise alone, discounting the proximity of hidden, sudden death, was enough to reduce strong men to wrecks, but not once did she succumb to female frailties. After one hair-raising sprint, when she arrived behind him a split second before a heavy machine gun opened up, the bullets ricocheting off the wall behind which they were cowering, he took her hand, now bleeding in a dozen places, as if to reassure her. She snatched it away. A moment later she replaced it and squeezed his hard. He now fully understood why Greenleigh had selected her for this almost suicidal mission, and he resolved quietly, almost unconsciously, that he would see much more of her if they were both lucky enough to come out of this alive.

She seemed to understand his silent vow, and she held on to his hand until Dunbar came thundering up from behind.

Yard by yard, hour by hour, ruin by blazing ruin, they came

closer to the protected area surrounding the Chancellery. Daybreak came and went, but because of the choking smoke and dust they were hardly aware of it.

By midday they were within sight of Voss-strasse, the inner base of the defense triangle that surrounded the Chancellery. But the Soviet T-34 tanks in Potsdamerplatz were laying down such an umbrella of fire that to make a run for it would have meant almost certain death.

Even through the smoke they could easily see the German defense positions and the troops who manned them, mainly riflemen and machine gunners but with antitank teams spaced at intervals still keeping the T-34s and the Soviet infantry away from their final goal.

An hour went by. It could have been ten. Or ten seconds. They were all so unbearably tired and shell-shocked by now that time had lost all meaning.

Dunbar tapped Lassiter on the shoulder. "Look."

Lassiter saw where he was pointing, and what he saw told him that they could not afford to wait any longer. Behind them, retreating across ground they had spent all night covering, were men of the SS division Nordland. That could mean only one thing: that the Russians were breaking through in force. It was time to make their final move for the triangle and to hell with the T-34s. If they did not go now it was possible that the men behind the barricades had, or would shortly be given, orders not to let anyone through.

It involved a sprint of sixty or seventy yards, no more, to the nearest of the defense dugouts, and Lassiter quickly made up his mind that it was pointless to go across one after another, Indian file. They would go together, shit or bust.

There were no dissenters to this strategy; everyone was far too weary. Valkyrie or no Valkyrie, what they all now needed most was rest.

"On my signal," said Lassiter, bent like a runner at the starting line. "Anyone goes down, unless it's Sara, he's on his own. Sara, you stick by me."

He counted up to five for no reason he could later think of. *"Go!"*

It might have been sixty or seventy yards on paper, but it

seemed like six hundred; and because they were compelled to weave as they ran, they almost doubled the distance.

Maclean's long legs took him out in front almost immediately, and Fodor and Dunbar were only paces behind. But Lassiter had Sara to contend with, and that involved half-pulling, half-dragging her. Twice she stumbled, but twice he managed to keep her on her feet.

Halfway across he saw, to his horror, the German machine gunner in the dugout become aware of them and arc his weapon in their direction. He tried to shout, but no sound came from his throat. Then, to his relief, the barrel swung away as the gunner recognized the SS uniforms.

They were almost there when bullets began kicking up dust just ahead of them. This time the gunner was a Russian and they were running into his killing zone. But either he ran out of ammunition or his gun jammed, because as quickly as the enfilade started, it finished.

Lassiter saw Maclean leap into the dugout, followed by Dunbar and Fodor. He pushed Sara ahead of him. Hands reached up for her. Last through, he caught his foot as he jumped. As he fell he struck his head, and all he remembered before passing out was the voice of Obersturmbannfuehrer Harmel saying, "I don't know why you bothered."

TWENTY-SEVEN

When Lassiter regained consciousness he was indoors, lying on a mattress in a room approximately twenty feet square. It appeared as if two smaller rooms, originally divided by a central partition, had been knocked together for the sake of convenience.

There were other mattresses on the floor, and on them other men. Female workers (if they were nurses they wore no uniforms) were doing their best with makeshift bandages to staunch blood and dress burns. He learned later that this was the area where minor injuries were dealt with. There were no longer any facilities to help those with major wounds.

Gradually his eyes came fully into focus. Sara was seated at the foot of the mattress, looking at him anxiously. Nearby stood Fodor, Dunbar and Maclean, MP 38s at the ready, watching for trouble. Obersturmbannfuehrer Harmel, their acquaintance from Markgrafenstrasse, was crouched on his hunkers.

"How are you feeling now?" he asked.

Lassiter tried to lever himself up on his elbows, but couldn't make it. He sank back and took several deep breaths. "Lousy."

"That was quite a crack on the head you took, but fortunately it didn't break the skin. Still, you people from the Das Reich have to be heroes. If you'd been wearing a *Stahlhelm* you'd have just heard bells."

"How long have I been out and where are we?"

"You've been out about half an hour and you're in the upper level of the Chancellery Bunker, in what used to be the servants' quarters and various storage rooms, but which is now, in part, a temporary field hospital and rest center for the SS." He indicated Sara with a nod. "And their guests."

His attitude toward Sara was not now so hostile. He had seen her run across open ground under enemy fire, and that had to be a plus in anyone's book.

"Incidentally," Harmel went on, "several other rooms on this level are occupied by officers of the SD. I'd advise you to keep clear of them. When I use the word 'temporary' I mean exactly that. You'll be allowed a couple of hours here, no more. After that it's back to the barricades. By rights, the uninjured men should be there now, but Sturmbannfuehrer Knopf"—he gave Fodor's pseudonymous German name—"has told me that you've been on the run all night, and it's no use to anyone if you fall asleep when the Russians are launching a major attack. I suggest you use your couple of hours in getting some rest."

Lassiter had to ask the question. "We lost touch with several of our men out there." He gave the adopted German names of Scipioni and Gallagher and added that of Kordt. "I don't suppose they've turned up."

"I wouldn't know." Harmel frowned. "I thought I remember you saying that your group and Kordt met by accident during the bombardment a couple of days ago."

"True, but he attached himself to us with some story about needing an escort to the Chancellery, back to his commanding officer. But as he never told us who his commanding officer is, we've no idea if he made it."

Harmel laughed. "Then he fooled you, my friend. I don't know Kordt and I've no idea who his commanding officer is, but one thing I can tell you: he was not a fighting soldier. He was probably on somebody's political staff. But ask around; someone may know him and the fate of your other friends."

"I might do that," said Lassiter. "I've no wish to get on the wrong side of some high-ranking politico."

"I don't suppose it really matters now, does it?"

Harmel got to his feet and massaged his thighs.

"Do as I say and get some rest. You may not get much more, except in eternity. As for me, you will observe that I did not get back to the Nordland. Which is really of no consequence, as the Nordland has now come back to me."

After Harmel had gone, Lassiter beckoned the others closer. When he spoke, he did so in whispers.

"How the hell did we get in here?"

"It was a piece of cake," answered Dunbar. "After you cracked your head Harmel got a couple of troopers to bring us

248

straight in through the entrance from the Foreign Office garden. Nobody stopped us, nobody asked any questions."

"Mind you," put in Fodor, "this is only the upper level. I managed to pump Harmel a little while you were taking your beauty nap. From what I can gather, the real powerhouse is another twenty or thirty feet below. That's where the brass are."

"Then that's where we're going. But not yet. What time is it?"

"Coming up to three fifteen."

"Then I suggest we do as the man says," said Lassiter, "and grab some sleep. We're going to need it."

Fifty feet from where Lassiter lay, in the lumber room across the general dining passage, Langendorf sat at an upturned tea chest that was his desk and waited. There was little else he could do. Either Koch and the Bauer documents would turn up or they would not.

Nearby squatted Zimmer, Scheller and half a dozen troopers. If there was an arrest to be made, Langendorf was going to need assistance. If there was not, they could help when the Russians came. There were to be no miracle weapons. One way or another, this was the last battlefield.

Thirty feet below, the founder of the Third Reich had already come to the same conclusion.

At 3:30 P.M., in the anteroom to his suite, Adolf Hitler picked up a Walther pistol. Near him, Eva Braun was already dead, slumped across a couch, poisoned by cyanide. A second unfired Walther lay on the red carpet beside her.

Hitler sat at a table, in front of a portrait of Frederick the Great. He hesitated only briefly before putting the barrel of the pistol in his mouth and pulling the trigger.

Throughout the next hour Otto Günsche, Hitler's adjutant, Heinz Linge, his valet, and Erich Kempka, his chauffeur, took the bodies of Hitler and Eva Braun up four flights of stairs and out of the emergency exit to the Chancellery garden.

Hitler's corpse was wrapped in a brown blanket and was carried by Linge, assisted for part of the way by Dr. Stumpfegger, the Fuehrer's surgeon. Kempka and Günsche carried Eva Braun.

No sooner did they reach the garden than a further Russian artillery bombardment began, though it seemed that no further damage could be done to the shattered remains of the Chancellery.

Hitler's body was stretched out in a shallow depression just a few feet from the Bunker entrance, with Eva Braun on his right. After waiting for a lull in the barrage, Kempka seized a jerry can of gasoline and poured it over the bodies.

By now the barrage was so intense that it was impossible to get near the corpses to ignite the fuel. Someone suggested tossing in a hand grenade, but Kempka found the idea of blowing the dead Fuehrer and his wife to bits repugnant.

Eventually Günsche solved the problem by taking hold of a large piece of cloth, dousing it with gasoline and putting a match to it. Unmindful of the shelling, he ran toward the open grave and tossed in the blazing rag.

It was a small fire compared with others raging in Berlin, but to those who supervised it, from time to time rekindling it with further cans of fuel, it was the most horrific any of them had ever witnessed.

Fodor awoke without prompting at 5:30 P.M. He quickly shook the others into consciousness. Lassiter had a bump the size of a hen's egg on the back of his head, but was none the worse for all that. In fact, the short sleep had benefited them all.

Outside in the general dining passage of the upper Bunker, bedlam reigned. In part, it too was being used as a dressing station, and the place was crawling with SS men, some on their feet, some on mattresses, some on the bare floor.

To their left, the way they had come in, was a bulkhead, no longer serving its original purpose of keeping out dust and noise. Left beyond the bulkhead were the stairs that led to the Foreign Office garden; right led to the Foreign Office itself and what remained of the Chancellery. But they had no intention of going out the way they had come in. Their destination lay in the opposite direction, to the spiral staircase that led down to the

Fuehrerbunker. They were no longer entering the lion's den; they were going down his throat.

But no one was checking passes, no one asking for identification; mere presence seemed to confer legitimacy of purpose.

It was Sara who decided that they should try to establish the name of Kordt's master before proceeding to the lower level. If they could obtain it, they could demand to be taken to him.

"Someone's going to smell a rat if we start asking too many questions," hissed Fodor.

"Not at all." Sara had been keeping her ears open. As was quite natural in such a situation, many of the men, and some of the women who were acting as nurses, were making inquiries about friends or people they loved. Few of the newly wounded could give answers, of course, but that still didn't stop the questions.

"She's right," said Lassiter. "We'll split up into two groups. I'll go with Sara; you three stick together. We'll each take one side of the corridor."

They began at the end nearer the outer bulkhead, and no one seemed to think it the least odd that a pretty young woman (even the dirt and the grime and the cuts and lack of sleep could not detract from Sara's looks) was asking for news of Sturmbannfuehrer Walther Kordt. But in each case the answer was "no" or a resigned shake of the head.

On the other side of the corridor Fodor was doing most of the talking. Lassiter could hear the American asking, though with a perfect accent, for whereabouts of his cousin. In fact, he was paying too much attention to Fodor's group, for when he next glanced around Sara was several yards ahead, engaged in earnest conversation with a youthful Obersturmfuehrer.

He did not have to be told that she had found what she was looking for; the sudden tensing of her whole body told him that. But in the hubbub all he heard the Obersturmfuehrer say was "... Reichsleiter's staff ..."

And then Sara was beside him, her face and eyes glowing with excitement. "I know who Valkyrie is," she said.

A battalion of Konev's First Ukrainian Front had occupied Markgrafenstrasse hours before and were now engaged in mopping-up operations. The cellar door behind which Gallagher and Scipioni were hidden looked as if it hadn't been opened in weeks, but the fake girders were meant to fool only those in a hurry. Anyone making a thorough search would be bound to see through the ruse, as a Russian patrol did at 6 P.M. on the thirtieth.

Although Gallagher and Scipioni had spent sixteen hours in each other's company, they had scarcely spoken. Each had his own private thoughts, and the old adage about men facing death growing closer to each other proved to be a lie.

The fact that Kordt had not turned up surprised neither of them. He could not have got through anyway. Since midmorning they had listened to the rumble of tanks overhead. They would not be German tanks.

The most they could hope for now was to be overlooked. In a few days, perhaps weeks, when the Soviet lust for blood had abated, they could make their escape. They had food and water aplenty. All they needed was luck and time.

It was not to be.

The Soviet corporal of the patrol was used to finding rats in cellars, and as one who had lost a mother, wife and sisters to the Germans in earlier years, he was prepared to miss no opportunity for revenge.

He felt the girders and found them to be false. He tried the door and discovered it to be locked or jammed.

No problem. There might be nothing down there but a few mice nibbling crumbs, but they were, after all, German mice.

He shattered the door with a burst from his submachine gun. When it hung from its hinges he threw in two grenades.

It would be fitting to say that Gallagher and Scipioni died nobly, if there is any nobility in death. But they were merely torn to pieces by the blast and fragments of shrapnel.

Unterscharfuehrer Lorenz, bearer of the message from Koch to Langendorf, also met his end at approximately the same time. In spite of being essentially a noncombatant, he had manned his few meters of barricade in Potsdamerplatz courageously until the advancing T-34s made the position untenable.

The Obersturmbannfuehrer who had commandeered his services as a rifleman in the first place ordered the unit to retreat to its secondary defense positions, but unaccustomed to moving at speed under fire, Lorenz was slower than the rest. Even so, he was within a few feet of the safety of the rear dugout when a T-34's machine gun picked him off.

They pulled him inside the dugout, but he was already dead.

The Obersturmbannfuehrer spotted the brown envelope protruding from Lorenz' pocket and saw that it was addressed to Hauptsturmfuehrer Langendorf. He put it inside his tunic for safety. He knew Langendorf vaguely by sight, knew him to be SD with quarters somewhere in the Bunker. He would deliver it himself if he got the chance. The way things were going, they would all be inside the Bunker within the next twenty-four hours.

Flanked by the others, Sara made for the spiral staircase that led down to the *Fuehrerbunker*. Apart from telling Lassiter that she now knew the identity of Valkyrie, she had said nothing. Lassiter was content to let her get on with it; the explanations would come soon enough.

At the head of the staircase they were confronted by two NCOs of Rattenhuber's *Reichssicherheitsdienst*, carrying machine pistols. But news, or at least hard rumor, was already spreading of Hitler's death and neither of the men was prepared to do his duty in more than a perfunctory manner, especially when faced with their own kind, troops of the Waffen SS.

"We have urgent business with the Reichsleiter."

Sara flashed her Gestapo papers. They were barely glanced at.

At the foot of the staircase they went through the same procedure. Again they were waved through without comment or hindrance.

The lower level of the Bunker was larger than the upper, the central corridor wider. But this too was thronged with SS troops and senior officials. Incredibly, unreally, Lassiter saw the diminutive figure of Josef Goebbels arguing with several high-ranking SS officers, and for a second he thought: Is this Valkyrie?

But Sara pressed on, apparently making for three men who

were standing on the near side of the partition that separated the general area of the *Fuehrerbunker* from the late Adolf Hitler's private quarters. Two of the men were Rattenhuber himself and Brigadefuehrer Mohnke, commander of the Citadel. Both appeared to have been crying, and it was to the third that Sara addressed herself, in spite of the fact that half a dozen SS troopers tried to intervene.

"Herr Reichsleiter . . . !"

The man turned to face her. He was below average height and round-faced. He was also wearing civilian clothes.

His eyes narrowed when he saw he was being spoken to by a woman, but that sixth or seventh sense which had kept him alive throughout a score of Machiavellian intrigues recognized her for what she was. He elbowed the troopers aside and came over.

"Yes?"

Sara caught her breath. "Herr Reichsleiter," she repeated, "Sturmbannfuehrer Kordt, you will be distressed to learn, did not keep his appointment, but Mercury did."

The man glanced from Sara to Lassiter, and from Lassiter to Fodor, Dunbar and Maclean.

"You'd better come with me," said Martin Bormann.

TWENTY-EIGHT

They were in one of the rooms on the northwest side of the *Fuehrerbunker* previously occupied by Dr. Stumpfegger. Bormann had assured them that Stumpfegger was in the process of preparing his escape; they would not be disturbed.

For the moment, they were alone. The Reichsleiter still had business in the corridor.

It was only now that Sara was beginning to realize why Greenleigh had chosen her as courier. Not more than a dozen British agents would have recognized the Deputy Leader of the Nazi Party, for outside Germany, and to a large extent inside it, his face was relatively unknown.

Quickly she went over what she remembered of the man from the intelligence files, filling in the gaps for Lassiter and the others as she went along.

He was in his mid-forties and something of a prolific father, he and his wife, Gerda, having produced ten children. There were also reports, though unconfirmed, that he and Gerda had something of a peculiar sexual relationship. Bormann was far from faithful to his wife and frequently wrote to her about his experiences with other women.

The records indicated that he was a confirmed atheist and had probably been drawn to National Socialism by its denunciation of the Church. Its nationalism had also appealed, of course, as well as the chance for personal advancement. While assistant to Rudolf Hess, he had played a minor role, and even later he had shunned publicity, spurning decorations and public honors which others grabbed by the handful. Photographs of him were rare; the half-dozen in the possession of SOE showed him as a mysterious figure, always in the background.

Yet of his power there was little doubt. Intelligence résumés had it—and doubtless postwar research would confirm—that as Number Two in the hierarchy he virtually controlled what documents Hitler saw. Everything was filtered through Bormann, and it was more than possible that he knew more than his master.

In looks he was short and heavyset, with a weight lifter's thick neck. His face was round but with prominent cheekbones and broad nostrils. His thin hair was combed straight back, and his eyes were cunning. There was little doubt that one of his major qualities would be brutality, though the total effect given —the sum of the manifold parts—was one of colorlessness.

Sara was about to describe his probable relationship with other Party leaders when the Reichsleiter returned. He stood with his back against the closed door.

"You have been extremely clever and resourceful," he told them. "When Kordt failed to return I felt sure he had been killed en route and that the whole operation was a failure. I see now that you were chosen well for this particularly difficult task, and I congratulate you on the successful completion of phase one. But now to phase two. You have some documents for me, I believe," he said to Sara, assuming correctly that the woman must be the courier.

Sara glanced at Lassiter, who nodded. Bormann noticed the exchange. Two of the men in front of him carried the rank of Sturmbannfuehrer, but it was obviously the harder-looking of the pair who was the leader. It was something to know.

Sara handed over a small sealed wallet wrapped in waterproof material. Bormann tore off the wrapper and broke the seal. He extracted several sheets of paper and flicked quickly through the contents before dropping his eyes to the signatures.

"These appear to be in order, but you will appreciate that I must check at least the signatures against documents I have in my own private files. In the meantme I suggest you get some rest and perhaps fortify yourselves with a little brandy." He pointed to a table that was littered with bottles and glasses. "No one will disturb you, not even Stumpfegger. I shall post an SS guard on the door with instructions that no one is to be allowed to enter."

But Lassiter had had enough of these niceties—the congratulations on a job well done, the offer of rest and brandy. In front of him stood the man who, at least in part, was responsible for the deaths of his wife and children. If he stayed in the same room with this apelike figure for much longer, he might be tempted to forget about the mission and blow the man to hell.

When he spoke there was no respect in his voice, nothing but barely disguised contempt. Had Valkyrie turned out to be a senior German general with an impeccable war record, he might have offered the courtesies accorded to rank. But this baboon was a murderer by proxy, a mere politician.

"We'll decline the brandy and the rest, if you don't mind," he said coldly. "I don't know how long it is since you've been up-stairs, but the Russians have overrun your forward defense posts. Unless your escape route is foolproof, we may already be too late."

Bormann seemed amused. "You do not approve of me, Herr Sturmbannfuehrer."

"I have no opinions at all on the subject. I'm here to do a job, that's all, and the quicker I can do it and get it over with, the better I'll like it."

Bormann raised his eyebrows with rare humor. "Merely doing a job? Obeying orders? You see, you're not so very different from us after all."

"Different or not," put in Fodor, "the Russians are not going to wait while you pack your pajamas."

"No doubt you're right, although I am probably better quali-fied to comment on the dangers of the current military situation than you."

"*Current military situation!*" Dunbar was aghast. "There is no current military situation. It's a rout."

"Perhaps so, but that doesn't mean it's an *immediate* rout, even if, according to the latest reports, there is at least one Soviet unit at present on Wilhelmstrasse. The last battle will not be over in minutes or even hours. As soldiers you must know that you can hold a good defensive position for weeks."

"This is not a good defensive position," retorted Lassiter. "The Russians are doing to Berlin what you did to Warsaw. You're low on everything: food, water, ammunition, manpower, and most of all morale."

Bormann seemed unperturbed. "The SS can hold out for another twenty-four hours. They know only too well what will happen to them if they do not. Even the *Volkssturm* and the Hitler Youth have a nuisance value far beyond their military capabilities. It will be twenty-four, perhaps thirty-six hours before the Russians close in for the kill, and that's all I need."

Twenty-four hours. Lassiter thought he was dreaming.

Bormann read his mind.

"As you seem so nervous about being taken captive by the Ivans, Herr Sturmbannfuehrer," he said sarcastically, "perhaps a word or two of explanation would not go amiss. In the first place you should know, if you have not already guessed by the panic and tears displayed by those buffoons in the corridor, that our Fuehrer is dead."

He allowed this to sink in. It took some time. The others looked at each other with vacant, disbelieving expressions. It seemed impossible that the man who had occupied the waking thoughts of most of the world for six years was no more.

"It's no trick, I assure you," went on Bormann. "Hitler has not been spirited away to some secret hideout to plan his next campaign. He killed himself at approximately three thirty this afternoon. If he were not dead I would not be sitting here with you now, planning my escape. I must confess," he added in a matter-of-fact tone, "that I fully anticipated his suicide—but sooner. Which was why I had you brought in on the twenty-sixth. While he was alive I could not make my plans. Now that he is dead, things have changed."

"So why wait another twenty-four hours?" demanded Dunbar.

"You do not understand politics, Herr Hauptsturmfuehrer. In particular you do not understand the politics of the Third Reich. You are, if I may say so, a mere soldier, and if Special Operations is running true to form, your rank in the British Armed Forces is equivalent to the one you have assumed in the SS—that is, captain.

"Hitler may be dead, but Goebbels and other powerful men are still alive. In the case of Goebbels, I don't expect that state of affairs to last much longer, but others such as Rattenhuber,

258

Mohnke and so on—some of these men may be taken by the Russians. If I leave now and am not found alive—which I certainly intend to be the case—captured Germans would undoubtedly reveal under interrogation that I was not in the Bunker on its last day. What, then, will the Russians think? That I have escaped to the West, naturally. Any information that I then pass on to your SOE will be devalued. I am sure you are not totally aware why your government is willing to grant me immunity, but it is, in part, for what I can tell them about Soviet ambitions in Europe—intelligence that I have been collecting from various sources for years. If I leave before the general exodus from the Bunker, the Russians will simply alter or put forward their plans accordingly, and SOE will not give me safe-conduct for information it cannot use. It will make me quietly disappear.

"This operation is not something which has been thought up on the spur of the moment, believe me. Its planning has taken months, and its success must depend upon the mystery of my disappearance. The Russians can think what they like; they will have no proof."

"And no body, either," said Sara.

"My dear child . . ."

Bormann fixed Sara with his piglike eyes and she saw instantly why he had such reputed success with women. Physically he was repulsive, but there was also something fascinating about the man. Rabbits would see the same thing in a snake.

"My dear child, have you any idea how many corpses there are at present in Greater Berlin? Thousands, tens of thousands. No one is going to examine each cadaver to see if it's Martin Bormann."

There was a short silence before Lassiter asked, "When is the breakout to be?"

"All being well, tomorrow night. We shall be going out in groups, but that's no concern of yours. The details of the route I'll explain to you later."

"In uniform?" asked Fodor.

"To begin with, yes. It may appear that because the Citadel is surrounded, the battle is over. That's far from the case. There are still isolated pockets of resistance all over the city, and I

259

know broadly where they are. You will all, however, be issued civilian clothes—workmen's clothes—which you will put on at the appropriate time."

Bormann cocked his head and listened to some argument going on in the corridor.

"And now I must leave you for a while," he said. "There are still things to be done even at this late hour and my absence is not passing unnoticed. There are toilet facilities through there, and what food can be spared will be brought to you by the guards. Do not speak to them. They are under the impression you are bearers of important dispatches from Vienna."

Sara got to her feet. "The documents, Herr Reichsleiter," she said politely.

"I beg your pardon?"

"The documents of immunity. I think it would be better if I held on to them. You can verify the authenticity of the signatures later. After all, if I let them go now you will have no further need of us, will you?"

Bormann hesitated. "On the other hand," he said cunningly, "now that I know they exist I am assured of immunity anyway, am I not?"

"No, Herr Reichsleiter. Unless you have them in your possession, you have no protection."

Bormann passed them back, reluctantly. But there was a certain admiration in his voice when he said, "We could have used you on our side."

"I doubt that," retorted Sara. "I am not someone who can speak of tens of thousands of corpses as though they were match heads."

Alone, the others congratulated Sara on her quick thinking.

"I'd never have thought of asking for them back," said Fodor. "The bastard could have been halfway across Europe before morning."

The brandy was nearby and tempting, and Lassiter signaled to Dougal Maclean to pour for all of them. As usual, Maclean was watching everything, saying nothing.

Glasses in hand, they all drank quietly for several minutes, nursing their private thoughts. So much had happened in the last few days that sitting in the *Fuehrerbunker* no longer seemed unusual. And the news of Hitler's suicide was almost a nonevent.

"I still don't see why we have to stick around for another twenty-four hours," said Dunbar between swallows. "His explanation sounded plausible enough, but for my money we should head for the hills without delay."

"I'd like to head there without Bormann." Fodor tapped his MP 38. "We'd be doing a lot of people a lot of favors if we put a magazine through his fat hide the next time he shows his face. And repaying a few debts, too."

"We're making the world a better place for democracy— didn't you know that?" The bitterness in Lassiter's voice startled the others. He usually kept his feelings on a tight rein. "We've beaten the Germans and now Bormann's going to tell us how to keep the Russians at arm's length. Jesus Christ, it makes you sick. We're doing a deal with someone who's killed millions just because Greenleigh or Dulles or whoever the hell else is involved thinks it's expedient."

He walked over to the drinks table and helped himself to a massive refill.

"Talking about Dulles," said Fodor, "do you think he knows our side's in on this?"

"No," said Lassiter, "and let's keep it that way. If he finds out he might not want to play. His deal's with us; let him keep on believing it."

"Maybe we'll get lucky and they'll string him up quietly when they've got what they want from him," suggested Dunbar.

"Not a chance." Sara shook her head. "Whatever else he's offering apart from Russian territorial ambitions in Europe, he can make it last for years. A slice of information here, a wedge there. And he'll make damned sure these immunity documents are kept in a safe place, to be released to the world's press if he doesn't ring a certain Swiss bank once every six months. It wouldn't be difficult. He's a clever man."

"He's a fucking killer!" spat Lassiter. "All that crap about not leaving for twenty-four hours because he's got to wait for the general exodus. He's sold out and he doesn't want his Nazi pals to know about it. He doesn't want history to regard him as a traitor to the Cause. You can bet your life that right here and

261

now he's sending telegrams to every surviving commander, showing that he's sticking it out until the last. Sure he wants his extra day, but he's only telling us half the truth. You'd better keep an eye on me, the rest of you, because it's just possible I'll put a bullet in his back if I get a chance. He's already cost us enough."

"Like Scipioni and Gallagher," said Maclean quietly.

There was an uncomfortable silence. Because of the heat of events, the speed at which they'd moved, the rapidly changing pace of affairs, not one of them—with the obvious exception of the tall Scot—had given a thought to Scipioni or Gallagher for hours.

"Like Scipioni and Gallagher," agreed Lassiter, walking back to his seat.

"Do you think they're still alive?"

Lassiter thought of the marauding Russian forces outside, how they themselves had barely escaped being cut to ribbons. "No," he said. "No, I don't."

He closed his eyes. They had hours to spare, they were all short on sleep, and Christ knew when they'd get any once they left the Bunker.

While Lassiter and the others slept and the night of April 30 became the day of May 1, an emissary, General Hans Krebs, was dispatched from the Bunker to discuss some form of limited surrender with General Vasili Chuikov, commander of the Eighth Guards Army. Chuikov in turn phoned Zhukov, who said that nothing short of unconditional surrender was acceptable.

Krebs returned at noon with this ultimatum, to be raved at by Goebbels, who accused the general of misrepresenting his proposals to Zhukov. Scarcely anyone listened. One thing was now self-evidently clear, and General Weidling put it into words: "We must stick to our breakout plan. To continue the Battle of Berlin is absolutely impossible."

This eminently logical proposal was accepted by all but Goebbels. While the others made their preparations to escape, he prepared for death. To begin with he asked Dr. Stumpfegger to inject his six children with poison, but Stumpfegger would not have this on his conscience. Goebbels therefore began looking for another doctor among the civilian refugees and wounded on the upper level of the Bunker.

Long before he reached there, the Obersturmbannfuehrer now carrying the letter from Koch to Langendorf was brought in with a thigh wound and laid on a mattress in the general dining passage. Caused by a fragment of a Russian shell, the wound was far from serious, but the pain, in the absence of local anesthetics, enough to make him lose consciousness from time to time. And although he would never know it, a piece from the same shell had removed most of the face of Obersturmbannfuehrer Harmel, killing him instantly.

Late the same afternoon, Bormann sent the following message to Admiral Doenitz. With typical cunning, he persuaded Goebbels to act as cosignatory.

> THE FUEHRER DIED YESTERDAY AT 1530 HOURS. IN HIS
> WILL DATED 29 APRIL HE APPOINTS YOU AS PRESIDENT
> OF THE REICH, GOEBBELS AS REICH CHANCELLOR,
> BORMANN AS PARTY MINISTER. WILL, BY ORDER OF
> THE FUEHRER, IS BEING SENT TO FELDMARSCHALL
> SCHORNER AND OUT OF BERLIN FOR SAFE CUSTODY.
> FORM AND TIMING OF ANNOUNCEMENT TO THE
> ARMED FORCES AND THE PUBLIC IS LEFT TO YOUR
> DISCRETION. ACKNOWLEDGE.

This done, Bormann decided it was high time he paid another visit to his rescuers.

They had all had as much sleep and rest as they could use and were raring to go. But Bormann was determined to stick to his timetable.

"Everything is ready," he said, "for the breakout to commence at around 2100 hours. There was a suggestion that everyone leave together, but I quashed that for obvious reasons. There will now be six groups leaving at fifteen-minute intervals. Ours will be number three or four and it will comprise, for your own edification, Doctors Naumann and Stumpfegger, Goebbels' adjutant Schwägermann, Artur Axmann, the Youth Leader, and Standartenfuehrer Beetz, one of Hitler's personal pilots. Needless to say, we shall attempt to lose these individuals as soon as it becomes feasible.

"It is important that you have as little as possible to do with them while they are with us. One or two of them might be curious to know why we are taking along a woman and four lower-ranking members of the Das Reich. You will refuse to answer any questions, referring the interrogator to me.

"To begin with we shall make for the Underground station in Wilhelmplatz, and from there follow the tracks as far as the Friedrichstrasse station, where we shall regain the surface and attach ourselves to what remains of Mohnke's battle group, which is still holding that area. With its help we shall attempt to cross the River Spree. After that, we shall head west. There is more to it than that, of course, but for the moment it's all you need to know."

None of them required spelling out of Bormann's reasons for keeping the remainder of the route secret. While he was the only one who knew it, they would have to make damn sure he stayed alive and in one piece.

The Reichsleiter glanced at his wristwatch. In keeping with the man's personality, it was the sort that could have been bought cheaply at any store.

"It's now six fifteen. I shall return for you at eight fifteen, bringing with me your civilian clothes. Until then, you will remain here."

"It's not much of a plan," said Chuck Fodor, when the door was closed. "We could be picked off in half a dozen places."

"It's not that that worries me," said Lassiter. "It's just that I'm beginning to feel less and less like the leader of this expedition."

At 6:55, Hauptsturmfuehrer Langendorf stepped from the lumber room into the general dining passage to stretch his legs. His mind, of course, was on other things, and it was several seconds before he realized he was being waved at by an officer

264

lying half upright on a mattress. The man wore the collar insignia of an Obersturmbannfuehrer, and in his hand he held a long brown envelope.

Langendorf was inclined to ignore him. The time had come, Bauer documents or no Bauer documents, to be thinking of getting away from this death trap of a Bunker, but something about the man's persistence made him curious.

Stepping carefully between the wounded, he walked across.

"Herr Obersturmbannfuehrer?" He vaguely recognized the man from some dealings they'd had in the past. But Christ—how he'd aged.

"Hauptsturmfuehrer Langendorf, isn't it?"

"It is."

"Then this is for you."

He passed over the envelope. Langendorf saw his name on the front, but turned it over and over without opening it.

"Where did you get this?"

The Obersturmbannfuehrer explained that he had taken it from the body of a dead runner, but by this time Langendorf sensed, knew, what the contents were.

Without thanking the Obersturmbannfuehrer and without much regard for whom he was treading on, he made his way back to the lumber room and sat down at the tea chest. At last!

Zimmer, Scheller and one or two of the other troopers present stared at him curiously as he tore open the flap of the envelope and examined the documents inside. He read quickly, feverishly, ignoring the details and looking only for names, authorizations. Bauer . . . Sturmbannfuehrer Walther Kordt . . . and . . . and . . .

It wasn't possible. There had to be some mistake, some clumsy forgery. The traitor could not possibly be the Reichsleiter.

Dazed, he read every word. There was no mistake. There it was in black and white. The documents that had authorized the fake Bauer to contact British Intelligence were countersigned by Martin Bormann.

Neither Zimmer nor Scheller understood the expression of bemused hatred on Langendorf's face, though each was willing to put his own interpretation on it.

As far as Scheller was concerned, Langendorf had uncovered some plot against the regime and was debating what to do about it. An ignorant, uneducated man if a devoted Nazi, Scheller would wait for orders, wait to be told his part in the proceedings.

Zimmer too had come to broadly the same conclusion: that Langendorf was measuring someone's neck for a noose. He'd seen that look too often to misread it—except this time he was determined to do something about it. Anyone Langendorf considered an enemy must have some good in him, and for far too long he, Ernst Zimmer, had stood by while Langendorf carried out what he called his duty. It wasn't only for Eismann, but Langendorf would not play the role of executioner again. It was all over anyway—the dreams, the victories. All finished.

Zimmer did not consider himself to be a noble man, but he knew, somewhere deep inside him, that Langendorf had long ago lost all right to live.

When the SD officer got abruptly to his feet and gestured to everyone in the lumber room to follow him, Zimmer was therefore in no way surprised to hear himself say, "No."

Langendorf glared at him. "No? Are you disobeying an order, Zimmer?"

"I haven't heard an order yet, Herr Hauptsturmfuehrer—but yes, when it's given, I shall disobey it."

He had his machine pistol cocked, though still in the "rest" position. He was unconcerned about Langendorf; the Hauptsturmfuehrer's Walther was still in its holster, the holster fastened. But Scheller's submachine gun was at the ready.

It was not in Langendorf's character to waste time.

"Kill him, Scheller," he commanded.

Scheller pulled the trigger like the automaton he was, but Zimmer was much faster. His first burst took the Scharfuehrer in the upper chest and throat, killing him instantly and wounding one of the other troopers. Langendorf was still fumbling with his holster when he realized that he was next on the list.

"You don't understand—" he began.

"Only too well," said Zimmer, and shot him through the head.

There was still half a magazine left. While the remaining SS troopers were backing away, wondering what the madman would do next, Zimmer put the muzzle to his forehead and squeezed the trigger.

The shots had, of course, been heard in the corridor, and the door to the lumber room was flung open by an SD Standartenfuehrer.

"What the fucking hell's going on in here?"

One of the surviving troopers tried to explain by pointing at Zimmer. "Sir, this man suddenly went berserk and started shooting in all directions."

The Standartenfuehrer had heard it all before; it was his third case in as many days. The pressure was too much for some of them.

"Never mind about that. Get those bodies outside and get this place cleaned up."

The corpses of Zimmer, Scheller and Langendorf were taken away. The Bauer documents, covered with blood, were tossed, unread, onto a fire.

At 8:45 P.M. Obersturmbannfuehrer Erich Kempka, who was to lead one group of thirty women from the Bunker, said goodbye to Josef and Magda Goebbels. The children were already dead, poisoned. Goebbels had found someone to do his dirty work for him.

With macabre humor the clubfooted former Propaganda Minister said that he and his wife would walk up the four flights of steps to the Chancellery garden in order that their friends would not have to carry them. Rach, Goebbels' chauffeur, and Schwägermann, his adjutant, followed them halfway up the stairway.

A minute later they heard a shot, and then a second. Schwägermann and Rach raced for the top of the stairs. There they found an SS man staring open-mouthed at the corpses of the Goebbelses. On their instructions, he had shot them.

Schwägermann and Rach wasted no time. They poured several jerry cans of gasoline onto the bodies and ignited it. Then they returned to the conference room of the Bunker and set fire to that also. There was to be nothing left for the Russians to put in a museum.

As the flames began to bite into what had been the scene

of so much bitter argument and recrimination, Brigadefuehrer Mohnke and Sturmbannfuehrer Günsche led the first group out into the night.

Lassiter had just become aware of the smoke when Bormann reappeared. He flung each of them a canvas bag.

"Your civilian clothes are in there and the fifteen-minute departure rule has been waived. As your nostrils no doubt tell you, the Bunker is now on fire."

They followed him into the corridor. It was bedlam out there, but the moment there was no arguing; Bormann was in command. Lassiter stuck to him like a leech, one hand holding Sara's.

Hours later, none of them really remembered leaving the blazing Chancellery near the corner of Wilhelmstrasse and Voss-strasse, amid the crack of rifles, the chatter of machine guns, the omnipresent artillery barrage. They only vaguely recalled disappearing down the Wilhelmplatz subway entrance opposite the Hotel Kaiserhof, and they had little recollection of pushing and barging their way past terrified civilians and military alike who crowded the Underground railway lines.

When they eventually reemerged at ground level at the Friedrichstrasse station, Bormann in the lead wearing the uniform of an SS-Gruppenfuehrer, it was 2 A.M. It had taken them five hours to cover a mile, but this was only the beginning. As they surfaced they saw, coming toward them, a man carrying a submachine gun.

TWENTY-NINE

Don't shoot," said Bormann, "it's Kempka. But where's the rest of his party?"

His face pale as death in the light from the flames of Berlin, Hitler's chauffeur's relief on recognizing the Reichsleiter's column was evident. With shells still falling from every direction, Kempka beckoned them toward him. They took shelter in the shadow of the ruins of the Admiral's Palace, a building that had once been a theater. Kempka explained that the remainder of his people were inside.

"There's no way across the Spree," he gasped. "The Russians have the north end of the Weidendammer Bridge under constant fire. They keep trying to send in a battalion of combat engineers to see if we've mined the stanchions, but our units there are holding them off." He giggled nervously. "Mined the damn thing! It's our only way out."

"What about Mohnke and Günsche's group?" demanded Bormann.

Kempka shook his head. "I don't know. They were first out. Perhaps they got across, perhaps they didn't. No one seems to know."

"We need tanks," said Bormann. "We could cross the bridge under cover of armor."

Standing a little way from the Germans but well within earshot, Fodor murmured to Lassiter, "If he's expecting to find a German tank that doesn't look like the losing side in a train crash, he's got another think coming."

But in this Fodor was wrong. Almost as he spoke, three Tigers and three armored personnel carriers loomed up out of the darkness.

Seeing the German uniforms, the commander of the leading vehicle stopped and introduced himself as Obersturmfuehrer Hansen. What they saw before them, he explained, was the last of an armored company of the Nordland Division.

"Do you think you can get us across the bridge?" asked Bormann.

The Obersturmfuehrer looked doubtful; he had been asked to do many impossible things in the last few days, but not by such an exalted personage. He did not recognize Martin Bormann for who he was, but he knew the uniform of a senior SS officer when he saw it.

"I could try, Herr Gruppenfuehrer."

"Then kindly prepare to do so. Kempka, get your people together. We haven't got all night."

While Kempka disappeared at speed to extricate his group from the bowels of the Admiral's Palace, Bormann—one eye open for falling masonry and an ear cocked for the telltale whistle of a shell that was about to land too close—walked over to where Lassiter and the others were standing.

"You heard all that, no doubt?" he asked. "That we're going to try to cross the bridge under the cover of armor?"

"I heard it," answered Lassiter grimly, "and you don't stand a chance. The Russians have got the range. They'll simply wait until you get within it and blast you to hell."

"Nevertheless, it has to be attempted. Can you think of a better method to cross the river?"

"I'd be able to answer that question more easily if I knew why we need to be north of the Spree in the first place."

Bormann shook his head. He was giving out no unnecessary information at this juncture.

Lassiter would not let it go. "Look," he said, "I'm a soldier and you're not. If I knew where we were going, I might be able to figure out a way of getting there. As it is, we're all likely to die on that bloody bridge or spend the rest of our lives in a Russian prison camp. Look at that lot."

Kempka was leading his group into the open. There were thirty or more of them, mostly women.

"My job," went on Lassiter, "is to get you out of here in one piece, though God knows I'm beginning to care less and less if we succeed. A small contingent—my people plus you—just might stand a chance. But fifty or sixty are cannon fodder."

"Then they have their advantages," said Bormann callously. "They may attract some Russian firepower, take it away from us."

"My God," breathed Sara.

"To whom you might as well start praying for your own survival, Fraulein," snapped Bormann. "As for me, I'll take care of my own."

"Ready," called Kempka.

With Obersturmfuehrer Hansen's Tiger in the vanguard, the tiny column made its way toward and across the bridge, coming under small-arms and antitank fire almost immediately.

The group crouched in the lee of Hansen's tank comprised Bormann, Doctors Naumann and Stumpfegger, Axmann, Kempka, Beetz and Schwägermann. Behind them Lassiter had one of Sara's hands clutched tightly in his and had so positioned Dunbar, Fodor and Maclean that the girl was protected from all sides.

At the north end of the bridge the Russians had constructed an antitank barrier, but somehow Hansen maneuvered his way around this. Miraculously, the Tiger had been hit by nothing likely to deal it a mortal blow, though rifle and machine-gun bullets were ricocheting off its armor like swarms of angry, insistent bees.

Beyond the barrier, Hansen's instructions were to make for Ziegelstrasse, some three hundred yards ahead, where remnants of Mohnke's battle group were still holed up. There were moments when all concerned thought they'd make it.

But finally a Russian antitank gunner, ironically using a captured *Panzerfaust*, got the range and scored a bull's-eye, touching off the magazine.

The Tiger exploded with a massive roar, and a sheet of flame leaped from the cockpit. The occupants were killed instantly, but those behind the tank suffered no more than minor wounds and burns—except for Kempka, who was knocked out and temporarily blinded.

In complete disarray and under continuous small-arms fire,

those who could stand raced back across the bridge; those who could not were pulled or dragged. The remaining two Tigers and the three armored personnel carriers had got no farther than the antitank barrier and were already retreating.

Once again within the comparative safety of the ruins of the Admiral's Palace, they took stock.

Kempka was now conscious and could partly see, but he had made his last attempt on the Weidendammer Bridge. Although he told no one as yet, he had already decided to abandon his group and get across the Spree by means of a small iron footbridge.

Beetz was bleeding from a wound at the base of his skull, and Axmann too was slightly injured. Bormann and Stumpfegger had been blown to the ground by the blast of the disintegrating tank, but had suffered no more than cuts and bruises. Lassiter, Dunbar and Fodor had escaped injury entirely, but Sara had received a cut above her left eye. Dougal Maclean was limping slightly but said it was nothing to worry about.

By now, however, Lassiter had had more than enough. There was no way across the Spree using the Weidendammer Bridge without the backup of an armored division and a brigade of Marine Commandos. Neither were they going to get much farther in such a large and unwieldy group. If Bormann continued to insist on making military decisions he was untrained for, they would all be dead within the hour.

Motioning to the others to remain where they were, he walked across to the Reichsleiter, who was conferring with Stumpfegger. Bormann turned toward him.

"Yes, Herr Sturmbannfuehrer?"

Lassiter glanced at Stumpfegger. Hitler's former surgeon got the message and moved off to join another group.

"It's time we had a talk," said Lassiter, as though addressing a very junior NCO. "We've tried it your way and it didn't work, and before I get involved in any more crackpot schemes I've got a few words to say myself."

Bormann was about to make some sort of arrogant retort; he was not accustomed to being spoken to in such a manner by the military, whatever their nationality. But some sixth sense and the look of anger on Lassiter's face made him hold his tongue. Besides, he reminded himself, he was Reichsleiter of nothing.

"I'll hear you out."

"You'll do more than that," said Lassiter. "In the first place, I'm not moving another step until I know what you've got in mind, where you're heading and why. If you refuse to tell me I'll leave you here and now, and the documents the woman is carrying will go with us."

"Your threats are idle," sneered Bormann. "One word from me—a suggestion that you are perhaps traitors—and the several dozen armed men you see around you will be your executioners. I shall then have freedom of action and the documents."

"Wrong," said Lassiter. "Any attempt to arrest us and you will be the first to die, I assure you of that."

Bormann was inclined to believe him. A man such as this did not make idle threats. "Go on," he said. "I'm sure knowledge of our destination is not all you require."

"Correct. It isn't. The second condition is that from now on I make all military decisions. Once I know where we're heading, how we get there is my business. You tell us where, I'll tell you how. It may not have occurred to you but our lives, to us, are as important as yours is to you. I will not leave my fate in the hands of an incompetent."

Bormann went white. "You dare to talk to me like that!"

Lassiter stood his ground, starting to enjoy himself. There couldn't be many British officers around who'd challenged the ability of the Deputy Leader of the Nazi Party.

"I can dare to say anything I like to a criminal with a price on his head. If I leave it to you this mission will end in failure. So just tell me where we're heading and why, and I'll guarantee we get there."

"You don't know what you're asking."

"I know exactly what I'm asking. I'm asking for a decent chance to get us all out of this rathole of a city in one piece."

"To show you properly I'd have to use a map. . . ."

Lassiter could see him weakening. "Then use the map."

"In front of these others? They would wonder what we were doing, what we were planning. They would want to come along also."

"Then get rid of them. Alternatively, let's leave them and make our own way home."

"You don't understand," said Bormann. "Think about it for a moment. Some of these people who go in other directions will be captured and interrogated. If they report that I was last seen talking to an officer of the Das Reich, there will always be a suspicion that I am still alive—somewhere."

"There'll be that anyway—because nobody's going to find your corpse."

Nevertheless, Lassiter could see Bormann's point. It was necessary, as the German had pointed out in the Bunker, that there always be some mystery about his disappearance, with the weight of evidence favoring his being killed in the ruins of Berlin. Many of those now trying to escape would make the American lines; some would be taken by the Russians. But whatever the outcome, someone would recall that Bormann was last seen consulting a map with an officer wearing Das Reich cuff bands. And someone else would ask what representatives of the Das Reich were doing in Berlin while the remainder of the Division was fighting in Austria.

But for the moment all that was academic. Bormann still hadn't given his consent to the new terms, to the revelation of their destination and to taking a back seat until they got there.

Lassiter put it to him again. He had played second fiddle in this operation for long enough.

Bormann thought about it for only a few seconds. He had risen to power because he bent with the wind, moving backward when there was opposition, forward where he met none. In this respect he resembled politicians of any ilk.

"I agree," he said finally, "but not until we are absolutely alone. There will be no further discussions of the matter, and neither will maps be displayed or destinations hinted at until I have convinced the others that we must, henceforth, make our own separate ways. Are we in accord?"

Lassiter nodded. "But bear in mind one thing," he added. "If it seems to me that you're betraying us to the others, that you are prepared to sacrifice us for the documents the woman is carrying, you will not live to enjoy their benefits. Even if we fail to kill you—and we are not without skill in that department—

the documents will be destroyed. Without those, your life won't be worth a postwar Reichsmark. Unless you can get them to a safe destination, to be published in the event of your premature death, SOE will extract what they can from you before standing you on a trapdoor."

Lassiter returned to the others.

"What the hell was all that about?" asked Dunbar.

"A little deal I was making with our Nazi friend. Unless he tells us where we're going and allows us to get him there, we're over the hills and far away, taking our own chances."

He also explained the difficulties, that it would be necessary for Bormann to persuade the others that each man/group would be better off on his/its own.

"What about the women?" asked Sara. "If they're left to try it alone, you know what will happen."

Lassiter was saved from being called upon to answer the unanswerable by Bormann's return. Hands on hips, the bullnecked Nazi looked at them with an expression for which the word hatred was gross understatement. He had been forced to place his life in the hands of others and he didn't like it one bit.

"It's been agreed," he said. "Kempka wants to make a run for it by himself, but many of the others, ourselves included, intend following the railway tracks to the Lehrter station. There we have agreed to separate. It appears that your views are shared by others, Herr Sturmbannfuehrer—that we will be better off in small groups. There is only one minor complication: Dr. Stumpfegger insists upon accompanying me."

"Then you must dissuade him," said Lassiter.

"He will not be dissuaded, but rely upon me. He will not bear witness."

Before Lassiter could query the precise meaning of this phrase, curiously biblical from a self-confessed atheist, Bormann was gone.

Sara tried hard not to look at the women—some old, some barely out of their teens, but all being left behind to handle the Russians as best they could now that their masters had decided it was every man for himself. They were a pitiful sight, not a spark of hope anywhere. They reminded her of cattle on first smelling the abattoir.

She forced herself to look away. There was nothing she could do, that was the hell of it.

"They're moving off," said Dunbar.

Following the tracks to Lehrter station proved easier than any of them had a right to expect. Although the sounds of battle could be heard in all quarters of the city, they did not see a Russian the whole way. It seemed that Zhukov was more concerned about mass breakouts using armor than the escape of any one particular individual on foot.

En route they lost Beetz, Hitler's pilot. One minute he was with them; the next, when they looked, he had gone. He was never seen again.

At Lehrter the Germans split up. There was no formality, no shaking of hands. The common denominator here was fear. Although the area seemed quiet enough by comparison with others, they were not to know whether a sniper was lining one of them up in his sights or whether a squadron of T-34s would suddenly round a corner.

Naumann, Schwägermann, Axmann and several others headed westward towards Alt Moabit. Bormann and Stumpfegger went east along Invalidenstrasse, making, it appeared, for the Stettiner station. This puzzled Lassiter; that way lay the Soviet strength.

He waited several moments to make sure that those who had chosen the western route would not suddenly change their minds, then beckoned to the others to follow him. Keeping well within the shadows and moving at speed, they caught up with the Germans within a couple of minutes, near the bridge where Invalidenstrasse crosses the railway line. At least they caught up with Bormann, for Stumpfegger was already dead, lying flat on his back, his eyes wide open.

No one had to ask what had happened, for Bormann had still not holstered his pistol. And with all the gunfire going on around them, it was hardly surprising that they had not heard a single shot from a low-caliber weapon.

Sara not excluded, they had all witnessed and sometimes participated in many acts of callousness and brutality, throughout the whole war as well as during the last few days, but this had to rank among the foulest they had come across. Stumpfegger was a Nazi, a member of the SS and Hitler's personal surgeon, but for him to have been shot in the back solely because he had chosen the wrong traveling companion made them all sick to their stomachs.

Lassiter was determined not to let them dwell upon it; himself included, each of them was within a hair's breadth of dispatching Bormann there and then. And that wasn't part of the scenario.

"What the hell's all this business of heading east?" he demanded.

Bormann spread his arms in a gesture of supplication.

"What else could I do? Axmann and the others wanted to head west. We'd never have parted company."

Lassiter accepted this as a reasonable explanation. But he still didn't trust Bormann and wouldn't until he had the escape route.

There was also another consideration. It would be light in a couple of hours.

"We've got our civilian clothes," said Fodor. "No one's going to bother a few workmen."

"I wouldn't be too sure about that," said Lassiter, "because in the first place the Russians will be throwing a ring around the city; they won't be letting anyone through, civilian or otherwise. In the second place, if we discard our uniforms we've also got to discard our weapons, and at the moment they're the only friends we've got. Thirdly, judging by the bloody racket you can hear going on all around you, the fighting's a long way from being over yet and won't be until whoever's got the power now Hitler's dead decides to surrender. The uniforms may yet be an asset if we can string along for a while behind a couple of tanks. And lastly, civvies or not, someone might recognize Bormann here. If his picture's on file in London, you can bet your life there's a dossier on him somewhere in Moscow.

"So holing up by day and traveling by night is our only chance. Of course, that all rather depends upon how far we've got to go and in which direction, and we won't know that until Herr Bormann has said his piece and shown us the map."

Bormann shrugged his broad shoulders. "It seems I have no

277

choice, though you can rest assured that your conduct will be reported to your superiors."

Lassiter almost laughed in his face. The bloody fool still thought it was 1942 and that his word was tantamount to a death sentence.

They took shelter in the gutted remains of a warehouse. It seemed otherwise unoccupied, by Germans or Russians, but Lassiter sent Maclean and Dunbar on a scouting expedition before he was satisfied.

As cover it was far from perfect, but cellars and the like, from now on, were obviously out. They were the first places the Russians would look. In any case, the fiercest fighting seemed to be taking place in the west, the Tiergarten area, and the south, around the Chancellery. Apparently much of the SS was prepared to continue the struggle until the ultimate decision was reached.

Dunbar reported back that all was quiet. Lassiter grinned to himself. Even on the outskirts of the battle, "quiet" was the understatement of the year. But he knew what the Scot meant: there was no immediate danger; and they had all become more or less accustomed to the scream of shells, the chatter of automatic weapons, the crack of rifles. In any case, so the legend went, you never heard the one that killed you.

Maclean and Dunbar were posted to keep watch while Lassiter turned his attention to Bormann. The Reichsleiter produced a bulky document case from inside his tunic. It no doubt contained matters of great interest to Greenleigh and Dulles, but all they wanted at the moment was the map.

Sara flicked on a penlight.

What they saw was a crude sketch of central and west Berlin, obviously made in a hurry but nevertheless showing the main thoroughfares and including a section of Lake Havel and one or two of its islands.

"We are approximately here," said Bormann. He jabbed a pudgy forefinger at a spot on Invalidenstrasse midway between Lehrter and Stettiner stations. "And we have to get here." He pointed out the island of Pfaueninsel, some ten kilometers down Lake Havel.

The total distance involved, from their present position, was approximately twenty-five to thirty kilometers—about fifteen to eighteen miles. Under normal circumstances they were talking about a journey that would take no more than four or five hours. But these were far from normal circumstances. To get to the island meant running the gauntlet of almost the entire Red Army.

"When do we have to be there?" asked Sara.

Bormann took a deep breath. "By this time tomorrow. To be precise, at exactly four A.M. on the morning of the third."

"You're insane!" exclaimed Fodor.

"Shut up, Chuck," said Lassiter. There were many more questions he wanted answered before deciding whether Bormann was asking the impossible in the time available.

"What was the original plan, the route?" he demanded. "If we're supposed to be heading southwest, what the hell are we doing northeast of the city?"

"Because that's the way we've been forced to come," answered Bormann. "The original conception was to cross the Weidendammer Bridge and join up with Mohnke's battle group. With them we would head west along Invalidenstrasse and Alt Moabit, circumvent the Tiergarten and join the East–West Axis at Bismarckstrasse. From there, depending upon conditions, we would either proceed directly along the Kaiserdamm or take the long way round via the Reichssportfeld Stadium. In either event we would end up at the Pichelsdorf Bridge and either follow the banks of the Havel or steal a small boat to take us to Pfaueninsel."

"And you call that a plan?" asked Fodor. "What did you think the Russians would be doing all that time? Acting as traffic cops? Waving you and Mohnke and every tank at your disposal through? I've never heard anything so lunatic in all my life."

Lassiter again told Fodor to shut up. He had to think. Certainly the chosen route would have been suicidal were they using tanks as battering rams, but for a handful of determined men it was within the bounds of feasibility.

He was beginning to understand why Greenleigh had sent in a team; there were a dozen other methods by which the German could have received his documents of immunity. But Bormann by himself would have ended up precisely where he now was: in the ruins of a warehouse off Invalidenstrasse. He needed professionals to take him out.

But there were still a couple of "whys" Lassiter wanted answered. Why that particular island, and why by 4 A.M. on the third?

"Because there and at that time—where the island juts out here, see?—we shall be met by a guide."

The lie sprang easily from Bormann's lips. If anything went wrong and one of his escorts was taken by the Russians, he or she would not be in a position, under torture, to reveal the rest of the scheme.

"What guide?" persisted Lassiter. "And where is the guide to lead us?"

"I don't know," lied Bormann. "All I have been told is that I, we, are to be at the northern tip of Pfaueninsel at precisely four A.M."

"*Told?*" demanded Lassiter. "Told by whom?"

But he did not need the answer to that. Neither did Sara. It was basic security that operatives were given only as much information as was necessary for them to complete their part of the task. If they had not threatened Bormann, they would not even know where they were heading. Greenleigh himself had arranged for the guide, and Lassiter guessed wrongly that Bormann himself did not know much more.

In any case, a moment later the whole matter became academic.

"All very interesting," said a voice from behind them, "but I regret to inform you that the Reichsleiter will not be going anywhere near Lake Havel."

Lassiter turned slowly. It all fell into place. Standing to one side of Maclean but in such a position that the tall Scot was included in his field of fire, Dunbar had cocked his MP 38. His finger was resting very lightly on the trigger.

THIRTY

The ensuing silence seemed to go on forever, though in reality it could not have lasted more than a few seconds. Fodor was first to find his voice.

"What the hell's going on?"

"Dunbar's a Russian," answered Lassiter. "At least, he works for the Russians, which is tantamount to the same thing."

The SAS officer was surprised. "You know?"

"Not names—just that one of us could be on Stalin's payroll. I thought at first it was Scipioni. In fact—God forgive me—I hoped it *was* Scipioni because Scipioni's now dead."

He noticed that Dunbar's back was literally to the wall. It was the perfect position; they could scarcely see him in the shadows, but he could see them perfectly owing to the flames from the street.

"I'd like you all to ground your weapons and take three paces backwards," said the Scot. "Officers to get rid of their side arms as well. That includes you, Dougal. Put your Schmeisser on the deck and join the others."

Maclean complied without a word; so did the others. But Bormann was a little slow fumbling with his holster. Dunbar sensed that he might be tempted to try something.

"You in particular, Reichsleiter, I'd advise to be very careful. My instructions are to bring you in alive if possible but dead if not. We know about the cyanide pill in your tooth, so it's likely to be dead. But it doesn't matter. You won't be talking to British Intelligence and you won't be living in the lap of luxury for the rest of your life. So the pistol, if you please."

Bormann hesitated only momentarily before tossing the Walther onto the pile of the MP 38s and Lugers. This so-called Russian was outnumbered five to one, and there was always the cyanide capsule if things turned out badly. Not that he wanted to use it, but it was better than being taken by the Ivans.

"I don't know whether you're Russian or British or hybrid," he said contemptuously, "but one thing I'm sure of: that this whole business smells, that it was a trick to lure me out into the open and kill me."

"Oh, no," said Dunbar lightly, "don't blame the others. They're as genuine as they appear to be."

"I don't believe you, any of you. Without the connivance of a senior member of British Intelligence you could not possibly have known that I was Valkyrie."

"We didn't." Dunbar's voice was quite calm in the semidarkness. "All we knew to begin with was that a team was being assembled for a special mission. Even then it might not have gone any further except that one of the names on the team—potential names, that is—was my own. It wasn't until much later that we learned the code name Valkyrie and not until yesterday that I realized who Valkyrie was. A magnificent stroke of luck has landed us with a prize of untold proportions."

Sara turned to Lassiter. Accustomed as she was, much more than the others, to playing the double game, she found one or two aspects of the business puzzling.

"I still don't understand how you knew there was an agent among us."

"Remember the phone call I got at Eindhoven before we took off? That was from Greenleigh, telling me that his damn fool of a secretary was sleeping with a Russian contact who now knew the name of every member of the squad. There was therefore a good chance we'd been infiltrated, that one of us was working for Stalin. His own guess was either Chuck or Scipioni. Sorry about that, Chuck. It made sense then, but it doesn't now.

"My own choice of personnel for the mission was either Dunbar and Dougal, or a Major Kennedy and a Sergeant Holmes. Kennedy and Holmes were unfortunately killed in a motor accident, which made Dunbar and Dougal their automatic replacements. I should have asked myself long ago whether that accident was an accident at all."

"But it must have been a million-to-one shot," protested Fodor, "actually being in a position to put an agent on the team."

"Not really," said Dunbar. "You see, there are many more of us than you'll ever know—right up to the top. All we needed was the information that something big was being planned. One way or another, after that, we'd have made sure one of our people was included."

"*Our* people?" questioned Lassiter.

"Our people, Jack, whether you call them Communists or Socialists or Marxists or whatever. The people who fought alongside Maclean and me in Yugoslavia, while the German Panzers were knocking hell out of them. People who'd attack Tiger tanks with Molotov cocktails or their bare fists." He jerked the muzzle of his MP 38 in Bormann's direction. "Anybody who's on the opposite side to bastards like him."

"*We're* on the opposite side," Lassiter reminded him.

Dunbar laughed quietly. "Are we, Jack? Are we really? Then what the hell are we doing protecting the lousy bastard's hide? We've beaten the shit out of the Germans and now Bormann's going to sell all he knows to save his filthy neck. And let none of us kid ourselves what that information's going to be, who it's going to be directed against. The Russians have lost more people in this war than the rest of the combatants put together, and we're doing a deal with a man who's killed millions of them just because Greenleigh thinks it's a good idea. The hell we're on the opposite side; if we were, we'd string Bormann up from the rafters."

Lassiter knew it was important to keep Dunbar talking until he could think of a better method of resolving the situation than a free-for-all grab for the MP 38s. Of one thing he was quite sure: the Scot would not want to kill any of his friends if it could be avoided. While he continued to pour out his hatred he would be less inclined to pull the trigger.

"Where did they recruit you?" he asked.

"Does it matter?"

"It matters. Stalin and Tito are different animals."

"Balls. Tito had Russian advisers while the British were still wondering whether to support him or the Chetniks under Mikhailovich."

"Tito was given Russian advisers and equipment because it suited Stalin to have Hitler's southern flank tied up."

"Maybe so, but one thing you can be assured of: when the war's over, neither Stalin nor Tito will be doing deals with Nazis. And neither will Bormann be hiding away in South America, living on a British pension."

"Then that leaves only one thing to be decided," said Lassiter: "how many of us do you intend to kill to get at Bormann?"

As he finished speaking he stepped in front of the Reichsleiter. Lassiter was the taller by a whole head. There was no way Dunbar could kill Bormann without killing Lassiter first.

Dunbar moved out of the shadows, his face pale but his hands as steady as a rock. His words were almost a plea.

"Jack, don't be a hero for this scum. You don't understand. The only man I want is Bormann, dead or alive."

"And what happens to you when it's all over? Are you going to make a run for it with the rest of us?"

"You know that's not possible. I know where to go when it's finished, who to see. I've been well briefed. You and the others can go, use the escape route he's given you. Just leave me Bormann."

"No," said Lassiter, "but hear me out before you make any rash decisions.

"I understand the way you feel, believe me, and by rights I should feel the same. This man was responsible for killing the only three people I ever really cared about. I don't mean he pressed the bomb toggle or anything like that; that was probably done by a nineteen-year-old kid who was scared stiff and wanted to go home. But somewhere along the line Martin Bormann took the decision to manufacture that bomb or train the pilot or support those who did. He's more responsible for the deaths of my wife and children than any nineteen-year-old—"

"Which is exactly what I'm saying," argued Dunbar.

"Let me finish," said Lassiter. "In the last few days I've lost two men I've known for years. Fodor has lost Joe Scipioni. If you intend to kill me—and that's the only way you're going to get at Bormann—I'm entitled to a hearing."

Lassiter sensed rather than saw Fodor and Maclean move into position alongside him, and he definitely felt Sara Ferguson touch his arm. Whether it was by accident or whether she was trying to reassure him, he didn't know.

"Like thousands, millions of others," he went on, half surprised that he was capable of making such a lengthy speech, "I don't know and haven't known for years why I'm fighting this war. To begin with it had something to do with beating the

Germans; then it was a matter of personal revenge. But for the last couple of years it's become a question of habit."

"War's not a habit, Jack. It's a continuation of capitalism by other means."

"Jesus, they really got to you, didn't they? Well, I'm not fighting for a better world or any of that other crap that's fed to us. I'm a soldier, Alex, whether I like it or not. Christ knows I've broken the rules often enough when it suited me, but I'm still a soldier with a job to do. I said the same thing to Greenleigh when he asked me if I had any qualms about bringing out a top Nazi.

"I don't know why they want Bormann, but I'm taking him back anyway. Not because I was ordered to, not because I can't disobey an order if I think it's wrong, but because it's my job and I agreed to do it. Besides, I don't believe even Greenleigh thinks it can be done. The odds are a couple of million to one against, and they're the sort of odds that appeal to me."

There was a long silence.

Lassiter's monologue had been conducted in German. Martin Bormann could not have failed to understand every word.

As an operational officer with the U.S. 17th Airborne Chuck Fodor had known several men like Lassiter. They were generically termed "pirates" because they fought for nothing but the right to hold on to their buccaneering instincts. They were unique individuals, not especially liked by their fellow officers because they seemed to have no tangible goal.

Maclean was in a state of semishock. He had worked with and served under Alex Dunbar for years; they were close personal friends; Dunbar was his son's godfather. There was no doubt about the incredible bravery of the Yugoslav partisans, but Dunbar was suggesting treason.

Sara came closest in her understanding. Her own husband had enlisted in Lord Lovat's Number 4 Commando when he could easily have applied for, and obtained, a safe job in the War Office. But that wasn't his way, as it wasn't Jack Lassiter's.

Lassiter moved a pace forward. Behind him Maclean and Fodor closed ranks; Sara joined them—protecting Bormann with their bodies. The Reichsleiter was now sweating profusely, prepared for anything, although one thought continued to preoccupy him: he would *never* understand the British.

"In a few moments I'm going to pick up one of these MP 38s," said Lassiter. "You can shoot me if you wish and after me, the others. If Bormann's death means that much to you, you won't hesitate."

Although they could not see it because of the angle, a light went from Dunbar's eyes. He had not expected Lassiter, of all people, to oppose him.

Lassiter bent forward, but he was still inches way from the nearest submachine gun when a voice behind him said:

"Captain Dunbar."

It was Maclean. In his hand he held a Luger pistol, which he had produced from inside his tunic. It was pointed at Dunbar's heart.

"You always did carry a spare, Dougal. I should have remembered."

"That's the way you taught me, Captain."

There was a single shot from the Luger and Dunbar pitched forward, dead before he hit the ground.

Lassiter turned and faced Maclean. On the tall Scot's face was as much pain as he, Lassiter, ever wanted to see again.

Bormann started to say something, but Lassiter reached him in a couple of strides. He held him single-handed by the throat until the Reichsleiter's face became purple.

"Nothing, you understand," he hissed. "Not one word!"

It was almost dawn, and there was nowhere they would be going in daylight. They covered Dunbar's body with a civilian raincoat from one of the canvas packs, and retreated to the rear of the warehouse.

To make doubly sure that no casual observer would take them for anything other than corpses, they lay under fallen girders and charred beams, carefully supported on piles of rubble, feigning death, their weapons hidden to deter souvenir hunters.

It was a nerve-racking experience, for they had only a low-level viewpoint and total immobility was essential.

Yet in spite of the fact that throughout the whole morning and most of the afternoon they could hear the sounds of war going on all around them—the shells, mortars, tanks, small-

286

arms fire, the dive-bombers overhead—no one came near them, neither Russian nor German nor civilian. At regular intervals squadrons of T-34s and their supporting infantry trundled past, but at this stage the Soviets were firing only at those who fired first. The mopping-up operations had not yet begun; the main objective was still the Citadel.

Toward dusk the shelling stopped, the dive-bombers went away, the small-arms fire became sporadic. The battle for Berlin, it appeared, was over.

Lassiter gave it another hour, until close to 8 P.M. Under normal circumstances, at this time of year it would still be bright outside. But the smoke and dust still rising from the city's funeral pyre brought an early, unnatural darkness broken only by the flames.

He had no idea what was going on outside, but he knew from past experience that it was virtually impossible for an occupying force to police every intersection, watch every street and alley. In any case, the victorious Russians would be mostly looking for drink and women this night, although they would be herding together any persons in uniform and putting them in temporary camps or shooting them. Certainly anyone wearing the insignia of the hated SS or carrying arms would be executed on sight. Regrettably, it was time to don civilian clothes and dispose of their weapons.

At the last moment, however, he hung on to one MP 38 and two clips of ammunition. The gun itself, with the stock folded, measured only a fraction of an inch over two feet and could easily be hidden under a raincoat. He also allowed each man to keep his dagger.

He gave the order to strip and change at once, Sara included, urging them to hurry. Bormann was reluctant to abandon his Walther at first, but a sharp rap across the knuckles made him think otherwise.

Speed was of the essence now. Lassiter had no doubt that with the knowledge of Berlin shared by Sara and Bormann they could bluff or bypass Soviet patrols and find their way to the Pichelsdorf Bridge at the head of Lake Havel. What concerned him more was whether they would reach Pfaueninsel by the stipulated time of 4 A.M.

THIRTY-ONE

Lassiter had already made up his mind to use Bormann's planned route as far as possible—with the obvious exception of the Weidendammer Bridge, of course, which the Russians had doubtless taken by this time anyway. Neither did it seem a particularly bright idea to include the Tiergarten area or Bismarckstrasse in their itinerary, though in both cases that might be unavoidable. As for the rest of it—making for the Pichelsdorf Bridge by way of the Reichssportfeld Stadium (where Jesse Owens had triumphed nine years earlier)—that seemed sensible enough, if sense and Berlin were not antonymous.

Whatever their route, somehow they had to cross the city, from northeast to southwest, and paradoxically it seemed as if the first part of their journey was going to give them the least trouble. The fighting might be all over except the shouting in central Berlin, but over in the west and southwest, to judge by the artillery flashes on the Havel, it was still raging.

Not that any of it was going to be easy, not in less than eight hours and with the fat Nazi in tow. If they intended to pass themselves off as harmless civilians bemused by it all and just waiting for the soup kitchens to open, ready to say "Da" or "Nyet" as the occasion demanded, they had to avoid areas of conflict or suspicious behavior resulting in a body search. Apart from the fact that such an examination would reveal (with the obvious consequences) that Sara—now dressed in dungarees, raincoat and a workman's cap—was a woman, they would all end up in front of a firing squad when the MP 38 was discovered.

Those were the minuses, Lassiter explained, as they prepared to leave the warehouse. On the plus side they had the following: it was night; they knew where they were going; many of the invaders would be drunk or well on the way.

"What's the first move?" asked Fodor.

"I suggest—" began Bormann.

Lassiter silenced him with a clenched fist under his nose. The Reichsleiter cut a ridiculous figure now that he was out of his tailored Gruppenfuehrer's uniform and into workman's overalls. It just went to show that Hitler had attained his power in large part by dressing up his followers in brown and black. Put them in off-the-peg clothes and they wouldn't have made Potsdam, let alone Poland.

"From now on you'll speak when you're spoken to and keep your head down. If the rest of us run out of ideas, I'll come to you. Until then, shut up and try to behave like the plumber you appear. Sara?"

Without referring to any map, Sara Ferguson knew that she could find her way around this part of Berlin as easily as she could from the Tottenham Court Road to Marble Arch. The trouble was, they were north of the River Spree. By following the tracks to Lehrter station, Bormann had succeeded in crossing the river but at the wrong place and the wrong time. To make matters worse, the Spree twisted and turned between here and the western boundaries of Charlottenburg (which was between them and the Reichssportfeld Stadium), involving half a dozen bridge crossings which the Russians would have covered as a matter of routine. They were up against a deadline of 4 A.M., and it seemed best to take the bull by the horns and plunge for the Tiergarten and the East–West Axis, using side streets as far as possible. At least that way they would be over the river and could make for the Stadium by a more or less direct route.

She explained her theory as quickly as she could. Bormann was horrified.

"You're absolutely mad! You don't know the Russians as I do. They kill people for the fun of it. Go toward the Tiergarten? We'll be lynched before we've covered a hundred meters. We'll do much better to follow the banks of the Spree through Charlottenburg until it turns south and meets up with the Havel at Pichelsdorf."

"Sara?"

"Well, apart from the bridges, which could hold us up for any length of time, we'd be taking the long way round, adding another eight or ten kilometers to the distance to be covered. I don't think we've got that sort of time. We'll be pushing it as it is. Unless everything goes like clockwork, we'll be lucky to see Pfaueninsel by four A.M."

"Will the guide wait?" asked Lassiter.

Bormann hesitated. Perhaps now was the time to tell them . . . But no, the habits of a lifetime prevailed. It was *his* escape route, not theirs. If something went wrong and one of them was captured . . . It was better to say nothing.

"Will he?" repeated Lassiter.

"No," answered Bormann.

"Then that settles it. We'll head for the Tiergarten."

Led by Fodor, the solitary Russian speaker among them, one by one they left the warehouse. Only Maclean looked back at the dark bundle that was Dunbar. He seemed about to say something until Lassiter, who was bringing up the rear, shoved him roughly in the back. "Come on, Dougal, we've got a long way to go."

Traveling by side and back streets proved a lot more difficult than any of them had foreseen because, in 1945 Berlin, there was little that resembled any sort of street; there were just mountains of debris juxtaposed with other mountains. But one thing worked in their favor: they were not alone in the night. On every bomb site south of Alt Moabit, German civilians were scrabbling through the rubble, possibly looking for a valued possession (their own or someone else's), possibly trying to identify the last resting place of a loved one.

There were Russians everywhere, of course, but they seemed totally uninterested in the average Berliner. This was their first night of victory, and they were intent upon savoring it. As long as you kept your head down, changed direction if a patrol waved you away from something they were guarding or someone they were about to shoot or rape, and played your part as a member of a defeated people, you were not bothered.

There was really nothing so strange about this. The Russian High Command was only just beginning to realize the magnitude of the problems confronting it. Apart from the fact that it still had to wipe out nests of hard-core resisters, it faced the massive task of making the city a viable entity again. Not necessarily for the Berliners; it was doubtful whether the Russians cared one way or the other if the whole of the indigenous population starved to death. But for the sake of their own troops they had to get the main supplies functioning. There wasn't a drop of water to be had from a faucet, not an ampere of electricity from a light switch. Sewage and decomposing bodies littered the streets, and typhus and cholera could be contracted just as easily by the occupiers as by the occupied. For the time being, as long as the Berliners behaved themselves, they would be let more or less alone.

It was not the first time Lassiter had found himself trapped in a beleaguered city—though on past occasions the Germans had been the conquerors and the French or Dutch the conquered—and he knew that the best time to get out was right after the city's fall, before the occupying authorities had an opportunity to get organized and begin issuing ration cards and identity papers.

Although trying to appear as though they were heading nowhere in particular and keeping far enough apart not to be taken as a group—but with Lassiter never more than yards from Bormann—they ran into their first obstacle just north of Bellevue, where the Spree had to be crossed for what they hoped would be the one and only time.

The bridge here was a main viaduct, connecting Alt Moabit with the Tiergarten, and needless to say it was guarded. The main function of the guard, however, appeared to be to keep the way clear for the tanks, half-tracks, trucks and armored personnel carriers that were rolling in from the north. Certainly they were making little attempt to disperse the crowds of Berliners, mostly sullen and silent, who had gathered on both sides of the road to watch their conquerors (of Zhukov's force) make for the main thoroughfare of the city, the East–West Axis.

Fodor allowed the others to catch up with him.

"They're not letting pedestrians through," he said. "I don't think there's anything sinister in that, but they've obviously got to keep the road clear for vehicles. Come tomorrow morning they'll be only too pleased to let the Germans see what beat them."

"Unfortunately," said Lassiter, "tomorrow morning will be

too late. We've got a long way to travel and the clock's still against us."

His head covered by a dark blue cap, an overcoat collar turned up to hide his bull neck, Bormann growled, "We should have kept north of the river. I told you so in the first place."

Lassiter put his face very close to the Reichsleiter's, so close that he could smell the other man's breath.

"Listen," he said, "I told you before that you speak when you're spoken to, when you're asked. One more word out of place and I'll announce in a very loud voice that I personally have captured the Deputy Fuehrer. You'll be damned lucky if the Russians get to you first, because this crowd here will tear you into a hundred pieces and feed you to the fish. So keep your mouth shut."

"We've got to make a move," whispered Sara, stating the obvious but making it clear that this was no time to be arguing with Bormann.

"You're right. Chuck, the ball's in your court. You speak the language and we don't."

Fodor thought about it. It was nice to be in the driver's seat for once. He'd felt like a passenger for most of this trip.

"It's got to be a bluff," he said eventually. "We stay here, we miss our rendezvous. We try to force our way across, they shoot us. But it occurs to me that the Russians are pretty much like anyone else when it comes down to it."

"Meaning?"

"Meaning that from what I know of their propaganda they've been told for years that only Hitler and his gang are their enemies, not the German people; that the German people would welcome them as liberators. Yet I don't see anyone throwing flowers or kisses. Remember what it was like when we rolled through France after D-Day? As many girls as you could handle swarming all over the tanks and enough flowers to cover Central Park."

"Go on," said Lassiter, although he could already see what the American was driving at.

"That's it," said Fodor. "We each of us hop onto the running board of one of the trucks and make like we're grateful. It'll help if you say something in pidgin Russian. Like *Voyna kaput*

292

—meaning, The war is over. There are five of us—three trucks at the most. With any luck some of these other Krauts will join the parade. We'll be across before the Reds know what's hit them, even if they're not delighted anyway."

It was just crazy enough to work, Lassiter thought. In any case, it was already 9 o'clock and they were running out of options.

"Okay," he said, "we'll make it two per truck. But we've got to be prepared for the fact that while they might be surprised and let one through, they could stop the rest. Which means Bormann goes first."

"Not without the woman," said Bormann, who had not missed a word of the conversation. "The woman has the papers of immunity."

Lassiter turned to Sara—but she was ready for him.

"Obviously I can't go with Bormann." She produced from within the folds of her raincoat the wallet containing the documents and passed it to Lassiter. "If anything goes wrong and our truck is the only one allowed through, I might not be able to get him to safety." She didn't mention that there was also a distinct possibility that Bormann would knock her on the head, take the documents and make his own way out.

Lassiter hesitated, torn between wanting to take a later truck to make sure Sara got through and sticking with his prime charge, Bormann. In the end he decided that Chuck Fodor had not become a major in the U.S. 17th Airborne because he had a pretty face. He would remain with Sara; Fodor could take Bormann across the bridge.

He handed the wallet to the American.

"You and Bormann first, Maclean second, Sara and I on the third truck."

"I don't mind going last," said Maclean.

But Lassiter was wary of this. Not a few hours since, Dougal had shot and killed his longtime friend and commanding officer —because he had to and because it was all that could be done. That did not mean, however, that Maclean had forgotten it, that he did not, in some way, wish to atone, even if it meant his own life. One day he would be able to rationalize, but this was not the day. Lassiter wanted no dead heroes or martyrs or plain suicides on his hands. For the moment, Maclean was safer where he could be seen.

"You'll go on the second truck and no arguments," he told the Scot. "And the sooner we're off, the better."

"Next three, then," said Fodor, "after these half-tracks. And remember: *Voyna kaput*."

Herding Bormann before him and yelling, "*Voyna kaput*" like a cheerleader at a football game, Fodor barged his way through the crowd and jumped up on the running board of the first truck, making sure that Bormann was half a stride ahead of him. The Red Army driver was startled but delighted. "*Voyna kaput*," he screamed back through the open side window.

Maclean went next, bellowing at the top of his voice, as though this were the glens and he were part of a clan massacre. After that it became a procession, with dozens of Germans surging forward shouting that the war was over. And far from clambering aboard the third truck, Lassiter and Sara were lucky to get on the fifth. It took a lot of elbowing and quite a few punches before they were ensconced on the running board, Sara in front, cap well forward, trying desperately to hang on with one hand and accept cigarettes from the driver with the other.

Far from being angry or showing any signs of belligerence, the guard on the near side of the road bridge, a *starshina*, or sergeant-major in command, seemed overjoyed. Had Fodor but known it, he had done the Soviet High Command a favor. Little worse can happen to an occupying power than to have a sullen and potentially uncooperative civilian population on its hands.

Clinging with one hand to the open window and with the other around Sara's waist, and howling "*Voyna kaput*" until he thought his lungs would burst, Lassiter recalled the speech he had made to Dunbar hours earlier, when he had said that only three people in his life had ever mattered. He'd been wrong about that. Sara mattered.

On the far side of the Spree, Germans and Russians were grinning all over their faces and slapping each other on the back. But this could be only a temporary state of affairs. Sooner or later word would get back to a political commissar that conquerors and conquered were fraternizing and an order would come down forbidding it.

Not that a gang of what were obviously Hitler Youth—lads of

fifteen or sixteen but now without their armbands and badges of rank—seemed to approve anyway. Propagandized since their cradles that Russians and Germans were implacable enemies, they were bewildered and resentful at this display of goodwill.

Lassiter had difficulty in picking out Fodor and the others as he and Sara leaped from the running board, and it was eventually the American who found them.

"Will you take a look at that?" he said, awestruck.

Through the smoke and the dust across the Tiergarten, lined up in review order along the East–West Axis were literally hundreds of Soviet tanks, with more joining them every minute. It was a sight to take the breath away, but Sara seemed hardly aware of it. She beckoned Lassiter to one side. Her face was lined and tired, but fatigue could not account for the worry in her eyes.

"What's the matter?" he asked her.

"The time factor," she answered bluntly. "If I had a dozen hours I could get you not only to Pichelsdorf but right down to Pfaueninsel. But I haven't; I've got less than seven, and I don't know what we're going to meet en route. We might have to double back or change direction a dozen times. It's not at Pfaueninsel we need the guide; it's right here and now— someone who knows the safest route to Pichelsdorf, who's done it often."

He saw where she was looking: at the lads of the Hitler Youth. There were twelve or fifteen of them, and they were being studiously ignored by their fellow Germans, for fear, perhaps, of guilt by association. After all, these young men would have been future SS officers.

"It's a risk."

Sara shrugged. "So is staying here."

Lassiter did not have to think twice. Sara was no helpless female upon whom tiredness and fear were now beginning to take their toll. If she said she doubted her ability to get them to the rendezvous in the time allotted, then that doubt was based upon careful calculation, not panic.

"Tell Chuck what I'm doing and keep Bormann occupied," he said. "I don't trust the cunning bastard not to get hysterical if he thinks I'm jeopardizing his precious neck."

He strolled casually over to the group of youngsters, who

looked up warily at his approach. Some of them could not be more than fourteen, and it was more than obvious from their expressions that each and every one of them had seen death and destruction in its many forms.

"I have relatives at Pichelsdorf," he said, deciding there and then that there was no point in beating about the bush. "Do any of you know what's happening at Pichelsdorf?"

"The same thing that is happening in Berlin." The one who answered was older than the rest, sixteen-plus, and had the cold blue eyes of a fanatic. "The civilians are taking cigarettes and the women are lying with anyone for a crust." He spat a mouthful of saliva into the dust at his feet.

"That's just rumor," said Lassiter, baiting him deliberately, testing his mettle. "You can see for yourselves that the Ivans are not the barbarians we were led to believe."

"Then you're a fool and a traitor," sneered the youngster. "I was there only yesterday, commanding a mortar team. So were Hans, Willi and Christian." Several of the others nodded at the mention of their names. "If our Area Leader had not ordered us to lay down our weapons we should be there still—no doubt as corpses, but a dead German fighter is better than a live German lickspittle. Now go back to your Russian friends. This time they may let you drink their piss."

Lassiter felt like taking the lad by his neck and snapping it, but this was the one he wanted: a born leader, someone who knew Pichelsdorf and who was disgusted by the attitude of his elders.

"I'd like a word with you in private before you condemn me and include me in the rest of this rabble," he said.

At first the youngster appeared unprepared to move, but finally he shrugged his shoulders and followed Lassiter until they were some twenty yards from the remainder of the group.

"Touch the front of my raincoat," said Lassiter.

The youth recoiled with distaste.

"If you're one of these filthy, degenerate—"

"I'm not. Just do as I say." Lassiter's voice contained the smack of authority the lad was used to, and he did as he was told without further demur. His eyes widened when he felt the outline of the MP 38.

296

"Now listen to me carefully," said Lassiter, "because we haven't got much time. First of all, what's your name?"

"Erich."

"Right, Erich—it should be obvious by the fact that I am armed, risking immediate execution if discovered, that I am not what I appear, not one of your civilians who accept cigarettes or someone who believes the war is over. For reasons that I cannot explain it's vital that I and four others get to Pichelsdorf in a great hurry and from there down the Havel. I need you to guide us to Pichelsdorf Bridge and possibly help us steal a small boat. We could probably find our own way through the Russian lines if we had more time, but we do not have that time. Which leaves me with just one more question: do you have the courage and the knowledge to provide us with what we require?"

Erich's eyes flashed with fierce pride. "They do not give command of a mortar team to those who lack courage, and I have also knocked out two Russian tanks with a *Panzerfaust*. As for the other, I have personally made the journey between here and Pichelsdorf many times, both in a vehicle and on foot. Before I was given my mortar team I was a messenger, as all Hitler Youth are."

"Then it's possible?"

"It will be difficult, but the Russians are creatures of habit. They like to stick to the main highways with their tanks. It's only the foot patrols that have to be avoided, but if one knows the route . . . Yes, it's possible."

"And at speed?"

"We could be at the Pichelsdorf Bridge, below it if it's your intention to go down the Havel, in three hours."

"And you'll help us?"

Lassiter held his breath. The youngster hesitated.

"How do I know that you're not just someone who wants to escape," he asked, "who has picked up a submachine gun from a dead soldier for self-defense?"

Lassiter played his last card. "*Meine Ehre heisst Treue*," he said. It meant "Loyalty is my honor" and was the motto of the SS. It was also the correct thing to say.

"I'll help," said Erich.

"Good." Lassiter exhaled a sigh of relief. "You must now go back to your friends and tell them that you are coming with me, nothing more. As good Hitler Youth, they should know better than to ask questions, but should any of them be inquisitive you will remain silent. Is that understood?"

"Yes, Herr. . . ." The boy paused expectantly.

"No ranks," said Lassiter. "For the time being—and for the foreseeable future—no more ranks."

THIRTY-TWO

The boy Erich asked no questions, although it was perfectly obvious at close quarters that one of the party was a woman in man's clothing. Now that he had accepted he was helping part of the remnants of the Third Reich, he guided them with bewildering speed through the side streets of central Berlin, always keeping to that area between Bismarckstrasse and Kantstrasse and always heading more or less due west.

Time became meaningless as they obeyed his every instruction without hesitation. Through there. Across there. No, hold it. Soviet patrol. Keep in the shadows. Watch yourself here—danger of collapsing masonry. Roadblock ahead. Never mind. Swing left. Go around them. Hold it again—marauding tanks and half-tracks. Never mind, never mind. They can't go where we can. Special care here. Don't worry about making a noise. So much noise going on in fucking Berlin that no one's going to hear a footfall or two.

The sights were the same everywhere. The dead and the dying, mostly German, some Russian, many women and children lying half in, half out of bomb, shell and mortar craters. The sickly-sweet smell of decomposition in the night air. Houses, shops, restaurants burning still. Would the fires ever end, the flames ever be extinguished? How was it possible for anything to be alive amid such chaos?

In the gardens of private houses German gun emplacements, many still intact although their crews either dead or vanished. A horse with its entrails in the gutter, already providing a banquet for the maggots. Vehicles burning.

But push on. Lassiter had asked for speed and speed was what he was getting.

As the eldest and least fit of the group, Bormann kept complaining sotto voce that he had to rest or he would die of a heart attack. Lassiter couldn't have cared less and kept prodding him forward, knowing that sooner or later, as on any forced march, the mind switches off and the limbs move of their own accord.

At Adolf Hitler Platz there was a choice of routes: right along the Reichsstrasse, taking the long way around via the Reichssportfeld Stadium, or due west parallel to the Kaiserdamm, through the northern tip of the Grunewald. There was also a third alternative which caused Erich, recalling what Lassiter had said to him earlier, to hesitate.

Lassiter came up to him. There were masses and masses of Soviet tanks, trucks and half-tracks pouring eastward along the Kaiserdamm, and he thought this the reason for the youngster's indecision.

"What's the matter?"

Erich explained his dilemma.

"The Pichelsdorf Bridge is almost certainly in Russian hands by now, otherwise we should not be seeing this armor. But if that's where you want to go, that's where I'll take you. However, you mentioned that you wished to travel down Lake Havel, and if that is still your intention it will be pointless to go to Pichelsdorf. You will have to cross an enemy-held position and you will still have to steal a boat. If you can tell me your destination, perhaps I can think of an easier way to reach it."

In spite of himself, Lassiter had to admire the young boy's guts and foresight. Many a fully trained British soldier had less. If only . . . But the world was full of "if onlys."

"Pfaueninsel," he said. "We're making for Pfaueninsel."

"Then the quickest way is southwest through the Grunewald."

"It'll be crawling with Russian infantry."

"There are paths, sir, trails. I know many of them, having spent much of my boyhood in the area." Lassiter almost smiled at the word "boyhood," but Erich's young face was deadly serious. "Besides," he went on, "it is my opinion that the Ivans will wait until they have fully occupied the east bank of the Havel before moving through the Grunewald from all directions, driving our own forces into a defensive ring. This will take time and can be done only in daylight. They will not risk shooting at shadows. But it is your decision. The other way still means crossing the bridge at Pichelsdorf."

Lassiter's admiration for the tactical sense of the youngster was increasing by the minute, and he had to remind himself severely that Erich would attempt to kill them or betray them in a flash if he knew the true purpose of their mission.

"Can you take us all the way to Pfaueninsel?"

"I doubt it. But I can bring you out somewhere north of the Schwanenwerder Peninsula. There I will find you a boat or a small canoe, and to Pfaueninsel is only a matter of four or five kilometers."

"We'll do it your way," said Lassiter.

Sara Ferguson's own anesthesia of the brain had come miles earlier. All she knew was that Fodor was immediately in front of her, Maclean behind, and that she ducked or crawled or climbed or changed direction without any conscious effort of will. Though after a while she realized that they were no longer traveling through streets but were among trees.

It was something she would be reluctant to admit to herself later, but there were many times when she would not have cared had they run into a battalion of Soviet troops. At least then it would all be over. But always there was Dougal Maclean—sometimes behind her, sometimes at her side—helping her when she stumbled, gently urging her forward.

At the rear of the tiny column, moving in tighter formation now that they were in the forest, Lassiter had not dared look at his wristwatch, not even during his brief conversation with Erich, since the beginning. His legs and lungs told him that they'd been traveling fast, but how fast he had no idea. For that matter, he had no idea how it was that the German youngster picked his way like a cat through the trees, or how he avoided—sensed would be a better word—encamped Russian infantry. Like any other commander, he knew that luck—and taking full advantage of it—played a major part in the success of any operation, and he muttered a silent prayer to the God he no longer believed in that theirs would hold.

They kept to the pattern they had adopted in the streets. Careful here. Move forward slowly. Small Russian unit up ahead. Another on its right flank. You can see their cigarettes no matter how carefully they try to conceal them in cupped hands. Backtrack and go around. Watch that gully. We're getting closer now. Hear the machine-gun fire? See the artillery flashes? Some units still holding out. What was over here? Hitler Youth? *Volkssturm*? No, 20th Motorized Infantry Division. And what the hell's that big blaze through the trees? Jesus Christ, don't tell me we're walking into a firefight.

Immediately in front of Lassiter, Bormann stopped so suddenly that Lassiter collided with him and gave vent to a sudden oath. But this was not Bormann being tired, refusing to go any farther. They were almost at the edge of the Grunewald, and Erich was coming back down the line. Through the thinning trees it was now possible to see that the huge fire was coming from a munitions ship blazing in the middle of the Havel. Russian batteries on both sides of the lake were still shelling it with relentless ferocity, and it presented the fugitives with another problem: it made the whole area of the lake for miles in either direction as bright as day. Stealing a boat might be one thing; sailing it down the Havel quite another.

But Lassiter already had one or two alternatives. Their success, to a large extent, depended upon Erich. First of all, however, he had to know exactly where they were.

"Approximately where I envisaged," answered the youth. "A kilometer or two north of the Schwanenwerder Peninsula, four or five above Pfaueninsel."

"Can we get closer to Pfaueninsel by skirting the shores of the lake?"

"Not moving at any great speed. The Ivans are bound to have units on the banks, and in any case we shall have to go around the Wannsee. It could take another three or four hours, perhaps more."

For the first time Lassiter chanced a look at his wristwatch: it was a little after 2:15 A.M. Under the circumstances they, all of them, had done magnificently, covering something like twenty kilometers in about five hours. But there was no more time to spare. Bormann had said the guide would not wait. Perhaps so, perhaps not, but he couldn't take the risk. It would have to be a boat. But no ordinary boat—no rowboat or canoe—or the Russian shore batteries would blow them out of the water before they'd covered half a mile.

"Do the Russians patrol the lake using captured powerboats," he asked Erich, "looking for people like us?"

"I don't know, sir, but I suppose they must. I doubt if they'll be out there at the moment, though—not with that going on." He indicated the barrage being directed against the munitions ship.

"Neither do I," said Lassiter, "which means they must be tied up somewhere alongside." He gripped the lad's arms. "Find me one, Erich. Find me a powerboat flying the Russian pennant and guarded by no more than two or three men."

Erich's eyes glistened. "You're going to kill the Ivans and take it?"

"Never mind about that. Just do as I ask and be quick about it. Report back here as soon as you have something. And be careful!"

Lassiter watched the lad disappear among the trees. He had no doubt that Erich could carry out his assigned task without getting himself killed, but much would depend upon how long it took him.

He turned back to the others. Sara was lying against a fallen tree, utterly exhausted. Bormann was sitting with his head between his knees. Only Fodor and Maclean, a result of long and arduous training, were still on their feet, eyes fully open for any signs of danger.

"I hope one of you people can run a powerboat," he said.

Fodor confirmed that he could. "You live in California, it comes with solid food."

"Then all we have to pray for now is that Erich doesn't let us down."

Lassiter nudged Bormann with the toe of his boot. The Reichsleiter was almost asleep.

"This guide of yours," he said: "you're sure he won't wait any longer than four A.M.?"

Bormann decided to come clean. They would know in any case in an hour and a half. And looking down the Havel from the present position he could see, across the Schwanenwerder Peninsula, that Pfaueninsel was being heavily shelled. It was no place to be, certainly if it wasn't necessary.

"There is no guide," he said softly.

Lassiter thought he'd misheard. "*What did you say?*"

"There is no guide. There never was. We're being taken out by flying boat."

Not only Lassiter but Fodor, Sara and Maclean also were now sure they were losing their minds.

"Flying boat?"

"It was the plan from the beginning," said Bormann, raising his head from his knees. "Your control officer was aware that I would be unable to leave Berlin until Hitler was dead, by which time the Russians would have surrounded not only the city but the suburbs as well, pressing on as fast as they could for the Elbe. An escape overland would be virtually impossible. It was therefore arranged months ago that I, we, would be at the northern tip of Pfaueninsel at four A.M. on the second day after the news of Hitler's death was officially announced. As you may or may not know, that announcement was made over Hamburg Radio at nine thirty P.M. on the first. Our rendezvous is therefore for four A.M. on the third, in a little over ninety minutes. The flying boat will land just north of Pfaueninsel, and the signal from us will be a series of Morsed 'Ws' by flashlight."

"It's insane!" cried Fodor, realizing to his horror that his voice had gone up an octave. "Land a flying boat in *that*?" He pointed lakeward, where the munitions ship was still under artillery fire. "And why the hell weren't we told from the beginning? Why all the fucking secrecy?"

Lassiter answered him. Now that the initial shock was over, it made sense.

"It's not insane because it's so illogical—and it's no more dangerous than what we've been doing up to now. The last thing the Russians will expect is a seaplane landing among them, and by the time they wake up to the fact that all is not as it should be, we'll be on our way. It's the best chance we stand. It'll probably be equipped with the same kind of synchronized searchlights we used on the 52 coming in, but the pilot is going to be getting all the light he needs from that ship out there."

Fodor was not in the kind of mood to be reasonable. Not that it mattered a damn in the long run, but he still wanted to know why they hadn't been given the same information as that fat bastard Bormann.

"Maybe one of us was," said Lassiter slowly.

Sara shook her head wearily. "No, it's as much of a surprise to me as it is to you—though I don't suppose, deep down, that I expected Greenleigh to let us cross fifty miles of Germany on foot. If something had happened to Bormann, we'd be left sitting in the middle of no-man's-land with a document case full of papers and nowhere to go."

Lassiter disagreed. "I think you're missing the point." He spoke of the Reichsleiter as though the man were not sitting there, listening to every word. "The documents are important enough, but they're probably in some personal code, one that only Bormann can interpret. For that, Greenleigh needs Bormann himself.

"We were expendable right from the start, and let none of us feel hurt or used because that happens to be the case. What we didn't know we couldn't tell, even if they worked us over with rubber hoses. Coming in, we weren't to know our target was Bormann in case one of us was captured and put through the hoop. The same applies going out. While only Bormann knew where we were going and what would happen when we got there, Greenleigh's operation was safe. The only one who could give it all away was the Reichsleiter himself, and there was little chance of his being taken alive. Greenleigh had everything to gain and nothing to lose. Our only function was to see that the bastard got here in one piece. If it comes off, Greenleigh's a hero. If it doesn't, all he's lost is a handful of men, the crew of a pilfered Ju 52 and that of a seaplane."

Fodor turned away, disgusted. "I thought I'd seen it all," he said quietly, "but I'm learning something new every day. You had it right when you were talking to Dunbar, Jack; all this crap we've been going through for the last few years has nothing to do with fighting for a better world. If it did, that bastard would be dancing at the end of a rope and Joe Scipioni and the others would still be alive. Where's the sense in that? Scipioni gets killed, Bormann gets plastic surgery and a South American passport, Greenleigh gets a promotion and Allen Dulles gets a pat on the head from the President. If I come out of this, I'm going to find me the highest mountain in the world and sit on top of it. Forever."

There was a long silence. Only Dougal Maclean had not

305

spoken, but that was Dougal's way. In any case, anything he might have wished to contribute was forestalled by the sudden reappearance of Erich.

No one had heard him approach, and Lassiter knew they were slipping, suffering from a combination of fatigue and low morale. But this was no time for self-recrimination. To judge by the look on the boy's face, he had found what he had been sent to look for. And not a moment too soon. It was now almost 3:05.

"About a thousand meters north," he said excitedly, "a small motorboat with a light machine gun mounted on the bow. It has a crew of four, but they're not doing anything, merely talking and smoking. There is nothing else, no Russians, for two hundred meters above and below the boat."

"And between here and there?"

"Some vehicles and several gun emplacements near the water's edge. But one can get past them easily by keeping among the trees."

"Thank you," said Lassiter, and meant it.

He put an arm around the lad's shoulders and led him to one side.

"You do realize, of course, that you cannot go where we're going."

"Naturally. My job was merely to get you this far. Afterward, I will return to Berlin. There will be much to do there. Perhaps Russians to kill."

"And a few to kill here before you go," Lassiter told him. "You will have noticed that one of our party is a woman and one a middle-aged man. Who they are doesn't matter, but neither will be able to tackle even one Russian at the boat, and speed and stealth will be essential. The remaining three of us can take care of three of them, but do you think you can handle the other one?"

"I will try."

"You'll have some assistance."

Lassiter took from the sheath at his waist his SS dagger and handed it over. Erich fondled it with pleasure.

"That's yours to do the job with, and then it's yours to keep. Think of better times—not so much those in the past but those in the future."

"I will. And I know how to use it. An arm around the neck, a slice across the jugular."

Lassiter stared at the boy for a moment in horror, then composed his face into the appropriate expression of command.

"Very good," he said. "Now I'd like you to stay here for a few minutes. I have something to say to the others which is private."

"Of course, sir."

Lassiter returned to the group. Although he would never know it, it was precisely for the qualities he was about to display that Greenleigh had chosen him to lead the team.

He knew he had to rally them for one last effort, otherwise the whole operation stopped right then and there. He had to alter Greenleigh's meticulously laid plans somehow without upsetting the structure of the whole, give his team the impression that they, not Greenleigh and/or Bormann, were calling the shots.

"Listen to me carefully," he said, "because we haven't got long. The lad's going to lead us to the motorboat and we're going to take it. Including Erich, there are four of us capable of putting four Russian infantrymen out of action without making a hell of a lot of noise about it. It'll be bare hands for me as I've given Erich my dagger, but you, Chuck, and you, Dougal, can use either your knives or any other method you like. Just make sure they go down and stay down."

"Is the boy capable?" demanded Bormann.

Lassiter looked at him with hatred. "That lad is just about the best thing I've come across in Germany. If it weren't for the fact that you bastards indoctrinated him from birth, I'd take him with us."

He tossed away his raincoat and unslung the MP 38, which he handed to Sara.

"Your job is to watch Bormann," he told her. "If he looks like making a movement or a noise that you don't think is necessary, give him the whole magazine through the stomach. We may be expendable, but if we don't get home, neither does our fat friend here."

"It'll be a pleasure," said Sara.

Lassiter thought for a moment. "Now comes the interesting bit. When we're in possession of the motorboat we don't make for Pfaueninsel. We hang around mid-channel until the aircraft appears. Then we make straight for it. If it puts the fear of Christ into the crew to see a powerboat bearing the Soviet pennant heading for them at speed, that's their lookout. But we'll make sure they don't take off and leave us with egg on our faces by flashing them 'Ws' as we approach.

"The order of boarding will be Sara first, then Bormann. Chuck will go third, Dougal fourth, and me last."

"And the boy?" asked Sara.

"He stays ashore. I've already explained that to him. Any other questions?"

There were none.

"Then let's go," said Lassiter. "It's three ten and we've got a lot to do."

With Erich in the lead they skirted the Havel, heading north, keeping within the cover of the forest's edge.

Several times they passed close enough to Soviet positions to hear the Russians chatting among themselves, but Erich had already traveled this route and he kept them well away from danger.

It was nevertheless 3:35 before the Hitler Youth NCO held up his arm for them to stop. Lassiter joined him up front. Beyond the trees, tied up to what appeared to be a temporary jetty, was a fifteen-foot motorboat. The four-man crew, or guard, or whatever it was were looking out toward the middle of the lake, fascinated by the blazing munitions ship, which seemed as if it would never sink. Fortunately they were standing more or less in a line, but to get at them still meant covering fifty yards of unprotected ground.

Leaving Sara with Bormann, Lassiter beckoned the others forward, indicating by gesture which of the Russians each man should take.

Fodor was to be on the extreme right of the assault; next to him Maclean; between Lassiter and Maclean came Erich. The German boy's eyes were already gleaming in the flamelight at the thought of one less Russian to go home bragging to Moscow.

They took their time, their beat, from Lassiter, running silently at the crouch. It was important that they strike simultaneously, for fear that a nervous finger on the trigger would alert the whole coastline.

In twenty seconds it was all over. Lassiter had his own man around the throat with his left arm, crushing the windpipe and with it any chance of his victim's making a sound, while with his right he wrenched the Russian's head sideways and slightly backward, snapping the neck.

He turned quickly to see if Erich was in need of assistance, but the boy was already wiping his dagger on the dead Russian's tunic.

There was no need to check on Maclean and Fodor. They knew how to kill silently and efficiently.

"Take their headgear and one of the flashlights," ordered Lassiter.

Sara had seen it all from the trees. With Bormann a stride or two ahead and at gunpoint, she swiftly reached the boat.

Fodor was already inside the cockpit, going over the controls. It was a German design, naturally, but powerboats, like automobiles, are more or less the same the world over. There was nothing unfamiliar, and a glance at the fuel gauge revealed that they had more than enough to make the five-kilometer trip to Pfaueninsel ten times over.

Erich remained ashore while the others clambered aboard. Lassiter was last. He shook the lad by the hand.

"Thank you for everything," he said formally. "Without you we wouldn't have made it."

"It was nothing." The boy shrugged modestly.

"Don't hang around," cautioned Lassiter. "Get to hell out of here as quickly as you can."

"I'll be back in Berlin—or wherever else I'm needed—before you know it."

He seemed about to raise his arm in the Nazi salute, but Lassiter stopped him. "Don't be a fool. You never know who might be watching. Good luck, Erich."

"Good luck, sir."

Lassiter turned to cast off the painter. When he looked back, the boy had gone.

"How fast will this tub go?" he asked Fodor.

"Hard to tell. It's not a military craft; probably some sort of pleasure boat before the Russians commandeered it. Say forty k.p.h., tops."

309

Lassiter again checked the time. It was 3:42. At forty kilometers per hour, that meant about eight minutes to Pfaueninsel, and if he knew Greenleigh the seaplane would be bang on the hour.

"Get going, then," he ordered. "Keep mid-channel as far as possible, but avoid that bloody ship. If we're anywhere near it if and when it goes under, it'll take us with it. Dougal, man that machine gun. I'm not expecting any trouble until the plane lands, but after that anything can happen."

Fodor turned over the engine. It fired on the first try. He opened the throttle and moved out into mid-channel.

To reach Pfaueninsel they had to pass between the Schwanenwerder Peninsula and the west bank of the Havel, and at this point the lake was no more than a couple of hundred yards wide. They could easily be seen from both banks. Indeed, this was part of the exercise, flying the Red Flag and wearing the dead Russians' headgear, with Sara crouched in the bottom of the cockpit. On more than one occasion they were hailed via loudspeaker. Fodor answered and translated as they went along.

"They keep asking where we're going and what we're up to. I'm telling them that we've been ordered to patrol this stretch."

The Russians seemed satisfied. At least, they did not send a boat out to check on the authenticity of the patrol. Which was just as well, as moored to the banks on both sides of the lake Lassiter counted up to half a dozen motor-powered boats, several of them much bigger and more heavily armed than the one they were in.

The closer they got to Pfaueninsel, the more they realized how suicidal it would have been to make a landfall on the island. The Russians were giving it a hell of a battering with light artillery, either because they had ammunition to spare or because they thought it held a German position. But there was no answering fire.

Forty k.p.h. might well have been tops for the motorboat in its heyday, but their speed down the Havel averaged less than thirty. It was therefore 3:58 before Lassiter ordered Fodor to heave to some three hundred yards north of Pfaueninsel, well out of reach of a wayward shell.

"But keep the motor running," he warned.

They waited. Four A.M. came and went. Then 4:05.

It was Maclean who first heard it, coming in very low from the south. Then they saw it, a Catalina bearing RAF roundels. It skimmed the trees of Pfaueninsel with what appeared to be inches to spare and waved-hopped upchannel, finally coming to rest some six hundred yards from the motorboat.

"Bastard," snarled Lassiter. "All right, let's get to hell out of here."

Fodor opened the throttle, and for a second everyone's heart missed a beat when nothing happened. Then the gears meshed and the boat careened forward.

"Listen!" shouted Sara.

They all did so.

"I don't hear anything," said Fodor.

"Precisely. The Russian guns have stopped firing."

"Give me that flashlight," bellowed Lassiter.

Sara passed it over. Lassiter stood next to Maclean on the machine gun, signaling "Ws" for all he was worth.

They were still a couple of hundred yards short of the seaplane when some Russian artillery officer ordered his gun crew to put a salvo across the Catalina's bows. Then just as quickly the firing stopped, perhaps because the RAF markings were recognized.

But the relief for those in the motorboat was short-lived. Setting out from the west bank of the Havel, though with a greater distance to cover to the Catalina, was a massive powerboat. This one had never been designed for a Sunday afternoon's pleasure cruising up and down the lake. It was moving at high speed, and mounted on its bows were a searchlight and a heavy machine gun. The Red Army was coming to investigate.

"Do something about that fucking searchlight!" shouted Lassiter, but Maclean shook his head helplessly. The distance was far too great for such a puny weapon.

Greenleigh was already in the side hatch when Fodor eased the motorboat alongside, closing the throttle but leaving the engine running.

Sara was first to be dragged aboard, followed quickly by Bormann.

"Move it!" screamed Lassiter at Fodor, and the American scrambled through the hatch.

The Russian boat was now only three to four hundred yards

away and via its searchlight could see the frantic activity going on around the Catalina. RAF markings or not, something was happening here that the Red Army should know about.

The commander ordered his machine gunner to open fire just as Dougal Maclean was climbing aboard, framed in the hatch. He took three or four heavy-caliber bullets in the region of his lungs. Chuck Fodor tried desperately to hold on to his tunic, but the material came away and the tall Scot sank back into the boat, his mouth foaming blood. One glance was enough to tell Lassiter that Maclean was dead.

"Hurry, Jack!" bellowed Greenleigh.

The pilot of the Catalina was revving his engines, already moving forward. The Russian machine gunner was still firing, knocking chunks off the fabric.

Out of the corner of his eye Lassiter could see that the Soviet vessel was now only two hundred yards off and beginning to alter course. He needed no second guesses to divine the commander's intentions. He was going to either place his boat in the takeoff path of the Catalina or ram it.

"Fuck off!" he yelled. "Get to hell out of here!"

He thought he heard Sara cry his name and Greenleigh shout something about ". . . bloody fool . . ."—but then his attention was fully taken up by the throttle. All he had to do was open it, and with both hands gripping the wheel he made straight for the Russian craft.

The Soviet commander could see what was going to happen long before it did. He screamed at his machine gunner to hit the helmsman of the other boat.

The machine gunner tried to comply. Lassiter could see the tracer hurtling toward him in a lazy arc and hear it ripping through the motorboat's woodwork. The caliber of the gun, he noted professionally, was at least .50.

He tried not to think of what was going to happen to him. He concentrated solely on the Soviet boat. It had been a long war, and he'd had more than his fair share of luck.

The gap between the two craft closed to eighty yards. It was virtually point-blank range. The Russian gunner couldn't miss.

The first of the shells caught Lassiter in the right shoulder; the next—perhaps it was two or three—tore a hole in his chest.

The shock was immediate, the pain excruciating, but he held on to the wheel. They'd come too far to be cheated now.

Fifty yards . . .

Five seconds . . .

No more . . .

There were no final thoughts, no images from the past. There was, perhaps, a moment when he saw, in his mind, a picture of a tall woman with dark hair; but his brain had no time to register it.

Ten yards . . .

Technically Lassiter was probably already dead when the two boats collided. Yet a fraction of a second before they went up in a mushroom of flame as the fuel tanks exploded, he seemed to raise his eyes skyward.

High above, gaining altitude rapidly, the Catalina climbed safely into the night.

EPILOGUE

"Mrs. Ferguson's here," said a voice over the squawk box.

"Ask her to wait," said Greenleigh.

There were four of them in the drawing room of Greenleigh's Mayfair house: Greenleigh himself, now a major general; Jake Bellinger; Allen Dulles, leg extended on a cushion, and Chuck Fodor. Originally scheduled for Berne, the meeting was taking place in London because Dulles and Bellinger had business there. It seemed easier to bring Fodor with them than have Greenleigh and Sara fly to Switzerland.

The war in Europe had ended officially six weeks ago, but the full extent of Nazi atrocities was only just being realized by the public, making newspaper headlines every day. It was in view of this that Dulles had suggested an ad hoc conference. Fodor he was sure about, but no one wanted Mrs. Ferguson suddenly developing a crisis of conscience, especially as she had remained a virtual recluse in Scotland since early May. It had taken more than a little cajoling to entice her out of purdah.

But there were other matters to discuss too.

"As I was saying," said Dulles, "we're getting some flak from the Russians to the effect that Bormann is alive and we've got him. I can deny that with my hand on my heart, of course, because he's still under British jurisdiction, but it'll be a bit different when you turn him over to us next month."

"With the proviso that we have complete access," Greenleigh reminded him.

"Naturally. In fact, I might have to ask you to keep him in Canada and let our people commute to him. Early days though it is, President Truman has one eye on the '48 election, and he

314

doesn't want a charge of harboring war criminals in the opposition's armory."

"Strange people, politicians," mused Greenleigh. "After congratulating me on the success of the operation, Mr. Churchill said almost the same thing—about how it would be a good idea if we could get Bormann out of Canada and into the United States."

Dulles grinned through yellowing teeth. "Well, they'll come and go, Prime Ministers and Presidents, but we go on forever. Not unless we kill these Russian rumors, however. Though Major Fodor has a few thoughts on that subject."

Chuck Fodor took his cue. "It seems to me," he said, "that it's not enough that we deny we've got Bormann. We should actively encourage contradictory stories that he's both alive and dead. I've even coined a word for it. Disinformation."

Greenleigh winced.

Fodor went on: "We know the Nazis have an escape line to South America. We're hoping to nail it, but maybe it can work in our favor for now. We spread the word that Bormann's been seen in, say, Paraguay. We can plant this pretty easily with the newspapers, maybe fake a couple of photographs. They'll be the real thing, of course, taken against backdrops of jungle and so on, and slightly out of focus. At the same time we grab an eyewitness or two to say they definitely saw Bormann killed in Berlin. This is better than a straight denial. Create enough confusion and no one will know what to believe."

"The boy'll go far," said Bellinger.

Greenleigh was sure of it. "I suppose it will work, though I can't help feeling we all underestimated Bormann. It was my original intention to grill him for a few months before quietly disposing of him. We could then have faked finding his body in our zone of Berlin and invited the Russians to see he was really dead. I did not expect him to have the names of so many German agents in the Soviet Union. Neither did I expect him to release their names to us piecemeal or to be the sole possessor of the key words to activate them. It'll be a good twenty years before every one is on our official payroll, and in the meantime we have to finance them via Bormann's nominees."

The look between Bellinger and Dulles said it all. The British were still amateurs at this sort of game, no matter what they thought.

"Still," said Dulles, "we need them. The Russians are going to seal off their part of Europe with a vengeance. The Nazis have had their deep-cover men in for a decade. We couldn't hope to put our own guys in before Stalin decides he wants to take over the world—or what's left of it. One day, however, we'll have finished with friend Bormann. Then we can arrange an accident."

"I doubt that," said Greenleigh. "The man's forty-five years old. I have a terrible feeling he'll live out his natural life. In comfort, too. Do you know what he asked me? He asked me why he couldn't be given a mansion in Scotland."

"He'll probably ask us the same thing," said Dulles. "Maybe we'll give him a gas station in Michigan."

"Which would be punishment enough," muttered Jake Bellinger.

Fodor cleared his throat.

"Something on your mind, Major?" asked Dulles.

"Not really, sir, but I was just wondering what does happen to him eventually."

"I don't think your security classification is high enough," said Dulles, "but I'll tell you this much. Long before we've finished with him, debriefed him, we'll have given him a new face, a new background, money. It's in our interest as much as his that no one knows he's alive. He'll grow old the way everybody else grows old and no one will know who he is. We'll teach him to speak English without an accent and dump him somewhere— maybe the United States, maybe right here in London. Whatever happens in your career, Major, and wherever you settle, always take a good look at your neighbor. Anyone over forty-five could be Martin Bormann."

It was a chilling thought.

"They'll still wonder, the Russians," said Greenleigh after a moment. "If they never find his body, I mean."

"Well, we've sort of covered that too," drawled Dulles. "There *is* a body, or there will be. Bormann's exact height, weight, build and so on. We've also arranged to substitute the corpse's dental records for Bormann's own. When—*if*—the skeleton ever

316

comes to light and the Russkies or anyone else decide it could be Bormann's, the first thing they'll do is check the dental charts. That should satisfy them that the bastard's really dead."

Greenleigh shook his head. "I'd hate to play poker with you."

Dulles chuckled. "Let's have Mrs. Ferguson in."

A few minutes later Greenleigh was saying to Sara, "It never happened. There was no Valkyrie, no Operation Horsetrade. Please remember that."

Sara said nothing.

"I don't have to remind you," Greenleigh went on, "about the Official Secrets Act, as I'm sure Major Fodor does not have to be reminded by Mr. Dulles of his own oath. The operation was a success, which is our only criterion."

Greenleigh cleared his throat and eased some of the sternness from his voice. Really, he was overplaying it, and he could tell from Sara's calmness that the tears were past.

"It goes without saying," he went on, "that we, the Americans and ourselves, would like to award the highest decorations to those who took part, but we all know that such a thing is not possible. Victoria Crosses and Medals of Honor require eyewitnesses. We have none who can testify."

There was an awkward silence. Greenleigh was aware of how inadequate he was in such situations, and he found himself unable to look into Sara's unblinking green eyes.

"What will you write on his service record?" she asked.

"Major Lassiter's? I'm afraid that too must remain an official secret."

"Killed in action, probably. That's the way these things usually work, isn't it?"

"I'm afraid I can't answer that."

"It doesn't matter." She smoothed her skirt. "May I go now?"

"Unless Mr. Dulles or Major General Bellinger has anything he wishes to add."

Both senior Americans shook their heads.

"May I see Mrs. Ferguson to the door?" asked Fodor.

Dulles nodded his assent.

In the street Fodor said, "I'll be based at the Embassy for a while. Perhaps we could have dinner some night."

"No, I don't think that would be a good idea at all."

London was waking up again. The victory celebrations were over and there was a city to be rebuilt.

"What will you do now?" asked Fodor.

"I don't know. Go to Canada, I expect, as I doubtless should have done in the first place. And you? What about that mountain you were going to find and sit on top of—forever?"

"They want me to stay on. Dulles is forming some sort of new organization and wants me to be part of it. And judging by the noises the Russians are making . . ." He stopped, embarrassed.

"But we do have an advantage there, don't we?" said Sara. "What do you Americans call it—an ace in the hole? We do have some knowledge, thanks to Jack Lassiter." She paused. "They didn't mention it once, you know, what he did for us."

"I don't think it was for us that he did it. It was for you."

She held out her gloved hand. "Goodbye, Chuck."

"Goodbye, Sara. They broke the mold when they made you."

"Not me, Chuck. Very definitely not me."

She turned on her heel and walked in the direction of Park Lane. Fodor stood quite still until he lost sight of her in the crowds.

Bormann Dead

Berlin—Thursday. It now seems certain that Martin Bormann, Deputy Leader of the Nazi Party and the last ranking Nazi to be unaccounted for, died in the ruins of Berlin on May 1 or 2. A British spokesman said today that there was no chance, as is being rumored by the Russians, that he had escaped and was somewhere in the West. Reports that an amphibious aircraft carrying RAF markings was observed landing on Lake Havel in the small hours of May 3 are denied. Major General Henry Greenleigh was quoted as saying that it was impossible for anyone to have fled the city. An American source confirmed that they too were closing their file.—AP

TABLE OF RANKS

SS	German Army	British Army	U.S. Army
Reichsfuehrer	Generalfeldmarschall	Field Marshal	General of the Army
Oberstgruppenfuehrer	Generaloberst	General	General
Obergruppenfuehrer	General	Lieutenant General	Lieutenant General
Gruppenfuehrer	Generalleutnant	Major General	Major General
Brigadefuehrer	Generalmajor	Brigadier	Brigadier General
Oberfuehrer	No equivalent	No equivalent	No equivalent
Standartenfuehrer	Oberst	Colonel	Colonel
Obersturmbannfuehrer	Oberstleutnant	Lieutenant Colonel	Lieutenant Colonel
Sturmbannfuehrer	Major	Major	Major
Hauptsturmfuehrer	Hauptmann	Captain	Captain
Obersturmfuehrer	Oberleutnant	Lieutenant	First Lieutenant
Untersturmfuehrer	Leutnant	Second Lieutenant	Second Lieutenant
Sturmscharfuehrer	Stabsfeldwebel	RSM	Sergeant Major
Stabsscharfuehrer	Hauptfeldwebel	No equivalent	No equivalent
Hauptscharfuehrer	Oberfeldwebel	Sergeant Major	Master Sergeant
Oberscharfuehrer	Feldwebel	QM Sergeant	Technical Sergeant
Scharfuehrer	Unterfeldwebel	Staff Sergeant	Staff Sergeant
Unterscharfuehrer	Unteroffizier	Sergeant	Sergeant
Rottenfuehrer	Obergefreiter/Gefreiter	Corporal	Corporal
Sturmmann	Oberschütze	Lance Corporal	PFC
SS-Mann	Schütze	Private	Private

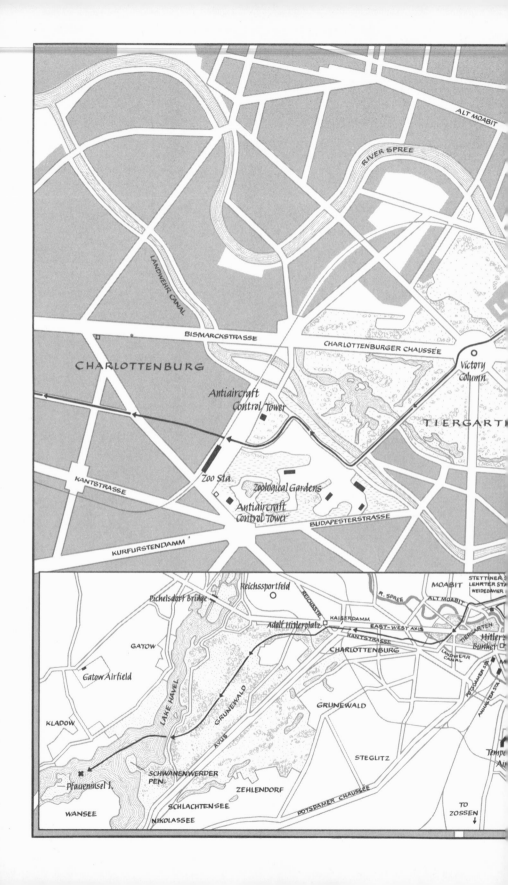

ALT MOABIT

RIVER SPREE

LANDWEHR CANAL

BISMARCKSTRASSE

CHARLOTTENBURGER CHAUSSEE

CHARLOTTENBURG

Victory Column

Antiaircraft Control Tower

TIERGARTEN

KANTSTRASSE

Zoo Sta.

Zoological Gardens

Antiaircraft Control Tower

BUDAPESTERSTRASSE

KURFURSTENDAMM

STETTINER
LEHRTER STA
WEIDEDAMER

MOABIT

Reichssportfeld

R. SPREE

ALT MOABIT

Pichelsdorf Bridge

REICHSSTR

KAISERDAMM

Adolf Hitlerplatz

EAST-WEST AXIS

TIERGARTEN

Hitler's
Bunker

GATOW

KANTSTRASSE

CHARLOTTENBURG

LANDWEHR
CANAL

Gatow Airfield

LAKE HAVEL

GRUNEWALD

GRUNEWALD

POTSDAMER STR

KLADOW

AVUS

STEGLITZ

Tempel
Air

Pfaueninsel I.

SCHWANENWERDER
PEN

ZEHLENDORF

WANSEE

SCHLACHTENSEE

NIKOLASSEE

POTSDAMER CHAUSSEE

TO
ZOSSEN